Marc Dupree's words threw Laney completely off guard, as did his soft tone.

"Are you still in need of money, Miss O'Connor?"

"Yes," she admitted before she could stop the word from rushing out. Why, *why* did she find herself wanting to lean on this man, when she knew he was dangerous to everything she held dear?

For a long moment Dupree stared at her, those blue-blue eyes piercing straight through her, as though he could see inside every one of her secrets. "Then I have a proposition for you."

A number of terrible possibilities came to mind. For the past twenty-four hours Laney had experienced nothing but fear and desperation. The feeling of falling into a pit with no way out had been dreadful, panic-inducing. Terrifying.

Was she about to fall deeper into that pit, thanks to this man and his…proposition?

No. She couldn't lose hope. For the sake of the children she had to believe good would come out of this awful situation.

"What kind of proposition are you suggesting?"

"Come work for me at my hotel."

Renee Ryan
and
Naomi Rawlings

Charity House Courtship
&
The Wyoming Heir

LOVE INSPIRED
INSPIRATIONAL ROMANCE

LOVE INSPIRED®
INSPIRATIONAL ROMANCE

ISBN-13: 978-1-335-97198-2

Charity House Courtship & The Wyoming Heir

Copyright © 2021 by Harlequin Books S.A.

Charity House Courtship
This is a revised text of a work first published as Extreme Measures by Dorchester Publishing Co., Inc. in 2002.
Copyright © 2002 as Extreme Measures by Renee Halverson
Published as Charity House Courtship in 2012 by Harlequin Books S.A.
This edition published in 2021.
Copyright © 2012 by Renee Halverson, revised text edition.

The Wyoming Heir
First published in 2014. This edition published in 2021.
Copyright © 2014 by Naomi Mason

Recycling programs for this product may not exist in your area.

This edition published by arrangement with Harlequin Books S.A.

For questions and comments about the quality of this book, please contact us at CustomerService@Harlequin.com.

Love Inspired
22 Adelaide St. West, 40th Floor
Toronto, Ontario M5H 4E3, Canada
www.Harlequin.com

Printed in U.S.A.

CONTENTS

Renee Ryan grew up in a Florida beach town where she learned to surf, sort of. With a degree from FSU, she explored career opportunities at a Florida theme park and a modeling agency and even taught high school economics. She currently lives with her husband in Nebraska, and many have mistaken their overweight cat for a small bear. You may contact Renee at reneeryan.com, on Facebook or on Twitter, @reneeryanbooks.

CHARITY HOUSE COURTSHIP

Renee Ryan

Do nothing out of selfish ambition or vain conceit, but in humility consider others better than yourselves. Each of you should look not only to your own interests, but also to the interests of others.
—*Philippians* 2:3–4

To Sheila Vittitow and Jean Smith.
Your dedication to serving the Lord always
humbles me. Thank you for your stellar example.
I'm honored to call you ladies my friends!

Chapter One

Denver, Colorado
June 1879

Laney O'Connor hesitated outside the legendary Hotel Dupree, unsure how best to proceed. Suspended in her moment of indecision, she took a slow, calming breath. The gesture did little to dispel her increasing agitation. She was, after all, about to commit a brazen act.

Could she pull this off?

Did she have any other choice?

A wave of doubt crested. With a hard swallow, she shoved the unwanted emotion into submission. This was no time for uncertainty.

Yet here she stood, motionless, hardly daring to breathe.

Lifting her gaze, she studied the ornate building in front of her. Not out of curiosity, but to gather the courage she would need to enter the most exclusive establishment in Denver and finish what she'd started this morning.

The Hotel Dupree was—as all the periodicals

claimed—the most elegant building in town. Although the sun had set hours ago, modern gaslights bathed the structure in a golden, welcoming glow. Nine stories high, and boasting large, wrought iron balconies on every floor, the beautiful stone structure brought to mind beloved childhood tales where happily-ever-after always reigned.

Would Laney find her own happy ending here tonight?

Doubtful.

But she had to try. She had to forget that time had run out for her, that a shady, unscrupulous banker wanted his money in less than three days.

Three. Short. Days.

An impossible deadline.

Tears pushed at the back of her eyelids, a frightening reminder of her own helplessness, of the sharp, terrifying fear that she couldn't raise the five hundred dollars in time.

For weeks, Laney had prayed for an answer to her dilemma. She had all but begged the Lord to reveal a solution, *any* solution. Silence had met her countless appeals.

Now, with the clock ticking and no one to rely on but herself, Laney had to obtain the money on her own.

In the only way she knew how.

Please, Lord, please let him show.

Squaring her shoulders, she pushed through the rotating doors and entered the hotel's main lobby. Stepping to the side, she stabbed a cursory glance through the large room. The rich fabrics on the furniture, the expensive mahogany paneling on the walls and the polished marble floors spoke of an attention to detail Laney appreciated.

As much as she admired the beautiful décor, the tiny alcove in the far corner captured the majority of her interest. Small, private, out of the main traffic flow, the nook was a perfect spot for her clandestine meeting.

Head high, eyes cast forward, Laney made her way across the lobby. She kept her steps slow and purposeful, but not too obvious. She had to draw as little attention to herself as possible. Hard to do, considering the dress she'd borrowed for this occasion.

She prayed her choice of clothing hadn't been a mistake. The gown wasn't meant to entice, but rather to remind a man of his duty. And why he had that obligation in the first place.

Once nestled in the hidden alcove, Laney placed her back to the wall and waited for her quarry.

Searching faces only, a sense of foreboding slipped through her resolve. Her pulse kicked into an erratic rhythm, punching ruthlessly against her ribs. *What if he doesn't show?*

No. She couldn't give into doubt.

Her entire plan hinged on Joshua Greene's cooperation. And his assumption that she was a woman of questionable character. Sighing past a wave of guilt, Laney shifted her position slightly, ran her gaze through the room once more, but found no one bearing the familiar mane of gray hair and ruddy features she sought.

Another adjustment to her stance and she felt her attention pulled to the left, inexplicably drawn to the most compelling pair of steel-blue eyes on a man she'd ever seen.

Their gazes locked. And held.

Why couldn't she look away?

Stunned at her own daring, she pressed her lips tightly together. Her breathing hitched in her throat. For a terrifying instant, every rational thought receded from her mind.

Riveted into immobility, she continued staring at the handsome stranger. He stared back. Boldly, relentlessly, with a bleak expression on his face. *That look*, that stern, unyielding glare sent a shiver tripping along her spine.

Laney quickly broke eye contact. Something felt off about this whole situation, now more than ever. A sense of impending doom urged her to leave the hotel immediately.

She ignored the sensation, knowing she couldn't leave. Not yet. Not without her money.

Against her better judgment, her gaze sought the handsome stranger once again.

He hadn't moved from his earlier position.

This time, his lips curved around a fixed smile. Distrust, suspicion, they were both in his gaze.

Who *was* he? And what did he think she was planning to do here tonight?

Knowing how she was dressed, sensing he'd come to the absolute wrong conclusion, she nearly rushed out of the hotel.

The children, she told herself. *Think of the orphans*.

The reminder helped her recover the necessary courage to finish what she'd come here to do. Yanking her gaze free, Laney melted deeper into the shadows of the alcove.

She held her breath, waiting, counting the endless seconds, praying the stranger would grow tired of watching her and leave. Finally, after shooting one more look in her direction, he disappeared into the adjourning restaurant near the bank of elevators.

Instead of experiencing joy over his departure, another bout of uncertainty reared.

Again, Laney disregarded the feeling.

She could do this. She *had* to do this. For the abandoned children who needed the safety of the home she alone provided.

A movement at the hotel's entrance cut through her thoughts. Joshua Greene had arrived.

Relief nearly buckled her knees, even as the well-dressed, gray-haired gentleman paused in the doorway. Laney eyed him cautiously, hopefully. Dressed in an expensive, hand-tailored suit, the cut as elegant as the man himself, Judge Greene looked every bit the distinguished Denver citizen that he was.

He glanced around the room with a caged expression on his face. Apparently, he was as unsettled by the nature of their impending transaction as Laney.

Wanting to ease his mind, she moved out into the open and flashed her brightest smile at him. He did not return the gesture. Instead, he tugged his hat over his face and set out in her direction.

Despite her impatience to be finished with this uncomfortable meeting, she waited until he was nearly upon her before speaking. "Good evening, Judge Greene."

A brief nod was his only answer.

So, he was going to play it that way. Laney sighed. "I'm sorry we had to meet this way." And she was. More than she could put into words.

"I, too, am sorry, Miss O'Connor." His lips twisted

into a frown. "But I suppose it's better than the alternatives."

It was her turn to nod in agreement. Given the unorthodox nature of their relationship, Laney could never have met him at his home, or hers. And certainly not his office in the courthouse. The Hotel Dupree provided them anonymity.

Wanting to protect his identity as best she could, Laney took his arm and pulled him into the shadows with her.

He followed willingly.

Once they were out of sight of the other hotel guests milling about, he wasted no times with pleasantries.

"Miss O'Connor." He kept his voice low, his words barely audible over the din from the lobby. "As much as I sympathize with your predicament, you must never again contact me as you did this morning. Such recklessness goes against our original arrangement."

The reminder slammed into her like a punch. "I had no other choice," she whispered.

"I know, my dear." Softening his tone, he patted her hand with a benevolent, fatherly touch. "I understand this is difficult for you. Truly, I do. If it's any consolation, you look very much like your mother tonight. Quite beautiful, really."

Instead of relishing the compliment, Laney's heart filled once more with guilt.

She hated putting this man in such a precarious situation. But what else could she do? Her loan had been called in six months early. And this former "friend" of her mother's owed Laney far more than she was asking of him tonight.

Considering the circumstances, he was getting off easy.

Keep telling yourself that.

As if wishing to finish their business as quickly as possible, he slipped a hand inside his coat then pulled out his wallet. A flick of his wrist and she was in possession of her money.

Surprised at how quickly the transaction had gone, Laney automatically curled her fingers over the large bundle and pressed it to her heart.

"Can I assume this settles our account?"

"Yes." She gave him a firm nod. "Thank you, Judge Greene. As per our agreement, you owe me nothing more."

"Excellent." He turned to go, then spun back around to face her. "I know I don't have to remind you of the necessity for secrecy, but under the circumstances, I feel I must verbalize my request so there is no misunderstanding."

Knowing what was coming next, Laney waited silently for him to continue.

"Never reveal who gave you this money, Miss O'Connor. Or why."

She clutched the bills tighter in her fist. "No, I won't. Your secret is safe with me."

"Thank you. I trust we shall not meet again. I…" As if only just realizing what he was saying, a sad smile crossed his lips. "Take care of my boy."

Such an easy request. "You may count on it."

Without another word, he pivoted on his heel. This time, he didn't turn around.

Light-headed from joy over her success, Laney slumped against the wall and sighed. She glanced after the judge's retreating back. He moved quickly, already halfway to the bank of elevators. At least he was stick-

ing to their plan. As agreed, he would ride to the ninth
floor of the hotel, and then exit the building by way of
the back stairwell.

Laney would leave the way she came, after she drank
a cup of coffee in the restaurant. Twenty more minutes
and she could put this whole ugly business behind her.

The thought that she'd jeopardized the reputation of
the most respected judge in town left her with a mild
case of regret. But then she drew on the image of the
children sleeping soundly in their beds. One in particular came to mind and her conscience eased.

Regardless of what Judge Greene told himself, he
hadn't come here tonight out of altruism. Nor had he
shown up to pay off the debt he owed, at half the cost.
No, he'd come to ensure Laney kept his son's parent-
age a secret.

He'd paid handsomely for her silence. Or so he'd
thought. What he didn't know, what Laney hadn't reveal during their transaction, was that she would have
kept his secret for free.

Now that Marc Dupree had taken over the day-to-day
operations of his hotel, he no longer tolerated dishonor-
able behavior. Not from his employees, *or* his guests.
After months of ensuring every member of his staff
adhered to this strict policy—and a handful of tussles
with unruly patrons—the Hotel Dupree was now considered the most elegant, well-run hotel this side of the
Mississippi.

Marc had worked hard to earn that reputation. He
would allow nothing to ruin what he'd built out of the
worst possible betrayal a man could suffer. Already cautious by nature, years of running the most dangerous

saloons in the West had taught him how to spot trouble before it began. Thus, the moment the stunning woman in the gold dress entered his lobby he'd known—*known without a doubt*—she was going to pose a problem.

The way she'd scanned the lobby with a calculating eye, searching male faces only, had told its own story. When she'd stared at him from across the room, as if daring him to call her out for some misdeed, Marc had taken it upon himself to do just that.

Once he had concrete proof. He was, after all, a fair man.

The fact that he'd been unexpectedly affected by the woman's striking beauty made no difference. He would not abide dishonest dealings in his hotel.

No matter the circumstances.

Careful to keep outside the woman's line of vision, he observed Judge Greene step inside the empty elevator closest to the restaurant. If Marc had been a betting man, he'd wager half his fortune that the woman would soon follow her "friend."

Swallowing his distaste behind a sneer, Marc found himself torn between tossing the little beauty out of his hotel and waiting to see how long it would take her to make her way to the elevators.

He guessed two minutes. Perhaps three.

She proved him wrong, by lingering in the alcove a good five more minutes than he'd predicted. Marc took the opportunity to study her more closely.

She'd arranged her rich, mahogany hair loosely atop her head, with several strands cascading free at random. The tousled effect was both captivating and enthralling, a sure sign she'd taken great care with her appearance. The gold dress complemented her figure to perfection, its tight-fitting bodice cut just high enough to avoid indecency. But only just.

Marc knew better than to allow such an artful display to send his logic disappearing into another room. If his experience with Pearl LaRue had taught him anything, it was that a man could trust no woman.

This one, no matter how exquisite, was no exception.

She set out, heading straight for the bank of elevators near the restaurant. Exactly as he'd predicted.

Uncommonly disappointed in a woman he'd never met, Marc cut across the lobby in a wide arc, keeping to the left of her so she wouldn't notice his approach. Two feet away, he reached out and caught her by the arm.

Ignoring her shocked gasp, he spun her around to face him.

For an endless moment his mind emptied of all thought. His heartbeat roared in his ears, making it difficult to concentrate on anything but the stunned woman blinking wide-eyed back at him.

Up close, her refined, delicate beauty took his breath away. In contrast with the bold cut of her dress, everything about her was soft and inviting. Her face, her figure, even her light amber eyes spoke of a kind soul and a generous heart.

Completely unexpected. Enough to render him speechless.

She stared back at him, unmoving, waiting, holding silent, as if trying to gauge his mood before making her move.

Wounded, that was the word that came to mind as he gazed into those exotic, heartbreaking eyes. Vulnerable. Desperate.

All a lie. Her kind *always* lied.

Marc gave his head a hard shake. "Miss," he said past the drumming in his ears. "I would like a word with you in private."

He felt her betraying tremble, an instant before she physically repressed the sensation and then smoothed a look of calm across her face. The alarming speed in which she regained her composure proved Marc's earlier assessment. Only a woman with something to hide would respond with such calculated control.

"If you would be so kind as to come with me," he added with an edge of warning in his words, "I'm sure we can avoid an unnecessary scene."

As if coming out of a daze, she tugged on her arm, hard. "Sir, I suggest you release me before *I* make a scene."

"I wouldn't do that if I were you." Marc tightened his hold, not enough to hurt her but enough to make his point.

"Who do you think you are?" An impeccable mix of indignation and shock sounded in her voice.

Oh, she was good. She looked *and* sounded generally taken aback by his behavior.

But Marc had seen that very same expression on another woman's face. The reminder was enough to harden his heart.

"My name is Marc Dupree," he said with hard-won authority. "The owner of this hotel."

"Well, then, Mr. Dupree." She swept a lock of hair behind her ear with a trembling finger, the only sign of her agitation. One he would have missed had he not been watching her so closely. "I must compliment you on your fine establishment."

She punctuated her words with a brilliant smile. The same one she'd given Joshua Greene earlier.

Marc had seen enough. He motioned to his security man, Hank, watching from across the room.

Well-versed in the need for propriety, the big man sauntered over in a casual manner.

"Hank, please escort Miss—" Marc leveled a look on the woman. "I'm afraid I haven't had the pleasure of learning your name."

A sound of despair slipped from her lips as she fixed her eyes on the rotating doors at the other end of the lobby.

"Now, now, that wouldn't be wise, Miss…"

She snapped her gaze back to his. "Oh, honestly, this is absurd." Indignation masked any signs of her earlier anxiety. "My name is Laney. Laney O'Connor."

"I trust that's your real name."

"Of course it's my real name. Why would you ask such a question?"

Marc lifted a single eyebrow. "I find women like you often use a variety of names."

"*Women like me?*" She frowned, as if trying to discern the meaning of his words. The moment understanding dawned, her eyes widened. "Oh…*oh*." She yanked once again on her arm. "You insult me."

He almost believed he'd offended her. Almost.

"Hank, please escort Miss O'Connor to my office." Marc lowered his lips to her ear. "This will go much easier for you if you cooperate without a fight."

"I…I don't understand. I've done nothing wrong."

They both knew that was a lie.

"Then you won't mind if I take a look inside your satchel." Giving her no opportunity to respond, he let go of her arm and commandeered the tiny bag dangling from her wrist.

Shock and fury flared in her eyes. "What do you think you're doing?"

"Ensuring that nothing unsavory occurs in my hotel."

Gaze locked on the tiny satchel, she lunged for him.

Marc shifted to his left.

She went stumbling past. One step, two, by the third she caught her balance and swung back around to face him. "Mr. Dupree, please. You…you've made a terrible mistake."

Panic sounded in every word.

Marc remained unmoved. How many times had Pearl given that very same appeal, with that precise look of distress in her eyes?

"A mistake?" He shook his head. "Not likely."

"Please," she whispered, her shoulders slumping forward. "You have to believe me when I say I've done nothing improper in your hotel."

Yet.

The unspoken word echoed in the air between them. Marc nearly called her bluff. Except…

Her desperation appeared real.

Something in him, some hidden part he thought long dead, reconsidered confiscating the ill-gotten money and returning it to its rightful owner. Perhaps, as Miss O'Connor had claimed, Marc had misjudged the situation.

He nearly relented and gave her back her reticule without further delay. But then he remembered what he'd witnessed moments earlier. One of Denver's most prominent citizens—a federal judge, no less—had given this woman a large sum of money. In a very secretive, clandestine manner.

Something unsavory was afoot in his hotel. And Marc needed to collect all the facts before he could act.

Of course, questioning Miss O'Connor would require privacy.

Decision made, he hitched his chin toward Hank. Needing no further instruction, the other man took her arm.

She didn't fight this time, nor did she try to appeal to Marc's compassion. She did, however, release a defeated sigh, as though she understood she had no other choice but to cooperate.

"Mr. Dupree." She wrapped her dignity around her like a protective shield. "Once I have explained my actions here tonight I trust you will return my reticule."

Marc leaned forward until their noses nearly touched. "That, Miss O'Connor, will depend completely on what you reveal."

Chapter Two

Laney tried to formulate a new strategy as the large, beefy man named Hank escorted her through the hotel lobby. Unfortunately, Marc Dupree followed closely behind them. So closely, in fact, that she could smell his spicy, masculine scent.

The heady aroma left her slightly light-headed, and her mind filled with the same hopelessness that had been gnawing at her all evening.

No. She couldn't give up. Not now. *Not ever.*

Maintaining her outward calm, she kept her steps slow and steady, her expression mild. Despite what the hotel owner might think, the five hundred dollars in Laney's reticule belonged to her.

Of course, per her deal with Judge Greene, Laney couldn't disclose the reason he'd given her such a large sum of money. She would have to come up with another explanation, one that would protect the promise she'd made and still satisfy Dupree's suspicious mind.

As if reading her thoughts, the annoying man moved in closer still, narrowing the distance to mere inches. "Thinking up a good lie, are you?"

Arrogant brute.

He thought he had the situation all figured out.

When he was so very wrong.

"I'm warning you now," he continued in his low, husky baritone. "I'm not a man easily fooled."

Her breath caught on a gasp. Oh, she had no doubt he was a sly one. The sense of danger pulsating out of him nearly overwhelmed her. But she coaxed her fear into compliance and focused on putting one foot in front of the other.

Hank's hold on her arm remained remarkably light. Laney considered making a break for the rotating doors behind her. But she sensed if she tried to escape, the hired ruffian would tighten his grip to painful proportions.

Mind working quickly, she considered other options. Even if she managed to get away from Hank, there was the matter of Marc Dupree. Laney could feel his suppressed anger as he walked directly behind her.

Again, he leaned in close. Too close. "I wouldn't try to run if I were you." The warning sizzled in the tiny space between them. "You're no match for Hank. Or me."

Laney seethed at the man's self-assurance. Nevertheless, she knew better than to fight at this point. Not without an escape plan.

Praying for a calm she didn't possess, she allowed Hank to usher her inside a small room in the back corner of the hotel.

Dupree entered a few steps behind them and shut the door with a resounding click.

The moment Hank released her arm Laney pivoted

around and took a step forward. Dupree shifted directly in her path, an ironic twist of his lips.

Out of ideas but not out dignity, she opened her mouth to express her outrage over his behavior. Unfortunately, words eluded her.

Eyebrows raised, Dupree stared at her, waiting, taking her measure, silently challenging her to defend herself.

The noisy din from the hotel lobby pervaded the cold mood in the room.

Laney ignored the racing of her pulse, putting it down to sheer desperation, and returned Dupree's glare with equal intensity.

The handsome, chiseled features and square jaw created a deceptively appealing picture, as did the thick black hair against his smooth, olive skin. In contrast to his severe good looks, the crisp white shirt he wore, red silk vest, and matching neck cloth added a refined dignity not often seen in the West.

For a brief moment, as she continued holding his stare, Laney detected a familiar restlessness in his blue-blue eyes, the kind garnered from a painful past much like her own. A kindred spirit?

Hardly.

This might be her first face-to-face meeting with Marc Dupree, but she'd heard all the rumors. His reputation as a ruthless businessman was legendary around town. Known for demanding unreasonably high standards from his employees—as well as everyone else around him—she doubted he had an ounce of mercy in his heart.

Such a man would never understand what had brought Laney here tonight. She would be wise to consider him no different from the heartless banker who'd called in her loan six months early.

Apparently finished with his silent scrutiny, Dupree turned to Hank and handed over Laney's reticule. "You know what to do with this."

"Sure thing, boss."

Pretending to misunderstand, Laney reached out as Hank swept past her. "Oh, how kind of you to walk that over to me."

Hank paused midstep.

"Ignore her," Dupree ordered.

Cocking his head, the big man eyed her cautiously. She thought she detected a note of sympathy in his eyes but then he shook his head and continued on his errand.

As if bored with the whole affair, Dupree leaned against the shut door and crossed his arms over his chest. His casual stance was an illusion, of course. Laney easily detected the concentrated focus behind that bland manner of his.

Recognizing the sensation in her stomach as fear, she forced herself to speak as though nothing was amiss. "Come now, Mr. Dupree. Considering the late hour, perhaps you would be so kind as to return my reticule now. I'm sure we can have our *little discussion* some other time."

His expression never changed, but his gaze narrowed ever so slightly. "Not a chance, honey."

Out of the corner of her eye, Laney caught Hank reaching out to a small, metal safe situated on the floor next to a sturdy-looking desk.

Renewed panic reared, abrupt and violent, stealing her ability to think logically.

Knowing Dupree watched her as closely as she eyed

Hank, Laney inched slowly into a new position, lowered her lashes and focused covertly on Hank's fingers working the dial.

The melodic tick, tick, tick, of the spinning lock filled the room, diminishing her chances of an easy escape with each turn. Another few clicks and Hank pulled opened the safe. He shoved her reticule deep inside then closed the door with a hard snap. Another twist of his wrist and the lock went spinning again.

As the tumblers cleared, her composure snapped.

She whipped around to glare at Dupree. "You can't do this." Her breath came in short, shallow gasps. "It's… it's stealing."

"Don't be so dramatic." Dupree waved his hand at her in a careless gesture. "I have no plans to keep your reticule indefinitely, nor its valuable contents."

"I don't believe you."

"No? What if I told you I plan to return the large sum of money to its rightful owner at once?"

Her throat tightened at the very idea. "You… Mr. Dupree, you can't do that."

"Can't I?"

"But you…" Her mind raced for a solution to this new, awful threat of his. "You promised to give me a chance to explain."

"Indeed, I did." He quirked an eyebrow at her. "Do proceed with your explanation, Miss O'Connor."

Her gaze automatically tracked toward Hank. Standing partly in the shadows the big man appeared deeply enthralled with his thumbnail.

Laney sighed. "Very well. The gentleman gave me that money for—"

She cut off her own the words, remembering Judge

Greene's adamant request. *Never reveal who gave you this money, Miss O'Connor. Or why.*

She'd given her word. Yet, due to no fault of her own, she'd already violated a portion of her promise. She could not reveal the rest.

"Joshua Greene gave you the money for..." Dupree prompted.

Laney pressed her lips tightly shut. How to respond? *Think, Laney. Think.*

In the ensuing silence, Dupree motioned to Hank. The other man dropped his hand and strode out of the room without a single glance in her direction.

With only the two of them left, a thick blanket of tension fell over the room. Laney prayed for divine intervention.

Please, Lord, show me a way out of this quandary.

No quick solution came to mind. She spun in a slow circle, taking in the room from the perspective of a captive—searching for a route of escape. There was no back door, only a small window high above the floor just to the left of the large desk.

Tossing a smile in Dupree's direction, Laney sidled in the direction of the window as nonchalantly as possible.

The size was right, but she'd never make it through the tiny opening in her borrowed dress. Perhaps there was still hope. Having eyed an armoire before setting out, she moved back to the other side of the room, and then threw open the cabinet doors.

"What's this? Several sets of trousers and shirts?" She slanted Dupree a look over her shoulder. "Don't you keep a room for yourself here in the hotel?"

He didn't answer her question directly. "As I'm sure

you've already concluded, Miss O'Connor, there are no additional exits in this room."

"I don't have any idea what you mean."

A patronizing grin slid onto his lips. "Naturally."

How she hated his condescension. The sneering attitude reminded Laney of Thurston P. Prescott III, the banker who'd refused to give her more time on the remaining portion of her loan. All because of a cold, judgmental heart.

Suppressing a scowl, she closed the cabinet doors and twirled in another slow circle. "Oh, my. You have a fireplace. I say, Dupree, your office is exceedingly well furnished."

"I like nice things."

"Of course you do."

She doubted a wealthy man like him knew what it meant to be penniless and scared, never knowing when the next meal would come. But Laney did. As did the children whose mothers had sent them to her orphanage for safekeeping.

Laney had pledged to those women that she would provide every child living in Charity House a Christian upbringing, the comfort of a warm bed and the promise of three meals a day. She would not fail them simply because a suspicious hotel owner had misread her transaction with a prominent judge in town.

Drawing confidence from the thought of her honorable mission, Laney made her way to the fireplace mantel. She immediately took note of the tin photographs arranged haphazardly across the handcrafted stone.

How odd, she thought. The man leaning against the door, watching her through narrowed eyes, couldn't possibly have loved ones. And yet, photographs meant family and friends. Drawn to one image in particular, Laney ran her finger along the pretty gold frame.

Concentrating on the photograph beneath her hand, she looked from the stunning woman smiling up at her, to Dupree, then back again. The resemblance was uncanny. Was this his sister? No. He seemed too hard to have a sister.

And Laney was wasting valuable time.

Glancing to the heavens, she prayed for guidance. *How do I proceed, Lord? What do I say to protect Charity House and the children?*

"Enough stalling, Miss O'Connor." Dupree pushed away from the door and made his approach. "Your failure to explain your actions here tonight speaks volumes. As such, the money you accepted from Judge Greene will remain secure in my safe, and *you* will wait in this office while I go in search of the man myself."

No longer caring about pride, or dignity, Laney met Dupree halfway across the room. "Please, I beg you. Don't involve Joshua in this."

"So now it's Joshua, is it?"

"I meant…Judge Greene." The correction came too late. She saw the censure in Dupree's eyes.

"I'm afraid, Miss O'Connor, *Joshua* involved himself—and consequently me—when he agreed to meet you in my hotel. Since I imagine he's smart enough not to use his real name on the register, I must ask an indelicate question. Which room is he waiting for you in?"

Laney stifled a groan that rose up in her throat.

This man seemed determined to think the worst of her. With very little evidence, he actually believed Judge Greene had rented a room in this hotel with the express purpose of spending the evening with her.

Laney would be insulted if Dupree wasn't so completely incorrect.

Then again…

Perhaps his mistake was a blessing. Perhaps Laney could use this man's ugly assumption of her character to her advantage.

Why not buy herself some much needed time while he went on his search. A search that would prove highly unsuccessful.

"Joshua is in room…" she paused, blinked, and then pretended to accept defeat at last "…912."

For an endless moment, Dupree studied her face. Laney held her breath. The look of disappointment in his eyes—disappointment in *her*—nearly made her rethink her plan.

Should she tell him the truth? Maybe he would understand her situation. Maybe he would care.

And *maybe* Marc Dupree was no different than the shady banker demanding his money before their agreed upon deadline. Simply because he thought the children in her orphanage didn't deserve a safe home in which to live. Not because they were bad children, but because of how their mothers chose to earn their living.

A living that Marc Dupree had accused Laney of conducting here tonight.

No. She couldn't trust him.

The risk was too great.

With renewed determination, she lifted her chin a notch higher.

Dupree's lips twisted into a frown. "Stay here."

Without another word, he turned on his heel and slammed out of his office.

At the sound of the lock striking into place, Laney blew out a hard burst of air.

Stay here. As if he'd given her any other choice.

At least he wouldn't find Judge Greene on the ninth floor. Or any floor, for that matter. Denver's most respected federal judge had already exited the building by way of the back alley. By now, he was probably enjoying the rest of the evening with his very proper, very naive wife.

Dupree would be furious when he returned to his office empty-handed. Laney didn't plan to stick around to find out just how angry. Of course, if there was no money waiting for him in the safe there could be no reason to approach the judge, now or in the future.

No evidence. No shady dealings.

Laney knew what she had to do. And she had precious little time in which to do it.

Pulling her bottom lip between her teeth, she looked frantically around the room. A new plan began formulating in her brain. One that would require a different ensemble than the ridiculously fancy dress she wore now.

She hurried across the room and flung open the doors to the armoire. Smiling wryly, she reached for a pair of worn trousers. Then thought better of her choice and dug deeper.

One by one, she tossed out clothing items until she found the most expensive pair of trousers and the finest linen shirt among the lot.

Kicking off her shoes, she made the change as quickly as possible. Her fingers shook over the buttons but she remained focused. Shoving up the too-long sleeves, she folded her discarded dress into a neat ball then rushed over to the safe.

Thankful she'd paid attention to Hank's fingers working the lock, she spun the dial around, clearing it, then proceeded to get down to business.

Three turns to the right, two more to the left, a final one to the right and…

Click.

Blessed success. It took both hands to open the surprisingly heavy door. She eyed the contents, took only what belonged to her, then pushed the safe closed.

Feeling contrary, she scribbled a quick note to the owner of the hotel—it was the only proper thing to do after all the hospitality he'd given her—then, with a bold sweep of her arm, cleared the desktop of all papers.

She jumped onto the desk.

Looking to the window, she let out a chuckle. She'd scaled too many walls, jumped on and off too many trains, to let a measly little slab of glass three feet above her head daunt her now. A quick flex of fingers, a check to make sure she'd secured her reticule tightly around her wrist and she was ready.

Mind focused on one task at a time, she grabbed the window's frame with one hand and felt around for the opening with the other. Finding the lever at last, she unlocked the latch and pushed the glass forward until she'd created a substantial slit. Careful to avoid catching the silky material on any random piece of wood or metal, she threw the borrowed dress out the opening.

Her foot found a toehold in the wall's masonry. Pulling with her arms and pushing with her feet she raised herself up. Once she was halfway through the window, she grasped the outside casing and tugged again. One final push and she was free.

Free.

Tumbling toward the ground, she used the momentum of the fall to gather her balance.

As always, Laney landed on her feet.

Smiling, she picked up the dress, checked the condition of her reticule and took off at a full run. She made it exactly five steps before colliding into a solid mass of silk-encased muscle.

"Oh!"

The dress plummeted from her clutches. Head reeling, mind focused on escape, Laney instinctively bent to snatch the garment as quickly as possible. Her progress was halted midreach.

Powerful arms trapped her from behind, while an annoyingly familiar voice rang in her ears. "It would appear, Miss O'Connor, you have no idea who you're dealing with."

Chapter Three

Laney tried to twist free, but Dupree's hold tightened around her waist. "Be still," he ordered.

His haughty tone slid over her, making her bolder than usual. "Or you'll what? Hurt me?"

His arms jerked, just a bit, enough to tell her she'd hit her mark. "I'm not in the habit of harming women."

"Then release me."

He had the audacity to chuckle. "Not a chance, honey."

Honey? Laney ground her teeth in frustration. But she wisely remained unmoving. As covertly as possible, she lifted her gaze and studied the window she'd just slipped through. How could Dupree have known she'd escape by way of that tiny opening?

He chuckled again. "I'm an observant man, Miss O'Connor. I watched you eye my window with the same longing that a land-bound sailor tosses at the sea."

"How dare you?"

"I dare because I can." He shifted his hold, drawing his arms tighter around her, as if he suspected she would make a break if he gave her an ounce of opportunity.

He was right, of course. The cad.

The knowledge that he could read her so easily sent a shiver of alarm skidding down her spine. Her bravado of only seconds before disappeared. Clearly, she'd underestimated the man.

A mistake she wouldn't repeat.

She had to get away. But how? At the moment, he had the advantage. Unacceptable. She couldn't allow him to keep her imprisoned in the alleyway where the dim light from the adjacent street made this encounter all too intimate. Terrifyingly so. "Let me go."

"Not until you hand over Judge Greene's money."

"Money?" She struggled with every ounce of her strength, and managed to lengthen the space between them by an entire four inches. "I don't know what you mean."

"So we're back to that. You might want to reconsider your denial in light of your present situation." He spun her around to face him, clamped his hands on her shoulders and dropped an assessing glance over her. "As you must agree, you are in no position to argue."

Far too aware of his hands on her shoulders, she swallowed back a sarcastic retort. She should be furious with indignation. Yet, as he held her trapped inside his gaze a strange, almost pleasant situation rippled through her.

What was wrong with her? This man was the enemy. The enemy! "You seem to be under the impression that you are in control right now."

His fingers flexed, then gripped her again. Not any harder, just more securely. "Wonder where I'd come by such an idea?"

His smug attitude quickened the fight in her. Calling upon the lessons she'd learned from the friendly Chinese man at the mining camp outside Cheyenne, Laney dropped low, then bobbed to her right. She managed to surprise Dupree long enough to free herself for a full half second.

But he reached out, grasped her again then lifted her back to an upright position.

"Release me, you oaf."

Placing her directly in front of him, he flattened his lips into a grim line. For a brief moment, their feet shuffled in a bizarre dance of wills while she tried to get free and he made sure she didn't.

Fully in control of the situation, Dupree concluded their perplexing waltz once he had her in a spot where her only route of escape was through him.

Apparently satisfied with this new arrangement, he released her shoulders at last. "Now." His low, gravelly drawl drifted through the air between them. "Where were we?"

A shudder of unease racked through her. "Your manly display of physical intimidation is rather pedestrian, don't you think? Especially in light of the fact that I have done nothing wrong here tonight."

"You claim innocence, yet you tried to make a quick escape before my return. And now that we're on the subject." His eyes narrowed over her. "I don't remember giving you permission to borrow my clothes."

She jerked her chin at him. "I'm not afraid of you."

"You should be."

Keeping her eyes locked with his, she faked to the right, then shifted quickly to her left. He shot out a restraining arm, and once again, moved her back to center.

"I'm warning you, Dupree—"

"Dispensing of the 'mister,' are we?"

Laney sniffed. "Mister implies a gentleman." She trailed her gaze across his far too handsome face, down to his fancy vest then back again. "Regardless of the manner in which you dress, we both know you are no gentleman."

"And since you are no *lady*, am I to assume we can dispense of any further pretense of good manners?"

Without waiting for her to respond, he reached out and captured a loose tendril of her hair, twined it around his finger.

For a long, stifling moment the strange sensation she'd experienced only moments before slipped through her again, freezing her into immobility. Why wasn't she slapping his hand away? Had she no pride left?

Yes, of course she did.

Calling upon every bit of her outrage, she said, "Release me this instant."

"In due time. But first." He let go of her hair. "I want that money."

"Well, you can't have it."

Even in the dim light she could see the exact moment his patience ran out. He grabbed for her reticule.

"Oh, no." She whipped her arm behind her back. "This money is rightfully mine, given to me for a very good reason."

"So you say." He stopped his approach and crossed his arms over his chest. "If you *are* innocent, as you keep claiming, then you should have no problem sharing with me why Judge Greene gave you the money."

"I…can't tell you."

"Of course you can't."

For reasons unknown to her, Laney again wished she

could tell this man the truth. Marc Dupree would be a powerful ally against the likes of Thurston P. Prescott III.

"All right, Miss O'Connor. Since you refuse to do so yourself, let me explain the situation for you."

She swallowed back a sarcastic retort and thought through her options. Except for crashing through him, she was stuck. For now.

"From your speech alone, I can only assume you're an educated woman. And since we both know an educated woman can earn money in a variety of ways, your presence here tonight can mean only one of two things."

Oh, how she hated that self-righteous tone in his voice, the one that sounded far too much like a banker she knew. "You have it all figured out, don't you, Dupree?"

"Sadly, I do." He dropped his hands to his sides and let out a regretful sigh. "The way I see it, you are either blackmailing Judge Greene or—"

"*Blackmail*?" Laney's breath clogged in her throat. The nerve of the man. The gall. Next, he'd be calling her out for prostitution.

"Or..." he leaned over her "...the judge was soliciting your services for the evening."

And there it was. The nasty accusation she'd feared. She barely resisted the urge to slap him, knowing the gesture would serve no purpose. Which only added to her frustration. "You scoundrel."

He continued as though she hadn't spoken. "Either way, neither activity is allowed in my hotel. So, again, I suggest you hand over the money with no more fuss so I may return it to Judge Greene."

"You seem to take great pleasure in thinking the worst in people."

"Not *all* people."

Out of patience herself, she placed her palms on his chest and shoved. Hard.

He didn't budge an inch. Provoking beyond measure, yet invaluable information for the future.

"I know firsthand what women like you are about, Miss O'Connor."

"Making assumptions again?"

"Absolutely. But I will admit, as reprehensible as I find your choice of lifestyle, I'm certain there are others who find you alluring and appreciate your, shall we call them...*talents*."

Laney sidled to her left.

Dupree scooted her back to the right.

"Talents?" she asked in an overly polite tone. "What sort of talents are we talking about?" As if she didn't know what he meant.

"For one, you dress like a well-bred lady with an accomplished eye for style." He dropped his gaze a moment. "Your present attire not included."

This time, she strayed to the right.

He hauled her back to center. "You speak with perfect diction, somewhat uncommon in these parts. And, most recently, you climbed out of my window with the finesse of a—"

"Skilled acrobat?"

"Precisely."

Not sure what she heard in his voice—grudging respect, censure?—she granted him her most unpleasant smile, the one she reserved for bankers and highborn gentleman in red silk vests.

Finally, an idea came to her. She could still get away with the money—*her money*—but before she resorted to such an underhanded tactic, she had to try to escape in a fair manner one last time.

Didn't she always tell the children to think before they acted? Didn't she warn them of the dangers of sinful behavior? How could Laney ignore everything she tried to teach the children and still face them in the morning?

Determined to hold onto the remaining scraps of her integrity, she scrambled to her right. Again, Dupree pushed her back to her original position.

So be it.

I tried, Lord. Truly, I tried. I pray, please, forgive me for what I'm about to do.

"You know, Dupree, I have other, equally impressive…talents."

"Oh? Do you cook, sew, ride a horse with great skill?"

Sniffing at his attempt to goad her, she took a step toward him and grasped the sides of his vest. "You are becoming redundant."

"As are you, honey."

Honey. She was really starting to dislike that word. Nevertheless, she touched her fingertip to the top button of his vest.

Eyes lowering to half-mast, he captured her hand in a light but firm grip. "I wouldn't advise continuing down this path, Miss O'Connor."

Allowing him to misunderstand her intent, she moved a step closer. "You sure you don't want to see what I can do?"

His look turned sardonic. "I'm afraid I must decline further demonstration of this particular skill."

"Once again," she tugged her hand free, "you have chosen to misread the situation."

He swallowed. Once. Twice. Then again more slowly. *Very* slowly. "By all means, honey, prove me wrong."

"Gladly." She shifted her weight, planting her left foot slightly behind her right. To keep his attention off her new position, she toyed with his lapel again. "You see," she said in a light, airy tone. "When cornered, I fight like I do everything else."

"You lie and cheat?"

"No." She gave him her most brilliant smile and took a step back. "I win."

She raised her right knee and, leading with her heel, slammed her foot into his chest. The blow landed exactly as her friend had taught her.

Caught off guard, Dupree stumbled backward. His gasp of surprise wasn't as gratifying as Laney would have predicted.

This was her one chance. With a quick snatch, she retrieved her bundled dress and tore around the corner at breakneck speed. She quickened her pace to a flat-out run as the bellowed promise to hunt her down like a rabid dog nipped at her heels.

Minutes later, Marc charged wordlessly to the back of his hotel. Holding on to his anger—*barely*—he released the lock and with a violent shove, plowed into his office. The earsplitting crack of door meeting wall punctuated his foul mood. Unfortunately, the jarring noise did nothing to eliminate the reality of the last ten minutes. Not since Pearl ran off with his fortune could Marc recall a time he'd suffered so complete a defeat.

Oh, he'd known Miss O'Connor would attempt to steal away with what she *claimed* was her rightful possession. He'd even expected her to resort to whatever means necessary to escape. Her kind always thought in terms of survival. What he hadn't imagined was to find room 912 empty and Joshua Greene long gone by the time Marc had arrived.

Had the judge known he was coming to confront him?

Not possible. There had been no time or opportunity for Miss O'Connor to warn him.

Rubbing the spot where she'd landed her heel to his chest, Marc let out a frustrated hiss. How could such a tiny, delicate woman land a blow with so much force? She hadn't hurt him, not by half. He'd suffered far worse from rowdy drunks and mean-spirited outlaws. Nevertheless, she'd taken him by surprise, enough to throw him off-balance and make her getaway.

The situation defied logic. And Marc was a man who relied solely on logic. Emotion, blind faith, he allowed neither in his life.

Shifting his angry gaze around what used to be his highly organized personal sanctuary, he slammed his fist into his open palm. He'd left the woman alone for fifteen minutes and she'd wreaked havoc. Risking a step through the clothes scattered on the floor, he tripped over a very delicate, very female slipper.

He kicked the offensive shoe out of his way and eyed the strewn papers at his feet. Papers that had once been in neat piles on his desk.

"Did she leave nothing untouched?"

Scrubbing a hand over his face, Marc fought for control. But then he spotted a slip of paper propped against a pile of books on his desk. A second later, he whipped the note from its perch with as much intensity as he'd used to enter the room.

If the miserable handwriting was any indication, Miss O'Connor had scrawled the words with as little care as she'd given his office.

Marc's irritation only increased as he read her parting jab.

> *My Dear Mr. Dupree,*
> *Thank you for your splendid hospitality this evening.*
> *But I'm afraid I must decline your offer to remain any longer. I have a much more pressing engagement with your window.*
> *Yours most humbly,*
> *Miss Laney O'Connor*

Crushing the paper in his fist, Marc stifled the urge to take off after the woman without formulating a plan of action. Not the most logical move. Calling upon his well-honed control, he shut his eyes and released all the air from his lungs.

Dark, ugly thoughts linked together in his mind until one emerged over all the others. Laney O'Connor had chosen the wrong hotel, on the wrong evening, to play out her little intrigue with a federal judge.

Five years ago, Marc had embarked on the greatest debacle of his life—marriage to Pearl LaRue. The events of the last hour merely added another layer of indignity to his rash, youthful mistake of thinking he could turn a bad woman good.

Having been raised by loving, Christian parents, Marc had operated on the belief *that all fall short of the glory of God* and that the Lord's unending grace was administered through His people. People with the means and desire to serve.

He'd been naive, painfully so. But Marc had learned his lesson, thanks to Pearl's betrayal. When she'd grown bored with him, she hadn't simply run off with another man. She'd robbed Marc blind. She'd emptied his bank accounts, his personal safe and, most humbling, his wallet—*then* she'd found someone else to share her spoils.

Marc's resulting years of poverty had taught him well. Back on his feet, his coffers fuller than ever, he was no longer in the business of saving souls.

That didn't mean he didn't offer women of questionable virtue a chance to change their lives. He provided them with an honest living, but left the condition of their souls to the local pastor. If they chose to return to their old way of life, who was he to stop them?

Which begged the question. Why was he so disillusioned with Laney O'Connor's behavior tonight? What about the woman made Marc want to give her the benefit of the doubt?

Was it the look of desperation he'd caught snatches of in her startling gaze?

He knew better than to trust her, or her lies. And yet, here he stood, on the night of what would have been his wedding anniversary, wanting to believe in a woman no different from the one he'd married all those years ago. He'd thought he'd learned his lesson.

An uncomfortable ache spread through him as he

realized just how much he'd wanted Laney O'Connor to be the innocent she'd proclaimed to be over and over again.

Even now, the thought of her making her way through the Denver streets, alone, with all that money, at this late hour, didn't sit well with him. He—

A loud rap against the doorjamb knocked Marc out of his musing.

"Mr. Dupree, I'm sorry she got away." Hank's gaze tracked through the room. "She...I mean, I never thought she'd climb out of the window. I thought—"

Marc lifted a hand to stop the stilted flow of words. "I know, Hank. She fooled us both." Remembering the way she'd toyed with his vest, drawing his attention away from the situation, then unceremoniously kicking him in the chest, he shook his head. "In more ways than one."

"She seemed, I don't know, honest." Hank visibly cringed as his gaze landed on the open safe. "I never would have taken her for a woman of such questionable...character."

The same thought had gnawed at Marc from the start, but he'd learned long ago that people were rarely what they seemed. He shouldn't have been surprised by Miss O'Connor's deception. But he was. Shockingly, profoundly, inexplicably shaken to the core.

"The world is full of dishonest people," he said for Hank's benefit as well as his own.

All sin and fall short of the glory of God.

His mother's favorite Bible verse and a truth that pertained to Marc far more often than not. Despite his efforts to remain above reproach, he made mistakes. Perhaps knowing he often *fell short* explained why Marc still wanted to believe Miss O'Connor wasn't what she seemed. That she was…somehow…more.

"I wonder how she figured out the combination," Hank said, still eyeing the open safe.

Marc rubbed his palm over his chest. "She watched your fingers."

"You…" Hank blinked at him. "You knew?"

Marc nodded. Pearl had pulled a similar stunt.

The abrupt silence that fell over the room stood in stark contrast to the noise echoing from the main part of the hotel.

In the ensuing hush Marc came to a decision. "I'm going out. While I'm gone, switch that," he pointed to the safe, "with the one in my rooms upstairs."

"Sure thing, boss."

Marc paced to the doorway. Hank stopped him before he could leave. "Where you headed? In case I need you."

Taking a deep, calming breath, Marc stated the obvious. "Holladay Street." Where the bulk of Denver's brothels were located.

"The Row? You think Miss O'Connor lives…*there*?"

"It's the most logical place for a woman like her."

Not that Marc thought she was a regular, run-of-the-mill prostitute. Considering her mode of dress and impeccable speech, he feared she was something far worse. A madam. One who employed the kind of girls Marc hired away for their own good.

This was no longer about money. In truth, his clash with Miss O'Connor had never been about the contents of her reticule. But rather, how and why she'd acquired the large sum.

Marc wasn't through with the woman.

Once he located her on The Row he would explain to her, in excruciating detail, why she could not use his hotel to conduct her unsavory business ever again. No matter how discreet or desperate she might be. He would then seek out Judge Greene and explain the situation to him as well.

This wasn't personal. Hotel Dupree's sterling reputation was at stake, a reputation Marc had spent three years honing to perfection.

"One thing's for certain, Hank. I'll root our little fox out of her lair before daybreak. And when I'm through with her, she'll be sorry she ever strayed into my hotel."

Hank's smile bowed with the same grim determination Marc savored in his own heart. "Happy hunting, boss."

Chapter Four

Home at last, Laney stood at the bottom of the front steps and admired the three-story house glowing golden under the streetlamp. She couldn't help but smile at the house that was now a home for nearly thirty abandoned children.

After four lean years, and two strapping loans, Laney had turned the ordinary structure into an enchanting brick mansion. The result was as fine as any house owned by her fashionable neighbors in the Highlands of North Denver. She'd come a long way from the grubby mining camps and saloons of her childhood.

In her overzealous attempt to provide more than a roof and bed for the children, she'd left no detail to chance. She'd furnished the twelve bedrooms, two sitting rooms, and three parlors with tasteful furniture. She'd hung expensive wallpaper, ordered rugs straight from Paris, and purchased assorted fineries for every room.

Perhaps she'd gone a bit overboard.

How could she not? What better way to demonstrate God's majesty than by providing the children with unspeakable beauty and grandeur in their everyday lives? Lives that had been filled with far too much squalor and despair prior to arriving at Charity House.

An image of Marc Dupree splintered through her thoughts and a sudden, ugly dose of conscience whipped through Laney. She hadn't behaved completely without fault tonight. In fact, she'd been intentionally misleading, deceptive even, practically lying to the man. Just how far was she willing to go to save Charity House from foreclosure?

The front door opened a crack, rescuing Laney from further reflection on the consequences of her behavior this evening. Katherine Taylor, the young woman she'd left in charge, came out onto the porch. "Well? What happened?"

Laney skipped up the steps. "We did it, Katherine." She pulled her friend into a fierce hug. "Our worries are finally over."

"You got the money? He gave you all of it?" Katherine pulled back and searched Laney's face. "All five hundred dollars? How did you convince him?"

"The details aren't important."

Stepping farther back, Katherine scanned Laney from head to toe. "What happened to Sally's dress?"

"Plans changed." Laney held up the gold silk bundle. "I had to switch clothes at the last minute."

Katherine planted her balled fists on her hips. "You didn't do anything unlawful, did you?"

"Of course not."

The truth, up to a point. She'd only allowed Dupree to *think* she'd planned to conduct a shameful act with Judge Greene. Her actions had been misleading, but not criminal.

Considering how Katherine would worry herself sick if she knew the full story, Laney decided to keep the details of her encounter with Dupree to herself. "I have in my possession the money we need to save Charity House. Now stop with the questions and enjoy our moment of triumph."

"Oh, I'm thrilled. But why won't you look me in the eye? I'm almost twenty. Plenty old enough to handle whatever it is you're hiding from me."

Laney squared her shoulders. But to her chagrin, she couldn't hold Katherine's gaze longer than a second or two. It was no use pretending all was well. She was going to have to tell her friend at least part of what had occurred this evening. "Don't start making judgments before you hear the whole story."

"Oh, Laney, what did you do?"

"Only what was necessary."

"No, I'm sure you did more, as always. Look at this place." She wound her hand in a circle. "It's a mansion. Orphanages are usually full of filth, misery and despair, especially for the likes of us, the unwanted children of prostitutes."

Uncomfortable with the turn in conversation, Laney grimaced. "I didn't do anything special."

"No, you just made a dream come true for children who have lived without hope most of their lives. You are a good, Christian woman with a big heart, Laney O'Connor."

If only that were true. "Don't make me out to be more than I am. When my mother moved us to Mattie's brothel, I couldn't get out fast enough. I didn't want to go it alone, so I took the rest of the children with me. That's selfish, not noble."

"Keep telling yourself that, but I know how hard you've worked to make Charity House a reality. You wouldn't intentionally jeopardize it by..." Katherine's voice trailed off. "Are you sure everything's all right?"

Laney looked over her shoulder, praying she'd done enough to ensure Dupree hadn't followed her. She'd darted up, down and across several streets, then doubled back three more times.

But just in case...

"Let's head inside for the rest of this conversation."

Frowning, Katherine allowed Laney to hook their arms together. "We're going to keep Charity House, right?"

The quick flash of terror in the younger woman's eyes, the same one Laney saw every time she looked in the mirror, called to the part of her that would do anything to save the orphanage. Unfortunately, her efforts never proved enough. Oh, she provided a home, material luxuries, and even love, but she had yet to figure out a way to erase the one thing the orphans all shared.

Uncertainty.

Mistrust and fear lived in all their gazes, in their very souls. It was one thing to teach the children about Christ's love, quite another for them to accept the Lord in their hearts, fully, and without reservation.

If only it were easier for them to believe they mattered, truly mattered, as precious children of God. But their pasts didn't allow for a straightforward, trouble-free path to salvation. The choice to believe was an individual matter, one Laney couldn't settle for anyone but herself, despite her desire to do so for the children in her care.

When she'd stared into Dupree's eyes, Laney had seen a similar restlessness and need for peace.

Could that have been why she'd come so close to sharing her troubles with him? Because something deep within her had recognized a hurting soul like her own?

No. Ridiculous, dangerous thinking. Clearly, she'd lost her perspective. Thanks to the harsh reality of life as the daughter of a prostitute who'd killed herself with too much laudanum, Lancy knew better than to rely on a man, *any* man. After witnessing her mother's choice of lifestyle and eventual destruction, how could Laney toss away her caution after one evening in the company of Marc Dupree?

A breeze kicked up, rustling the bushes lining the porch. The ominous quiver in her heart urged Laney to pull Katherine toward the house. "Inside. Quick."

"Why the urgency?" Katherine looked behind her. "Laney? Are you in trouble?"

Concentrating on hustling the other woman inside the house, Laney tugged harder. "Quickly, Katherine. Quickly."

Once in the front parlor, with the dark night firmly locked outside where it belonged, Laney tossed Sally's dress on a blue velvet couch. Katherine moved through the room lighting candles. Laney waited, savoring the moment of serenity passing through her. How she loved the soft, warm glow of real candlelight.

Katherine lit the last candle, turned and centered her gaze on Laney's bare feet. "What happened to your shoes?"

Waving her hand in a dismissive gesture, Laney moved deeper in the room. "Nothing to concern yourself over."

"Perhaps it's time you shared the details of your evening with me."

Laney worked her reticule free from her wrist then handed over the bag. "This is all you need to know."

Fingers shaking, Katherine opened the satchel and caught her breath inside an audible gasp.

"It's real," Laney said with a smile.

Almost reverently, Katherine touched the money with a delicate caress, as though afraid it would disappear if she handled it improperly. "Oh, Laney." Unshed tears pooled in her eyes. "Our troubles are truly over."

Drawing closer, Laney peered inside the reticule as well. Why didn't she feel the same joy she heard in Katherine's voice? Perhaps because she'd come so close to losing it all. She hadn't been prepared for Marc Dupree. Or her strange reaction to him. Or the inexplicable need to profess her situation and ask for his assistance, no matter how fleeting.

A thousand ripples of unease churned in her stomach, reminding her of the weakness she'd discovered in herself tonight, the unthinkable wish to rely on a man, a man with impossible standards she could never hope to meet.

"All right, Laney. What happened? You might as well tell me whatever it is you're hiding behind that scowl."

Sighing, she lowered to a brocade settee and gave up pretending everything had gone as planned. "I went to the Hotel Dupree to meet Judge Greene at the agreed upon time…"

She stopped midsentence, unsure how to continue. How could she tell Katherine about Marc Dupree and their strange run-in? "I don't know if you should hear this, Katherine. You're not like the rest of us."

"Of course I am."

"No, you're not." Laney softened her words with a smile. "Your mother only turned to prostitution after your father died. She never made you live among it. That alone makes you different. You're also formally educated. You went to that prestigious school back East. What was it called?"

"Miss Lindsay's Select School for Young Ladies." Katherine sat beside Laney and set the reticule between them. "But that was my past. I'm here now, as much a part of Charity House as the rest of the orphans."

"Not by choice. You'd still be living in Boston, probably married to a wealthy gentleman, if that school hadn't expelled you when they found out about your mother's profession. Even now, you could get a teaching job in any number of places."

Eyes blinking rapidly, Katherine swiped at her wet cheeks. "But Charity House is my home. Where I belong. I'd do anything to keep this orphanage running."

"As long as it was ethical."

"Well, yes, that goes without saying." Katherine took Laney's hand. "All right, enough stalling. Let's have the rest of it. You went to the hotel, and…"

Laney bit her bottom lip as she searched for the right words. Katherine might have been forced to return to Denver, but she was still a product of her years back East, educated, moral, raised with Christian values, an example for the others. Would she understand the desperation that had led Laney to withhold information from Dupree?

She didn't want to find out. Not tonight. "*And…*the judge handed over the money. His debt is canceled. Charity House is saved. The end."

"So, it's that simple."

Laney drew a quick breath of air. "Yes."

"Don't you think I deserve to hear the rest, the portion you're hiding from me? Please, I've lived with the fear of losing Charity House just as deeply as you have. Maybe more." A shadow fell over her face. "I have no skills, no real life experiences to speak of."

"You have an education. You could teach school, just as you've taught me."

"Who would hire a woman like me, an infamous madam's daughter?" Katherine shut her eyes a moment and sighed heavily. "I have nowhere else to go. Now convince me I have nothing to worry about."

Taking a deep breath, Laney began her tale, but Katherine cut her off almost before she begun. "The hotel owner witnessed the transaction?"

"It gets worse." Laney proceeded to tell her friend the rest.

When she reached the end, Katherine gaped at her for several long seconds. "He confiscated the money? But why?"

"He runs a *proper* hotel, Katherine, something I can't fault him for." Dupree, for all his other unsavory characteristics, was clearly a man of integrity. Hard on others, true, but probably just as hard on himself.

Before she started sympathizing with the cad, she shook her head and continued. "When he saw me speaking with Judge Greene and then witnessed money changing he hands, he thought...well, he thought the worst."

"Oh, Laney."

"I never admitted to any wrongdoing. Why would I? I'd done nothing improper. But I couldn't reveal my reason for meeting with Judge Greene, per his adamant request. Nor did I try to dissuade Dupree's misconception of my character." And that had been wrong of her, dreadfully wrong. "When he locked me in his office—"

"He didn't."

"He did."

"But I don't understand." Katherine shook her head. "How did you get the money back?"

She touched the reticule, pulled on one of the strings, then the other, toyed with them. The gesture reminded her of the way Dupree had captured her hair around his finger, how he'd stared at it for an endless moment, and how—

She cut off the rest of her thoughts and focused on answering Katherine's question. "I had to...um...climb out of his office window, hence the change in attire."

"Oh, Laney."

She glossed over the part about breaking into his safe, making sure to tone down her use of physical violence to make her final escape from the alleyway.

"Oh, Laney."

"Would you stop saying 'Oh, Laney' in that disenchanted tone of yours? You sound like a shocked, elderly aunt instead of a young woman barely twenty years old."

"Well, someone needs to think like an adult." Katherine jumped to her feet and paced through the room. After her second pass, she turned back to face Laney. "Tell me more about this hotel owner."

A shudder quickened Laney's pulse. Dupree had been a formidable foe, far more clever than the banker she'd sparred with this morning. Prescott incited only disdain in her heart. While Dupree called up a mixture of emotions that confused her, and blunted the edge she usually relied on to aid her in sticky situations.

"I never want to see that man again. He's judgmental, arrogant and enjoys jumping to conclusions without a shred of evidence."

Eyebrows traveling upward, Katherine wrapped her arms across her waist and said, "Not a shred?"

Laney broke eye contact. "All right, maybe I sent his mind in a few wrong directions."

"I read in the *Denver Chronicle* that he's impossibly handsome."

"You have no idea."

Silence fell over them as each considered the events of the evening from their own perspective.

"Laney?"

"Hmm?"

"Do you think Mr. Dupree will leave the situation alone now that you've taken the money?"

"I…" A shudder of apprehension passed through her. "I don't know."

"Will he still try to confront Judge Greene without the evidence in hand?"

She could lie. She could pretend matters weren't as dire as they really were. Their long-running friendship deserved better. "He might."

Hands trembling, Katherine sank back on the settee. "What are we going to do?"

"The only thing we can do. We'll pay off the loan the moment the bank opens in the morning." The idea swelled within her, creating a sense of peace she hadn't experienced in days. "That way, no matter what Dupree decides to do next, we'll already own Charity House.

Even if he confronts Judge Greene there won't be much either man can do at that point."

"Other than make trouble for us, in all sorts of awful ways."

Laney batted away Katherine's objection with a flick of her wrist.

"No. Don't dismiss my concerns like that. What if Judge Greene teams up with Mr. Dupree, if for no other reason than to save face? What if they try to shut us down for some unknown, yet perfectly legal reason? What if they—"

"Stop, Katherine. Just stop. We must stay positive, and pray that Dupree will drop the matter now that I'm gone."

"You really think he'll leave us alone?"

"Yes, as long as he doesn't find us."

Katherine sighed heavily.

Looking at the clock on the mantel, Laney shoved her worries behind a brilliant smile. "Three hours, Katherine. We only have three short hours before the bank opens for business. By the time Dupree finds me, *if* he finds me, he'll be too late."

"You seem awfully confident." Rising to her feet once again, Katherine moved to the window and looked out. "You're sure he didn't follow you home."

Laney joined her friend at the window. "I was careful to lead him far away from Charity House. If I'm as good as I think I am, which I am, Dupree is looking for me on The Row."

"*The Row*?" Katherine's mouth dropped. "He thinks you live in a…a…brothel?"

A slow smile spread across her lips. "That would be my guess."

"You're reckless. That's what you are." Although Katherine's tone held far too much worry for Laney's peace of mind, a loving glint filled the other woman's gaze.

Visibly relaxing, Laney smiled in return. "Perhaps I am more than a little reckless. But thanks to my quick thinking, Marc Dupree is chasing shadows on the other side of town. Now, stop worrying and trust me." She squeezed Katherine's arm. "I have matters completely under control."

Katherine rubbed her temples. "Why is it every time you say that we end up in worse trouble than before?"

Chapter Five

Precisely three hours after arriving home from the Hotel Dupree, Laney bypassed the tellers, skirted along the high railing on her left, then charged toward the bank owner's private office. Unwilling to wait for a response to her knock, she turned the knob and pressed forward. "I'm here to discuss my loan."

Thurston P. Prescott III didn't bother looking up as he waved his fleshy hand in bored indifference. "There is nothing more to say, Miss O'Connor. My terms stand."

Outlaw, she wanted to scream. *Cheat*. Just yesterday, he'd adopted that same thinly veiled scorn, then shamelessly called in her loan six months early. No warning. No viable explanation. Merely the end of all her dreams for the children.

Exhaling slowly, Laney forced aside her hostility and coaxed her lips into a pleasant smile. "I have one final item to address."

His attention riveted on the papers before him, Prescott scratched his salt-and-pepper beard and patently ignored her. Laney widened her stance, calling upon the patience she'd lost the day before while standing in this very spot. The constant, even ticking of the wall clock beat in stark contrast to the banker's furious scribbling. The rich smell of polished mahogany and perfectly aged leather extolled power, ownership.

Laney refused to be intimidated.

She poked at the stack of papers nearest to her, sending them scattering to the floor. "Oh, my, look what I've done."

Prescott's head snapped up. Frustration knitted across his bushy brows. "I thought I made myself perfectly clear. As of this morning, you now have two days left to come up with the money." He dipped his pen in the inkwell on his left, then returned his gaze to his paperwork. "You know the way out."

Oh, no. He wasn't sending her away yet. Not before she'd settled her loan. "I will take only a moment more of your time."

Silence was his only reply.

Laney released a small sigh of satisfaction and plucked the neatly wrapped bundle of money from the hidden pocket in her skirt. "Perhaps you'll be interested in what I have to say now."

With a steady hand, she set the sizable pile directly where he'd fastened his attention after dismissing her so coldly.

In one swift movement, he snatched the money off the desk and looked up. His small, sharp eyes hardened. Sputtering, he flung his ugly glare from her face to the money in his hand and back again.

"It's all there." Laney granted him her most pleasant smile. "All five hundred dollars."

For a moment his gaze filled with disdain, but then

he set the money back on the desk and cleared his expression of all emotion, save one. Suspicion. "How did you come upon this much money in one day?"

A flicker of conscience ignited, making it no longer possible to escape the truth any longer. Yes, Judge Greene had owed Laney the money for Johnny's room and board over the past three years. And, yes, he should have been paying all along for his son's care. But that didn't make what Laney had done the most ethical of routes she could have chosen to raise the money.

She'd used the man's former "friendship" with her mother—as well as his current one with several other women in Mattie's brothel—to insist he pay off his debt. Worse, Laney had led him to believe she would make his life difficult if he didn't do so at once.

That had been wrong. Justified, perhaps, but wrong. *Forgive me, Lord.*

Drawing in a slow breath, Laney fought to keep the shame out of her voice as she spoke. "Does it matter where the money came from?"

Eyes narrowed, Prescott slapped both palms on his desk and leaned forward. "Yes, Miss O'Connor, it matters significantly. I must know, without a single doubt, that every dollar of this money is truly yours."

Laney sighed. She should have been prepared for such a reaction. But she'd been so relieved Judge Greene had cooperated without a fuss she hadn't thought much further. After convincing Katherine all was well, she'd changed clothes, helped with the children's morning routine, then hurried to the bank.

Tired now, and more than a little frightened, she did what came naturally. She fought for what was hers. "Telling you where or how I got this money was not part of our agreement. All you said was that I had to pay off my loan in three days. And there is my payment." She pointed to the money.

A succession of creaks and groans exploded in the air as the banker shifted his considerable frame into another position. Resting his elbows on the chair's arm, he steepled his fingers under his chin. "Did you steal it?"

"No." The very idea.

"Then I'll ask just one more time, before I throw you out of my office. Where did you get the money?"

How she detested that smug condemnation in his eyes. A man like Prescott, with his fancy clothes, obscene wealth, and judgmental nature exemplified all that threatened her children's chance of a secure future. "Let's just say I have a…benefactor."

Now why had she said that, as though she were a woman cut from the same cloth as her mother? She had no doubt Marc Dupree would positively go apoplectic if he heard what she'd just claimed, all but confirming his bad opinion of her.

Disturbed by the direction of her thoughts and that she'd think of the handsome hotel owner at a time like this, she batted at a stubborn curl falling loose from its pins below her hat. What did it matter what Dupree thought of her? If she'd done her job properly last night, and had fully misled him into thinking she lived on The Row, she would never see the man again.

A pity.

No. Not a pity. A blessing.

Studying her with narrowed eyes, Prescott rose from his chair and made his way around the desk.

Laney threw her head back and held his stare, refusing to stir as the banker drew closer. No matter what happened in the next few minutes, she would not let this man see how much she abhorred his self-serving attitude. The one that led him to give and take money whenever it pleased him.

"You have a…benefactor?" He practically spat the word.

"I do."

"You expect me to believe some misguided soul gave you five hundred dollars? Your friends on The Row may help you out on occasion, as well as a few saloon owners, but I know for a fact that none of them have the kind of money you just delivered here today."

Laney swallowed back a nasty retort and concentrated on remaining calm. "Is it so hard to comprehend?"

"I find it impossible. No one would give money to you or that…*home*…of yours. A place filled with illegitimate children with mothers working on The Row." His face inflated with fury. "It's beyond repulsive."

Laney recoiled at the callous words. "No child is repulsive." *Let these little ones come to me.* "There are many people in Denver who see the need for my orphanage."

"You mean the shamed mothers of your kind who need a place to discard their brats."

Her knees buckled at the venom in his tone. Hands trembling, she grasped the side of the desk to steady herself. This man, with his refined eastern accent and overfilled belly, had never cared about Charity House. Or the children. But surely, he held a fondness for one of them. "What about your son?"

"Don't ever mention that boy in my presence again." His rage reverberated in his voice.

"But I thought you wanted to provide for Michael's future, if not for the other children."

"That was never my intention." Prescott's lips twisted in a snarl. "He's Sally's problem, not mine."

Hypocrite. Just like the men who'd come to Laney's mother, wanting their pleasure and paying handsomely for it, then cursing her unholy profession once back in their daily lives on the righteous side of Hollady Street. "If that's how you feel, then why lend me the money in the first place?"

"Simple." He let out a bitter laugh. "I knew you could never pay back that much money in time. I gave it to you so you would fail. And then Denver would be rid of you and your brats for good."

He'd wanted her to fail? He might as well have grasped her heart and squeezed the very life out of it. She clamped her lips tight shut, shunning the weak tears that would proclaim her despair to this man. All this time, Laney thought Prescott had loaned her the money for the benefit of his six-year-old son. She'd been wrong. So...very...wrong.

"It doesn't matter what you think," she said, realizing the truth as she spoke it out loud. "You signed our agreement. That makes it legal. You can't deny me the right to pay off my loan."

He blinked, his insults held in check for the first time during their association. Sensing victory, Laney clutched her small advantage and pounced. "Take the money and let's be done with this distasteful business between us."

Prescott paused. "I'll have to count it."

Hardly daring to breathe, Laney nodded. "By all means, take your time. My morning is yours."

As he rounded his desk and lowered back into his chair, a sense of euphoria built inside her.

Almost there.

Counting one bill at a time, he made slow work of checking the amount.

Almost there. Almost there.

His gaze unreadable, Prescott set the last bill on top of the pile and looked up at her.

"You lose, Mr. Prescott." Laney allowed a full smile to lengthen across her lips. "And now I own Charity House."

I own Charity House. The thought coiled in her head, making her dizzy with relief.

All she had to do was endure a few more tense moments in this awful man's company and she'd never have to deal with him again.

"Before I leave this morning I want the deed to Charity House. And I want you to put in writing that I have no more debt owed to this bank. Or to you."

"I'm afraid that won't be possible."

What? "Why not?"

"You're short the full amount." He patted the stack of money.

"Short?" That couldn't be correct. "The full amount is there, all five hundred dollars. I counted the stack myself, just this morning."

"You didn't include the interest."

Every fiber of her being froze at the look of pleasure on Prescott's face. "Interest?"

"You can't think I would have given you three extra days on your loan without a penalty."

He had the audacity to look sorrowful now, as though the matter was out of his hands. A lie. They both knew he was the owner of this bank. He could add or subtract any terms he liked, on whatever whim suited him.

"Have you no decency?" she whispered, trying to reconcile the man standing before her with the one he presented to the good people of Denver. He attended church every Sunday, pretended piousness while in the pew, and then conducted shameless usury the rest of the week.

"How much interest are you talking about?"

"Ten percent."

She gasped.

"But to prove I'm a fair man, I'll extend your loan through the end of the month without adding any additional fee."

Fifty dollars. He wanted an *additional* fifty dollars in less than three weeks. It might as well be five thousand. How would she ever raise more money, when she'd already tapped all her normal sources, a few not-so-normal, and then one more?

She'd failed. When she'd come so close to victory.

And somehow Prescott knew she had no more resources at her disposal.

No. *No.* She couldn't give up. Not with nearly three weeks left to formulate a plan. Surely Laney could find the extra fifty dollars in the allotted timeframe. She could go to the children's mothers, again, or even Mattie Silks herself. Laney could cut costs to the bare bone, or maybe find a job.

What sort of job would pay that kind of money?

Something…anything…

Please, Lord, show me the way.

"All right, Mr. Prescott. I accept your terms." As if

she had any other choice. "You will have the additional fifty dollars by the end of the month."

"Good enough."

Not by half. Laney had learned her lesson. She knew better than to walk out of this office with only a verbal agreement between them. Not this time. Not ever again.

"Before I go," she said, "I want the new conditions of my loan in writing, spelled out in clear language, signed by us both with at least two witnesses present."

Owl-eyed and motionless, he blinked up at her.

Laney held his stare, boldly, fearlessly, silently calling his bluff as though they were in a high-stakes poker game with both their livelihoods on the line. "I'll wait while you draw up the document."

Hours of walking countless streets and alleyways in the wee hours of the morning had helped Marc's anger simmer to a low boil. He'd searched the length of The Row—Denver's notorious red-light district—but had not discovered Miss O'Connor's brothel or her alternate place of business.

The slippery woman had vanished completely and the suspicion that she was not what she seemed thrashed to life all over again.

Where was she? And more importantly, what could have possibly birthed that look of desperation in those beautiful, expressive eyes? Had she incurred a sizable debt that required quick payment?

A possibility, to be sure.

Perhaps that shifty banker Prescott would have some answers. Not long after moving to Denver, Marc had discovered the man's uncanny knack for asserting himself into almost every major financial transaction in the city. If Laney O'Connor owed money to someone in town, there was a high possibility Prescott would know the particulars. Or worse, had involved himself in the matter personally.

Marc wouldn't wish that cruelty on anyone, not even Miss O'Connor.

When he entered the bank, the clerk told him he would have to wait his turn to speak with Prescott. The owner was already conducting business with another customer.

None too happy, Marc thrust aside his impatience and sat in a chair facing the glass-encased office split into three sections by polished wooden planks. The elegant interior of the bank called to mind his youthful days in New Orleans, before the war had destroyed the opulence in which he'd been born. He knew it was a time that could never be regained. Yet the soothing memories of that simpler life flooded his mind, sending a sharp homesickness for family, and what might have been.

He'd lost so much, not just the only way of life he'd ever known, but far too many loved ones as well. Perhaps that explained why he'd been fooled into thinking he could reclaim some of his joy with Pearl by his side.

Pearl. What a debacle their marriage had been.

If only he'd caught up with her before she'd died in that train wreck, he wouldn't feel such regret, or such disgrace. But after three arduous years of searching, the last two conducted by an overpaid Pinkerton agent, Marc still didn't know where his wife had hidden the remaining portion of his fortune. All he knew was that she'd spent the bulk of the money in Cripple Creek during the first few months after she'd left him.

Unwilling to allow the melancholy he'd banished years ago to return this morning, he diverted his attention back to Prescott's office. At the sight of the woman jerking her chin at the banker, Marc straightened in his chair.

He knew that particular gesture, *and* that defiant angle of delicate female shoulders. The familiar prickling on the back of his neck confirmed her identity more surely than if she'd turned around to face him. "Laney O'Connor."

Outfitted in a pale pink, really very homely dress, she still managed to catch his attention and hold it fast.

The moment she squared her tiny shoulders and jutted her nose in the air, Marc stood.

No wonder he hadn't located the woman on The Row. The little con had been conducting affairs of a very different nature this morning. Was she starting her own brothel? That would explain the odd, hushed-mouthed reticence of the madams he'd questioned throughout the night and early-morning hours.

How he wished it weren't true, but what else would explain the need for such a large sum of money, money she was using to conduct business with the shadiest banker in town? Marc could hardly bear the thread of disappointment braiding through him.

Surprisingly heavyhearted, he continued to watch Miss O'Connor deal with Prescott. She shrugged in response to something the man said, and then turned to look out the office windows. Her gaze roamed the bank in the same cool, calculating manner she'd used to survey Marc's hotel last night.

He took a step forward, ensuring she saw him when her gaze crossed in his direction. The instant those amber eyes met his, he nodded. Her wide-eyed flush prompted him to add a bit of sarcasm to the moment. He delivered a two-finger salute.

She shifted her stance, shot him a frown and then purposely turned her back to him. Her slight tremble told the true story of her reaction to his presence in the bank. She should be worried.

The time had come to finish their conversation from last night, with Marc the ultimate victor. And he knew just how to orchestrate his triumph.

Chapter Six

After a brief spasm of panic and several long seconds of contemplation, Laney came to the conclusion that she had no other choice than to face the tall, well-dressed bundle of trouble waiting outside Prescott's private office.

The wisest decision would be to confront Dupree alone, before the banker insinuated himself into the matter. Taking a quick, uneven pull of air, Laney sauntered into the main foyer with the most nonchalant gait she could muster.

For additional courage, she clutched the signed document Prescott had reluctantly drawn up, per her unwavering insistence. All Laney had to do now was come up with fifty dollars and Charity House would be hers.

After she faced Marc Dupree, of course.

Prepared for their upcoming encounter, she almost regretted the anticlimactic sensation upon discovering the man's absence in the bank lobby.

Capitalizing on her good fortune, Laney turned toward the back door, but thought better of her chosen route after only three steps. She'd seriously underestimated Dupree the night before. He most assuredly would expect her to exit by way of the empty alley again.

Or would he discount the obvious?

Front entrance? Back door?

Decisions. Decisions.

The apprehension she'd previously held at bay uncoiled, making each step a brand-new torture. Insisting her brain cooperate, Laney made her choice. After carefully folding her new loan agreement, she stuffed the document into the hidden pocket of her skirt and burst through the bank's entrance.

Squinting into the blinding sunlight, she breathed the fresh pine scent so much a part of the bustling city and took her first step toward home.

"Well, Miss O'Connor, isn't this a happy coincidence?"

She stopped cold. The shiver grazing along her spine had very little to do with the breeze riding on the air, and everything to do with the man standing directly behind her.

"Indeed, it is," she said through clenched teeth.

"I say, you do get around."

A choked gasp seemed the most appropriate response, and the only one she could force past her quivering lips.

"You know—" exasperating confidence resonated in the deep tone "—of all the ensembles I've seen you wear in our short acquaintance, this one is by far the ugliest."

Now that wasn't fair. Her dress might not be as elegant—or nearly as pretty—as the one she'd borrowed for last night's adventure, but the simple cotton garment was respectable.

Insulted to no end, she whipped around to face the confounding hotel owner. Failing to account for the difference in their heights, her gaze engaged nothing more than gold and black-threaded silk. As calmly as possible, she looked up. And up farther still.

Dupree was tall, to be sure, with very broad shoulders. The kind a woman could dump her troubles upon and know whatever problem plagued her would be handled with absolute skill.

Shocked at where her thoughts had led and unable to formulate a proper response, Laney scowled at the man.

Dupree's rumble of laughter locked her voice into further silence. He seemed happy enough to continue their one-sided conversation. "Imagine my surprise when I saw you conducting business with the shiftiest banker in Colorado."

Shiftiest banker, indeed. Laney could hardly stomach the way Dupree made the scenario sound like two thieves cavorting with one another, as if she were made of the same unethical ingredients as Prescott. Her throat instantly unclogged.

"Rude, unconscionable, mean-spirited—"

"Now, now, Miss O'Connor, I wouldn't go that far. You do have a few redeemable qualities."

Sorely tired of the man's lack of control when it came to vocalizing his low opinion of her character, Laney tilted her head at a wry angle. "Slinking in the shadows again, Dupree? I wonder why that image continually rings true."

Seemingly amused, a slow smile spread across his lips.

Her traitorous heart skipped a beat, and then another.

Why did she find it so hard to think clearly when he looked at her like…like…*that*?

Still smiling, he devoured the space between them with a single stride. Obviously unconcerned with propriety, he plucked an imaginary speck of dust off her shoulder, then brushed the cloth smooth. "I almost didn't recognize you in this rather boring dress. The woman I met last night had much better taste."

Standing so close, she couldn't help but inhale the masculine scent that wafted off him. Pure male elixir clogged her nose, her lungs, her every thought.

Oh, my.

"The other dress suited your figure to perfection."

Laney refused to react to his words. Yet the way he took his time assessing her, with that hooded gaze, made her insides turn into nothing more substantial than biscuit dough. "To what do I owe this unfortunate visit? Not to mention your shockingly inappropriate commentary on my attire?"

"You might find it interesting to know I was out hunting this morning. For you, of course."

"Of course."

He reached down and tugged on the tendril of hair that had defied cooperation all morning. "Why would anyone hide this lovely hair under such an unremarkable hat?"

"You are offensive, Dupree." She nudged his hand aside. "The epitome of bad taste."

"All part of my appeal. But let's not continue to argue over the inconsequential."

"And here I thought we were getting along so well."

"Enough." Every bit of amusement fled from his gaze. "We have important business still to discuss."

Of its own volition, her body strained toward him. She snapped her shoulders back. "Do we? I was under the impression we said everything we needed to say last night."

"Not even close." He reached for her again, but then dropped his hand and frowned. "You never explained why you chose to meet Judge Greene in my hotel. And why such a large sum of money changed hands between the two of you."

Laney shivered at the intelligent glint in Dupree's gaze, the one that told her he would immediately recognize a lie.

If this man found out about Charity House, and if he turned out to be no better than Thurston P. Prescott III...

No, she couldn't let that happen. "You are becoming redundant, Dupree."

"As are you. So that we understand one another from this point forward, let me make myself perfectly clear." He leaned over her, his superior height effectively intimidating her into silence. "Under no circumstances will you entertain men in my hotel. You will not meet them in my lobby, nor eat with them in my restaurant, nor stay with them in any of the private rooms."

"And we're back to that?" She silently demanded her mind to concentrate on the conversation and not her uncomfortable awareness of the handsome man glaring down on her. "How many times must I tell you? Last night was nothing more than two old friends catching up with one another after a long absence."

There. That sounded perfectly misleading and cryptic, with just the right amount of impatience to indicate her frustration.

"What do you suppose, Miss O'Connor, Prescott would say if I told him where you got the money to pay off your loan?"

Everything in her froze. How much did this man know about her business at this bank? Did he know about Charity House, and the children?

He couldn't know. She'd been careful last night, even more so this morning. That meant it was time to call Dupree's bluff. "I never said anything about paying off a loan."

"Then you were making a payment *on* a loan."

"You can't know that I—"

"Don't bother denying it. Should I go searching for the document Prescott gave you before you left his office? I can only imagine where you've hidden it." He leveled his gaze directly on the hidden pocket in her skirt.

The man was insufferable. "Let's say I've taken out a loan with Prescott's bank."

He crossed his arms over his broad chest. "You did."

Shutting her eyes a moment, Laney prayed for guidance. *Please, Lord, please help me through this conversation.*

"*If* I did, what business is that of yours?"

"Actually…none."

At the shockingly straightforward answer, Laney searched Dupree's face, measuring, assessing. "Then why persist in uncovering my motives behind meeting Judge Greene?"

"Your motives are yours alone." He waved his hand in a casual manner, as if he was the embodiment of reason. "I only sought you out this morning to extract a promise, nothing more, nothing less."

"And what would that promise be?"

"I want you to agree, right here and now, that you will never enter my hotel, either alone or with another patron. I won't leave until I have your word."

Such an easy request to give. One tiny promise on her part and this whole, ugly affair would be over. Then she could return to Charity House and begin formulating her plan to raise the remaining fifty dollars on her loan.

Simple. Uncomplicated. The end of a sticky situation. Yet she found she couldn't walk away. Not without first asking, "Why is this so important to you? Why do you consider me such a threat?"

He looked slightly taken aback by her question. Good. He'd pushed her enough this morning. It was comforting to know she'd finally gained a portion of the upper hand.

"I've worked hard to earn the reputation of my hotel. I allow no drunkenness in the lobby, or other public areas. I do not tolerate gambling of any kind, not even in the private rooms. I insist there be no lewd behavior from my employees or patrons, behavior which includes…" He touched his finger to her nose. "Prostitution."

He thought she was a prostitute. A prostitute! If she wasn't so horribly offended she might be impressed by his dedication to keep his hotel above reproach.

As awful as his opinion was of her, or perhaps because of his terrible assumptions, Laney wanted Dupree to know who she really was. She wanted this man to know she agreed with him, agreed that propriety mattered, and that she was a moral woman, down at her core.

But then she remembered why he thought so little of her. For the sake of Charity House she'd sent him on a merry chase through the most dangerous parts of Denver, with the express purpose of misleading him.

She wanted—no, needed—him to continue in his misconception. But, as much as she believed the Lord's opinion of her was all that mattered, the woman in her couldn't bear this man thinking ill of her. Not completely. "I'm not a prostitute."

"Then there is only one other alternative. You're a madam."

Now he was just being mean. The very idea that she would sell other women's favors—to men—for a large percentage of the price—made her sick to her stomach.

Hurt by Dupree assuming her capable of something so vile she raised her palm, with the notion of slapping his face. But reason returned and she lowered her hand.

This is what you wanted, Laney. For the safety of the children, you wanted him to misunderstand who you are.

"What? No denial this time?"

She curled her fingers into a fist. "You're so sure you have me all figured out."

"Enough to know that whatever you've gotten yourself into, it can't be legitimate, not with Prescott involved." He shook his head at her, and the sorrow in his eyes appeared genuine. "I find it disheartening that a woman with your brains and talent should waste her life on such a lowly profession."

There was simply no response to that. Other than the slap he so richly deserved.

No longer able to control her outrage, she raised her

hand and swung. He caught her wrist in midair. "Stay out of my hotel, Miss O'Connor. I mean it."

"Or you'll what? Have me arrested?"

"Well, well. You read my mind." He pulled her a fraction closer to him, enough for her to feel his anger. "I'd like you to look across the street."

She jerked on her hand. "What game are you playing now?"

"Do it."

Laney raised her eyebrows. "Perhaps if you would release my wrist, I could oblige your request."

"You'll manage."

Momentarily beaten, she pinned him with an insincere grin, then shifted to her left.

Unsure what he wanted her to see, she concentrated on the teeming streets of Denver. The mix of cowhands, women dressed in a variety of styles, merchants and even gunslingers made the city the perfect place for anonymity. Often Laney would walk along this very street, or stroll in front of the Wells Fargo office a block away, and never encounter the glint of disapproval she'd endured her entire childhood.

Here, in the richly populated part of Denver, she could almost accept the reality of God's grace and unconditional acceptance. The Lord had given her a second chance in this city, with her mission at Charity House. She would do anything necessary to honor her God-given blessing.

"See that gentleman over there—" Dupree's voice glided past her ear "—dressed in black?"

She focused on several possible candidates. "Would you like me to look at that tall, lanky one with the black trousers, black shirt and black coat standing to my

right? Or that shorter one over there?" She jabbed her
parasol toward the left side of the street. "The one with
the black trousers and black shirt and, surprise, black
coat? Or perhaps you mean the one with the black—"
She turned back to face him. "Well, you get the idea."

If she wasn't mistaken, she thought she caught Dupree's lips twitch before he said, "I meant the one with
the matching six-shooters and U.S. marshal's badge
pinned to his chest. And, would you look at that, he's
watching us in return. Or rather, he's watching *you* in
return."

Resigned, Laney centered her gaze on the man in
question. The tall, imposing figure was indeed eyeing
her from across the street. In fact, he made a grand show
of tipping his hat at her. Even from this distance, she
could tell his gaze was as sharp as a hawk's.

The man looked harder and more threatening than
any Laney had ever met, and that included the one holding on to her wrist with the light but firm grip.

"So you know a U.S. marshal. Is that supposed to ter-
rify me?" She didn't add that, of course, she was scared
spitless. She had the requisite dry mouth and tongue
stuck to the back of her teeth to prove it.

"Marshal Scott is very anxious to meet you."

"He is? Wh-why?"

"I told him all about how you broke into my safe last
night. He was extremely interested in the particulars.
Seems there's been a rash of robberies in the area over
the last two weeks."

"How fortuitous for me," Laney muttered.

Dupree's chuckle sounded much more pleasant than
the circumstances warranted. Just how well did he know

this Marshal Scott? Would the lawman arrest her on Dupree's word alone?

"Now, we can either handle this between ourselves or I'll call the marshal over and you can contemplate the situation behind a row of bars."

She nearly choked on her gasp. "Are you threatening me? That sounds like a threat. I think you're threatening me."

"I am. And you're babbling."

Pressing her lips together, Laney buried her panic behind a hard swallow. "Look, Dupree, I get it. You don't want me to enter your hotel ever again. Well, I won't. There, you have my promise. Now let me go."

He immediately relinquished his grip. "I knew you'd see things my way, eventually."

Yanking her arm back to her side, she refrained from rubbing her wrist where his fingers had been. She had some pride left, as tattered as it might be at the moment.

Now that their conversation was over, Laney really, *really* needed to get home. To sit down, alone, and figure out where she was going to come up with the money to pay off the interest on her loan. "Since we have nothing more to say to each other, I'll bid you goodbye."

Not waiting for his reply, she turned and started out.

"Not so fast." With two ground-eating strides he walked around her and then widened his stance, just as he had the night before in his back alley. "Was your meeting last night with Judge Greene truly innocent, as you claim?"

"Yes."

"Yet you won't tell me why he gave you the money."

"No." She looked across the street. And directly into Marshal Scott's hard, ruthless gaze. That was a very scary-looking man. One Laney had no desire to meet anytime soon.

"You have to believe me, Dupree, the money was rightfully mine." Panic made her voice raise an entire octave. "I just can't give you the specifics behind the why."

"You can't, or you won't."

She sighed. "Both. Either. Does it matter?"

It was his turn to sigh, in disappointment, at her. She'd let him down with her response, and that realization hurt far worse than his earlier insults.

Would Dupree hand her over to the U.S. marshal now, for breaking into his private safe and taking back what was hers?

Would he be that cruel?

His next words threw her completely off guard, as did his soft tone. "Are you still in need of money, Miss O'Connor?"

"Yes," she admitted before she could stop the word from rushing out. Why, *why* did she find herself wanting to lean on this man, when she knew he was potentially dangerous to everything she held dear?

For a long moment, Dupree stared at her, those blue, blue eyes piercing straight through her, as though he could see inside every one of her secrets. "Then I have a proposition for you."

A number of terrible possibilities came to mind. For the past twenty-four hours Laney had experienced nothing but fear and desperation. The feeling of falling into a pit with no way out had been dreadful, panic-inducing. Terrifying.

Was she about to fall deeper into that pit, thanks to this man and his…proposition?

No. She couldn't lose hope. For the sake of the children she had to believe good would come out of this awful situation.

"What kind of proposition are you suggesting?"

"Come work for me at my hotel."

Chapter Seven

No matter what Miss O'Connor thought of him or his motives, Marc was serious about the job offer. He put women to work in his hotel all the time, with the hope of turning them from their former ways to a life of respectability.

No condemnation. No hidden agendas. Just an authentic chance at a new beginning.

Yet, to witness the skepticism in Miss O'Connor's gaze, a random passerby would suspect Marc had just made a vulgar suggestion.

He tried to harden his heart—what did he care if she trusted him or not?—but her obvious distress touched a part of him he'd thought long dead. For the second time in less than an hour, Marc recalled better days, when he'd been a godly man who saw only the best in people.

Now, years after his wife's betrayal, he didn't bother looking below the surface. He simply made a job offer, and left the rehabilitation to the individual.

"I assure you, Miss O'Connor, this isn't the first time I've asked a woman to come work for me."

"Of that, I have no doubt." Her words came out

haughty, but he caught a twinge of hurt beneath the despair in her eyes.

How could the woman look so guileless, when Marc knew she could crack a safe in a matter of minutes and climb out a window with accomplished ease? Such a woman could not be honest. Or trustworthy.

So why did Marc want to believe her when she said she'd taken Greene's money for a good reason? Why did he want to assure her he had no secret motive for hiring her, other than to offer her a second chance in life?

A spurt of guilt softened his tone, as well as his resolve. "I promise you, Miss O'Connor. Your position at my hotel will cause you no harm."

"So you claim."

He deserved her cynicism, he knew that.

Unable to stop himself, he touched her shoulder in a show of comfort. Her corresponding flinch cut straight through him.

Dropping his hand, Marc let out a slow hiss of air. Perhaps he'd gone a bit overboard with the intimidating scowls and threatening comments. He didn't want this woman to be afraid of him, just sufficiently wary. "Miss O'Connor, I—"

She raised her hand to stop him from continuing. "What duties would I have to perform at your hotel, and what would be my pay?"

Straight and to the point. He admired that particular quality in any person. "We can discuss the particulars on your first day of work."

"I prefer to discuss them now."

"With your speaking ability, and general comportment, you'll be best suited at the front desk. Registration," he clarified when she shook her head in confusion.

"And the pay?" she asked, persistent to the end.

Surprising even himself, Marc quoted an outrageous amount, three times the normal rate. He tried to convince himself he had a reason for offering such a large sum. If he wanted to prevent this woman from starting her own brothel on The Row he had to pay her handsomely for the debatable honor.

But that hadn't been the only reason. He actually wanted to help her, despite everything he'd discovered about her in the last twenty-four hours.

Caught in her own thoughts, Miss O'Connor pressed a finger to her lips. After a moment, her eyes filled with… Was that relief he saw in her gaze?

"I suppose the salary is fair," she said at last.

"More than fair."

She acknowledged his words with a slight nod. "What would be my hours?"

"I will expect you to work the evening shift, from six at night to two in the morning. That's nonnegotiable." And the best way to keep her out of the red-light district during the busiest times.

When she didn't balk at the hours, Marc wondered if he'd misjudged her. Why did he continue to suspect there was more to her than she was letting him see?

"May I start tonight?"

"Of course."

"Very good." She presented him with a tremulous smile, one that made her look exceedingly grateful.

A trick of the morning light? Or was she that in need of money?

"Well then, Dupree, if there is nothing else to discuss I will see you this evening."

She turned toward the street and set out.

Marc followed one step behind. "I'll walk you home."

"That won't be necessary." The caged look she tossed him said more than her words.

What was she hiding from him now?

"After all we've been through I owe you the simple courtesy."

"Don't worry, Dupree. I said I would take your job and I will. You're going to have to take my word on this."

Against his better judgment, he wanted to do just that, wanted to trust that she would return to his hotel tonight as she promised.

Or was there another reason he didn't want to escort her home? Perhaps he didn't want to find out she lived on The Row, and that he'd been right about her from the start.

For a tense moment he held her gaze, trying to understand the silent appeal in her eyes, and his own unwillingness to force the issue. "All right, Miss O'Connor. I'll see you this evening."

"Yes, *Mr.* Dupree, you will." She set out once again. This time Marc let her go. She sidestepped her way through the morning traffic and crossed the busy street.

The moment she was out of earshot, Marshal Trey Scott, Marc's childhood friend, joined him on the planked sidewalk.

"You know, Trey, I can't help thinking things are not what they seem with that woman. She's hiding something, something big, something that's thrown her into a state of desperation."

Trey grinned, looking like the boy he'd once been rather than the man who hunted outlaws with a vengeance. "You like her."

Not the response Marc was expecting, nor the one he wanted to hear. "Not at all. The woman is frustrating, annoying and definitely more trouble than she's worth."

"Not only do you like her, you're attracted to her." Trey's laugh belied his hard exterior. "Don't bother denying it."

"Yes, I find her attractive. But I wouldn't read too much into it, if I were you. She's a master at mesmerizing men. I only want to rehabilitate her before it's too late."

"Miss O'Connor is not in need of rehabilitation."

"You didn't see her in action last night."

"I saw the truth this morning." Trey looked across the street, smiled when the woman in question leaned over and scratched behind a stray dog's ears. "And you would see it, too, if you'd look past that black fog in your brain."

Marc bristled. "There is nothing coloring my judgment, not in Laney O'Connor's case."

"On the contrary, you see everything through jaded, cynical eyes. Miss O'Connor is not your wife. Pearl was a liar and a thief. That woman across the street is neither."

"She's in business with Prescott."

Trey inclined his head. "Perhaps. But I got a real good look at her a moment ago. My take? She's a decent, honorable woman in a lot of trouble."

Pressing his lips tightly shut, Marc mulled over Trey's words. His friend's conclusion was too close to the one he'd struggled against ever since he'd first discovered Miss O'Connor in his hotel last night.

But Pearl had taught him well. His wife's betrayal made it impossible for Marc to believe in any woman, especially one who outwardly showed herself to be concerned with earning a lot of money as quickly as possible. How could such a pursuit be deemed honorable?

"I take it she agreed to your job offer?"

Marc nodded, his gaze still fixed across the street. He couldn't help noticing how men of all ages stopped to stare at her as she passed them by. She was remarkable, even in that ordinary pink dress.

"You paying her the usual rate?"

"Three times more," Marc admitted.

The other man's low whistle sent Marc's gut tangling into a tight ball of unease.

"Don't worry, Trey. I plan to make Miss O'Connor earn every penny of her exorbitant salary."

As though hearing the remark, she wheeled around to face him directly and then released an identical two-finger salute as the one Marc had given her in the bank.

Chuckling low in his throat, Trey ran a hand over the dark stubble on his chin. "She looks like a biddable employee already."

"Oh, she will be. Once I explain the rules."

"Right. Keep telling yourself that." Trey slapped him on the back. "Now that I've witnessed the two of you together, I wonder who's in more trouble. Miss O'Connor? Or you?"

Marc had a feeling it was him.

At five minutes to six, Laney watched the sun edge behind the western peaks, trailing golden pink fire in its wake. The dusky-hewed sky added to the gloom in her heart. If only she'd stuck to Charity House's original design a year ago, she wouldn't have needed the extra loan from Prescott. And she wouldn't be standing here now, facing her greatest threat yet. Marc Dupree.

Laney must never let him find out about Charity House. The risk was too great. If he wasn't the honorable man he portended to be, he could ruin all her plans. And then Prescott would win.

Before leaving the orphanage, she'd done some quick calculations. If she moved a few expenses around, cut more corners and Dupree actually paid her the salary he'd quoted her, Laney would raise the remaining fifty dollars in time.

Unfortunately, her ultimate success hinged on Marc Dupree's honor.

She could only pray he proved to be a man of his word. *Please, Lord, let it be so.*

Drumming nervous fingers against her thigh, she turned her gaze to the spectacular building in front of her. "The Hotel Dupree."

She spoke the name aloud, as though the gesture alone would provide her with the much-needed courage to walk inside.

A ribbon of light streamed out of the hotel lobby, beckoning Laney deeper into the drama she had set into motion last evening. What had she been thinking? She should have met Judge Greene somewhere else, anywhere else. With a vigorous toss of her head, she flung aside her agitation.

This was not a time for second-guessing.

She'd made her choices, and now she would accept the consequences. Just as she taught the children to do every day.

Head high, shoulders back, she started forward. After a few steps, she swerved to her left and looked through the large plate glass window beside the entrance.

Activity was high inside the lobby and her apprehension grew. Once she walked through the revolving door, she would be at the mercy of Marc Dupree. Her gaze swerved through the hotel, hunting for the tall, overwhelming man who held the children's future in his hands—even if he didn't know it.

The longer she stood on the outside looking in, the more she realized she couldn't go through with this. She couldn't rely on a man, *any* man.

She would raise the money some other way.

Decision made, she turned to leave and stopped midstride as her eyes connected with Dupree's lazy scrutiny. How long had he been watching her scan the activity in his hotel? Long enough, she realized, and felt heat rush to her cheeks.

Hoping to gain a portion of the upper hand, she swallowed several times and returned his open perusal.

Similarly to the night before, the simple elegance of his clothing added a measure of sophistication to his chiseled features. He had the bad manners to look handsome, calm...*awake*.

Worse, with the sky a rainbow of color behind him, he looked every bit like her romantic notions of a dime-novel hero.

Cringing at the whimsical thought, she purposely filled her tone with artificial politeness. "Dupree, always a pleasure."

He angled his head, peering at the window behind her. "Were you planning to clean those nose prints off the glass before you ran away?"

The temperature in her cheeks burned hotter. "I

wasn't running away." The lie skidded past her lips in short, halting syllables.

"Certainly looked that way to me."

A portion of the truth spilled out of her mouth. "If you must know, I was gathering the courage to walk inside."

That earned her a dry chuckle. "You may be a lot of things, Miss O'Connor, but cowardly is not one of them." He dropped his gaze. "I see you didn't feel the need to change your clothes from this morning. Didn't I already remark on what I thought of that dress?"

Welcoming the surge of irritation his question provoked, Laney scowled. "You did, in very unflattering terms."

He leaned against the streetlamp behind him and produced a full, stomach-bumping grin. Smiling like that, he looked so…appealing. Approachable even. For a dangerous moment, Laney forgot why she distrusted the man.

"Let me guess," he said. "You wore that pink concoction primarily to irritate me."

And now she remembered why. "You do catch on quickly."

His smile widened, shoving open the door to her heart by a mere crack. With a hard blink, she slammed the tiny slit shut. Hopefully for good.

"You ready to come inside now?"

She couldn't tear her gaze away from his. Why this compulsion to catalog every line, every groove, every feature of his rugged, handsome face?

"Through with your inspection?"

Beast. "Almost."

She forced her body to relax, her mind to clear, but

nothing could stop her pulse from working itself into a frenzy. She had a sudden, shocking urge to reach out and cup his face, to stare into his eyes, to know this man on a deep, personal level.

Was it true then? Was she more like her mother than she realized, deep at her core? Was she flawed in her very character, like so many of the bad women of the Bible? Was she a Delilah, at heart? Or a Jezebel?

No, that couldn't be true. She made mistakes, yes, and bad decisions at times, but she wasn't wicked.

Mouth twisting at a sardonic angle, Dupree withdrew his watch from a pocket in his vest then made a grand show of releasing the clasp and looking at the time. "Ticktock, Miss O'Connor."

His sarcasm hurled her into action. "Yes, yes. I'm ready now."

"After you."

Determined to maintain her dignity, she pirouetted quickly, driving her feet forward with sheer will alone. Once inside the hotel lobby, she nearly gained control over her foolish senses, but then Dupree closed in from behind.

"I'll meet you in my office. You do remember the way?"

His whispered words hovered too close to her ear. The tiny shove on her lower back sent a chill navigating down her spine.

She really, *really* needed to get a handle on her emotions. "Yes, of course I remember."

"Excellent." With catlike grace, he shifted around her and trekked toward the restaurant. Strangely beholden to watch him stride through the lobby, Laney stood stationary, blinking after him, her heart keeping time with his fast moving feet.

He glanced at her over his shoulder, stopped. "Move along, Miss O'Connor. Dole reluctance doesn't suit you."

Making a face, she trudged toward the back of the hotel, all the while searching for an ally. Any would do. She passed her gaze over several people, then linked eyes with Hank.

Why not?

Determined to make her time at the Hotel Dupree as pleasant as possible, she waved a happy greeting.

After a brief hesitation and a slight shake of his head, Hank grinned at her in return. Warmed by his response, Laney allowed a brief smile to linger between them. At his encouraging nod, she continued forward with renewed confidence.

Inside Dupree's office, she scanned the perimeter of the room, registering every nuance of the immaculate interior. All that she'd upset the night before had been put to rights. Even the books she'd used to prop up her sarcastic note were back on the shelves in their proper order.

Or so she assumed.

Out of some perverse need to know what sort of books Dupree enjoyed reading, she tugged a chair to the bookshelf and hopped on top. She scanned the closest titles, making murmurs as she went.

Oliver Twist, one of her favorites, a compilation of Shakespeare's tragedies, *not* a favorite. She liked the comedies. Two Bibles, one written in English and one— she checked the spine—was that…Latin? She'd have to ask Katherine what Vulgate meant. Both books were well-worn, an indication they had been read often.

By Dupree? Or someone else?

Just as Laney began perusing the rest of the titles, Dupree's commanding voice boomed through the room. "What are you doing on that chair?"

Startled, she twirled around on one foot, then fought to find a spot for the other.

Blocking the doorway with his impossibly broad shoulders, the man had the nerve to scold her as though she were a child. "Get down, now, before you fall down."

"Oh, honestly, I'm in complete control." She jammed her hands on her hips to prove her point. And promptly lost her balance.

Teetering from one foot to another, she waved her arms back and forth, praying the momentum would help her regain her balance.

It didn't. She was going down hard.

Resigned, she thrust her hands out in front of her.

Dupree rushed forward, moving quickly enough to catch her around the waist. Thanks to his timely assistance, Laney's face careened to a halt mere inches from smacking into the floor.

"You, Miss O'Connor, are a menace."

Considering her current position, she couldn't exactly argue the point.

Chapter Eight

Bent at the waist, her arms pinned in useless immobility, Laney remained perfectly still. One slip on Dupree's part, one pucker on her part, and she'd be kissing the fashionable Oriental rug beneath her nose.

Not the best of scenarios.

"Seems we have an interesting situation here." The grin in Dupree's voice stole any chance of Laney finding the desire to thank him for his prompt rescue.

With more than just her pride inches from the floor, she couldn't muster the poise to speak calmly. Or politely. "Help me up." She gritted her teeth to avoid moving a muscle. "I mean it. This isn't amusing anymore."

As if it had ever been.

"You know," he said, his tone full of easy camaraderie, as if they were enjoying a spot of tea, "after all we've been through, sort of seems appropriate to leave you…dangling."

To her shame, tears formed. But Laney refused to let them fall. She did, however, squirm. Just a bit. Enough to have Dupree's arms tighten around her waist.

"I find it necessary to advise you not to move like

that. You just might find yourself with a face full of splinters."

He was admonishing her? Again? As though he'd caught her with a toy that didn't belong to her? "Dupree, I'm warning you…"

"Considering our current positions—you down there and me, well, up here—I wouldn't be tossing out threats if I were you. Now," he adjusted his hold, "since I have you where I can keep an eye on you, shall we discuss the weather, that lovely sunset outside, or your upcoming duties in my hotel?"

Although her muscles screamed from her clenching them too tightly, Laney said in her firm, mother-of-the-house voice, "Let me up. This. Instant."

"Ask nicely."

A beat passed. And then another. "*Please.*"

He responded with a full-out, booming laugh.

"You've made your point." She tried to sound in control of the situation. Hard to do with her head growing lighter by the minute. Truly, the man was beyond rude. "I'm starting to get dizzy."

"Good, maybe it'll plop some sense into you."

"*Dupree…*"

"Right, right. Help you up." He twisted her in his arms, and then shifted her to an upright position. "There. How's that?"

"Unacceptable." Her toes barely touched the ground.

Grinning, he lowered her all the way down. "Better now?"

No. His hands still gripped her waist. He didn't seem to realize how much his touch bothered her. Or maybe he did. The rat.

"Yes." She forced out the word with extreme care. "I'm fine."

She expected him to release her then. But several seconds fled by. Then several more. And *still* his hands remained on her waist.

Tick, tick, tick, went the clock on the mantel.

Click, click, click, went her heart against her ribs.

With each intake of air, breathing became harder. Words eluded her. Common sense vanished.

Laney needed to step back, away from this man and his intense stare. She needed to put some distance between them. But a hidden part of her, a secret place she kept locked deep inside her soul, urged her to move a step closer.

What was wrong with her?

What was wrong with him? Why wasn't *he* stepping back?

As they continued staring at one another, a silent message passed between them, something new, something unsettling. Something…almost…pleasant.

Her vision blurred and her throat clogged.

If only she could get her voice to work properly.

"Are you all right, Miss O'Connor?"

She managed a nod.

"Truly?" He cocked his head at a concerned angle. "Your face is draining of color."

No doubt. Her head felt lighter now than when she'd been hanging upside down.

"Laney?"

She tensed at the use of her given name, instinctively holding back a sigh. Of contentment. *Oh, Lord, please, no. Don't let me start liking this man now.*

Too late, came the disturbing thought, *too, too late.*

Until this moment, Laney hadn't realized how safe she felt in Dupree's presence, as though he were a barrier between her and certain disaster.

And not just from the fall. But from all harm. For the first time in her life she wanted to rely on someone other than herself, someone who would take care of her and Katherine and the children.

What would it be like to be cared for by a man, by *this* man? To admit she needed help. To…simply… let…go?

Laney's mind reeled at the sense of longing that came with the question.

It is better to take refuge in the Lord than to trust people. Good, solid, Biblical advice. Yet the foolish longing in her heart remained.

Dupree's fingers flexed on her waist, squeezed gently, and then…

Intent filled his gaze and his head inched toward hers.

Was he going to kiss her?

Did she *want* him to kiss her?

Her pulse drummed a rapid staccato in her ears. She *really* must step back. Yes. Yes. She needed to step back.

She leaned forward instead.

The look in Dupree's eyes turned soft, affectionate, and his hold gentled. For several eternal seconds he stared into her eyes. He didn't utter a word—not, one, single, word—but Laney knew why he hesitated, knew why he didn't close the distance between them.

He was waiting for her permission to proceed.

This was her chance to push him away. But a pleasant, warm emotion spread through her, one she'd never experienced before. Trust.

This man, for all his faults, would never hurt her. Laney knew it as surely as she knew the dollar amount she still owed Prescott.

Was it any wonder she was the one to take the final step toward him?

Smiling softly, Dupree wrapped his arms around her, his hold firm yet protective. Laney had never felt precious in her life.

Yet, now, inside this man's embrace, she felt special, cherished even. She closed her eyes.

The smell of clean male mingled with tangy citrus filled her senses, settled in her heart, creating a memory that would last her a lifetime.

At twenty-five, she was about to experience her very first kiss. With Marc Dupree.

In spite of the explosive nature of their relationship, one word slipped out of her mouth. "Yes."

"At last, we agree on something." He ducked his head toward hers.

As though sensing the gravity of the moment, his lips stilled a hairbreadth away from hers, touching and yet not quite touching.

Her heart stuttered to a halt, then began beating again, picking up speed with each quick, painful breath she took.

Why wasn't he pressing his lips fully to hers? "Marc?"

"Say my name again, Laney, without the question in your voice."

"Marc," she whispered.

"Very nice."

Finally, he sealed his mouth to hers, in such a gentle, careful manner that Laney found every preconceived notion she'd ever had about men vanishing. All her life she'd considered men the enemy. She'd seen firsthand what they wanted from women. Nothing good or kind, but shameful acts that had to be paid for in advance, then hidden inside shadows and locked behind closed doors.

She'd never suspected tenderness could exist between a man and a woman, never thought a kiss could be sweet and affectionate.

Her mind slowly let go of all thought. Then awakened so quickly physical pain hammered behind her eyes.

This was Marc Dupree kissing her. He didn't respect her. Or trust her. Or even like her. Was this some kind of ploy, a test to see how far she would go to earn money from him tonight?

Panicked at the thought, she pushed against his chest.

"Please, Marc." She twisted to the right. And then to the left. "Please. Let me go."

Palms up, blood rushing in his veins and pounding in his ears, Marc took a large step away from Laney. He'd never seen a woman react like that to a simple kiss, especially not a woman with Miss O'Connor's vast array of life experiences and given...talents.

"Laney?" He used her given name on purpose. Despite her confounding reaction to their kiss, they'd gone far beyond the need for formality.

Doe-size eyes connected with his and Marc found himself fighting off a wave of guilt. Taking in her erratic breathing, large pupils and pale cheeks, he realized

Laney was in a state of panic. No, not panic. Terror. She was terrified. Of him. Of what they'd just done.

Marc shook his head in bewilderment.

The gesture seemed to jolt her into action. Her hand flew to her throat and her eyes widened even more. "Why…why did you kiss me?"

Good question, one he wasn't sure how to answer. But at the sound of her very real distress, and the genuine fear in her eyes—*fear!*—he decided to respond as truthfully as possible.

"Because I wanted to. And *you* wanted to kiss me in return. Regardless of this innocent routine of yours." And, yes, her behavior had to be a calculated response.

If not…

He'd made a terrible mistake. And had kissed a woman who deserved better treatment than him pawing at her in his office.

Lifting shaky fingers to her lips, she blinked up at him. The look of shocked innocence appeared real.

Oh, she was good. Marc almost believed she was as stunned as she looked. *Almost*, but not quite. He couldn't ignore the bits and pieces he'd already learned about her.

"Look, Laney, we both know you are no untouched maiden. So let's forgo the rest of this ridiculous act of yours."

"Act?" She fell back a step, looking as though he'd slapped her.

Marc had to admit, her performance was certainly first-rate, one of the best he'd ever seen.

Was he judging her unfairly?

Perhaps. Perhaps not.

"You, Marc Dupree, are ill-bred, rude and…and…"

She tossed a loose strand of hair out of her face with a violent shake of her head. "Pigheaded."

"Pigheaded?" He released a laugh lacking all humor. "Is that the worst you got for me, sweetheart?"

"Who gave you the right to judge me? You don't even know me."

"Oh, I know you." Or did he?

Miss O'Connor is not your wife. Trey's words came back to him, making Marc wonder if his judgment was indeed colored by his past. Had his experience with Pearl turned him into a cynic? A man who expected women to lie and cheat because his wife had done so over and over again?

Did that make him jaded, as Trey had claimed?

No. It made him cautious, a wise man who relied on his own power of reasoning. Every instinct told him that Laney O'Connor was hiding something from him, something monumental. And if Pearl had taught him anything it had been that nothing good came from secrets.

So why, then, wasn't he demanding answers from Laney? *Why* was he experiencing this gut-wrenching guilt?

They stared at one another for five full seconds, or perhaps five eternities, Marc wasn't sure which. He raked a hand through his hair, his puzzlement growing by the minute.

Who *was* Laney O'Connor? Her kiss called to mind innocence. Yet, in a single day, she'd broken into a locked safe, scaled a wall, climbed out a window and conducted business with the shiftiest banker in Colorado.

Was the woman a wolf in sheep's clothing or a sheep

in wolf's clothing? Marc couldn't be sure. And until he was certain, he would treat her with the same suspicion and distrust as before.

"Much as I'm enjoying this fascinating stare down," he began. "We can't stand here all evening glaring at each other."

"No? Then what do you suggest we do?" Her eyes flashed amber fire, alerting Marc that her former spunk was well on the way to returning.

Just to be sure…

He leaned forward. She scooted back a step, hiding the move behind a quick toss of her chin. The gesture came a second too late. Marc had caught the fear underlying her actions. *Fear of him.*

Unable to explain why that troubled him so much, he scrubbed a hand over his face. "I'm sorry, Laney. I was out of line. I apologize for kissing you."

She took another step back.

"I won't try to kiss you again. I promise."

The relief that filled her eyes belied the tart words that came out of her mouth. "I plan to hold you to that."

"From you, I'd expect nothing less. Now." He cleared his throat. "Perhaps we should go over your job duties."

"That sounds like a good idea."

He picked up the dress he'd tossed to the floor when he'd seen her teetering on the verge of disaster. Grimacing, he shook out the layers of silk until the majority of wrinkles disappeared. "You will wear this while on duty at the front desk."

"You want me to wear…that?"

"Yes."

"But it's so…so…" She trailed off, apparently lost for words.

"Respectable?" he offered.

"*Black*."

"That's right. The color and design are simple but elegant, just like my hotel. All my female employees wear identical dresses to this one." He lifted the garment to make his point. "And while we're on the subject, let me reiterate one final time. I run a respectable hotel, Laney, my guests rely on me to provide a comfortable, memorable stay that surpasses their wildest expectations."

"So you've said. More than once. Ten times at least."

"Save your sarcasm. I'm not in the mood to engage in another verbal battle."

She sighed. "Nor am I."

"Good. Now, for the rules of your employment."

"Rules? What rules?"

"You will live a clean, wholesome life while working inside the hotel and on your own time. Any unseemly behavior, whether here or anywhere else, will be grounds for immediate dismissal."

For once, she didn't argue with him. "I understand."

"You will be held to the same standard of behavior as all the women in my employ. Break one of my rules and you'll be fired on the spot."

"My, that sounds ominous."

"I mean what I say."

"Yes, I get that."

A pall of silence fell over them. They eyed one another with equal amounts of suspicion. And something else. Something Marc didn't dare define.

"So, *Marc*." She said his name in that soft, throaty voice of hers that left him blinking at her like a fool.

"Am I to have the rest of these rules spelled out for me, or am I to guess at them?"

"Right." He'd almost forgotten. "My requirements are simple and straightforward. No drinking, no cheating the customers, no lying, no stealing and, definitely, no—"

"Kissing the boss?" she asked with a deceptively innocent batting of her eyes.

"I was going to say…" He had to look away to hide his smile. "No breaking into any of my safes."

"Spoilsport."

He did smile at that, then instantly wiped his expression clean. He couldn't allow this woman to gain the upper hand in their highly irregular relationship. "Did I mention that Marshal Scott will be here later this evening?"

"You don't have to threaten me." She held up her hands in surrender, but ruined the picture of compliance by winking at him. "I promise to play nicely. As long as you do the same."

And he was holding off another smile. "I'll expect you to show up on time and work hard while you're here. In return, I'll pay you the salary I quoted this morning. Are these terms acceptable?"

"Yes, they are. Thank you."

Uncomfortable at the gratitude he heard in her voice, he turned to leave, then caught himself. He still held the black silk dress in his hand.

"Here you go." He tossed the uniform in her direction.

She caught the garment with a quick swipe of her hand. Marc didn't miss the fact that she'd moved with lightning speed. The woman certainly had a unique range of talents. And Marc was starting to become impressed by nearly every one of them.

Careful to keep his admiration out of his voice, he spoke with a bland, flat inflection. "Once you've changed into your uniform, join me out at the front desk."

"Gee, you make it sound so fascinating." She pressed a hand to her heart and sighed dramatically. "I'm all aflutter. I can hardly hold back my excitement."

Right then, right there, Marc gave up the fight and smiled directly into the woman's beautiful, amber eyes. Catching her playful mood, he gave her a wry smile. "Try to contain yourself, Laney. For both our sakes, please, *try*."

Chapter Nine

With her mind in turmoil, Laney gaped at the door Marc had just shut behind him with a soft click. Just this morning, confronted with her worst nightmare, she'd prayed for guidance and a solution to her money problems.

The Lord had answered her dilemma through an unlikely source. Marc Dupree.

His job offer was a blessing. An answer to prayer.

But, truly, what had she gotten herself into, putting her future into his hands?

Sorting through the events of the last hour, she worked the black silk of her "uniform" through her fingers. The fact that Marc had felt the need to spell out the rules of her employment left Laney wondering about the type of women he employed. Women of ill repute, no doubt. But why did he bother?

To save them from their chosen profession?

Was he that humane, that kind?

What would Laney's childhood have been like had someone given her mother a job like the one Marc had given her?

Would Laney have been raised with love and a sense of belonging? If so, would she have felt the need to start Charity House? After all, her chaotic, unpredictable childhood had led her to provide a safe home for the children in her care.

Tapping her finger against her chin, she sighed over another thought plaguing her. She hated Marc thinking she belonged in the same category as the other women he hired, women like her mother.

Isn't that what you wanted? In an attempt to protect Charity House and the children, Laney had sent the man on a merry chase down The Row, leading him to conclude she was a shady lady seeking money for shady purposes.

Oh, she'd done it for the right reasons, but what a mess she'd made for herself.

Laney squeezed her eyes closed, praying for clarity. Her mind blurred with the memory of Marc's tender kiss. She shivered in response. The moment their lips touched everything had changed between them. Their *relationship* had changed.

For the better? Or the worse?

Because of her "willingness" to partake in the kiss would Marc always believe she belonged on The Row?

Letting out a rush of air, Laney pounded a fist against her thigh.

The memory of the countless men who'd paid their money and then lain with Laney's mother, should be enough to quell any silly, romantic notions she might have about Marc Dupree and his kiss.

Dirty, nasty, filthy. That's what she knew of intimate relations between a man and a woman. But would it be different with the right man? Would it be special?

The thought brought shameful heat to her cheeks.

At least facing the man again wouldn't be a problem. Learning her new job duties would demand her complete concentration. She wouldn't even have to acknowledge him. Unless he chose to instruct her himself, conveniently keeping watch over her.

"He wouldn't dare," she whispered to herself.

Oh, yes he would. Especially if she kept him waiting much longer. With grim determination Laney quickly stripped off the plain dress she'd worn to spite Dupree—just as he'd suspected—and stepped into the black gown.

Pulling the garment over her shoulders, her breath caught in her throat. The dress was a perfect fit. She sighed, releasing some of the built-up tension in her neck then spun toward the mirror standing next to the armoire. Taking a long look at herself, she studied the profound changes.

She barely recognized the stranger that stared back at her. Was it just the refinement of the black silk and the elegant cut of the dress, or did Dupree's kiss have something to do with the alterations she now saw in her reflection?

What would the children think if they saw her in this dress?

The children.

Her heart sank at the memory of the sullen, terrified faces as she'd kissed each of them good-night. She'd been confident all would work out as she'd left them in Katherine's capable care. Until one of them actually begged her not to go. That was when Laney had realized the magnitude of trouble in which she'd landed herself, and Charity House.

Johnny, Judge Greene's boy, had been frantic when he'd seen her leaving the house as the sun was setting. He'd reacted as though he knew exactly where she was headed and what she planned to do.

He'd been wrong, of course. But at the age of twelve, he'd seen too much of the ugly side of life thanks to his prostitute mother whose money went to feeding her opium addiction instead of her son.

Only time and a lot of love would heal Johnny's unseen wounds. Laney prayed that one day he would accept that grace and mercy were real, that he was a deserving child of God. Worthy of love, not because of something he did, but because he believed.

At least tonight Laney would return home before dawn, as promised. Perhaps then Johnny would accept that she wasn't living the same life as his mother.

Letting out a sigh, she smoothed her hands down her skirt and forced back the last of her uneasiness.

It was silly to worry any further. She could manage whatever came her way. She always did. As such, she could certainly handle a certain arrogant, way-too-big-for-his-britches hotel owner.

After all, he was just a man.

With a penchant for suspicion and distrust.

He deserves grace and mercy, too.

Shoulders back, sighing one last time, Laney twisted the door handle and pushed into the hotel lobby.

The first thing she noticed was the noise. Laughter and countless conversations twined with one another to create a chaotic harmony of sound. People of all sizes, ages and genders milled about the main lobby.

Most wore fashionable clothing that matched the un- mistakable opulence of the Hotel Dupree. Every piece

of furniture had been plumped to comfortable round-
ness, each rug was spotless, every slice of marble flooring shined.

The obvious wealth and power emanating throughout
the décor reminded Laney just what a man like Marc
Dupree held dear. Status and money. Money and status.

She needed to keep that reality in mind.

As though drawn by some unseen force, Laney connected gazes with the hotel owner himself.

He made a twirling motion with his finger. Oblig-
ingly, she turned in a slow circle, arms outstretched.

A lopsided smirk tugged his lips into a captivating
angle, calling to mind their kiss. As though unable to
support the weight of her thoughts her knees froze, then
suddenly gave out. Thankfully, Laney had the presence
of mind to reach out and steady herself on the edge of
a nearby chair.

Well, then. Clearly, she'd fooled herself into thinking Marc was *just* another man. On the contrary, he
was unlike any person she'd ever met, capable of making her feel the most frightening emotion of all. Hope.

What gave him the right to do this to her? Before
tonight she'd been a woman who could handle any
challenge thrown her way. Now, as she clutched white
knuckles to the chair, she had a sick feeling that there
would be no easy answer to the problem called Marc
Dupree.

With far more attentiveness than he'd like, Marc had
followed Laney's progress through the hotel lobby. He'd
known the exact moment she'd exited his office, perhaps because he'd pasted his gaze to the door for the
last fifteen minutes.

Ever since their kiss, he'd been unable to concentrate on anything or anyone but her.

After leaving her in his office to change dresses, he'd waved off Hank, ignored his customers and set out to find a quiet spot to think. As he'd silently considered all that had transpired, he'd almost convinced himself that what they'd shared had been merely a kiss. But he knew better. He and Laney had captured something profoundly deep. Maybe even life changing.

Now that was disheartening beyond measure. He was heading right down the same path as the night he'd committed the ill-conceived decision to marry Pearl LaRue and save her from herself.

What a fool he'd been all those years ago. As he'd stood in front of the preacher, reciting his vows, he hadn't considered that Pearl might have liked her role as temptress to every living, breathing male. That life on the stage hadn't been enough to fund her lifestyle as she'd claimed the night he met her. Aside from singing on the stage, Pearl had enjoyed taking money on the side in return for her "special" favors.

Was Laney O'Connor the same? Marc had learned that a man couldn't change a woman's heart, or her hidden dreams, no matter how hard he tried. Although, now that he allowed his mind free rein, Laney's display of panic after their kiss made him want to reconsider his opinion of her.

Watching her now, clutching at the chair beneath her hand, he wanted her to be exactly what she looked like. A brave young woman caught in a series of unfortunate mistakes, yet willing to see the consequences of her actions through to the end.

Needing to gain some perspective, Marc broke eye

contact and surveyed the activity in the hotel. It didn't take him long to notice how the men stared at Laney with varied levels of masculine interest.

And why not?

There she stood, magnificent in that black dress. Glowing, radiant. She had the look of both frailty and strength. Innocence with a hint of mystery—a powerful combination a man couldn't ignore for long.

Even now, Marc wanted to wrap her in his embrace and protect her from the bad things in this world. His gut twisted tighter and in that moment, he knew he should have never hired her to work in his hotel.

Trouble. The woman had trouble written all over her.

Releasing a hiss, Marc set out. He looked down at the tight fist he'd formed with his hand. Relaxing his fingers, he strode across the lobby with a clipped stride.

He stopped next to Laney and looked into her amber eyes. Some unnamed emotion robbed him of his ability to speak. Since she didn't try to talk, either, and instead raked her gaze across his face, Marc took a moment to study her attire up close.

The dress added a touch of refinement to her already graceful form. He took a deep breath of her unique, lilac fragrance that was hers alone.

Tenderness gripped his heart and he had to stifle the urge to brush his lips against her forehead. "The dress suits you."

Her gaze snapped to his. "Did you just give me a compliment?"

He enjoyed the shock flashing in her eyes, it added to the image of innocence that unfolded a little more each time they met. He finally accepted that he wanted, *needed*, her to be as innocent as she looked now. And that scared him far more than anything Pearl had dished out during their two years of marriage.

But not enough to stop him from adding, "Truly, Laney. You look lovely."

Clearly confused, she shook her head at him. "I simply don't know what to say."

He grinned down at her. "Thank you is the customary response."

She lowered her head, smoothed the skirt with shaking fingers then raised her gaze to his again. He liked the way she looked him directly in the eyes.

"Thank you," she whispered.

He suddenly wanted to shock her again, replace that slight smile of delight quivering on her lips with another kiss. But he'd promised not to kiss her again. And he always kept his word.

"Let's get you started, shall we?"

With a line of worry creasing her brow, she nibbled on her lower lip. "Will you be instructing me on my duties tonight?"

"No. I'll leave that task to Rose." Marc pointed at the older woman watching them from behind the front desk.

Catching Laney's eye, Rose waved at her.

Laney waved back. "She looks like a nice lady."

"She is. She'll teach you everything you'll need to know to do your job well. She's my best front desk clerk." Which was true enough. Marc didn't add that Rose had once been a notorious madam in Cripple Creek. "Come on. I'll introduce you."

He placed his hand at the small of Laney's back and led her through the lobby. He couldn't explain why the sudden feeling of protectiveness that whipped through him felt so good.

Trouble.

Yeah. Marc's association with Laney O'Connor promised to be nothing but trouble.

Chapter Ten

For the next few days, life at the Hotel Dupree fell into a routine. As he'd done every evening since taking full control, Marc surveyed the interaction between his employees and customers from a corner of the lobby. He drank in the finely honed rhythm and waited for the surge of pride that came with ownership. Unfortunately, this night the sights and sounds didn't bring their usual satisfaction.

Why wasn't he content?

And why couldn't he shake the notion that something was missing? The longer he beheld the workings of what had become his home, the more a strange sense of disquiet tugged at him. It was as though tonight, instead of seeing the fruits of his labor, he saw just another fancy hotel.

His gaze continued to rove, pausing at the front desk.

Laney. She smiled at an elderly couple she was helping register for the night, no doubt charming them with her poise and wit. A favorite of the guests already, she was fast becoming indispensible.

The now familiar jerk of Marc's pulse was just as

unwelcome as the last time he'd experienced the sensation, and the time before that. The woman had spent far too much time in his head. He wasn't about to allow her to continue making him crazy just because she smiled at every guest that came her way. That was, after all, her job.

Determined to concentrate on anything other than his growing awareness of Laney O'Connor, Marc shifted his gaze to the restaurant on his right. They had a nice crowd this evening. Yet, despite his best efforts to engage his mind on business, his gaze wandered back to Laney. His heart made one hard kick against his ribs.

What was it that drew him to her? She'd shown up for work every night since they'd come to their agreement, and he had yet to get used to her presence. If he were a wise man he'd discover her secret, the one that kept her silent whenever he questioned her as to why she'd needed Greene's money.

Perhaps if Marc knew the truth, she'd no longer have this power over him. In the hopes of finding out something, anything, he'd attempted to walk her home each night after her shift. But every time he offered she turned him down.

He knew he could have insisted, could have forced the issue, but he'd rather remain in ignorance than discover he'd been right about her all along. And since she always came to work punctual and ready to do her best, he didn't really need to know more.

At least, that's what he told himself.

The man standing next to him chuckled, and then pounded him on the back, gaining his full attention. "When you gonna quit gaping at that woman and offer me something to eat from your fine restaurant? My gut's practically pressing against my backbone."

Marc snapped his gaze to Trey and frowned. "I wasn't gaping at Laney."

"Right." Trey divided a look between Marc and the front desk. "But you knew exactly who I was talking about, didn't you?"

Deciding the question didn't deserve a response, Marc focused on a more important matter. "You want the food or not?"

"I want."

"Then stop trying to annoy me and come on." A few moments later Marc stepped into the restaurant and waited while Trey placed his order with the maître d'hôtel. When he was through, Marc added, "Please have the food served in my office."

"Very good, Mr. Dupree."

Without waiting for Trey, Marc left the restaurant and made his way to his office.

A few seconds later, Trey entered behind him and shouldered the door shut. Folding his arms across his chest, he leaned back against the wood. "Can't help but notice how Miss O'Connor has been the model of hard work these last three nights."

"She's shown up, that's what matters."

"The male guests certainly seem to enjoy her undivided attention. What do you think?"

Marc bristled at Trey's goading tone. "I think subtlety never was one of your finer points."

"So I've been told." Trey tossed his hulking frame into an empty chair and set his boots on top of an expensive table.

"Have you no decency?" Marc hissed. "I had that

piece of furniture imported straight from Paris last week."

Pretending not to hear him, Trey leaned his head against the back of his chair. "You never did tell me what Miss O'Connor said about that outrageous salary you're paying her."

Marc lifted a shoulder. "I don't remember what she said." The lie slid easily through his lips. He remembered every moment of every encounter he had with the woman, including the kiss they'd shared. The one that came to mind far too often.

Trey chuckled. "She was pretty shocked, I take it?"

"No. She was…grateful." And that reaction warmed him clear through to his soul, reminding him of the man he used to be. A man who assisted people in need without attaching conditions to the offer. Laney O'Connor had slipped beneath his defenses and Marc wasn't altogether sorry for it. He felt the betraying smile on his lips just before he realized it was too late to hide it from his friend.

Trey's eyes narrowed. "You got something you want to tell me?"

"No."

"You sure about that? Don't want to share why you haven't bothered finding out more information about our little safecracker? Or why you won't let me do it, either?"

"No."

"Don't want to tell me why the poor little dear couldn't look you straight in the eye that first night of her employment, or why she keeps sliding glances toward you when you aren't gawking at her?"

"She doesn't glance, she scowls."

"You noticed that, too?"

Marc stifled the urge to kick Trey's feet off the table, and not only because his boot heels were chafing off the shine. "I'm warning you, Trey."

"I know. I know." Trey lifted his palm in the air. "Change the subject or get out."

"And here I thought you'd lost your gift of perception."

Trey leaned forward and picked up a glass off the table where his feet rested. He twirled it under the light and a rainbow of color shot through the air. "Lead crystal?"

"Imported from Ireland."

"You've certainly left nothing to chance."

No, Marc hadn't. "What's your point?"

Trey set the glass back on the table. "Who said there was a point?"

Answering the rhetorical question was beneath them both, so Marc waited for his friend to continue.

"Over the last five years I've traveled across most of the West." He dropped his feet to the ground and leaned forward, his eyes glassy as he gathered his thoughts. "The Hotel Dupree has no rival, except maybe in San Francisco. But even there, I'm not so sure."

"I planned it that way."

"Why go to so much expense?" Trey asked.

"You know the answer."

"*Pearl.*" Trey spat the word as a curse. "Is she the reason for all this opulence?"

Furious at his friend's lack of understanding, Marc paced through the room in hopes of settling his anger. "This has nothing to do with Pearl."

"No? Then tell me why all this." He waved his hand in a wide arc.

Marc stopped pacing and swung around to glare at his friend. "You of all people should understand, especially after what we went through in Louisiana after the war."

"You still riding that horse?" Trey cocked his head. "That was fourteen years ago."

"Look, Trey—"

"No, you look, Marc. Look around you. Look real hard and tell me what you see."

"I don't have to look around to know that I like what I've created here."

"What *you've* created? Do you hear yourself?" Trey rested his elbows on his knees, his eyes filled with genuine concern. "You're talking blasphemy."

"Blasphemy?" Marc drew in a tight breath. Quelling his temper was becoming harder by the second. "You're overstating matters."

"Am I? You used to know where your blessings came from, Marc."

"I still do. Hard work, focused discipline and ruthless drive."

Trey snorted. "Go ahead and tell yourself that, but I know better. You're worshipping the creation of your own hands instead of the Creator."

The man might as well have gut-punched him, which had been Trey's goal. Too late, Marc remembered why he hated these heart-to-heart talks with his friend. "This, from you? You haven't stepped inside a church in five years."

"No, I haven't. But we aren't talking about me, we're

talking about you and why you refuse to turn back to God."

"Do I look like I care what you think about me or my relationship with the Lord?"

Trey went on as though he hadn't spoken. "Everywhere I look I see shocking displays of wealth."

Marc shrugged.

"But do you want to know what I really see? Things."

Waiting for his friend to continue, Marc barely concealed his impatience. This wasn't a new conversation between them, and he was getting sorely tired of Trey's condemnation. But the marshal remained silent, as if there was nothing more to say on the matter.

Well, Marc wasn't finished. "That's right, Trey. I have things. *Nice* things that bring comfort and security, not only to me but my employees as well." He paused for a moment, then dug deep into the bitterness rooted inside his soul. "As firstborn sons, our futures were secure. We were destined to be planters, like our fathers and their fathers and their fathers before them. Then the war came and we lost *everything*."

Trey ran his fingertip across the lip of the glass, studying the crystal as though it was a complicated puzzle waiting to be solved. "I'd say you're a long way from poverty, my friend."

"What do you know about it? You own a pair of six-shooters, a tin star and a horse."

"I…*know*."

The whispered response cut deep and Marc flinched at the realization of his insensitivity toward his friend's loss. At what they'd both lost with a single rifle shot. "Look, I'm sorry. I didn't mean—"

Cutting him off, Trey raised his hand between them.

"The people that come with your wealth aren't real. They only want what you can give them. What kind of future can be found here?"

"I'll never be poor again. *That's* my future."

"I find it necessary to point out that you said that once before. And then you met Pearl."

Marc's jaw clenched. With great effort he forced himself to relax. "Pearl might have run off with my first fortune, but no woman will ever steal from me again."

"You know, Marc, if you weren't so bent on comparing the two you'd see that Miss O'Connor is different from Pearl." Trey searched Marc's face with the shrewd skill of a lawman. "But I'd say you already know about their differences."

"You've got it all figured out, don't you?"

"Maybe not all of it." Trey shook his head. "But I've noticed how you watch Miss O'Connor."

Marc hated that smug tone. "How do I watch her?"

"Like you can't stop thinking about her, can't stop wondering what it would be like to know her better." Trey laughed. "Like it or not, my friend, you look at Miss O'Connor as if she's the only person in the room."

"If I do look at her more than anyone else it's because I need to keep an eye on her. Laney O'Connor can't be trusted," Marc said. "Didn't she prove that the other night in my office?"

"She's definitely clever. And wily—"

"So we agree."

Trey frowned. "Not completely. She's also a woman of integrity."

"All of a sudden you know her so well?"

"I've watched her these last three nights, too."

Marc pretended the spasm of white-hot jealousy was just a trick of his imagination. "Have you now?"

"I'd stake my life on the fact that she took that money from Judge Greene for a good reason. Have you even asked her why she needed it?"

"I've asked, ten times at least."

"What'd she say?"

"She didn't say. She just stared at her toes or made a glib remark or pretended she didn't hear the question or…well, you get the idea."

"Ask her again."

Marc swallowed back a quick retort. Trey had no understanding of women like Laney since the only woman he'd truly known had been pure and sweet, made to share his life. Trey was comparing Laney to the wrong woman. "I don't need to ask her again. She took a large sum of money from a man in a clandestine manner. If she'd had a good reason to do so she'd have told me already."

"If you really thought that, she'd be out of your life by now," Trey pointed out. "Deep down, you know I'm right."

"I see you're determined to defend her." And there went that spasm in his gut again.

Trey started to open his mouth, seemingly rethought his words then started again. "Hasn't she shown up every night on time and worked to the end of her shift without complaint? That says a lot about her character."

"You're putting more into her actions than her behavior warrants."

"It's my job to make quick judgments on a person's character. As far as Laney O'Connor goes, I'd say she needs your protection, not your lack of trust."

Marc didn't like what Trey said, didn't like that he desperately wanted to believe his friend was right about Laney. Before meeting the woman, he hadn't realized how tired he'd become of meeting disreputable characters, tired of never finding that one person in the world he could trust. The part of him that wanted to believe in Laney warred with the part of him that needed to shun all she appeared to be.

Under the circumstances he did the only thing he could. He attacked Trey. "You have the gall to tell me Laney needs protection? What do you know about it? All you know is vengeance. Ever since Ike Hayes killed Laurette, you've lived for nothing else."

Trey slammed a fist into his palm. "She was my *wife*."

"And she was my sister."

Shoulders slumped, Trey sank farther into his chair. "We've been through this too many times to start again."

"I miss her, too, Trey."

"Then leave it alone."

Marc choked down his own pain. What he had to say was too important to hold back the words any longer. "I can't. If she knew what you'd become, her heart would break. It's been three years. Let go of the past."

Bitterness filled the other man's eyes. "Like you've done?"

Marc said nothing. Trey was right. He hadn't let go of the past any more than his brother-in-law had. In this, they were the same.

Unable to find the words to soothe Trey's grief, Marc watched helplessly as the man rose from his chair and went to the mantel. As though he didn't realize what he was doing Trey's touch gentled the moment his finger ran along the frame surrounding the photograph of Laurette. A shuddering sigh slipped out of him.

"We aren't talking about me anymore, or Laurette."

Trey pulled his hand to his side, clenching his fingers into a tight fist. After a moment he turned back to face Marc, all expression cleared from his eyes. This was familiar ground for them, both too filled with pain to continue discussing the woman they'd each loved too much and lost too soon.

"Listen, Marc. Take your own advice and move on. Stop letting money mean so much to you and start living your life as the godly man you were meant to be."

The need for honesty overruled any desire to defend himself. "My life isn't all about money."

"No? Then give Miss O'Connor however much she needs. No questions asked. Let her have the money free and clear, without making her work for it."

Marc thought hard about Trey's suggestion. Ever since he'd pulled Laney into his arms and discovered she held secrets in her lips that called to a part of him no woman had ever touched, he'd considered helping her out of whatever spot she'd gotten herself into.

But something in him, the part the war had pillaged and Pearl had helped destroy, couldn't let go of everything he'd come to believe. One earth-shattering kiss didn't mean Laney was worthy of his trust.

A knock interrupted his thoughts. Trey's dinner had arrived. Grateful for the distraction, Marc called out, "Enter."

The door cracked opened and a very lovely head spilled through the tiny opening. "I need to talk to you."

Just for a moment, Marc allowed himself to enjoy

the rush of pleasure elevating his body temperature at Laney's habit of looking him straight in the eye.

"Come in." He barely managed to hold back his grin. "We were just discussing you."

She wrinkled her nose. "We?"

Marc indicated Trey with a nod of his head.

She took a step forward then halted as her eyes focused on the U.S. Marshal badge clipped to Trey's chest. "Oh. Um. I'll just leave you two to finish your business. What I have to talk about can wait."

She backed out of the room but Marc pressed forward and caught up with her. "I said come in, Laney. It's long past time you officially met the esteemed marshal."

Popping her head back into the room, her wary eyes filled with frustration. And a good dose of trepidation. "I'd rather not tonight."

Marc reached out, clasped her arm and urged her back inside. "All the more reason for me to insist."

She batted at his hand. "Perhaps another time?"

"Now works for me."

The flash of alarm in her eyes made all the agony he'd suffered since he'd first met her much easier to swallow.

Time for a little fun.

Chapter Eleven

The last thing Laney expected when she'd knocked on Marc's office door was to encounter Marshal Scott's very large person. Over the last three days her avoidance of the lawman had been nearly flawless, a work of artistry and manipulation that would appall Katherine but made Laney rather proud.

Even now, she might have thought of a way to continue avoiding this inevitable meeting but for Marc's disdainful behavior. When she considered his performance of only seconds before, ill-mannered was the word that came to mind.

With perhaps more frustration than sense, she pushed aside care and strode into his office with her best imitation of nobility.

Hands on hips, she stared down her upturned nose. "Look, Marc, I get what you're trying to do." She threw a scowl at the Marshal, then turned back around. "Let's forgo the charade. We both know if you wanted to send me to jail, for taking what was *mine*, you would have tried to do so by now."

The marshal laughed outright. "Well, now. Beautiful *and* smart."

Marc sneered at his friend but aimed his words at her. "If you're so confident you know what I will or will not do, why bother coming back to work every night?"

Deciding to go with the truth, she lifted her chin higher. "I need the money."

"Hate to say it, Marc, but I told you that was the case."

Marc cut the marshal another hard glare. "Shut up, Trey."

Laney bit back her own suggestion as to what the marshal could do with his opinions. Staggering as the notion seemed, for once she and Marc were in complete agreement. The last thing she needed right now was an interfering U.S. marshal.

"So, what did you need?" Dupree asked her.

"Since the front desk has been slow all evening Rose suggested I head home. But I need your approval first. So here I am, asking. May I leave?"

Marc just stared at her, a grin twitching at the corner of his lips. When she realized he wasn't going to answer her request, Laney sighed. "Is that *yes* or *no*?"

Releasing a smug smile, he chuckled at her. "Pushy, aren't you?"

It was a shame that boyish grin on his oh-so-handsome face took the punch right out of her anger. "Fine. I'll take that as a yes."

"Not so fast. I'm still weighing my decision."

Well, of course he was. In the face of that all that masculine arrogance, Laney nearly gave into her frustration. Tired from a full day at the orphanage and an even fuller night at the hotel, she considered telling a certain hotel owner and his pesky U.S. marshal side-kick what she thought of them both.

All night, they'd watched her from their usual vantage point in the lobby. She'd tried not to notice them, but the two together were hard not to notice. If a girl were the romantic sort—which, praise God, Laney was not—she'd be hard-pressed to ignore such a pair. There was the dark and brooding one, the marshal badge adding a hint of respectability to his roguish good looks.

And the other?

As she eyed Dupree now, she realized he was equally as handsome as his friend, but his refined elegance made him much more intimidating to her. And that frightened Laney more than she cared to admit. Never before had a man held so much authority over her emotions, especially one who made it clear what he thought of her character.

"Why not just give me your answer?" To her mortification, she couldn't keep the shake out of her voice. "May I go or not?"

"You all square with Rose?"

"Didn't I already say my leaving was her idea? Just say what you really want from me so we can end this ridiculous game."

Eyes narrowed, Marc's lips crushed into a hard, thin line. "What I want is an explanation as to why you're in business with a banker like Prescott. I also want the exact location where you live and, finally, I want to know the reason you accepted money from Judge Greene."

Holding his arrogant, forceful graze, Laney sniffed delicately. "Is that all?"

"No." Visibly relaxing, his lips curled toward that

thrilling smile again. "I could use a decent meal and a strong cup of coffee."

She hated how she had to fight not to return his smile. Like a dog on point she made her request for a third time. "It's real simple, Marc. Either I can go home now or I can't. Make your decision or I'll make it for you."

She'd forgotten all about the other man in the room until a choked bark of laughter caught her attention. She swung a disapproving glare in his direction. "Something funny?"

"No, ma'am. Just enjoying the show."

"Then keep out of this."

He raised his hands in a show of surrender. "Whatever the lady says."

At least one of the men in this room knew who was in charge.

Turning back to the more stubborn of the two, Laney tapped her foot on the carpet. "Well? What's it to be?"

"Where are my manners?" His tone filled with mock politeness as he grabbed her hand and tugged her deeper into the room before shutting the door behind her. "You've never *officially* met my friend, U.S. Marshal Trey Scott."

"Perhaps I don't want to meet him."

"Sure you do."

She yanked on her hand, but Marc pulled her closer until they stood inches apart. His scent filled her head, making her think of the last time she'd been in this office.

With a lift of her hand, she could reach up and drag Marc's head toward hers, finally discovering whether the kiss they'd shared the other night had been real or just a figment of her imagination. She didn't do it, of course.

In an attempt to harden her defenses against him, she fired off insults at will. "You are the most fallible, self-deluded, bullheaded man I know."

"There you go again, making me all aflutter with your fine words regarding my character."

She poked a finger against his chest. "A swine, that's what you are."

"You're too kind, really." He leaned over her and dropped his voice to a mere whisper. "Watch out, Laney, you might turn my head."

"I'm completely unimpressed with your clever responses, *Marc*." This time when she pulled on her hand, he released her.

She spun to leave.

Unfortunately, two steps forward and she found herself eye to eye with a shiny tin star that had U.S. marshal branded in the metal.

Where was the fear? The trepidation?

Strange, even though this man towered over her, she wasn't at all scared of him. And she experienced *none* of the confusing emotions whenever Marc stood this close to her. She looked up, and up some more, before she finally noticed that the marshal was grinning at her. The gesture made him appear almost boyish.

Maybe her absence of fear was due to lack of sleep, or maybe it was that very likable smile. Or maybe it was simply because the man had shaved off the dark stubble that usually covered his jaw.

"I'm pleased to finally meet you, Miss O'Connor." His voice was a deep, soothing bass rumbling in his chest.

Unsure if he meant what he said or was playing a game with her, she stared at him for a long moment. But then he winked at her, and she finally released a returning smile. "You, too, Marshal Scott."

"Call me Trey."

"I think I'd like that."

From behind her Marc released a growl from deep in his throat. "You're done for the evening, Laney."

She spun around at his sudden acquiescence. Forgetting for a moment what she'd come into the office for in the first place, she scrunched her eyebrows together. "What?"

"You may go home."

"I… Wait just a minute. Why are you letting me go all of a sudden?"

"Why not?" His gaze didn't quite meet her eyes. "Like you said yourself, we aren't that busy this evening."

No, they weren't. But still, why was he capitulating?

"Well, now that Marc has made his decision at last," Marshal Scott cleared his voice, "won't you allow me to escort you home, Miss O'Connor?"

Laney turned back around. "You? No…" She quickly gained control of her spinning thoughts. "No, that won't be necessary. I can manage on my own."

The sudden heat at her back told her Marc had stepped forward, trapping her in from behind. "No, Trey. *I'll* escort her."

"You have a hotel to run. While I'm free for the rest of the evening." The marshal dropped a grin on her. "It would be my pleasure to escort you home, Miss O'Connor. A real pleasure."

Too much musky, hulking male surrounded her. Her

insides started to tremble, alerting Laney to the fact that the man behind her was far too close and the one in front of her was far too unfamiliar for all this personal closeness.

Twisting slightly, she thrust out her palms, landing a hand on each of their chests. With a hard shove she pushed at both men.

Neither budged.

She tried again. This time, Marc placed a restraining hand over hers. "I said I'd do it, Trey. End of discussion."

Laney looked from one man to the other. Neither acknowledged her in return. They were too busy glaring at one another.

"It's really no problem," Trey said, his words rumbling over her head as he spoke directly to Marc. "I was leaving anyway."

"You haven't had your supper yet." Marc squeezed Laney's hand softly, but he didn't move his gaze away from his friend. "I insist you stay here and eat."

"Oh, well." Trey shrugged a very large shoulder. "If you insist."

"I do."

Trey shrugged again. "All right."

"Then it's settled."

Not for Laney.

She couldn't afford either man escorting her home. The children's safety demanded she make her way back to Charity House like she had every night since taking this job, *alone*. Neither Marc nor Trey could find out about the orphanage, at least not until Laney owned the house free and clear. Only then would she rethink her options.

For a moment, she watched the two men, measuring, gauging, trying to determine what was really going on between them. The two stood glaring at one another, neither moving. This had to be some sort of male stand-off. Laney had seen a similar scenario just this afternoon when two of the older boys had fought over a toy.

She didn't much like the idea that they might consider her a *toy*. "As much as I appreciate all this chivalry, I can find my way home on my own."

Arms up, palms out, she quickly backed away, but a knock had all three of their heads turning toward the sound.

"Enter," Marc and Trey said simultaneously.

The door swung open and a waiter carrying a platter on his shoulder stepped into the office. The delicious scent of ham and potatoes filled the air.

Sniffing in appreciation, Trey moved toward the smell. "Well, if you'll excuse me. I have a plate of food to devour." He glanced at Marc before exiting. "I'll be in the restaurant if you need me."

Motioning for the waiter to follow him, he strode out of the room without a backward glance.

Laney stared after him, his departure barely registering until the door shut with a soft click.

Her stomach dropped at the sound.

She was with Marc. In his office. For the first time since he'd kissed her three days prior. With no one to act in the role of buffer.

Trying to gain some semblance of control over her hammering pulse, Laney blew out a slow breath and faced the man head-on.

All thought vanished from her mind, except the fact that here she stood. Alone. With a man who was looking exceptionally handsome in a gray vest, crisp striped shirt and red tie.

Holding her stare, his expression slowly changed, turning into something both frightening and exciting in its intensity.

Oh, my. Laney knew that look, had seen it was once before on his face.

Marc Dupree planned to kiss her again.

And Laney—Lord, help her—planned on letting him.

Chapter Twelve

Shoulders tense, gaze riveted, Laney braced herself for Marc's kiss, feeling as though she were about to go to war. But then his eyes darkened to a deep, stormy blue and the emptiness she'd battled all her life gave way, beckoning her to let go and allow this man inside her heart.

He moved a step closer.

Sighing, she breathed in his spicy scent. Suddenly her daily burden of raising a houseful of children became a thousand-pound weight atop her shoulders. If only she could find a moment's relief, just this once.

Perhaps kissing Marc wouldn't be so terrible. Perhaps kissing him would bring a respite.

A rush of contentment surged through her blood as he reached around her and spanned his fingers against the small of her back.

Holding her breath in anticipation, she waited for him to lower his head.

He simply stared at her.

Afraid she wouldn't be able to stop her heart from latching on to his, Laney prayed he wouldn't press his lips to hers. In the next breath her prayer tumbled into the hope that he would kiss her.

Adding to her agitation, he continued to hold her gaze with his. He captured a loose curl falling from its pins and roped it around his finger.

"You have beautiful hair, Laney." His already turbulent gaze filled with a yearning her soul recognized. "One of the first things I noticed about you."

His words fell across her cheek like a warm, welcoming caress.

"I don't think this is a good idea," she whispered.

"Probably not."

Letting the tendril bounce free, the storm clouds faded from his gaze. He leaned forward and pressed his lips to her...*forehead.*

Shocked at the tenderness in the gesture, at her own hopeful reaction that they were on the verge of something more significant than a kiss, Laney wrestled between relief and disappointment. Before she could sift through which of the two emotions bothered her most, Marc gave her cheek a sweet, almost tender tap, tap with his finger.

"You look tired," he said.

Unfair. Really unfair.

She knew how to defend against his arrogance, his condescension, even his masculine superiority. But how could she hold out against such sweet affection? He wasn't supposed to like her, or worry about her. That would mean they could become friends. And then... maybe...something more.

Her eyes started watering. Big, fat tears threatened to spill down her cheeks. She blinked rapidly, desperately trying to gain control over her strange reaction to a simple gesture of concern.

Skimming his gaze across her face, his eyes narrowed. "You're not getting emotional on me?"

And to think she'd almost allowed herself to believe they could become friends. Swiping the back of her hand across her cheek, she flicked him a look. "I'll try to restrain myself."

"That's my girl." He touched her bottom lip with his fingertip, his eyes still dancing with soft emotion. "I knew I could count on you."

She couldn't manage to speak past the burst of sensations rushing through her. Hope, anticipation, faith. Such dangerous emotions when she knew how this ended between them. How this *had* to end between them, with her walking away once she'd earned the money to pay off her loan. And him never the wiser about Charity House or the children.

"How much sleep are you getting, Laney?"

"Enough." For one insane moment she wanted to share the strain of her schedule and the burden of her worries and, most of all, her fear of losing the orphanage. But the part of her that had survived too many years alone couldn't give into such a weak, selfish need.

This wasn't about her. It had never been about her.

Gentling his touch further, Marc traced his fingertip along the curve of her cheek then across the shadows below her eye. "Now why don't I believe you?"

Even though she heard the twinge of sarcasm in his voice, she couldn't muster her usual rancor. Mainly because she believed he was truly worried about her. And that scared her far more than Prescott's threats to foreclose on Charity House.

Laney had to remember why she didn't trust Marc Dupree, why she *couldn't* trust him. Or she would fall into his arms and beg for his help. In an attempt to prevent such a disaster, she blurted out the first thing that came to mind. "Can I have tomorrow off?"

"No."

"How very kind of you to spend so much time considering my request."

"Always willing to oblige." His grin switched into the smile that turned her legs into nothing more substantial than cooked gelatin.

She locked her knees to keep from dropping to the ground. "I thought you were concerned I wasn't getting enough sleep?"

"Tell me why you really want the day off and maybe I'll reconsider your request."

"Never mind." She pushed him away from her with a hard shove to his chest. Knowing she needed to remain calm, she kept her gaze pinned to the third button of his shirt.

Placing his finger under her chin Marc applied enough pressure to force her to look at him eye to eye. "You know, Laney, withholding the truth can lead to telling bigger lies."

She wrenched her chin free from his grasp and swallowed several times. Each time the beating of her heart grew louder in her ears. "Well, that settles it then. I'll see you tomorrow night at six o'clock sharp."

"Laney—"

She elbowed around him then tossed him a mock salute as she swung open the door and stepped into the lobby. "I'll be heading out now. Enjoy the rest of your evening."

"Wait a moment. I'll escort you home, like we agreed."

She looked over her shoulder and saw that he was closing in fast. "No. No." She increased her pace. "That won't be necessary."

Two long strides and he drew alongside her. "Don't be contrary. Bad things happen to women alone on the streets at this time of night."

The genuine concern in his tone stopped her retreat. Placing her hands on her hips, she spun around to face him. "I can take care of myself."

His lips smoothed into that smile she was growing to dread, mainly because she liked it so much. "You overestimate your own strength, sweetheart."

He sounded as if her safety was his main concern. She knew better. "Watch out, Marc, your paranoia might be mistaken for caring."

He threw his head back and laughed. Really laughed. The gesture looked entirely too appealing on his handsome face.

"All right, you win. I won't see you home. *Tonight*."

Wondering why he'd given in so quickly, she angled her head and studied his face. His expression gave nothing away.

"Have a nice evening." He took her arm and steered her toward the door.

Her feet began to move despite her shock, while her jaw opened, closed. Why couldn't she get any words out?

"Laney?" He touched her arm. "I've changed my mind. You can have tomorrow off."

No. No, no, no, no, no. He didn't get to be kind, or

understanding, or play the bigger man. It simply wasn't fair. "I…thank you, Marc. But I'll be here as always."

"*Because…?*"

"I need the money."

"Right." He smiled. "I guess that settles it then. I'll see you tomorrow night."

"Yes." More confused than ever, especially since his eyes still had that warm glow, she started out.

"Don't forget the rules of your position here."

"Wouldn't dream of it." She waved her hand over her head to punctuate her words.

Smiling at her retreating back, Marc watched Laney saunter through the lobby, saucy attitude in every step she took. Unable to take his eyes off her, and not caring who saw him staring, he waited until she walked out of the hotel before motioning for Hank to join him.

"Yeah, boss?"

"You know what to do."

Hank straightened. "You want me to follow her all the way home this time? Or only part of the way like last night?"

Just as he had every evening he'd given the order, Marc puzzled over his reluctance to send Hank on the errand at all. He wanted to know where Laney lived. But what if he found out he'd been right about her all along? What if she lived on The Row, after all?

Then again, what if Trey was right, and Marc had misjudged her? What if the woman needed his help, not his mistrust?

One way or another, the time had come to end the mystery that was Laney O'Connor. "Follow her the whole way."

* * *

A shadow rode in her wake. Out of the corner of her eye, Laney watched a hulking form dart in and then back out of the alley immediately to her left.

Hank. He'd heeled her ever since she'd first left the Hotel Dupree. She'd like to think Marc had sent his man to follow her for her protection. But from his parting shot, she figured the handsome hotel owner wanted to find out whether or not she was breaking any of his precious rules.

That brief moment of concern he'd displayed in his office must have been an illusion. Shaking off a sudden wave of melancholy at the thought, she considered her options. She could lose Hank easily enough. Sure, he was big and scary on first sight, but under all that gruffness and hard muscle was a gentle heart. With a little charm Laney might be able to get Hank to talk.

Perhaps she could find out why Marc had sent the man to follow her.

Heading down the next alley, she melted deep into the shadows. Hank entered a moment after her. Tentatively looking around, he leaned to his right and squinted into the inky black. Shaking his head, he squinted harder and continued forward with a large show of hesitation.

Laney waited until he was directly next to her. "Looking for me?"

The sound of Hank's responding high-pitched holler sent a swirl of guilt coursing through her.

"Hank, it's me. Laney." She reached out to touch his sleeve.

"That was *not* funny, Miss O'Connor." With the

petulance she'd witnessed in very young boys, Hank pushed her hand away. "Not funny at all."

"I know. I'm sorry."

"What are you doing slinking in the dark?" he asked, his gaze darting around the alley.

"Waiting for you."

His audible gasp told its own story. "You knew I was following you?"

"You're sort of hard to miss." She touched his sleeve again. This time he didn't push her hand away.

For the benefit of his dignity, she made a suggestion. "Let's step back into the light. I can't even see my own shadow."

"Good idea." He turned and started out, leading the way without bothering to see if she followed.

Once they were back in the full light of the street, Laney got straight to the point. "Why are you following me?"

"Just doing my job."

"I figured that. But why?"

"As much as I like you, Miss O'Connor—" he gave her a sympathetic grimace "—I can't tell you any more than I already have."

"If it's for my protection…?" She paused, waiting for him to affirm or deny the suggestion, but old tight-lipped Hank pretended grave interest in his right thumbnail.

His silence confirmed her suspicions. Marc wasn't worried about her safety. The tenderness, the concern over her lack of sleep had been an illusion.

After another moment she softened her tone and dripped sugar into the air. "You really won't tell me why you're here?"

"I can't."

A little more sugar. "Not even a hint?"

Nothing.

"Hank, please?"

He sighed. "Miss O'Connor, I like you. Really, I do. Even when you did all that fancy safecracking and wall scaling the other night, I thought you were someone special. But I work for Mr. Dupree. And he doesn't trust you. That means I can't, either."

She couldn't keep the bitter taste of disappointment from filling her mouth. "Does your boss trust anyone?"

Hank looked down the street, as though checking to see if anyone was listening. "Sure. Just not…"

"Me."

"No, it's not you in particular. It's all women." He looked behind him again. "And believe me, he has a good reason not to trust your sort."

Laney tried to remind herself that she'd long since accepted that Marc considered her just another woman of questionable virtue. But she couldn't make herself believe it, not in the dark recesses of her mind. Saddened, she lowered her lashes to hide the hurt running through her.

Hank must have seen something of her pain. "Oh, no. I didn't mean it like that. I meant Mr. Dupree doesn't trust women, period."

"No?" A small portion of her sorrow lifted, replaced by a different sort of pain, one for a man who had material wealth and comfort yet little faith in mankind. Or rather, womankind. "Why doesn't he trust women?"

Hank slammed his mouth shut and shook his head.

Now that the subject had been broached, Laney

couldn't let the matter drop. "If you must follow me home, can't you at least tell me the rest?"

"I already said too much."

"You know, I have my own reasons for not wanting Marc...I mean Mr. Dupree...to know where I live."

Hank blew out a puff of air. "I have to follow you anyway."

Time to change tactics. "I always show up for work, don't I?"

"Can't argue with that."

"And I work hard when I'm there."

"Of course you do."

"Seems silly that you follow me home." She lifted an eyebrow. "What difference could it possibly make where I live?"

"It's not that Mr. Dupree doesn't think you'll show for work, he just wants to know—" Hank cut his own words off, scowled and pointed a finger at her. "Oh, no you don't."

Think, Laney. *Think*. She hated manipulating this big, kind man, but she had to protect the children. "No one would have to know that you didn't follow me home."

"I would know. And that means Mr. Dupree would figure it out eventually. He's smart like that."

"What if you accidentally lost me?"

Hank rubbed his chin. "No. That could never happen."

Before he had time to consider the possibility further, Laney darted down the alley again. Fifty feet later, a wooden fence blocked her passage to the other side. With considerable reaching, a good toehold and a solid jump she scrambled over the barrier.

Hank's bark of shock and thudding pursuit motivated Laney to lift her feet faster off the ground. With no time to check behind her, she sped around the next corner then wove her way through two other streets. After a few more turns Laney gave in and looked over her shoulder.

Hank wasn't following her anymore. She slowed her pace and sighed with pleasure. But guilt reared quickly. She'd like to think she and Hank had become friends. Not that she could count on that, not with so much at stake.

For now, she had to operate on the assumption that both Hank and his boss were threats to Charity House. Perhaps she'd played a rotten trick on the big, kind man but, in the end, she'd managed to protect her children for another night.

Chapter Thirteen

The next day after sending Laney home early, Marc went about his daily business. He still couldn't fathom how Hank had lost her the evening before. Although he knew the woman was crafty, something about Hank's story didn't make sense. Had Hank lost her intentionally?

That would mean the two had become…amicable. At the notion a quiet, shocking jolt of jealousy burned through Marc's soul. He wondered how long he could continue pretending he wasn't growing attached to the woman.

The answer was painfully obvious.

Not long enough.

The time had come to find out exactly who she was and where she lived. Marc would ask the one man who knew the truth—Thurston P. Prescott III. And if the banker wouldn't cooperate, Marc would introduce him to Trey. Amazing the plethora of information a tin star could get out of an otherwise reticent source.

Now that he'd decided to take action, Marc was anxious to solve the mystery of who Laney O'Connor really was beneath her pretty smile and evasive manner. Unfortunately, before he could question Prescott, he had to check in at Mattie's first.

All week long he'd had a bad feeling about one of the restaurant's waitresses. Julia had left early three nights in a row, with the obvious lie of not feeling well. Marc hoped he didn't find the girl working for the infamous madam again. As much as he'd hate to do it, if Julia had broken the rules he would fire her. If for no other reason, he'd have to release her for the sake of the other women who wanted to make the change permanently.

His gut told him Julia had lapsed. And his gut was never wrong. Except once. Even now, he couldn't squelch the onslaught of painful memories over his wife's betrayal and subsequent self-destruction. Till the end of his days, Marc would never understand what made a woman like Pearl indulge in a lifestyle that she'd hated as much as she'd craved.

It was too late to save Pearl. He just hoped it wasn't too late to help Julia.

Clutching the gold dress in her arms, Laney made her way along the upstairs hallway of Mattie's brothel. She stopped at the end of the corridor, shifted the neatly folded garment to one arm and knocked on the closed door.

No answer.

She tried again. "Sally, it's me, Laney. I've come to return your dress."

While she waited again for an answer, Mattie Silks sauntered down the hallway toward her. "Laney, my dear girl, Sally's not up for visitors. She had a bad bout of coughing this morning and it's worn her out."

"Why didn't you tell me this when I first arrived?"

Concentrating on smoothing a nonexistent wrinkle from her sleeve, Mattie shrugged. "It's none of my concern, as long as that lunger does her job in the evenings, I don't care what she does during the day."

Choked with anger, Laney took a long, hard look at the petite madam. Pretty and plump, the blonde, cold-hearted woman had the audacity to wear a cross studded with diamonds around her neck.

Laney's anger boiled deeper as she realized the expensive piece of jewelry had been purchased with the commission Mattie earned off her girls. Girls who knew no better when the madam demanded an outrageous percentage of their evening wages.

"How could you not care?" She strained to keep every bit of emotion out of her voice. "Sally's been with you for years, since before my mother came to work for you. That lovely British accent of hers brings in the fancy men *and* their money."

"I run a business, not a charity house." Mattie giggled at her pun on words. "Oh, that's funny."

Jaw clenched tight, Laney focused on the dress in her hands, sickened at the sinful deeds that had been committed to pay for the expensive garment. Mattie drove all her girls hard, literally enslaving them with her demand that they work every evening in dresses imported from Paris and supplied with their own money.

Reaching out, Mattie's eyes turned shrewd as she touched Laney's shoulder. "You've got it all wrong. The life I provide my girls is really quite comfortable. Your mother certainly didn't mind it. You just have to look at it from the proper perspective."

"Proper perspective?" Laney practically choked on

the words. "Don't forget who you're talking to. I know what this life does to women, how it steals their youth, their futures, often even their lives."

"Now, now, don't be so dramatic." Mattie pulled at a loose thread on her collar. "If you ever get tired of taking care of other women's mistakes, I could use a girl like you." Her gaze roved past Laney's hair, across her face, and slowly along her body. "You'd bring in the fancy money, too."

"My answer is the same as always." Laney shuddered. "I'm not interested in working for you, Mattie."

"If you change your mind…"

"I won't." Laney turned back to the closed door, knocking with more force than before. "Sally, open up."

Coughing erupted in answer.

Hating to ask but not having much of a choice, Laney turned back to Mattie. "Would you unlock this door, please?"

Like a dog with a bone, Mattie continued the previous conversation. "Sally won't be around much longer. You could take her place. She has the best room in the house."

In an attempt to gather her patience, Laney squeezed her eyes shut for a moment. "Just open the door."

"Rude, that's what you are." Mattie shook her finger inches from Laney's face. "I should kick you out of here."

"But you won't. Like it or not, you need me. I keep you in business."

"How do you figure that?"

"I care for your *girls* when they get into trouble, and then I care for their children so they can come back to work for you. You'd be out of half your income if it weren't for me."

"I'd manage." Mattie leaned against the opposite wall and flashed a false smile. "By the way, a man came around a few days ago asking about you."

Laney's hand froze on the door handle. "What man?"

Mattie plucked out a handkerchief from her sleeve, waved it in front of her face, sighed. "Handsome devil, that one."

"You get his name?"

Smiling an I-got-you-now smile, the madam paused for several long beats. "It was that hotel owner, Marc Dupree."

No. "What did you tell him?"

Instead of answering, Mattie fired off her own question in response. "What does he want with you?"

"It's personal. And I'd rather you not tell him how you know me."

Mattie rolled her eyes. "I'm not stupid, Laney. No one outside our circle knows what service you provide me. Or rather, what service you provide several of my girls."

"Thank you." With that settled, she turned her attention back to Sally's door. "Since we understand one another, I'd like to check on Sally now."

"You better watch out, girl." Mattie pushed forward, unlocked Sally's door and then moved aside. "Marc Dupree isn't like most men."

Laney didn't need anyone telling her something she already knew, especially not a woman like Mattie Silks.

"If he wants to find you," Mattie said, shaking her finger in Laney's face again. "He'll find you."

Hearing the truth spoken so casually, with Mattie's knowing grin on her face, Laney could only pray the madam was wrong.

* * *

Marc consulted the large double doors outside the fancy brothel, hoping once again that Julia hadn't gone back to work for Denver's notorious madam. True, Mattie ran the most elegant parlor house in town, but a brothel was still a brothel.

Pushing open the door, he stepped into the gaudy foyer and strode into the main parlor. Though nothing in particular assaulted his sensibilities, everything about the chosen décor was too much. Alone, each piece of furniture and various adornments could almost pass for tasteful. But together, the red velvet divans, the paintings, the gold fixtures and the bold wallpaper defined bad taste.

As with the décor, Mattie Silks overdid everything. She only served champagne while her girls dressed in the height of Parisian fashion. Marc surveyed the interior with a critical heart and a twinge of conscience got to him. Here he stood, judging the woman for the very offense Trey had accused him of—the acquisition of nice *things*.

Was Marc turning his need for wealth and security into a modern-day form of idol worship? Was he putting more stock in what he could accomplish with his own hands instead of turning to the Lord for guidance?

Perhaps. But that didn't make him an idol worshipper, and it certainly didn't make him similar to Mattie Silks.

Concentrating on the task at hand, rather than dwell on his own uncomfortable thoughts, Marc nodded to Mattie's bouncer walking toward him. "Jack."

"Dupree."

"Mattie around?"

Jack smiled, the diamond in his tooth twinkling under the soft lantern light that glowed day and night. "She's not talking to you. Not since you stole Julia, Ruth *and* Lizzie right out from under her nose like that."

Shrugging, Marc pulled out a ten-dollar bill. "Tell her it's important."

Jack grunted while quickly palming the money. "She won't like it."

"Just tell her I'm waiting."

Moments later Mattie sauntered toward him, taking her time and striking a pose every fifth or sixth step. Carrying a flute of champagne, she wore an immovable smile on her overly painted face. Marc decided she looked older than her reported twenty-nine years. At least twenty years older.

Stopping close enough for him to get a whiff of her cheap perfume, she offered her cheek. Out of politeness, Marc leaned down and touched his lips to the plump curve, the taste of grease and pungent roses slipped into his mouth.

In the next second, he found he couldn't prevent his mind from comparing Mattie's offensive smell to Laney's soft, pleasing scent. Shaking his head, he stepped back and offered his usual greeting. "You're looking well."

"Don't you use those sweet words on me." Tapping him on the arm, she added, "I'm still mad at you, Marc Dupree."

"I know."

"You've stolen a total of five of my best girls. And for what?"

"An honest job and a second chance."

Mattie sidled to the nearest chair and hitched her

hip against one of the arms. "Such righteousness I hear in your tone. My girls are entertainers, Marc, nothing more."

They both knew that wasn't the truth. At least not the full truth. "Ruth and Lizzie are happy working for me."

"Ha. You make them wear dreary black."

"They aren't complaining."

"*Yet.* But they will. And just like Gretchen and Patsy, they'll come back to work for me in the end."

Marc didn't bother commenting on the two he'd lost recently.

"So, what brings you here this morning?"

"You mean afternoon." Marc's lips twisted into a grimace. "The sun rose hours ago, Mattie."

"You will call me Madame Silks."

Marc inclined his head, trying not to laugh at the way she attempted to pronounce the word like the French but failed horribly. "It's pronounced *Madame*."

Mattie relaxed into a pose, her tone full of begrudging affection. "You are the most rude, impolite man I know."

He doubted that. "That's why you love me."

Without taking her eyes off him, she took a long, slow sip from her glass. "We should go into business, the two of us. With your brains and my looks, we'd make a fortune."

"I'm not looking to go into the…entertainment business. I'm looking to get women out of it."

With her free hand, she tossed a few curls off her face. "So they can work in your hotel for slave wages, compared to what they can make here?"

"It's not about the money, Mattie. I give them a better living than what you give them, an honest one where they can look themselves in the mirror at the end of every shift. That's why they leave you and come to me."

He had to give it to her, though Mattie visibly stiffened at his words none of her outrage showed on her face. "I should throw you out of here right now."

"Probably." Marc edged toward her, glancing up at the staircase. "But you like me too much to send me away just yet."

"You're a rogue, Marc Dupree." Fanning herself with her hand, she sighed. "Pity I like rogues so much. So, what can I do for you this morning?"

"I'm looking for a woman."

"I have several."

"Not that kind."

She rode her gaze across his face and down to his toes. "Maybe I'll break a rule or two and take care of you myself."

"Not today." *Not ever.*

"You are a man of phenomenal willpower."

Tired of the game, Marc shifted his weight to a more intimidating stance. "Let's get to the point. I'm looking for Julia. Is she here?"

Her eyes darted to the staircase then back to him. She couldn't quite hide the satisfaction in her smile. "Did you say Julia?"

"She's here, isn't she? I see it in that smug smile of yours."

"I don't know what you mean."

"Let's make this simple, I want to know if Julia is still one of my employees, or if she's back to working for you."

"You know, Marc, this is the second time in less than

a week you've come looking for a woman. Having a hard time keeping track of your girls?"

"I was looking for Laney O'Connor for a very different reason."

"*Personal* reasons?"

"You could say that."

Mattie locked eyes with his, interest fringing the edges of her gaze. "I knew you had a secret. But I never thought it was...*that.*" A giggle danced from her lips.

"You know Miss O'Connor?"

After a final searching glance of his face, her expression cleared. "Now, I didn't say that I did and I didn't say that I didn't."

This was far too familiar territory. He'd gotten this exact behavior from every other madam on The Row. What he didn't understand was why the tight-lipped runaround? "So what you're saying is that you know her, but you won't tell me *how* you know her."

"My, you are a smart man."

"What is it about that woman that keeps all you madams on The Row so determined to remain discreet? Does she have something on you? Is she a blackmailer?"

"Laney? You must be joking."

"So you do know her. Is she a crib girl?"

"You mean to tell me, you really don't know what she does and why?"

Marc took another step toward Mattie, using the difference in their heights to make his point. "Are you planning to continue this game or are you going to solve this mystery for me here and now?"

Nonplused, Mattie took another sip of her champagne. "You're going to have to find this one out on your own, you arrogant brute." She tapped a finger on his chin. "It'll serve you right for stealing my Ruth and Lizzie with promises of legitimacy. But, at least I have Jul…" Covering her mouth with two fingers, she fluttered her lashes. "Oops, it almost slipped."

"I knew it. Julia *is* here."

"Of course she is, silly man. You can't change a woman like her. I predict Ruth and Lizzie will be back as well."

"Don't count on it."

Marc swallowed his disappointment. He'd lost another woman to the allure of fine clothes, expensive champagne and the illusion of glamour Mattie offered. Three in one month.

Well, Julia was the last. As long as he owned a means to save these women from themselves, he'd fight to keep the rest straight. *Especially* Ruth and Lizzie.

"Oh, look. I've upset you." Mattie rose to her full height, pressed her palm against his chest and pushed him back a step. "But you're in luck. Since I'm feeling generous this afternoon I'll give you a little hint about your Laney."

Not trusting himself to speak, Marc held his tongue.

"You're looking in the wrong place. She doesn't live here on The Row."

His heart soared. Could Trey have been right about Laney? "You mean, she's not a—"

"Oh, you have the right idea. Sort of. Well, not really, at least not the *complete* right idea."

Marc felt the muscles in his jaw tighten, and his nerves bowed to near snapping. "Could you confuse me any more?"

"I could, but like I said, I'm feeling generous this morning."

"Afternoon, Mattie. It's early afternoon."

Jack came up from behind Mattie and whispered in her ear.

Eyes narrowing, she shook her head violently. "No, not now." She flicked a sideways glance at Marc. "Just keep her in her room until I'm through here."

"Julia?"

Pretending confusion, Mattie cocked her head to the left. "Julia, Laney, which woman were you looking for again?"

"Either. Both."

A crash shot out from a back room, followed by a feminine wail of anger. Mattie grasped Marc's arm and directed him toward the door. "So good to see you. We'll have to finish our discussion some other time." At the sound of another crash, Mattie released Marc and nodded to her bouncer. "Jack, please show Mr. Dupree the way out."

She was already hustling off in the direction of the commotion by the time Marc asked, "What's the hurry?"

Knowing the question fell on deaf ears, he turned to go. But a familiar voice washed over him, and he spun back around.

"Mattie, Jack, where are you? I need some fresh water for Sally and—"

The words stopped abruptly.

Unable to stop himself, Marc steered his gaze toward the staircase. His eyes locked onto Laney O'Connor. He'd never experienced true torment before. Until this moment.

For days he'd hoped against hope. He'd put off finding concrete answers. But now he had to face the truth.

Laney was one of Mattie's girls.

The reality of how close he'd come to losing his objectivity—again—over a woman—again—struck him to the core.

In one word he managed to convey all the anger, the pain and the disappointment he felt. "*You.*"

Wide-eyed, Laney continued to stare at him, unmoving, eyes blinking rapidly. "Marc, please, it's not what you think."

Refusing to accept that any of the emotions flitting across the woman's face warranted consideration, he attacked. "I knew I couldn't trust you."

Just as she opened her mouth to respond, Jack took his arm and physically escorted Marc to the front door.

Too stunned to fight, Marc went willingly.

Chapter Fourteen

Several hours after leaving Mattie's brothel, Laney stood outside the Hotel Dupree, shifting from foot to foot. The wind tugged bits of her hair free from its knot, while pure dread sliced through her.

How could she face Marc after this afternoon? How could she not? She had to explain herself, had to make him understand that her presence in Mattie's brothel wasn't as scandalous he thought.

Would he be willing to listen?

As if to mock her agitated mood, day inched slowly into night, dragging a ribbon of blues, pinks and purples behind it.

Needing a moment to gather her thoughts—and her courage—Laney turned toward the distant peaks. No comfort came from the mountains' snowcapped beauty. Only more apprehension. The memory of Marc's eyes when their gazes had connected, the condemnation and disappointment, made Laney's heart grew heavier, and more troubled than before.

All her lies, all her deceptions had caught up with her in a single moment of recognition.

What did you expect? a tiny voice chided. *You've intentionally misled him every day of your brief acquaintance.*

In her attempt to keep Marc away from Charity House she'd allowed him to think the worst of her.

Having spent the last three hours coming to terms with her unrequited feelings for Marc, she'd gained insight into the future that lay before her. Like a barren cloud blowing over a parched field, promising much but producing little, any chance of earning Marc's respect had disappeared.

That didn't mean she wouldn't try.

The soft glow of light and low murmurs flowing from the hotel lobby compelled Laney forward in a strange, mesmerizing summons. Answering the call, she entered through the revolving doors.

As if he'd been waiting for her arrival, Hank drew alongside her. "Mr. Dupree wants to see you in his office."

She smiled up at him. "Thank you for letting me know."

"Just doing my job." His accompanying scowl warned her he hadn't yet forgiven her for the trick she'd played on him in the alley.

In serious need of a friend, she grabbed his arm. "Hank, wait. I'm sorry about last night. I know you won't believe this, but I had to lose you."

A myriad of emotions waltzed across his features before his lips cracked into a tentative smile. "I understand."

"I'm glad. One day, I'll explain my actions fully."

"When you're ready."

Well, at least she'd healed one relationship. "Thank you for understanding."

His face reddened. "Go on," he urged. "Mr. Dupree won't bite."

"I wish I had your confidence."

He nudged her forward. "You're better off facing him sooner rather than later."

If only that were true. As the shut office door loomed ahead of her, several concerns grappled against one another. What would she do if Marc fired her, before she'd earned enough money to pay off the interest on her loan?

What if he found out about Charity House, would he threaten to shut her down as Prescott was trying to do?

As nerve-racking as Laney found that unlikely possibility, another, more selfish, concern rose to the top of her fears. How could she face Marc, knowing the feelings she had for him were too strong to deny? And how could she keep from begging him to feel for her a tiny portion of what she felt for him?

With each step she sent up a silent prayer for courage, but she doubted God listened with a sympathetic ear. She'd done enough in the last few weeks to ensure that the Lord turned away from her. If not for good, at least for now.

Aware of how very alone she felt, Laney rolled her trembling fingers into a fist then knocked twice on Marc's office door.

"Enter."

A wave of white-hot terror slithered through her stomach, but somehow she managed to trek into the room.

With his attention riveted on one of the photographs on the mantel, Marc didn't turn around. "Shut the door."

She did as he commanded and waited for him to face her directly. When he finally turned and met her gaze, she wished he'd kept his back to her a little while longer. Although his expression held little emotion, his clenched jaw and muscle ticking in the side of his throat told of the battle that waged inside him.

"I see you wore the black dress." He spoke in a near whisper, but the underlying misery in his tone shouted at her to cross the space between them and beg him to listen to her side of the story.

She stayed rooted to the spot. "I've come to work my shift as usual."

He skimmed his gaze over her and the expression in his eyes changed, turning shattered, as though the world had let him down one too many times.

Heart hammering against her ribs, head whirling with sorrow, Laney could hardly keep from rushing forward and pulling him into her arms. She wanted to soothe away his agony and perhaps end a little of hers as well. Staring at him now, feeling his pain as though it were her own she could deny the truth no longer—she was falling in love with Marc Dupree. And like a dangerous reef that shipwrecked the mightiest of boats, she knew her feelings for this man could easily destroy her.

As his eyes held hers, silently communicating the full of his disappointment, her soul died a silent death—one she feared was the first of many more to come.

"Do you remember the rules of your employment?" His voice dripped inside the stiff tension between them.

She nodded. "I am to live a clean, wholesome life. No drinking, no cheating, no lying, and no stealing." Surprised at how clear and strong the words came out of her mouth, she continued. "I'm to partake in no unseemly behavior, either here or outside this hotel."

"And yet you're standing in my office, after what happened this afternoon in Mattie's brothel."

"Yes. I have broken none of your rules."

He searched her face, his eyebrows drawing together as though he puzzled over what to say next. Laney returned his stare, silently willing him to believe in her just this once.

"Ask me, Marc. Ask me what I was doing at Mattie's." Urgency raised her voice a full octave higher than usual. "Then ask me how I'm acquainted with the madam."

"I don't want to know why you were there. God help us both, I don't want to know." He moved quickly and wrapped his fingers around her shoulders. With one great tug he pulled her in his arms. "Don't you understand? I *can't* know."

"But it's not—"

His mouth pressed against hers, cutting off the rest of her words.

For weeks she'd held back her anger, anger at his inability to see who she really was, deep at the core. She'd blamed herself for his misconception. But now her disappointment in him caught up with her anger at herself.

Couldn't he tell she was different from the women Mattie employed?

Apparently not.

This was not a pleasant kiss, nor was it purely physical. It held more intimacy than she'd ever imagined possible between a man and woman. Her very soul understood this man, better now than ever before. As deep as her anger went, she wanted to soothe the pain she felt in him.

Finally, he pulled his head back. He tried to draw away from her completely, but she wouldn't let him. Not yet. Not until she proved to him who she really was, not the woman he seemed determined to see.

Cupping his face, Laney put all her answers to his unspoken questions in her gaze. After a moment, she softened her hold and gently touched her lips to his temple then let him go.

Breathing hard, he stared at her. But he didn't back away.

Progress.

She held his gaze, watching, waiting, praying he understood her silent message declaring her innocence.

Raking a hand through his hair, he stepped back, turned and walked again to the mantel. He ran his finger along the frame of a single photograph, as though drawing strength from the image of the young woman who looked so much like him.

With his attention focused elsewhere, Laney let her eyes rove over him. Her heart swelled with emotion, with something that felt like gratitude.

Despite their turbulent history, Marc Dupree had given her a precious gift these last few weeks. Before meeting him, she'd thought intimacy between a man and woman was dirty, sinful. But now she knew it could be different, maybe even beautiful.

His hand stilled over the frame. "Why were you at Mattie's?"

Laney took a deep breath, hoping the right words would tumble from her lips. "I had to return the dress I borrowed from one of her girls." When he didn't respond, she explained further. "You remember the gold dress I wore that first night we met? It wasn't mine."

He spun around and shot her a chilling look, clearly unwilling to believe her. "You weren't carrying a dress when I saw you this afternoon."

"No. I'd already returned it." His raised eyebrow was enough of a question. "Sally, the girl who loaned me the dress, has consumption. When you saw me on the stairs, she'd just had a terrible coughing fit. I'd gone in search of some water to help soothe her throat."

There. The truth was out.

Would he believe her now? Would he ask for answers to the rest of his questions?

Or would he send her away, with no further chance to explain herself?

Oh, Lord, please, soften Marc's heart. Help him hear the truth in my words and the ones I can't say just yet.

Marc's heart pitched in his chest. A twisted, ruthless spark of hope rode him hard. Laney had been nursing a sick woman? Could the explanation for her presence in Mattie's brothel be so simple?

"Do you work for Mattie?"

"No."

He had to know the rest, had to stop dancing around the real issue and get to the truth at last. "Are you a… prostitute?"

She smiled at him. "No, I am not."

"Were you ever?"

Her smile deepened, as if she'd been waiting to have her say for a very long time. "*Never.*"

"Then how do you know Mattie?"

A shadow darkened across her features, but in the

next instant she threw her shoulders back and looked him directly in the eye. "Before she died, my mother worked for Mattie."

"Your mother? Was she a—"

"Yes, she was." Laney's voice hitched, but she maintained unrelenting eye contact with him. "I spent most of my childhood traveling from mining camp to mining camp, wherever men were willing to pay for my mother's time. Eventually she grew weary of traveling so she went to work for Mattie."

"I'm sorry." He reached out to touch her, to prove he meant every word.

She pushed away from him. "My mother was not a happy woman, nor did she trust anyone but me. You see, Marc, while you were kicking up your heels at fancy balls and parties I was keeping time and collecting money for my mother."

Unable to bear the pain he saw in Laney's yes, Marc reached out to touch her again.

She shook her head and held up a hand to stop his pursuit. "Don't. We have to finish this now."

As much as he wanted never to speak on this topic again, he knew she was right. Just because she wasn't a prostitute didn't mean she wasn't associated with the business on some level.

Although he had a strong suspicion that wasn't the case, Marc still had to ask the toughest question of all. "The money you took from Judge Greene, was it to start your own brothel?"

She gave him a blank look. "Is that what you thought? That I needed money to open a…a…brothel?"

"Why else would you need that much money?"

As soon as the words left his mouth he finally understood their absurdity. From the start, he'd measured Laney against Pearl. Not because she was like his wife, but because he'd been afraid to see the truth. Laney had stepped into his hotel and stolen his breath the moment he'd laid eyes on her. He'd lost trust in his own objectivity years before. So, instead of sorting through his initial impressions of her, as well as his attraction, he'd assumed the worst.

Her next words stamped across his guilty conscience. "There are a lot of things money can buy besides a brothel."

She had every right to her anger, but he wasn't through. He had to know the rest. "Then why did you need the money?"

"Because Prescott—" She broke off, her brows drew together before her expression closed inside itself. "I can't tell you. There are others who could be hurt if you decided to stop me."

"Stop you from what?"

"I can't say."

"At least tell me who else is involved in your business venture, the one that required a large loan from Prescott's bank."

The shadows in her eyes turned into storm clouds, brewing for combat. "The loan is mine and no one else's."

Marc didn't understand her reluctance to tell him the entire truth. What could she possibly be hiding? "If the loan is yours alone, then how is this not your secret to tell?"

She opened her mouth to speak, then promptly shut it. "We made a deal, Marc. I've stuck to my end, you *must* stick to yours."

Her vehemence stunned him. Had others let her down so badly that she couldn't trust *his* word? "Laney, secrets and deceptions are the same as lies. Haven't you learned that yet?"

"You don't understand."

"Trust me."

She released an unhappy laugh. "You want me trust you?"

"Would it be so hard?"

"Oh, let's see. Mere seconds ago you assumed I needed money to start my own brothel. You suppose something like that might hold me back from complete honesty?"

"I was wrong. And I'm sorry."

"I could also remind you of the countless little threats you've made in the last few weeks. For instance, the ones involving a certain U.S. marshal."

"You played your part in this deception as well. Correct me if I'm wrong, Laney, but you wanted me to think you lived on The Row."

She had the cheek to break eye contact with him. "All right, I'll give you that."

"So we start clean. A new beginning."

It was her turn to become the skeptic. "How do we do that? Even now, can you honestly tell me you believe I've had nothing but good intentions?"

"I'm no hypocrite. I won't pretend it hasn't crossed my mind that if you had nothing bad to hide, you'd tell me the truth now."

She threw her hands in the air. "And you want me to trust you?"

"I'm not the one keeping secrets."

"Is that a fact? You want to tell me why you don't

trust women? Or why you so readily assumed I was a prostitute, without once asking me if it were true? You can't expect trust, Marc, unless you're willing to give it in return."

"All I know is that nothing good comes from deception." He took a step closer. "What are you hiding from me, Laney?"

"Please, don't keep asking me the same question and expecting a different answer."

"Tell me."

"Would you settle for a compromise?"

He tucked his hands inside his pants pockets. "A compromise?"

"You know, it's when each person gives a little, and both get something back in return."

"I know what the word means." He gave a short laugh. "I'm just not overly fond of the concept."

She grazed him with another penetrating look. Under the circumstances he supposed she had every right to be leery of him, but knowing it and accepting it were two different things.

"Here's how it would work," she began. "Once I pay off the rest of my loan, I'll tell you everything."

Looking at her as though seeing her for the first time, he realized that if Laney said she would tell him the truth eventually, she would.

From the beginning, he'd measured her against Pearl, all the while refusing to admit that Laney just might have a good reason for her behavior.

He remembered the silent desperation underlying her actions on that first night. Her despair had been real. Maybe he could help her with whatever had put the look of desperation in her eyes. Maybe by helping her he would find his own redemption.

Maybe this was his way back.

"All right, Laney. I won't ask any more questions." At her sigh of relief he added, "For now."

Not in the least discouraged, she relaxed into her smile. "So, you finally accept that I'm not a woman of questionable virtue?"

How could he believe anything else, when the evidence had been in front of him all along? "Yes."

"And I'm not fired?"

"Not tonight."

She touched his sleeve. "Thank you, Marc."

He covered her hand with his. Overcome with the sudden urge to pull her into his arms and kiss her again, he blew out a painful rush of air and focused on the matter at hand. "Ready to charm our guests?"

"It's what I do best."

Chapter Fifteen

Over the course of the next week, Laney's days settled into a pleasant, if somewhat hectic routine. She worked at the orphanage all day, visited an increasingly ailing Sally in the late afternoon then worked her shift at the Hotel Dupree in the evening. Though on the verge of exhaustion, she'd never felt happier in her life. And she knew the source of her joy.

Marc Dupree.

No longer her enemy, she now saw him as a person, with worries and burdens and flaws just like her. Instead of finding fault with his imperfections, her admiration deepened.

She was in love. Or, if not, very close to getting there.

Smiling, she spread flour on the chopping board and pressed out more dough. The clock on the table told her she had two hours to finish with her morning chores before serving lunch to the children. No matter how hard she tried to concentrate on her long list of tasks, her mind kept wandering back to Marc.

She'd see him again soon. A rush of anticipation tingled along her scalp.

What had happened to her restraint, her need to guard her heart? A single thought of the handsome hotel owner and her stomach turned all shaky and quivery inside.

Sighing, she pressed a flour-tipped finger to her lips. Though he'd not kissed her again, there were times when Marc looked at her in a way that had her thinking of the future, of happy endings, of forever.

Laney looked forward to the day when there would be no more secrets between them. On countless occasions she'd opened her mouth to tell him the truth about Charity House, but each time something in her had halted her confession. Perhaps it was the habit of caution, or perhaps simple fear, but she could never quite find the words to tell him about the orphanage.

And Marc hadn't pressed.

If she told him the truth, would he finally trust her? A very selfish part of her wanted it to be that simple. But she'd learned her lesson well, thanks to Thurston P. Prescott III. The children needed her protection. Until she was certain of their safety, she had to maintain her silence.

Kneading the dough a bit harder than necessary, Laney sighed. Why couldn't she have met Marc under different circumstances? Despite her limited knowledge of relations between a man and a woman, she sensed her feelings for the man were special, different, *good*.

Laney wanted to throw caution to the wind. She wanted to trust in someone other than herself and a silent God who seemed too far away at the moment. She wanted to—

The back door burst open, jarring her out of her daydreams. "Miss Laney, come quick, Katherine just hit a home run."

Pure delight filled her. The very idea of prim and proper Katherine whacking a ball hard enough to cross over the backyard fence was quite a thought indeed. "Megan, are you certain of this?"

"Yes." She pointed to her left. "See for yourself."

Laney wiped her hands on her apron and glanced out the window above the sink. Half the kids were jumping up and down, screaming and carrying on in childish enthusiasm. The other half looked positively bleak. They slapped leather gloves against their legs or scuffed toes in the grass. "Well, what do you know? She finally did it."

Laney watched Katherine skip from one base to the next, taking her time, giggling all the way.

Megan tugged on Laney's hand. "Hurry, Miss Laney. The Hawks need you, or else those awful Panthers will beat us again."

Laney smiled to herself. Baseball. Who'd have thought one tiny suggestion to try out a new game she'd read about in the *Denver Chronicle* would end in such success? As a whole, they were a little fuzzy on the rules, but everyone had a good time anyway. And that's what mattered most.

Megan tugged harder. "You can't let us down when we need you to help us even the score."

Laney wouldn't dream of letting the children down. *Ever.* If that meant playing a game of baseball, or continuing her silence with Marc Dupree, then so be it.

"I'll be right out. Just let me finish this pie and put it in the oven first."

Megan looked out the window and gasped. "She's

almost all the way around the bases." Hopping on one foot, the girl snorted in impatience. "Hurry up, will ya?"

Laney hurried.

Marc turned to Trey as they walked down Ogden Street, unsure what words to use to stop his friend from making a big mistake. He went for the direct approach. "You'll send word if it turns out Ike and his gang are holed up in that shack outside Cripple Creek?"

Trey nodded, his gaze set on the mountains in the distance.

Drawing to a stop, Marc waited for his friend to halt as well. "You sure you don't want me to come with you?"

Trey shook his head. "This is my quest."

"I want justice served, too."

"*Justice*?" Trey ground out his word. "After what Ike and his gang did to Laurette, I don't want justice. I want vengeance."

Sick of the same argument, Marc slammed his clenched fist into his palm. "It won't bring her back."

"Easy for you to say. You weren't the one who got her killed."

How could he convince his brother-in-law that Laurette's death wasn't his fault? "Trey, you couldn't have known they would attack your ranch that day, that your foreman would turn out to be a coward, that Ike—"

"No, Marc. Don't try to rewrite history. We both know I wasn't there to protect my wife when she needed me." He glared at an invisible point in the distance.

Marc didn't like the unbending look he saw in his friend's eyes. Trey was in his uncompromising mood. Someone was going to end up dead. And that someone could be Trey. "Maybe I should come with you, after all."

"You'll only get in the way." Trey shook his head decisively, the gesture clearing his expression at last. "You have issues of your own to settle while I'm gone."

"Nothing is as important as keeping you from getting yourself killed."

"I'm not going to die. Ike, on the other hand…" He let his words trail off, the unspoken message clear. Trey planned to ensure the man who'd murdered his wife didn't make it out of their skirmish alive.

Not liking what had become of his once peace-loving friend, Marc let out a slow breath. "Trey, you can't let your anger rule your actions. You're not thinking clearly."

"I'll be back in Denver once I'm through in Cripple Creek. I shouldn't be gone more than a week. And when I return I want to hear how matters are progressing between you and Miss O'Connor."

"Now isn't the time to discuss Laney and me."

"I disagree. It's the exact time to talk about the two of you." The bitterness in Trey's eyes softened. "When this is over, I want a niece or nephew to spoil. You and that fiery lady of yours can give me that."

Though his gut rippled in anticipation at his friend's words, Marc knew Trey was trying to divert his attention from the more volatile subject. "Trey, you can't win this fight, not with your current mind-set. Find peace in Laurette's memory. Then go after Ike."

"Oh, I'll get my resolution. Once Ike is dead. Now that I know where he's hiding, it's time I settled the matter once and for all."

A familiar wave of helplessness marched through

Marc. "There's nothing I can say to talk you out of this?"

"I'm leaving in an hour." Trey's gaze hardened again. "*Alone*. And you're going to stay here and find out what Miss O'Connor is hiding. My guess, she's going to surprise you, in a good way."

Before Marc could respond, Trey clasped him on the shoulder. "Take care, my friend."

Without another word he turned and charged down the street toward the jailhouse.

Knowing his words would fall on deaf ears, Marc didn't bother calling after Trey. Perhaps his friend was right. Perhaps it was time for Trey to face Ike Hayes at last.

Lord, keep him thinking clearly. Keep him safe.

As far as prayers went, this one wasn't very fancy. But Marc wasn't used to talking to the Lord on a regular basis anymore. He should probably work on that.

For the first time in years the idea of relying on God seemed possible.

After a few moments of pausing over the thought, he continued on his own path toward the bank. He allowed his head to fill with the business that lay ahead of him. He liked taking care of his own financial affairs. Pearl had once convinced him to take on a manager, and he'd ended up broke.

Never again.

Marc joined in the crowd on the sidewalk, the hurried energy soothing away his frustration over Trey. He liked the personality of Denver at this time of day. The honest people milling about reminded him of better times, simpler times. Here, on Ogden Street, he saw real people with a penchant for hard work and honest living.

With the clean scent of pine riding along the breeze, Marc experienced pure contentment. He didn't particularly miss Louisiana or the South, but he missed his family and his life before poverty had stolen his youthful innocence. At heart, Marc was a man of strong family bonds, which was why Trey's destructive quest concerned him.

Was he any different from his brother-in-law? His need for wealth and drive for the material security had hardened his heart as sure as Trey's quest to avenge Laurette's death had hardened his.

They'd both turned away from God.

Marc couldn't say exactly when he'd lost a handle on his own perspective. Perhaps when he'd made the mistake of marrying Pearl. Her death had freed him legally, but he hadn't been the same since.

His frequent contacts with Laney O'Connor had begun to change him, though. And now he realized he wanted to change, wanted to become the man he was before poverty, before Pearl—before bitterness had spread through his soul. He wanted to turn back to God.

He prayed the road wouldn't be a long one.

So focused on his thoughts, he failed to watch his steps as well as he should. Swerving at the last moment, he barely avoided colliding into a small child slouching straight for him. Unfortunately, in his attempt to avoid crushing the boy, he ran into another, taller one.

The second kid tipped forward, fell hard into him then leaned back.

"Sorry, mister," he muttered, keeping his eyes cemented to Marc's waistcoat.

"My fault entirely." Marc locked his gaze on a bent

head of black curls. A half-second later he felt the whisper of a touch against his vest.

"Sorry again, sir." The boy shrugged away. The quick flick of triumph in the kid's gaze was all it took for Marc to figure out what had just happened.

As the boy swaggered off, Marc reached out and grabbed him by the shirt collar. "Not so fast."

The kid pulled hard to free himself, but Marc had too firm a hold for an easy escape. Out of the corner of his eye, he caught sight of the smaller kid lingering just out of reach. He took a step closer, dragging his captive along with him.

Just as he was about to clutch the smaller kid, the bigger one yelled, "Run, Michael."

Michael dodged Marc's grasp and took off running toward the opposite end of the sidewalk. At least Marc had the presence of mind to keep his grip around the older of the two.

He waited a beat. When the kid simply blinked up at him, Marc broke the silence. "You have something of mine."

"No, sir. I…I don't have anything of yours." The boy's gaze darted across the street, searching, gauging.

Marc was in no mood to play games with a young thief a third his size. "Hand over my wallet."

"I don't know what you mean."

"Yes, you do." Marc made sure the look on his face squelched any desire for the boy to continue denying his crime.

Shoulders slumped, he reluctantly pulled Marc's wallet from his pocket. "I…I'm sorry, mister. I don't ever do this sort of thing. Well, not anymore. It's just, we need the money. And you looked like you have a lot, enough that you wouldn't miss a few dollars."

Although the kid's gaze was never at rest, Marc caught a glimpse of the desperation in eyes.

Marc's thoughts jumped immediately to Laney and the similar look she'd had in her eyes that first night in his hotel. "What's your name, boy?"

"Johnny. Look, mister. We didn't mean no harm."

Marc followed Johnny's glance across the street. "We? As in, you and Michael over there?"

"Yeah, so I took your wallet. I didn't do it for myself. I did it for—" Johnny sighed "—oh, boy. I'm in big trouble now." He gave Marc an imploring look. "Please let me go. I don't want her to find out what I did."

"Her? A woman told you to pick my pocket?"

"*No.* She didn't tell me to steal, but she needs the money. For the orphanage. I heard her say so. She…"

Again, the kid stopped his explanations without giving a complete answer. Marc tried not to bark out his next question. "What orphanage?"

"Charity House. Where me and Michael live with the other kids."

"So, the orphanage needs money?"

"Yeah, that's what I just said."

The swift bunching of muscles under his hand warned Marc what the kid planned. "I wouldn't try it."

Johnny tried it.

Marc tightened his grip, making it harder for the kid to move at all.

"You're not going to let me go, are you?"

"Not until I get some answers." He placed his free hand firmly on a bony shoulder. "Tell me more about this orphanage."

Defeated, Johnny sighed in resignation. "A few weeks ago, I heard Miss Laney tell Katherine she had to get five hundred dollars or we'd lose Charity House."

At the familiar name and the exact amount he'd counted in a certain woman's reticule *a few weeks ago*, Marc's gut twisted.

Everything else forgotten, he moved a step closer to the kid and pressed for more answers. "Did you just say...Laney?"

The kid kept talking, suddenly spewing words out as fast as they could come. "Yeah. She's the reason me and Michael have a home now. She's the nicest lady I know." A dark sadness flicked in his gaze. "But she's working too hard. Every night she goes somewhere and stays till real late. She's promised me she's not doing what Mama does for Miss Mattie, but I'm not so sure."

Tears filled the boy's eyes, but he kept them from spilling with a few hard blinks.

"This Laney you mentioned, she about so tall?" Marc placed his hand in the air near his chin. "Real pretty, with dark hair and light brown eyes?"

"You know her?"

An ugly thought rushed to the top of the others. "Did she teach you how to pick pockets?"

Johnny's eyes got as big as billiard balls. "Oh, no. Hey, you're not gonna tell her what I did? She's going to be so disappointed in me."

As she should be. Suddenly Marc's head couldn't quite take in all the information Johnny had expelled fast enough. An orphanage. A large loan. A woman named Laney.

The facts aligned together, making perfect sense. And yet, no sense at all. If Laney needed money to help fund an orphanage why not just tell him that straight out? Why the secrets? Why the deception?

One sure way to find out. "Let's go."

"Where you taking me?"

"Home. It's time I saw this orphanage. And you're going to direct me there."

"I'm not taking you anywhere. Not till you promise not to tell Miss Laney what I did."

Marc wasn't about to bargain with a twelve-year-old pickpocket scamp. When he caught sight of the other little boy peering around a building from across the street, he roped his fingers around Johnny's arm and started out. "We'll just follow your friend over there."

Johnny pulled back, dug in his heels using his full body weight for leverage. "You can't tell on Michael, either. He's already in trouble for running away last week."

That got Marc's attention. "Is it so bad at this orphanage that you have to run away?"

"Oh, no, he didn't mean to run away. Not really. He just kind of got lost, looking for his dad."

"Seems reasonable."

Johnny missed the sarcasm in Marc's tone. "Yeah, that's what I said. But Miss Laney made Michael promise not to ever come to this side of town again. She'll get all sad and gloomy if she finds out he came with me today. Then she'll give us both that 'I'm really disappointed in you' lecture."

"She will, huh?"

Johnny shuddered. "Oh, yeah."

Seemed like a pretty good punishment to Marc. After all, he'd known Laney long enough to understand how particularly moving her 'I'm really disappointed in you' speech could be. She'd given it to him twice in the past week.

"Please, mister, her lectures are the worst. I'd rather take a whipping. But she never whips me, says that wouldn't teach me anything."

Not quite sure why he did it, he started bargaining with the kid, after all. "Take me to the orphanage and I won't tell on you or Michael."

"Promise?"

"You have my word." He'd let Johnny confess on his own.

As though sensing the direction of his thoughts, Johnny looked hard at him, searching his face with the shrewdness of a man twice his age. Marc held his glare, allowing the kid as much time as he needed. "All right, mister. You have a deal."

Marc lifted his hand from Johnny's shoulder, then thought better of it. "Before I completely release you, I must point out that I'm bigger and faster than you."

A hint of disbelief whisked across Johnny's features. "In other words, don't try anything foolish?"

"Precisely."

Marc let go of the boy. Prepared for a break, he caught Johnny in two strides.

Johnny slid him a sheepish grin. "Just checking."

Marc slapped him on the back then looped his arm across his shoulders. "Wouldn't have expected anything less."

After a few blocks of silence, another question came to him, one he couldn't hold back any longer. "This Laney you mentioned. What does she have to do with the orphanage?"

The boy's grin widened. "She's the owner."

Chapter Sixteen

After making a diving catch, Laney jumped to her feet with the ball securely in her glove. "Got it."

The sound of her team's happy cheers filled her ears as they changed sides for a new inning. She did a quick head count, coming up two short. "Anyone know where Michael and Johnny went?"

"I do." Megan stepped forward. "They went to—"

One of the other kids elbowed her into silence, then finished the sentence for her. "We don't know where they are."

Megan's scowl said otherwise.

Sighing, Laney let the matter drop. For now. If the boys didn't show up soon she'd ask again, and again, until she received the proper answer. The truthful one.

Before she had time to worry any longer, Michael came screaming around the front of the house. When his gaze landed on Laney he skidded to a halt, and then walked more slowly, head hung low.

She waited until he stopped in front of her. "Want to tell me where you've been?"

Michael shook his head.

Laney knelt in front of him and ran a hand across his forehead. "You might as well confess. I'll find out the truth eventually. I always do."

The boy shuddered. "I was with Johnny. We didn't mean to get into trouble."

"Oh, baby, what happened? Where's Johnny?" She looked over the child's head, peering toward the front gate. The *empty* front gate. "Isn't he with you?"

"I didn't want to leave him, honest. But he told me to run when he got caught."

"Caught?" *Oh, Lord, not again.* "Doing what?"

Michael clamped his lips shut and dug his foot in the grass.

Laney sighed. She'd get nothing more out of the boy.

The sound of voices in the distance had her glancing over Michael's head again. Her heart sank. "Oh, no."

Marc Dupree was striding straight toward her, tugging a very reluctant Johnny along with him.

Laney's first instinct was to pretend she knew neither man nor boy. But Marc's steady gaze told her the secrets between them had come to an end.

So be it.

Dreading the coming confrontation, she rose to her full height. "Go on, Michael, go play with the others."

She sent him off with a tiny shove on his back then waved her hand in a small circle, motioning for Katherine to continue the game without her.

Katherine looked at her with a questioning expression. Laney cocked her head in the direction of Marc and Johnny. Katherine's eyes widened but then she got straight down to business. "All right, everyone. Let's play ball."

Once the game began again, Laney trudged across

the yard with leaden feet. The moment she opened the gate Johnny burst into a run and launched himself into her arms.

"Please don't be mad at me, Miss Laney. I was only trying to help." Tears trickled down his cheeks.

Her breath hitched at the sight of the boy's obvious despair. She couldn't remember Johnny ever crying, not even the night she'd rescued him from jail.

Putting Marc Dupree out of her mind for a moment, Laney concentrated on calming Johnny. She held him tightly against her and patted his back. "I've never seen you this upset. What's happened?"

A strangled sob was his only answer.

She pulled away and bent down, searching his face. "Are you hurt?"

A curt, masculine snort lowered over her. "He's not hurt."

Laney snapped her gaze up. "What did you do to him?"

"I'll let him tell you the story."

She reached behind her and pried the boy's hands from her waist. "Johnny?"

"I…I…" He wailed and threw himself back into her arms. "I stole this man's wallet."

Of all the scenarios she'd expected, this was the one she'd dreaded most. "Oh, Johnny. We talked about this."

"I know. Miss Laney, I'm sorry. Please, don't give me *the lecture.*"

Her heart thumped in her chest, a deep sense of defeat magnifying all her other emotion. In the past months she'd tried to teach Johnny right from wrong, tried to help him understand that stealing was never the answer.

Clearly, she'd failed. "I don't understand why you did this."

She'd hoped to keep the hurt out of her voice, but at the sight of the boy's grimace she knew she hadn't.

"I did it for Charity House." His hiccupping sigh sent guilt rushing through her. "You told Katherine we were in trouble."

"You—" *oh, Lord, no, please no* "—heard us talking?"

"I couldn't sleep the other night so I went to the kitchen for a snack. You and Katherine were already there. I didn't mean to listen in but I couldn't help it."

"Oh, Johnny, I'm so sorry." She'd never guessed one of the children would overhear her confessing her worries to Katherine.

"I heard you say we might lose Charity House." The boy choked on a sob. "I couldn't let that happen."

"You needn't fret over money. That's my job."

Johnny didn't seem to hear her. "But you have to go to work every night, like mama."

"I'm not working in a brothel. I promise."

"Then why do you look so tired all the time?"

"Listen to me." She pulled him back into her embrace and pressed a kiss on the top of his head. "You don't have to worry about money or anything else while you're living here at Charity House. It's my job to bear the burden of responsibility, not yours."

Johnny shook his head as though he didn't understand what she was saying.

Laney tried to explain. "It's really simple. All you have to do is be a kid, nothing else. Just a kid."

When he still looked confused, Laney realized the boy didn't know how to be *just a kid*. The realization broke her heart. Not knowing what else to say, she glanced up at Marc.

The look of encouragement in his gaze gave her the courage to add, "I'm going to get the money to save Charity House." It was a promise she intended to keep. "In fact, I'm nearly there. Now, no more worrying for you. Go join the game and have fun. You can take my place on Megan's team."

Johnny stuck his bony chest out. "I'll hit a home run."

"I like that idea."

With the resiliency of youth, the boy swiped a hand across his face and took off toward the backyard.

Heart in her throat, Laney watched Johnny run to a group of boys and slapped the closest one on the back in greeting.

"You going to keep pretending I'm not here?"

She kept her eyes on Johnny. "The idea occurred to me."

"You're not afraid to look at me, are you?"

"Not at all." She threw her shoulders back, but still didn't turn to face him. She'd told Johnny she'd handle matters. Now she had to make good on that promise.

But not here.

"It might be best if we went inside for our conversation." She drew in a calming breath. "I don't want the children to overhear us."

"No, we wouldn't want that. By all means, Laney, lead the way."

Marc didn't need to look into Laney's eyes to know she was worried. Why was she acting as if he was the one in the wrong? Marc hadn't lied and deceived and evaded throughout their short acquaintance. Nor had he tried to pick anyone's pocket.

"I'm curious to see the inside of your home," he said with a hint of irritation as he followed her across the large expanse of perfectly manicured lawn. "The one you took out a loan with Prescott to pay for."

She spun around then, a swathe of outrage turning her eyes a golden, liquid brown.

"Am I wrong?"

"No. The loan was for Charity House." Without explaining further, she turned back around and continued toward the row of stairs leading to the front door.

Glancing around, Marc noted the immaculate lawn, the flowers and shrubs planted in tidy rows. Everywhere he looked he saw order and charm, comfort and beauty. He hadn't seen this much concentration to detail in a long time, maybe never, except in his hotel, of course.

Apparently, he and Laney had a lot more in common than he'd originally thought.

Why didn't that make him feel better?

Crossing the house's threshold, the smells of home greeted him. The tangy odor of soot from the fireplace mingled with the lemon wax from the floors and furniture. The lingering aroma of fresh-baked pies transported him back in time to his childhood. For a brief moment, Marc experienced a peace that transcended all understanding.

The sensation unnerved him.

"This doesn't look like an orphanage to me."

"That's the general idea." Still not looking at him, she directed him into a parlor.

Again, he was met by a combination of luxury and warmth all around. "*Definitely* not a typical orphanage."

"Charity House isn't an orphanage. It's a place where prostitutes and women of questionable virtue can leave their precious children because they can't care for them in the brothels, saloons or wherever they choose to conduct their business."

She connected her gaze with his. The sadness in her eyes captured a part of him long dead. He wanted to comfort her, to tell her he wasn't here to hurt her or the children. No, he wouldn't harm her. He did, however, want answers.

In the silence hanging between them, Marc took his time studying her face, enjoying her beauty as he hadn't allowed himself to do since discovering her in Mattie's brothel. He'd been afraid to look at her like this, afraid he'd want her in his life, permanently, even knowing she'd deceived him on purpose.

Now he knew why. Except, he didn't. Why had she withheld the truth from him?

"Help me to understand why you kept your orphanage a secret from me."

She linked her gaze with his, holding him in place with the intensity of her stare. "The children who live here aren't typical orphans. In fact, the majority aren't orphans at all. Most of their mothers live on The Row."

Marc took her hand in his, squeezed gently, let go. "Go on."

"There's not much more to tell. Here at Charity House we turn no child away. My goal is to offer boys and girls a chance to break the cycle of sin so rampant in their parents' lives. I try to give them a solid, Christian upbringing. No condemnation. No judgment. Just love and unconditional acceptance."

A noble pursuit, to be sure, but she was leaving

something out, something important. "How do you fund this place?"

"The children's mothers pay a monthly boarding fee, when they can. Some of the fathers help out as well, but not many." She dropped her gaze to the floor and sighed. "Most men deny responsibility when a woman who isn't his wife finds herself in trouble."

As he silently studied Laney's bent head, Marc wondered about her father, no doubt a member of the group of men she'd mentioned. Marc saw the true beauty in her now. The kind that came from a heart that sacrificed everything for children no one else wanted, not even their own parents. Children like she had once been, scared and alone.

When she looked up again, he noticed the dark circles and lines of exhaustion dancing across her face. Her schedule had to be grueling, working here during the day and at his hotel at night.

Marc understood a lot about Laney now, and admired her all the more.

But she hadn't shared any of this information with him willingly. Had it not been for Johnny's fast fingers, Marc might never have found out about Charity House. He had to remember that, or else he might find himself doing something foolish. Like falling in love with Laney O'Connor.

A woman who hadn't trusted him enough to share the most important part of her life with him—her home, and the children she cared for.

"I take it the loan you have with Prescott was for this place."

"Renovations were needed."

Marc looked around him, drank in the luxury. Moving through the area he touched a vase, a crystal ornament, a porcelain pitcher. "Don't you think you overreached necessity a little?"

"Perhaps." She looked around, sighed. "But most of this came with the house. Understand, Marc, this is the only home most of these children have ever known. I want to keep it intact, down to every trinket. I want to provide a sense of permanency that never changes, no matter what comes at us from the outside world."

That was her reasoning for the fancy furnishings?

"What if you fail to raise the rest of the money for your loan with Prescott?" He couldn't keep all the anger out of his voice. "What happens then?"

"I won't fail."

How could she possibly know that? "Laney, you aren't thinking about the long-term consequences. So you pay off your loan, *this time*, what happens if you get strapped for money again? Sell the furniture, the trinkets?"

"If I have to, then yes."

He looked around him again, gauged the value of the furniture and trinkets, found himself becoming the voice of reason. "A house this size, with so many mouths to feed, takes more money than these furnishings would bring in, a lot more."

"You make it sound as if I'm fighting a losing battle."

"Aren't you?" She'd already admitted funds didn't come in on a regular basis. "You still didn't answer my question. What happens if your money runs out again?"

"Then I find another way to stay afloat."

She wasn't thinking like a businesswoman. Marc had to make her see beyond the moment, beyond the now. "I don't doubt your resolve, or your abilities, but what if something happens to you, Laney? What then?"

Hands shaking, she smoothed a strand of hair off her face. "The children know how to survive on their own."

"By picking pockets?"

Her shoulders flinched. "I didn't tell Johnny to go out and pick pockets."

"Maybe not. But haven't you taught him that the end justifies the means? That as long as everything turns out all right, then do whatever it takes to survive?"

She threw her hands in the air and twirled to face him. "You're intentionally misunderstanding."

"Like it or not, I have a stake in this orphanage now."

"You have no say here, you are only my employer."

That hurt, but not enough to let her push him away. She was scared, desperate. In that, at least, he could offer her some relief. "Let me pay off your loan with Prescott."

"I… *No.*" Her expression closed. "I can't accept your money."

"Why not?"

"I'm trying to teach the children the importance of facing the consequences of their actions, by doing so myself."

"The pace is killing you."

"I'm fine." The fatigue in her eyes told a different story.

"No, you're not. Johnny saw your exhaustion, and it terrified him enough to go out and steal from a stranger. You're fortunate that stranger was me."

The look she gave him said she wasn't so sure.

He tried a different approach. "You're pushing yourself too hard trying to prove you can take care of everything on your own."

"It's the only way I know how to live."

"What if you aren't alone anymore? What if I'm here now? Please, let me help you."

"If I accept money from you, then all I'm teaching the children is how to take charity." Tears welled in her eyes. "That's not a lesson I want them to learn."

Marc crossed the divide between them. He linked his fingers with hers and squeezed gently, as though he could will her to comprehend what he was trying to do for her, and maybe for himself, too.

"Taking my money could also teach the children how to accept a gift that's freely given, with no hidden agenda, no expectations."

"Nothing is free in this world."

"God's grace is free."

She yanked her hand out of his. "That's not the same thing."

"It's *exactly* the same." And in that moment, Marc accepted the true meaning of grace, finally understood the need to give a gift to someone who hadn't asked for anything in return.

"Let me pay off the rest of your loan."

"I…can't, Marc."

Considering what to say next, what to *do* next, he paused. Maybe he should allow her to continue working for him to earn the money she needed. What better way to protect her from men like Prescott and to make sure she didn't exhaust herself beyond reason?

Marc could always fiddle with the numbers. Maybe give Laney a bigger percentage of her earnings sooner than planned.

"All right. If you're determined to do this on your own, I won't stand in your way."

Tired, dull brown eyes rose to meet his. "I have to finish what I started."

And now...so did he. "Answer me this, Laney, why didn't you tell me you needed Judge Greene's money for Charity House?"

In answer, she grabbed onto his sleeve, pulled him toward a window overlooking the yard where the children played. "Look at them."

He did. He saw youthful energy and happiness. The things this woman had never had as a child. She'd been too busy keeping time and collecting money for her mother.

Was it any wonder she didn't trust him, or any man for that matter?

Well, one day she *would* trust him. Marc would make sure of it.

He looked at her again, caught her smiling indulgently at the children outside. The puzzle pieces fell neatly into place. "You didn't tell me why Greene gave you the money because you were protecting the children, not him."

"Exactly." In a halting tone, she told him the full story behind her loan with Prescott, including the banker's attempt to shut the doors of Charity House by demanding the bulk of his money six months early.

"So you see," she said, taking an unsteady breath. "I had to take Judge Greene's money, money he owed for one of those children out there." She turned to face him. "The one you escorted home this morning. I'm trusting you to keep this secret for that boy's sake, not mine."

"I'm not like the other men you've come across in

your life, Laney. I won't hurt you, or the children and certainly not Johnny."

She nodded. "I realize that now, but when we first met I couldn't take that chance. There was too much at stake."

"I understand." And he did.

Unable to stop himself, Marc pulled Laney to him. He brushed his lips along the slope of her cheek. But the sound of footsteps tripping down the hall kept him from touching his mouth to hers.

He let his hands drop to his side and stepped away from her. "I'll see you at the hotel later tonight."

"I'll be there."

Chapter Seventeen

Marc stood on the fringes of the nightly activity of his hotel, watching Laney work the front desk with her usual poise and efficiency. In a few short weeks she'd become his best clerk, managing to charm his guests with a ready smile and willingness to address their every concern.

For two days now Marc had avoided her, speaking to her only when necessary. He'd needed the time to sort through his thoughts, to mull over the secrets he'd discovered about her orphanage.

Charity House. Had a nice ring to it.

Though he didn't fully approve, Marc understood why she'd gone to Prescott for a loan all those months ago. He hated that she wouldn't accept his help with her debt to the shifty banker. But he admired her determination to accept the consequences of her actions.

Narrowing his eyes, he gauged the visible signs of fatigue he could see even from this distance. Exhaustion was etched in her features, weariness circled her eyes. No longer able to deny the need to alleviate her suffering, he made his way to the front desk.

Although it wasn't yet nine in the evening, the night was long from over for Laney. A spasm of guilt hiked across his conscience. Instead of worrying about his own need to understand her actions, he should have tried harder to get her to take his money, thereby giving her relief from the grueling schedule she forced upon herself.

Stepping behind her, he whispered into her ear. "When you get a moment come and talk to me. I'll be waiting outside the restaurant."

She nodded but kept her focus on the guest in front of her. Treading toward the restaurant, Marc made idle conversation along the way. When Laney eventually joined him, he knew what to say to her. "I have a gift for the children."

"A…gift?" His words seemed to surprise her. "What are you up to now?"

"Who says I'm up to anything? Honestly, Laney, you're so suspicious."

"You've practically ignored me for two days and suddenly you're generosity itself. Why the sudden change of heart?"

He liked the miffed look playing across her features, enough to quit bantering with her. "Nothing to upset yourself over. And you can feel free to say no, but one of our guests from South America wanted to show me his gratitude for his exceptional stay—his words, not mine—by giving me a bushel of fruit."

"Fruit?"

At her confused expression he laughed softly, the sound rumbling deep in his chest. "That's right. *Fresh* fruit, the kind we don't usually find in Colorado. Oranges, grapefruits, tangerines."

She considered him for a moment, tucked her arms around her waist and sighed. "The children would love that. Thank you, Marc."

"You're accepting my gift?" The significance was not lost on him. "No questions asked?"

"No questions asked." Her smile nearly blinded him.

Although, this wasn't the same as her accepting his money, it was a start. And as he stared into her beautiful face he realized he'd do anything to see that smile of hers, directed at him, only him, always.

"Let me retrieve the fruit, and then I'll escort you home."

Her smile disappeared. "My shift is only half over."

"I'm releasing you early."

"I thought we talked about this already. I need to work, Marc. I need the money, I—"

"I'll still pay you for tonight."

"But—"

"Don't get too excited. I'll expect you to work your entire shift tomorrow. Now, come." Cutting off the rest of her arguments, he looped her arm in the crook of his. "You can wait in my office while I fetch the fruit."

That way she wouldn't get caught up helping another guest. *Brilliant, Dupree.*

Eventually, she nodded at him. "All right, Marc. I'm tired enough to let you send me home early."

"I like you in this accommodating mood."

"Don't get used to it." She tried to look fierce as she spoke, but he was on to her now. Laney O'Connor was a woman with a large heart, tender affection and deep convictions.

The kind that were running her into the ground.

Marc wanted to lighten her burden a little, by offering a moment of respite and a special treat for her children. It wasn't personal. He'd do the same for any employee.

Right, Dupree, keep telling yourself that.

Before Laney could protest, or change her mind, Marc steered her toward his office.

With a flick of his wrist he opened the door then stepped aside to let her pass.

The soothing comfort hit her like a punch. She breathed in deeply and nearly stumbled over her own two feet. Too many sights washed into too many smells, making her fully aware of a man she already thought about more often than she should.

Holding back a sigh, she headed toward one of the wingbacked chairs facing his desk with the idea of resting her tired feet while he retrieved the fruit.

"Oh, no, not there." Marc placed his palms the back of her shoulders and urged her toward the sofa instead of the chair. "Sit here, where you'll have more room to stretch out."

She stared longingly at the piece of furniture, tempted by the mounds of soft, plush fabric and fluffy throw pillows.

"Go on, Laney, stretch out your legs while I'm gone. I might be a while."

She spun around to ask him what he meant by *a while* but he'd already slipped out of the room.

After a moment of staring at the closed door, exhaustion took hold. She sank onto the sofa. Bouncing a few times, she resisted the urge to fall back and sleep through the next eternity.

Promising her tired body rest—when she made it

home and all the chores were complete—she hopped up and paced through the room. Eyeing the armoire, she smiled broadly, remembering the first time Marc had shut her in this room. They'd come so far since then. She no longer had any desire to escape, out the window or by any other means.

In the mood to reminisce, she thought about opening the large cabinet, to see if Marc still had his clothes neatly arranged by color and style, but the sofa beckoned. She drifted across the floor and plopped down again. With Marc's masculine scent lingering in the air, she leaned her head back and sighed deeply.

Now, this was one seriously comfortable piece of furniture.

Determined not to wake her just yet, Marc stood on the threshold of his office, watching Laney sleep. Cuddled on the sofa, her dress a mountain of fabric around her, she looked peaceful for the first time he'd known her.

At last, he thought. She was getting the rest she needed. Maybe he should let her sleep a bit longer. But he'd already been here and gone two other times and he knew her well enough to know she wouldn't appreciate being left to sleep too long.

The woman was many things, strong, resourceful, stubborn. But she was no lady of leisure. Pity that. Marc could get used to spoiling her.

Decision made, he entered the room. Turning, he clicked the door closed and pressed his forehead against the wood. "Just wake her up, Dupree, then quickly escort her home like you promised," he whispered to himself.

Fine advice, for a man of iron will. He stepped toward her sleeping form. Then stepped back. Maybe he should go get Rose and have her wake Laney.

At least she snored. Unfortunately, instead of annoying him, the delicate, feminine sound left him charmed beyond reason.

The woman slept with as much abandon as she went through her waking life. Laney O'Connor had the grit and determination of eight sailors fighting a hurricane in a two-man boat.

She's just a woman, he told himself. *One who put the lives of innocent children ahead of her own.*

Even before he'd known about the orphanage, Marc had already concluded that Laney was unlike anyone he'd ever known.

And now, he let the truth take hold.

He loved her humor, her courage, her willingness to accept her mistakes and see them through.

He loved…her.

He *loved* Laney O'Connor.

He wanted to spend his life with her, to stand by her side, through the good times and the bad, to protect her and keep the world from hurting her any further.

But he also wanted to laugh with her, fight with her, and let her smooth his cares away while he conquered hers.

He reached out and touched her cheek, wondering when he'd managed to cross the room.

She sighed contentedly.

"Laney, honey. It's time to wake up. We need to get you home." Before he did something they'd both regret.

Another sigh. A slow, secretive smile.

He swallowed. "Laney?"

"Mmm."

"Come on, honey." He rubbed his hand down her arm. "Wake up."

She snorted—she actually snorted—then mumbled something in response. It sounded like she said "sleepy," but he couldn't quite make out the word.

Right. That was one exhausted woman.

And Marc's heart was melting by the second. "You're not making this easy on me," he muttered through his very tight jaw. "*Laney.*"

Her lids slowly opened, fluttered shut, then snapped back open.

"Hello," he said, grinning at her like a besotted fool.

She rubbed a fist against her eyes. "What time is it?"

"Time to get you home."

As if only just realizing where she was, she shot off the sofa and looked frantically around her. "How…how long did I sleep?"

"Two hours."

"Oh, I…" She glared at him. "Why didn't you wake me earlier?"

"You looked so peaceful. I didn't have the heart."

Her hand went to her hair. "I must look a fright."

Tenderness swept through him. "You look beautiful. Now, come." He reached out his hand. "Let me walk you home."

She hesitated, staring at his hand for an endless moment. After a quick intake of air, she placed her palm against his. "Thank you, yes, I'd like that."

Finally. She was beginning to trust him.

The next morning, Laney struggled to keep her emotions even, but her growing feelings for Marc nearly overwhelmed her.

In a flurry of activity, she completed her share of the household chores earlier than usual and found herself with too much free time to think. Needing something to do with her hands—and her mind—she went to the kitchen and busied herself with making biscuits.

Once the preparations were complete, she grabbed a fistful of flour and flung it onto the dough waiting to be spread out. The air clouded with white powder, making her eyes water and setting her lungs coughing themselves clear.

She punched the dough with a fist. "Not only did I fall asleep in Marc's office last night, now I'm going to choke myself to death," she said with a groan.

Marc. Oh…Marc.

She couldn't stop thinking about the way he'd looked at her when he'd said good-night to her at the front gate. Adoringly. Lovingly. Though there had been no actual declarations, no promises made, she knew he cared for her deeply. Perhaps even loved her. Her heart told her to trust him.

Trust. It always came back to that.

Could she let Marc into her heart, into the world she'd created for herself and the children? She'd have to battle a lifetime habit of relying only on herself. A habit that would be difficult to break, no matter how much she cared for the man.

So intent on ridding herself of her troubling thoughts, she didn't hear Katherine approach. "You're going to beat that dough to death."

Jumping, Laney wiped her forehead on her sleeve then started back to pounding. "The idea has merits."

Katherine poured a glass of water and offered it to her. Laney shook her head. "No, thank you."

"You want to talk about whatever's troubling you?"

Laney's hands stilled. "Who says there's anything troubling me?"

Pointing, Katherine indicated the mutilated dough. "Just a hunch. Here." She set down the glass of water and handed Laney a towel. "Wipe your hands and come sit with me on the porch."

"I have biscuits to make."

Fingers wrapped around her wrist, and squeezed gently. "Leave it for now."

Biting back a sigh, Laney snatched the towel with exasperation. "Oh, all right."

She followed Katherine on to the front porch. Settling herself in one of the rockers, she looked out at the Rocky Mountains, seeing them but not really seeing them. "I don't know what's wrong with me."

Katherine perched on the edge of the railing and smiled down at her. "No?"

"Well, yes, I do. I just don't want it to be like this." She spread her palms across her skirt. "It's not supposed to be so complicated."

"It?"

Laney dashed a glance behind her, ensuring they were alone. "Falling in love."

"Ah. Does Mr. Dupree know how you feel?"

"Who says I'm talking about Marc?"

Katherine waved her hand in the air. "You've been in love with him since the first night you two met. So, have you told him?"

"No."

"What are you waiting for?"

"I…don't know." For the first time in her life, Laney couldn't handle a situation alone. And the only person who could help her, the person who could give her the answers she needed, was Marc, the very person who could cause her the most pain.

Closing her eyes, she fought off a wave of trepidation. "What am I going to do?"

A minor commotion at the gate had Katherine rising to her feet. "Looks like you get to find out."

The very object of their discussion called out a greeting as he released the latch and entered the front yard. Looking carefree and happy, Marc set a large wooden crate down by his feet. "Anybody want some fruit?"

Laney's eyes connected with his. All the emotion of the night before came rushing back. Right then, right there, she gave up the fight, gave up pretending this man wasn't important to her. That he didn't hold her heart in his hands.

"Laney? Are you all right?"

"I forgot about the fruit." Forcing a delighted smile on her face, she climbed hastily to her feet.

Marc started forward, a jaunty gleam in his eyes. "Guess you had too much on your mind last night. My wit and stellar conversational skills made you scattered. I do that to women."

She took to the game as though the banter could make her forget the other, more dangerous emotions brewing just below the surface. "Oh, sure. As far as you know."

He drew up next to her. "Good morning, Laney."

"Good morning, Marc."

His eyes swam with all the words she needed to hear but he had yet to say to her.

A crash came from somewhere inside the house.

They jumped apart in tandem. Marc was the first to

recover. Amusement dancing in his eyes, he pointed to the crate at his feet. "Where should I put this?"

Peering inside the box, she let out a happy laugh. He'd really brought fresh fruit for the children. She couldn't think of a better treat or, with money tight right now, a more thoughtful gift.

"Katherine, look what Marc Dupree brought us."

Chapter Eighteen

After introducing Marc to Mrs. Smythe, their sometimes housekeeper, Laney left the fruit in her care then directed Marc on to the porch.

She clasped her hand over his and looked into his eyes. "The children are in for a real treat tonight at supper. Thank you."

"You're welcome." He angled his head, studied her face a moment, then frowned. "You still look tired."

"I am, a bit. But not as much as yesterday. My unexpected nap and early night helped."

"I'm glad."

Silence fell over them. As the moment turned into two, and then three, they continued to stare at one another. So much had been left unsaid between them last night. And yet, now that the time had come, Laney couldn't find the words to start the conversation that would be the beginning of their future.

She wanted to be a part of Marc's life, and he a part of hers, but she didn't know what that meant. Or how her days would change with him in them.

She'd always been on her own. She only knew how

to rely on herself and her limited resources. With sheer grit and determination, she'd carved out a place for her and the children in a world that didn't want to make room for them.

Could she change so drastically? Could she open her heart and life to a man? To *this* man?

Did she dare take that leap of faith?

Faith is being sure of what we hope for and certain of what we do not see.

So easy to recite in her mind. So hard to put into practice.

As if understanding her worries, Marc's features turned compassionate, intense. "There's so much I want to say to you I don't know where to begin."

He'd spoken her thoughts aloud. Were they that connected? Yes. Yes, they were. "I know exactly what you mean."

He blew out a puff of air. "I'm not a man of pretty words."

"I don't need pretty words."

"Yes, you do. And I need to say them." In a single swoop he crushed her against his chest. "Maybe I should start with an apology."

Wrapping her arms around his waist, she rested her cheek on his shoulder. "You've already apologized."

"It's not enough. It'll never be enough. Not after the way I treated you the first time we met and the next and then the next."

He wasn't the only one with regrets. "I guess we both have some things to atone for."

Little worried lines appeared between his sharply arched brows. "Is it too late, then?"

"I don't know. But I'm willing to find out."

"Me, too." His mood turned even more serious. "Come back to the hotel with me. I want to be alone with you, to say the words you deserve to hear without anyone overhearing or misinterpreting."

"I'd like that. Just let me make sure everything is taken care of here and retrieve my uniform for later." She tossed him a smile over her shoulder. "I won't be long."

"Take your time. I'm not going anywhere."

Less than an hour later, Laney followed Marc into his office. Emotion clogged her ability to speak as he nudged her forward then struck the lock in place.

She turned to face him.

A slow smile eased onto his lips. "You look a little shaky."

"I am."

His eyes proclaimed his love as he opened his arms wide. "Come here."

Without hesitation, she wrapped herself in his embrace. As she looked into his gaze, her stomach knotted. "Oh, Marc."

He kissed her then. But after only a moment, he pulled back and put distance between them. "What you do to me, Laney."

"I think it's what we do to each other that could prove a problem."

She saw the struggle in his gaze, wondered at it. "You look so serious."

He grasped her shoulders and placed her at arm's length. "I'm trying to tell you how I feel."

She smiled. "Yes?"

"Stop looking at me like that." He practically growled the words.

"Well, that's a nice, snarly declaration." She planted her hands on her hips. "You really weren't kidding when you said you weren't a man of pretty words. You're far more likeable when you aren't talking."

His smile turned deliciously roguish. "Well then, no more talking."

He stepped toward her.

She edged slightly out of reach.

"Now you're just being difficult," he said.

"Careful, you silver-tongued brute, my heart can't take much more of this tender affection from you."

He laughed, reached for her again but she shifted to the left this time.

He tried again. Missed again. Growled. "Would you let me catch you?"

She edged closer, then dodged to her right.

"Laney, Laney." He threw his head back and laughed. "How I love you."

The air hissed out of her lungs in a single whoosh. "What did you just say?"

"I. Love. You." He crooked his finger. "If you come over here I'll say it again, maybe put a little more feeling into it."

She walked straight into his embrace and smiled up at him. "I love you, too. You big brute."

The affectionate, lopsided grin on his face said more than words. She'd been right. He was far more likable when he wasn't talking.

Hours later, her shift only half over, Laney peeked inside Marc's office. "Hank told me you wanted to see me."

He swiveled in his chair and smiled into her sparkling eyes, dazzled all over again. Would he ever get tired of looking at her? "You ready for me to take you home?"

She aimed a sleepy grin at him. "More than ready, but I still have another hour left on my shift."

"I'd rather take you home now."

"No, Marc. *No.* I still have a debt to pay, and time is running out."

He'd like to wrap his hands around Prescott's throat. In fact, the idea had such merit he decided to make a trip to the bank in the morning. In the meantime... "I could always give you an advance on your wages."

"No."

Why had he expected a different answer? "The independent woman to the end."

She glided over to him. "You either take me as I am or not at all."

Marc rose and pulled her into his arms. "Are those my only choices?"

"I wish I could think of something insulting to say to you, but I'm too happy to work up enough lather."

"And here I was looking forward to that sharp tongue of yours." He kissed her on the nose, then buried his face in her hair. "Did I ever tell you I love the smell of you?"

"No."

"How about the sound of your voice?"

She laughed. "Not that either."

He kissed her jaw.

She sighed. "Marc?"

He wrapped a piece of her hair around his finger. "Hmm?"

"I have to ask you something."

"Go ahead."

"Do you…do you think I'm like my mother?" she blurted out.

Marc stilled. Something in Laney's tone alerted him that she was upset, worried. He shook his head, trying to remember what they'd been talking about, but he couldn't. Giving up, he let go of her hair and stepped back. "What did you just ask me?"

"Do you think I'm like my mother?" With each clipped word, her jaw clenched tighter.

Confusion knit his eyebrows together. "Why would I think that? I never knew your mother."

"That's not what I meant."

Marc threaded his fingers through his hair. Slowly, understanding dawned. The fear laced inside her question came straight from her childhood.

How could he have been so thickheaded? So intent on kissing her, he'd completely forgotten where she came from, and the fears that accompanied a past such as hers.

He concentrated on alleviating her worries with the truth. "Laney, honey, I don't think you're like your mother."

She lowered her lashes, a tremble slicing through her calm. "But we've kissed. A lot."

"Yes, that's right. And there will be many more times to come, if I have my say."

Her gaze shot up, undisguised panic pouring into her eyes. "You, you don't think I plan to keep kissing you, that is, I don't think I can keep—not that I wouldn't want to—but… We, you, me. Oh, Lord, I'm really spoiling this, aren't I?"

Marc smiled, his heart filling with affection for her.

He took her hands in his, determined to pledge his life to her. "Ah, honey, stop worrying. I love you. Not your mother, or where you came from, but *you*."

She took a shaky breath. "You mean my pedigree, or lack thereof, doesn't matter to you?"

"Of course not." So that's what was bothering her. "Let me tell you a little story and then maybe you'll understand."

He tucked her into a chair and told her about his life in Louisiana after the war, the burning of his home, the scrimping for food, the poverty. Even the humiliation.

Her eyes widened with each portion of his tale. When he finished, she rushed to him, pulling him into her embrace.

"I didn't know, Marc. You've always seemed to leak wealth, straight out of your fancy, expensive clothes. You're so confident, so…*rich*." She shook her head, as though still unable to grasp the details of his story. "And all this time you were warring with those kinds of memories."

He rested in the circle of her arms, stroking her hair as she leaned her head against his shoulder. For a moment, he wasn't sure who was comforting whom.

"I've worked hard to regain the wealth that was taken from me." He let out a short laugh. "Funny, isn't it? You want nothing of the life you led as a child, and I want every bit of mine back."

"Marc," she paused, thought for a moment. "I'm not sure how to say this so I'm just going to say it. The pursuit of money and worldly things can be dangerous to your soul."

He didn't argue. He wasn't that much of a hypocrite. "Perhaps you're right, in some circumstances.

But money can also serve the greater good, such as, oh say, starting orphanages or paying off loans called in too soon."

"I didn't say money wasn't important." She cupped her hands along his face. "But why accumulate wealth if all you plan to do with it is hoard it away, or use it only for yourself?"

"You sound like Trey."

Her lips spread into a self-deprecating grin. "I suddenly like that man."

"Laney, I told you the story of my past so you would understand. I'll never be poor again."

As he said the words he realized how shallow they sounded, how self-centered.

Needing a moment to think, he pulled out of her embrace and sat in his chair. He rubbed his palms against his thighs, and shuddered. His preconceived notions of who he was and what he wanted out life were tumbling around him at rapid speed.

All this time, he'd thought he'd be less of a man if he didn't have the wealth and success taken from him all those years ago. But this woman, as she stood calmly staring at him, gave him a glimpse of something deeper than wealth. Something stronger and longer lasting.

Something eternal.

"You're right."

"I know." She softened her words by smiling very patiently at him, as if he were one of her children who'd just learned a very important lesson the hard way.

She was good for him, made him want to be a better man. Was it any wonder he loved her?

Smiling, he rose and went to her. But just as he pulled

her into his arms a loud knock on the door jolted him back a step.

Without waiting for an answer, Hank shoved inside the office. The sound of chaos and high-pitched shrieking trailed behind him.

"Hank? What's wrong?"

"Mr. Dupree, you need to come quick. We...*you*... have a problem." Hank's gaze darted to Laney, broke back to Marc just as quickly. "A real bad one."

"I'll be right there."

"Hurry, boss."

Marc tossed Laney an apologetic smile. "I'm sorry, honey. I have to take care of this."

She touched his arm. "Go on."

A jolt of foreboding had him clutching her to him. "Wait for me."

"Take your time. I'm not going anywhere."

The same words he'd said to her just this morning at her home. Holding her tightly against him a moment longer, Marc couldn't shake the feeling of loss stealing his breath, as though he'd never again enjoy this easy, open affection with her after tonight.

He buried his face in her hair, breathed in deeply. "I'll be right back."

Striding into the hotel lobby, the heightened level of noise hit him like a physical blow. His hotel had never seen such chaos. And all from the ranting of a small, emaciated blonde woman throwing anything she could get her hands on.

With her back to him, Marc couldn't see her face but her shrieking was impossible to ignore. A part of him recognized the voice, another part refused to accept what he heard.

He shot Hank a swift glance. Even as the man's pinched expression warned Marc what he would see once the woman turned around, he denied the truth in his mind.

The slurred words of the small human hurricane spoke of too much drink or too much laudanum, or perhaps both.

"Where's my husband?" the woman demanded, picking up a handful of theater flyers and flinging them in her rage. "I know he's here."

Hank circled to the front of the woman while Marc moved in from behind, his gut churning with dread.

"Well? Where is he?"

Dear Lord, it couldn't be. God just couldn't be this cruel, not when Marc had found happiness at last.

"I know this is his hotel," the woman said, and a little more of Marc's world came crashing down around him.

She kicked over a chair, grabbed an empty glass off an end table. "I want to speak to Marc Dupree, now."

"I'm right behind you."

She swung around, the glass forgotten as it slipped through her fingers.

"Marc, darling." The purr in her tone sounded more like a croak. "Aren't you going to greet me properly?"

When he didn't move, she reached up and yanked him to her.

He stiffened, fighting the urge to fling her away from him.

The impossible had happened. Pearl LaRue had risen from the dead.

Chapter Nineteen

As Marc stared at his wife, one thought swept though his mind. The years had been unkind to her. She looked harder, paler, more calculating and a little desperate. Though she'd changed much since he'd seen her last, one thing had remained the same. Pearl hadn't lost the use of her acid tongue.

Spewing out a litany of foul words, she reached up to slap him, lost her footing and tumbled to the floor. From a tangle of legs and skirts, she glared up at him. "You could have helped me up."

Right, and have her claw his hand to shreds. Pearl had never been a fair fighter, not even in their early days of marriage. "I could." He folded his arms across his chest. "But I know better."

Spitting more curses, she scrambled inelegantly to her feet. After inspecting him from head to toe with a sneer on her lips, she turned and surveyed the hotel. "Well, well. I see nothing can keep Marc Dupree down."

"That's right." He lowered his tone. "And it seems, dear wife, nothing can keep you dead."

"So you're upset." She lifted a shoulder, as though

she didn't have a care in the world, but the simpering that crept into her voice belied her calm. "I just knew you'd hold a grudge."

Angrier than he'd ever been in his life, he swallowed back the urge to toss her out of his hotel. "Now that you've broached the subject, where's my money?"

Ignoring him, she picked at her fingernails.

"Pearl, I'm talking to you."

"What was the question again?"

"My money," he ground out. "Where. Is. It?"

Eyes still lowered on her hand, she lifted a shoulder again. "All gone."

"I don't believe you." He reached for her, intent on shaking the truth out of her, but he stopped his own pursuit in time. He was a man of control, not one ruled by base emotion.

Never render evil for evil.

Refusing to sink to Pearl's low level, Marc took a slow, steadying breath. He circled his gaze around the hotel. All activity had stopped. The sudden hush—the stares, the questions, the unmistakable fascination—made him inwardly cringe. He needed to conduct this conversation where Pearl couldn't wage more chaos.

"Go back to your business," he said, connecting his gaze with the closest patrons, the ones unabashedly watching him in return. "There's nothing to see here."

When no one moved away, he wrapped his fingers loosely around Pearl's arm, resisted the urge to tighten his hold and then lowered his voice for her ears only. "Come with me. We'll finish this in my office."

She brushed up against him. "Why not in your suite of rooms?"

His stomach rolled. "My office is private enough."

"Private. I like the sound of that." The smell of stale whiskey wafted out of her and his stomach heaved again. He held his breath as she ran her finger along the top button of his vest. "We used to do our best talking in private. Remember?"

Revulsion continued moving through him. Though this woman was his wife, he didn't love her—had never loved her. He knew that now, knew he'd married her for all the wrong reasons. In the hope of saving her from herself.

He'd been young and idealistic. Foolish. He'd told himself he could change her into a woman of integrity. But Pearl was no Laney O'Connor.

Laney. He was so stunned and twisted up in his anger, he'd nearly forgotten about her waiting for him in his office. He'd been on the verge of asking her to become his wife, to merge her future with his for all time.

An impossible dream now. He was already married.

He'd nearly turned the woman he loved into an adulterer.

The depth of his sin weighed heavily on his soul. He looked up and saw Laney standing near the edge of the crowd, her eyes round, her expression hurt, her bottom lip quivering.

In one word she managed to cast her remaining hope at his feet. "Marc?"

He wanted to reassure her, wanted to tell her everything would be all right. But he loved her too much to lie to her.

How could Pearl LaRue still be alive? And how could he ever make Laney believe he hadn't betrayed her like this, hadn't intentionally withheld information about his marriage?

The most he could hope for now was that he didn't destroy the woman he loved completely.

"I'm sorry," he said, willing her to believe him, to see his love for her in his eyes, even if he could never act on his feelings.

Her eyes clouded with warring emotions then went blank. "Who is this woman?"

Before he could answer, Pearl pushed around him and wove through the crowd. Stopping inches away from Laney, she placed her hands on her hips and glared. "I'm his wife. Who are you? Another one of his projects?"

Fast on Pearl's heels, Marc stepped between her and Laney. Too late, the damage had been done. The pain shimmering in Laney's eyes, in her unshed tears, was real.

"She's your...wife?" The silent plea in her eyes begged him to deny the truth.

He reached out to her, needing to touch her, to assure himself she was real, that what they'd shared was real.

Stepping away from him, she lifted her chin. "You're married."

How could he hurt the only woman he'd ever wanted in his life, the only one he'd ever truly loved? *Because she deserves the truth.* "I thought she was dead."

Eyes blinking rapidly, Laney looked from him to Pearl and back again. "She doesn't look dead to me. And you don't look surprised to see her alive."

Maybe he wasn't. He'd truly believed Pearl was dead, but she'd always been like a cat with many lives. By now, she had to be well past the usual nine.

Laney's lips lifted into a tight smile. "Please excuse me, Mr. Dupree, I have to finish my shift."

This was the women he'd met that first night. Desperate and closed off, hiding behind her bravado.

He'd done that to her. He'd betrayed her trust, after only just earning it.

"Laney, wait."

She kept walking, head high, chin jutting forward. Marc stifled the urge to beg her to stop, to listen to him. But after what he'd just done to her, he owed her this moment of dignity.

Pearl's snicker tore through him like a dirty, jagged blade. "Your little girlfriend doesn't seem too happy to meet me. I'm shocked at you, Marc. Did you forget to tell her about us?"

In a voice barely above a whisper, he snarled out his warning. "Don't you ever speak to Laney again. Don't even look at her. You got that?"

He must have communicated his threat well because Pearl closed her mouth.

"Let's go."

Rage threatened to explode as he steered his wife toward his office. Too many questions ran into one another in his head to make coherent speech possible.

But the words would come, and he *would* get his answers.

He shouldered into his office, waited for Pearl to join him before banging the door shut behind them. He didn't see the need to waste time with pleasantries. "All right, Pearl, start explaining. I was told you died in that train wreck."

She spun around and gave him a saucy grin. "As you can see, I'm very much alive."

Her expression turned calculating. Reeking of smoke and stale liquor, she sidled up to him. "You've aged well, husband. I'd say you're more handsome than ever." She touched his cheek, ran her finger along his jaw. "That suppressed wildness in your eyes makes a woman want to tame you."

He clutched her roving hand. Before releasing her, he added enough pressure to get her attention without hurting her.

She blessed him with the look that had once made him pity her, made him want to take care of her and ease her burdens. But that was before he'd learned to recognize the hardness, the hint of cruelty behind her smile.

Naive and far too trusting for his own good, he'd thought Pearl glamorous and worldly. Now he saw the cunning, the bitter heart, the self-absorption he'd missed before.

"You haven't changed," he said, realizing the truth as he spoke the words.

"Oh, but I have, my darling." Her voice lowered to a husky drawl. "I could show you some of the new tricks I've learned. Just say the word."

The sinful woman in her shone like a tarnished nickel in a handful of gold. He saw it now, the cold soul, the undisguised hardness of heart.

"You used to enjoy my company." She moved forward, stopping inches from him. "Remember?"

He moved away. "Don't start. We may be married, but I'm not going to be intimate with you. Not now, not ever again."

She looked at him for a long moment, her eyes turning dark with hatred. "Always such a man of control. Just like that brother-in-law of yours, the one who's now a U.S. marshal. The holier-than-thou duo, that's what I used to call you behind your backs."

He didn't respond.

"Want to know how I made you believe I was dead?"

He knew she was goading him now, toying with his mind, but after years of wondering what she'd done with his money he needed to know the truth. "Yes, Pearl. Tell me how you faked your own death."

Her eyes filled with artifice and obvious intent to hurt him.

Marc simply waited for her to give him her worst.

She sat on his desk, scooted back a bit then dangled her feet over the edge. The gesture revealed dirty, bare feet. Where were her shoes?

"Did you know the Pinkerton agent you hired actually found me that very first month of searching?"

"No."

Laughing, she swung her feet back and forth. "He was very good at his job, among other things."

Despite his raging emotions, Marc held perfectly still. "Go on."

"I had a lot of money back then." She tapped her finger against her chin and slid a glance at him from the corner of her eye. "It must have been several thousand dollars, if I recall."

"You took five thousand, nine hundred and eighty-three dollars of mine."

She threw her head back and cackled. "I figured you'd know the exact amount. The money meant more to you than I did."

"Let's not rewrite history, Pearl. You knew who I was, and what I wanted out of life. Now, you were telling me about the Pinkerton agent."

"Oh, yes. By the way, got anything to drink around here?" She hitched her dress above her ankles, opened the top desk drawer with her toes. "What? No whis-key?"

"No."

"You always were predictable and boring. I hated that the most about you."

He could tell her a few things about hatred. "Just finish your story."

"Well. That Pinkerton… Oh, what was his name?" She shrugged. "I can't remember. Anyway, he was very official at first. He even went so far as to cuff me." She grinned in an ugly manner. "But he wasn't expecting my special brand of persuasion. I wore him down quickly enough."

Marc couldn't believe what she was saying. It was too absurd to contemplate. "You seduced a Pinkerton agent."

"With my wiles and, of course, *your* money. We had three lovely months together. When he was called back to Chicago, I gave him twice the rate you were paying him to help fake my death."

"You bought off a Pinkerton agent?" It was unbe-lievable, mind-boggling. Pinkertons were known for their honesty. That had been the reason he'd hired one in the first place.

"Everybody has a price, darling."

He thought of Laney, of her determination to forge her own way in the world for herself and the children of Charity House. "Not everyone."

"I'd wager even your pretty little girlfriend has a price."

Marc moved fast. Before she could stop him, he wrapped his hand around her arm. "I told you to leave her out of this."

Pearl didn't even have the good sense to look scared. "Let me go."

"Why should I? You're dead. And not just to me, but to the world. That's the trouble with faking your own death." He tightened his grip. "No one is looking for you or wondering where you are."

She snorted at him, her eyes full of contempt. "You never could bluff with me. Face it, Marc, you don't have it in you to hurt a woman. Not even me."

Two warring desires battled one another in his head. Get rid of Pearl or do his duty by her. He wanted to be free of the woman, for good, but not enough to go against everything he believed.

He was guilty of many sins, but he wouldn't sacrifice his integrity, not ever again. He released her arm with great care. "Where's the rest of my money?"

"Like I said, it's gone."

"You went through six thousand dollars in five years?"

"Four years, actually. I ran out a year ago."

"And you're just coming to me tonight? Why now?"

She picked at her dirty, ragged fingernails again, no longer able to meet his eyes. "I didn't need you before now. If you remember, I do have several rather enjoyable ways of earning money for myself."

Silence filled the moment as she measured him from below her lowered lashes. "Give me a little more money and I'll be out of your life again."

She hopped off the desk and stumbled, before a coughing fit bent her over at the waist.

Marc moved to her side. "Are you sick, Pearl?"

"I'm…" She coughed again, harder and longer. "Fine."

No, she wasn't fine. Nor was she drunk, well, not

completely. She was ill. Extremely ill. And highly medicated. He guessed with laudanum.

No matter the nature of their relationship, Marc wouldn't abandon her. He'd vowed to stay with her in sickness and in health, till death parted them.

He no longer wanted anything to do with Pearl, but they were married. He would never love her, not the way a man should love his wife, but he wouldn't let her suffer alone.

"Let's get you something to eat and then I'll set you up in your own room. We'll talk about money after you've rested."

"Now you're talking sense." She smirked up at him. "I knew you couldn't resist me for long."

Chapter Twenty

Cracking open the registration book, Laney thanked God that helping guests and addressing their various problems required her complete concentration. Though outwardly calm, her heart ached. Numb from the pain, she couldn't even collect enough anger to hate Marc Dupree.

She couldn't comprehend why he'd given her a reason to hope for a future, with him, when all along he'd been *married*.

Agony stole her composure, making her hands shake. Or had she misunderstood? Had he planned to ask her to be his mistress instead of his wife? Had she been one request away from becoming just like her mother?

How could Laney have been so foolish to fall in love with a married man?

Focusing on the guest in front of her, an elderly gentleman in an elegant suit, she positioned a friendly smile on her face. "How may I help you, sir?"

"Can you tell me what time the restaurant closes this evening?"

"Ten o'clock."

"Lovely." He turned toward the open doors. "Thank you, miss."

"My pleasure." She smiled after him, just as the hair on the back of her neck stood at attention.

Turning her head, she caught sight of Marc escorting his wife out of his office, his hand in a solicitous hold on her elbow.

With a gulp, Laney forced down the anguish choking her. The ache in her heart multiplied as Laney watched him steer the woman into the elevator. He was taking her to a room. To his room?

Again, she wished she could summon up at least some hatred but, *again*, she simply couldn't do it. The pain in her heart was real, and yet the love Laney felt for Marc wouldn't let go of her. Love didn't work that way, she realized. It didn't come and go on a whim, or even at the introduction of an unknown wife.

Laney willed Marc to look at her. As though hearing her silent plea, he turned his head in her direction. She'd already discovered she had few defenses against him, so she wasn't surprised when the expression on his face fractured the last of them.

The pure sorrow in his gaze joined with her answering despair. In that moment Laney knew that no matter what happened in the future, a part of her would always live inside Marc. She'd given him a piece of her soul. And he'd left a part of his with her.

His expression never altered, his silent pledge shouting over the divide between them. But he had a wife—a wife!—and that meant they could be nothing more than friends, perhaps not even that.

Determined to survive the loss with dignity, she turned away and focused on another patron's request.

Out of the corner of her eye she watched the elevator door shut.

For a heartbeat, she considered fighting for Marc. But she knew she wouldn't. Marriage was sacred. With God's help she would find the courage to live the rest of her life alone.

One step at a time.

For now, she focused on doing her job.

She even managed to answer several more questions without thinking about anything other than the individual guests in front of her. So focused on shutting out the world she didn't notice when Marc returned. "We need to talk."

She tried for calm, but her broken voice betrayed her despair. "I'm working."

"Rose will take over for you."

Without saying a word, the other woman moved into place, scooting Laney out of the way with a none-too-subtle shove of her hip.

Laney glared at the woman, but Rose just smiled at her with sympathy. "Go on, dear, Mr. Dupree will explain everything to you. Give him a chance."

Laney sighed, wanting to do anything but *give him a chance*. Putting her resolve in place, she faced the man who'd given her such lovely hope one moment and had shattered her heart in the next.

Marc reached out to take Laney's elbow but the look she shot him quelled that idea. Relenting, for now, he allowed her to walk ahead of him. He wished he knew what she was thinking, then thought maybe he didn't want to know, after all.

She moved inside his office, heading straight to the

fireplace. The moment he shut the door, she broke the silence. "You don't have a photograph of your wife. You never spoke of her. Why?"

He wanted only truth between them. "I thought she was dead."

He raised his hand to touch her, but she jerked out of his reach as soon as he laid his fingers on her back. "Don't."

He knew she hurt, could feel her pain as sure as his own. He tried again, resting his hand lightly on the top of her shoulder. "Look at me, Laney."

She shook her head, then dropped her chin to her chest. "I...I can't." Her words came out in halting, choked syllables. "If I look at you, I might be tempted to forgive you."

"Would that be so terrible?"

"You know the answer to that."

"I don't want to keep talking to the back of your head. At least turn around and face me."

She slowly did as he requested, but she kept her gaze firmly locked on the floor.

Marc exhaled. "I love you."

Her gaze shot up. "Don't say that." The anger and suffering mingling together in her eyes hurt him more than if she'd kicked him in his gut. "Don't lie to me, Marc, anything but that."

"I've never lied to you."

"What about your *wife*? I don't recall you mentioning her. Not once."

"I thought she was dead." He repeated the words as if they would eventually make sense to them both.

"You expect me to believe that?"

"It's the truth." He rifled through the top drawer of

his desk, searching for the document he'd nearly forgotten he had. Finding it at last, he urged her to take
it. "Look at this."

"I don't see the point—"

"Do what I ask, please."

Laney tugged her bottom lip between her teeth then
lowered her eyes to the piece of paper. She took the
document from him and read the inscription aloud.
"It's a death certificate from the state of Colorado,"
she gasped. "For Pearl LaRue Dupree."

"I was given this three years ago by a Pinkerton
agent I'd hired to find my wife."

She handed the document back to him with shaking
fingers. "I don't understand."

"No wonder. I hardly understand it myself." Marc
raked a hand through his hair. "Apparently, Pearl paid
the man to help her fake her own death."

"Why would anyone do such a thing?"

An excellent question. The magnitude of Pearl's
treachery was starting to sink in. She'd stolen from
him and then faked her own death. All because she
hadn't been able to bear the life he'd tried to offer her.
He'd wanted to care for her, to lighten her burdens. All
she'd ever wanted was his money.

Trey had warned Marc that his pursuit of wealth
would lure the ugliest of hearts. How right he'd been.

"Marc?"

"Oh, she had a reason. Actually, she had six thousand reasons."

"What do you mean?"

"It's a long story."

Laney gave him a forced smile. "Should I sit down
for this?"

"I didn't tell you I'd been married before because, well, it never came up." She opened her mouth but he stopped her with a wave of his hand. "I know that's not a good enough excuse. The other reason was that I didn't want you to know what a fool I'd been."

Laney angled her head. "You? I can't imagine you doing anything you didn't want to do."

"I wish it was that simple." Marc blew out a slow breath. "Do you remember I told you I grew up as part of the wealthy elite?"

"What does that have to do—"

"Let me finish," he said, stopping her midsentence. "Please."

She nodded. "All right."

"We went from wealth to poverty in a matter of years. When my father died of malaria and my mother shortly after him, I was through being poor."

"Oh, Marc. You don't have to tell me this."

He scrubbed a hand down his face. "After those hard, lean years I didn't just want money, I *needed* it. I was obsessed. Gambling was the quickest route to reaching my goal. I moved out West, traveling from card game to card game. By the time I was twenty-five, I'd earned enough wealth to never see poverty again."

She sighed.

"When I went to Cripple Creek I met Pearl LaRue. She was ten years older than me and the most exotic woman I'd ever met." Laney flinched at his words. He laid his hand on her sleeve. "I'm sorry this is hurting you."

"Go on. I want to hear this."

"Having grown up in New Orleans I thought I'd seen every kind of woman there was to see. But Pearl was different, unique, exciting. I had to have her for my own."

Laney's heart leaped to her eyes. "You loved her."

Marc smoothed his finger down her cheek. "No, my relationship with Pearl was never about love. At least, looking back now, I realize love hadn't been the driving force. At the time I thought I'd die if I didn't win her."

"So you married her?"

"Not at first. When I met her she was a dancing girl and a prostitute. I wanted to rescue her from that life, so I offered to put her up in her own home with the promise I would take care of her."

"Not much different from what you do for the women you hire here."

Touched by the compassionate look in her eyes, he wanted to go to her and let her smooth away all his pains, like she did for children in her care. But Marc was no little boy. He was a grown man. One who had to answer for his sins.

"What I didn't count on, was that Pearl liked her chosen lifestyle. She refused to quit seeing other men. She did, however, vow to change her mind if I made a more permanent commitment than just offering her a nice cottage and a little cash."

"That's when you married her."

"I knew it was a mistake almost from the start. As soon as I was bound to her for life, the excitement disappeared."

Her eyes widened with disappointment. "You don't believe in marriage then?"

"Quite the opposite. Marriage is holy, a promise made before God, and should be honored as such. The two married couples I'd known intimately were my mother and father, and Trey and my sister. I wanted what they had but what I got with Pearl didn't come close. I was looking for an ideal that didn't exist."

He'd been young and idealistic. Now he realized how much he'd lost by trying to do the right thing with Pearl.

"I'm assuming you tried to make your marriage work."

"A losing battle. It didn't take me long to realize that I couldn't change a woman who didn't want changing. But there wasn't much I could do. I was married. And marriage means forever."

"So what did you do?"

"I turned to my only solace. Accumulating wealth. Lots of it, as fast as I could. I continued gambling and didn't dare allow myself to think about what Pearl was buying with my money or doing while I was playing cards all night."

"Oh, Marc."

"*No.* I can handle your scorn, your anger, but not your understanding. I was young and stupid and set on using one sin to erase another. I'd made my mistake so I lived with it as best I could." He frowned. "I've since repented of that lifestyle. The Lord always offers mercy and forgiveness, but he doesn't always take away the consequences of our sins." As evidenced by Pearl's appearance tonight.

Her expression still full of bafflement, Laney shook her head. "You mentioned you hired a Pinkerton agent to find Pearl. What happened? Did she run off with some of your money?"

He sniffed. "She stole all of it."

"Oh, my. How?"

"At the time, I wanted my money as close to me as

possible. I kept some of my money in the bank but the bulk of my savings I put in a safe much like that one." He pointed to the small safe behind him. "Pearl learned the combination by watching my fingers."

"Just like me." Groaning, Laney buried her face in her hands. "No wonder you thought so poorly of me and believed I wasn't trustworthy."

"Don't, Laney. Don't compare yourself to Pearl. You aren't like her. You only took money that belonged to you." Everything in him softened as the truth hit him. "Deep down, I always knew you weren't the kind of woman who stole and conned your way through life. Perhaps that's why I let you get away so easily that first night."

"And that makes my kicking you in the chest all right?"

"No." He rubbed the spot where she'd landed the blow. "But it makes your actions understandable. I didn't give you a chance to explain yourself."

"I didn't try very hard to make you hear me. In fact, I intentionally led you to believe I was just like…like… your wife."

This was the first time they'd ever really talked about the night they'd met. It felt good to clear the air, to get it all out in the open. But nothing was solved.

"So, now you know," he said. "I was as shocked as you to see Pearl standing in my hotel tonight. Maybe more so."

"She wasn't exactly standing."

"No. She wasn't." A strange sort of pity spread through him. "Although Pearl's timing wasn't perfect, perhaps it was best she showed up when she did. You realize I was just about to ask you to marry me?"

Tears formed in her eyes. "Oh, Marc, we might have married not knowing, then what would we have done?" He reached for her but she shook her head. "We can't."

No, they couldn't.

"You should know, Pearl isn't the same woman who ran away all those years ago. She's ill. And as much as I know this hurts you to hear, I have to take care of her. She's my wife. I can't abandon her."

"I wouldn't expect any different from you."

"I love *you*, Laney. But I'm married to Pearl."

Her unshed tears wiggled to the edges of her lashes. "Because you're married, you realize I can't be anything more than your employee."

For a moment, he thought about asking her to run away with him. But too many people depended on them both. And neither of them was selfish enough to think only of their own pleasure.

Marc placed a tender kiss on her temple. As he pulled back, he put a silent pledge in his eyes, praying she understood what he couldn't say. "You are a part of my heart. But we can't be together."

"I know. Oh, Marc, I realized that the minute I heard you had a wife."

Chapter Twenty-One

Determined to survive one day at a time, Laney turned to routine for solace the next morning. Unfortunately thoughts of Marc, and what they might have had together, never left her mind for long.

It helped to focus most of her energy on getting the children ready to start the school year. She spent the morning rushing around, amazed at the amount of effort it took to get so many girls and boys fed and out of the house on time.

At two minutes past eight, Laney collapsed in a chair and shut her eyes. Pleasantly exhausted, she took a moment to collect herself before facing the rest of the day's chores.

A smile curled on her lips. As of today, her children were no longer just the sons and daughters of prostitutes. They were normal schoolchildren.

She couldn't wait to hear about their day, but that would be hours from now. In the meantime she would fill every moment with activity.

The hardest challenge would come later, when she went to work at the hotel. She would see Marc and pretend the tentative friendship they'd forged was enough. But with that lie came unspeakable pain. She nearly had the money to pay off her loan with Prescott, two more nights at most, and then she'd be out of debt. There would be no more need to work at the hotel. No more reason to see Marc again.

That thought brought even more sorrow.

Katherine's sympathetic voice skidded across her thoughts. "Do you want to talk about it?"

Laney slowly opened her eyes. "What is there to say?"

"I don't know. But in my experience talking seems to help. Remember when I came back from Miss Lindsay's?"

"You were so hurt, so confused." Laney swallowed her anguish in a sigh.

"You listened when I needed to talk." She wedged a chair close to Laney's. "Let me do the same for you."

Touched, Laney swiped at a tear escaping down her cheek. "Oh, Katherine, I'm trying not to wallow in self-pity. But it seems God is punishing me for all the mistakes I've made lately."

Katherine shook her head sadly. "Laney, God doesn't punish us for our mistakes. He just allows us to make them."

"And then leaves us to suffer the consequences? Like falling in love with a man I can never have?" She clutched the chair. "Why did I have to meet Judge Greene in Marc's hotel that night? There were so many other places I could have chosen."

She paused as her words sank in. What was she saying? If she hadn't gone to the Hotel Dupree she'd have never met Marc. She would have gone through the rest of her life never knowing the man, never knowing the beauty of loving him.

No, she couldn't be sorry for that.

There were other regrets, though. "Maybe if I hadn't taken out that final loan, I wouldn't have needed the money, and then I wouldn't have needed to force the judge's hand."

"I suppose you could look at it that way. But I like to think we find out who we are when we make our choices and then live with them."

When had Katherine become so wise? "It just seems I've been given a much harder road than others."

Katherine's expression shifted into sympathy. "No, Laney. You're where you are now because of choices you've made. Pure and simple."

Laney didn't deny it. "What other choices could I have made?"

Stitching an age-old wisdom into her words, Katherine touched her hand. "Only you can answer that."

For a moment, Laney thought hard about what else she could have done. She could have tried another bank, one run by a more honest man. She could have bought a smaller home. In reality, she could have made any number of other decisions.

But she hadn't. And, in the end, every choice had led her to Marc Dupree and the anguish she suffered now. Even knowing this, she still couldn't regret meeting him.

She was saved from further reflection when Megan burst into the house, tears streaming down her face.

Her own worries forgotten, Laney jumped from her chair and rushed to the girl. "Megan, what's the matter?"

"We…" She choked over a hiccup. "We were sent away."

"Sent away from school? But why?"

Entering the house a few steps behind her, Johnny said, "It was awful, Miss Laney."

One by one the rest of the children scuttled through the front door.

Surveying the downtrodden faces, Laney's heart sank. Only a few had tears falling, while the others were red-faced with anger. What concerned her most were the various hues of shame in each of their gazes.

Laney couldn't make words come out of her mouth. Thankfully, Katherine spoke for her. "Tell us what happened?"

"They laughed at us, called us names."

Laney instantly found her voice. "The other schoolchildren called you names?"

"Yeah, and then this man came and told us we had to go home."

Megan added, "He said we could never come back again."

A sick feeling tumbled in Laney's chest. "What did this man look like?"

"It was my—" Michael's lips trembled on a sob. "My daddy."

Prescott.

"He said he wouldn't tolerate brats like us mingling with the children of the good folks of Denver."

Katherine gasped. "Oh, no."

Laney raised her eyes to the ceiling, praying for an answer or, at the very least, wisdom to know what to do.

Think, she ordered herself. After a moment, an idea

formulated in her mind and she felt a surge of excitement. If she and Katherine could pull it off…

"Mrs. Smythe made cookies and candy." She pointed behind her, urging everyone to look in that direction. "Johnny, take everyone to the kitchen and tell her to serve the treats now."

He stared at her as though she'd turned into a fish trying to swim up the middle of downtown Denver. "But what are we going to do about school?"

"You leave that to me." Laney gave him her most confident grin. "I have an idea."

At the groan coming from Katherine, Laney spun to face her friend. "Well, I do."

"Yes." Katherine gave her a soft, understanding smile. "I know."

"It's a good one, too."

"It always is."

Laney tried not to sigh. "Go on, everyone." She ushered the bulk of the children toward the kitchen. "Either I or Katherine will join you in just a minute to tell you what we have planned."

Michael pulled on Laney's skirt, the look of sorrow wiping away his usual youthful enthusiasm. "We won't have to go back to that awful school again, will we?"

"Never again, I promise."

"Laney," Katherine warned, "Let's not be hasty with our promises. No good can come from—"

"You don't even know what I have planned." Laney poked a finger in the air between them. "So calm your worries right now."

"Why don't you calm them for me, by explaining what you have in mind?"

Laney waited until all the children were out of earshot, then explained, "It's really very simple. *You* will teach them."

"Me?" Gasping, Katherine covered her heart with a shaky hand. "Have you gone mad?"

"Of course not. It's a brilliant idea."

Katherine shook her head. "You're not thinking clearly, that's it."

"I'm thinking very clearly."

"Oh, really? What about supplies? Desks? Chalkboards? Books?"

"Minor details, the kind we'll work out as we go. Just like we always do." Excitement swelled, making Laney dizzy with all the possibilities running through her mind.

"We'll need to purchase a building, at some point, but not now." She held up a hand to stave off Katherine's objection. "In a few years, perhaps, once we've saved enough money."

There would be no more loans. Laney had learned her lesson on that score.

"Laney, you're getting drunk on excitement." Katherine grasped her by the shoulders and shook. "Sober up. There are more than a few details involved with starting a school."

Laney looked pointedly at Katherine's hands still gripping her.

She immediately released her hold, but didn't let go of her argument. "Where are we going to get the money to buy all the supplies and books? Books are expensive."

"I'll keep my job at the hotel for as long as necessary. And if that doesn't bring in enough money…" Laney looked around her, at the luxurious furnishings Marc had pointed out "…then we'll sell off some of the best pieces in the house."

Though that last idea wasn't her favorite solution, it might be the only way they could raise the necessary funds.

The grim twist of Katherine's lips did not bode well for her agreement to Laney's scheme. "Might I remind you, this is the kind of thinking that got us into trouble *all* the other times?"

Eyes narrowed, Laney tilted her head to look Katherine straight in the face. "Don't you want to teach the children?"

Katherine took a contemplative pause. "Well, yes. Yes, I do."

"Then leave the details to me."

"Perhaps you should discuss this with someone else, maybe get a man's perspective? Mr. Dupree's, perhaps?"

For a moment, Laney considered Katherine's suggestion. Marc had told her she wasn't alone anymore. She'd nearly believed him. But that was before his wife had shown up. "He has too much to worry about on his own to bother him with our problems."

"He'll want to help us with this. You should give him that chance."

"I have to do this alone." Like always. "And the first thing I'm going to do is go down to the school and tell that teacher just what I think of her. How dare she refuse them admittance? Doesn't she know what damage she's done?"

Katherine raised her eyes to the heavens. "Laney, I can't help but think it would be a mistake to go over there right now. You should calm down first. With the mood you're in, you'll only make matters worse."

"Nothing could be worse."

* * *

Laney marched along Market Street angrier than before she'd entered the schoolhouse, now that she knew the full story. The schoolteacher hadn't wanted to send the children away. She'd only been carrying out Prescott's orders. And since the shifty banker owned the school's building and paid the bulk of the teacher's salary, the woman hadn't had much choice in the matter.

Well, he wouldn't get away with this.

Before she lost hold of the outrage propelling her forward, Laney smoothed her palms down her skirt then stepped inside the bank. No matter what happened, she wouldn't leave until Prescott had made restitution for this unforgivable offense.

Her steps slowed as she reminded herself to pay off the interest on her loan *before* tearing into the banker. She had the bulk of the money on her, had thought to plan ahead despite her blinding anger when she'd left Charity House this morning.

The children, she reminded herself. *Remember their faces when they'd arrived home from the school.*

The reminder was enough to give her the courage she needed to confront Prescott.

The children deserved an education, without the banker's nasty interference.

She gave the clerk her name and waited. Like all the other times she'd come to this bank, Prescott didn't keep her wrestling in her anticipation for long. She might have thought that odd, if she didn't have so much else on her mind.

"Miss O'Connor, what a surprise." The lie slid smoothly from smirking lips.

Hiding her dislike behind her own smile, she allowed

him to lead the way to his office. As she watched him jut out his chest, Laney was reminded of that crazy rooster in the Montana mining camp that used to swagger around the streets, crowing all day long. A train had hit the stupid bird. She wondered if there would be a train passing through the bank anytime soon.

Once inside the office, Prescott wasted no time getting to the point. Without offering her a seat, he asked, "What can I do for you this fine morning?"

Squaring her shoulders, she held his gaze. "You know why I'm here."

His expression drew into a blank. "I can think of several reasons."

Forgetting all about her resolution to pay off her loan first, she laid into him. "Let's not continue the pretense, Prescott. You had my children banished from the local school."

"Come to beg for their readmittance?

"No."

"Ah." He scratched his beard. "Then you must be here to talk about your loan. But you're a few days too late, aren't you? Your *benefactor* already paid your outstanding balance."

"My benefactor?" What was Prescott talking about?

"Marc Dupree. He paid off the remaining interest on your loan days ago."

She stared at him, her heart pounding in her ears. Had she just heard him correctly? "When, exactly, did he come to you?"

"Tuesday morning."

The day after Pearl had shown up at his hotel. Marc was trying to make restitution for the pain he'd inflicted on her in the only way he know how. With his money. A kind gesture, if completely misguided.

"You had no right to take Marc's money for my loan without my authorization."

"*Marc*, is it?"

Her hand itched to slap that smug grin off Prescott's face. "Don't read too much into my use of his given name. I'm nothing special to the man. I'm simply his employee."

"No, Miss O'Connor, you are much more than his employee." He leaned forward. "People talk, you know."

"People gossip."

"Call it what you will. But word's out you're his mistress."

Outrage had her gaping at him. "That's a lie."

Flattening his hands on the desk, he leaned forward. "Tell that to his wife."

One sentence and Prescott made her relationship with Marc sound disgusting and sinful. Perhaps it was, on a certain level. Didn't she love a married man? Didn't he just pay off her loan as though she was his mistress?

She would deal with Marc later. For now, she had another, more pressing problem standing in front of her. "I want to discuss what happened at the school this morning."

"Certainly. But first, this is for you." He pulled out an official-looking document from the bottom drawer of his desk. "*Marc* insisted I give you this when next you came to see me."

Snatching up the document, she looked down and gasped. "The deed to Charity House." In *her* name.

"You win, Miss O'Connor. You officially own the house free and clear."

A surge of excitement whipped through her. How she wished she could just walk away now, never to return. But she couldn't. Not yet. She had to have her say, had to stand up for the children.

Prescott's smirk warned her how he would respond. Because of people like him and their dirty accusations, the children had to deal with more than their share of shame.

It was so unfair, so infuriating.

"All right, Prescott. Now that our business is complete, I want your word that you will leave my orphanage and the children who live there alone."

"You know, Miss O'Connor, you can't keep calling that place you run an orphanage. Very few of those children are truly orphans."

Laney bristled. She could accept the slurs about herself, but she would not listen to any more about the children. "Your word, Prescott. I want you to promise this is the end of our battle."

A hint of respect flashed in his eyes. "You've really learned your lesson."

"I have. Now that our association is over I will never step inside this bank again, and I ask you never attempt to undermine my efforts to create a home for the children at Charity House."

For a long, tense moment, he watched her through his beady eyes. The respect she'd seen earlier disappeared, only to be replaced with something that looked like pure loathing. "So this is goodbye."

"Yes."

"Then I suggest you leave at once." With his big beefy paw he shoved her toward the exit.

She went willingly.

Never again would she have to face Thurston P. Prescott III. Instead of feeling triumphant, instead of experiencing a wave of relief, a sense of foreboding filled her.

Lord, why am I not more pleased?

She knew the answer, of course. She might have the deed to Charity House tucked in her reticule. She might have learned a valuable lesson about living within her means, but she'd lost something precious in the process. She'd lost the man she loved with all her heart.

She'd lost Marc Dupree.

Chapter Twenty-Two

Settled in his private office at the Hotel Dupree, Marc worked on his accounts. Unfortunately, the numbers ran together in his mind, one big blur of black ink and incomprehensible marks. All he could think about was Laney and the fact that she would arrive for her shift in a matter of hours.

Although Marc wouldn't seek her out, or try to talk to her unless absolutely necessary, at least he would know she was near, in his hotel, earning wages she no longer needed to save her orphanage.

A smile of satisfaction spread across his lips. With a handful of dollars Marc had put an end to Prescott's hold over Charity House. No doubt, Laney would have something to say about his interference. Marc would let her lecture him, silently smiling while she did so, because nothing could change the fact that the orphanage legally belonged to her. Her future was secure, as was the children's.

As though his thoughts could summon the woman's very presence, Laney's fresh lilac fragrance filled the air.

Marc looked up from his ledger and connected gazes with the woman he loved.

Standing in the doorway, watching him with a closed expression, Laney looked both fragile and beautiful. So delicate and yet so strong. He wanted to beg her to run away with him all over again.

He would never dishonor her like that. Nor would he trample on the vows he'd said in front of a preacher five years ago. Still, his heart picked up speed at the sight of Laney hovering on the edge of his private domain. "Hello."

"Hello, Marc." When she didn't move deeper into the room, he narrowed his eyes and studied her more closely for clues to her mood.

Her casual stance gave nothing away. They could be strangers for the lack of emotion in her gaze. This new distance between them was yet another consequence of Pearl's unexpected return.

Marc hated that he couldn't tell Laney how precious she was to him. But if he did something that foolish, he'd profess his love to her in the next breath, and then he'd no longer be able to survive apart from her.

But survive he would. For the sake of a vow he'd made five years ago and the honor of the woman who stood before him now.

After another painful moment of silence, Laney jammed her hands on her hips. "I understand you recently made a bank transaction on my behalf."

Ah. So she'd been to the bank this afternoon. Marc should have known by the lack of warmth in her gaze. "I won't apologize for paying off your loan." He held up his hand to keep her from interrupting him. "And before you say anything more, I did it for the children, not you."

"Talk around town says otherwise."

He set down his quill very slowly, very deliberately. "What *talk* around town?"

"The gossips are saying I'm your mistress." She pressed her fingertips to her temples and rubbed. "Paying off my loan has only added proof to their assumptions."

That hadn't been his intention.

"It never occurred to me that my actions would put you at the center of the gossip mill."

"Don't get the wrong idea. I don't care what people say about me." She flicked her wrist in the air as if to make her point. "I've heard far worse in the past."

Angry on her behalf, he rose quickly and crossed to her. "Nevertheless, I'm sorry." He pulled her deeper into his office and shut the door behind them. "I wanted to help alleviate your burdens, not add to them."

Remaining just out of his reach, she drew in a shuddering breath. "Oh, Marc, I know you meant well. And I truly appreciate the gesture. So…thank you."

"Excuse me? What did you just say?"

"I said thank you."

The significance of those two little words spoken so boldly made his heart soar. "You're welcome, Laney."

He took a step toward her, but she warded off his approach with a shake of her head. "I have more to say."

"All right."

"Although I certainly appreciate what you've done for Charity House and the children, you can't continue giving us money, not even indirectly."

"Why not?"

"Because…" She blew out a slow, careful breath, as if she were formulating her argument very methodically in her mind. "The gossip could turn toward the children. They already suffer enough. I don't want to add more strain to their lives."

A valid point, to be sure, but a bit shortsighted. "They would suffer far worse than a little gossip if you lose the orphanage. No, Laney, I can't promise not to assist you if you get into trouble again."

"Marc, please." Her head turned away from him. "I need you to—"

She broke off midsentence, her gaze connecting with the cot he'd set up next to his desk. "Is that where you're sleeping at night?"

"The hotel is at full occupancy," he said, as though that was enough explanation.

He should have known better. Laney was too smart for that. "But you have your own permanent suite of rooms."

"Pearl is living there for now. Alone. Under the circumstances, I find this an acceptable arrangement."

"Acceptable, maybe." She turned to face him again, her eyes softening. "But surely not comfortable."

"Are you worried about me, Laney?" He rather liked the idea.

"Of course I'm worried about you." The longing in her eyes cut him to the core, made him wonder what his life would have been like with this woman by his side, a woman who cared enough about him to worry about something as minor as his comfort.

He stared at her for a long while, wishing he could reach out and smooth his finger down her cheek, maybe touch her hair. Both very bad ideas, as was spending any more time with her alone in his office.

"Let me walk you home and you can tell me how your conversation with Prescott went. And I'm warning you now, I want every detail, no matter how small."

She stiffened at his request.

"Did something happen while you were in Prescott's office? Did he threaten you? Hurt you in any way?"

"Nothing I haven't endured from him before." Her bright smile was clearly forced.

"Tell me what happened."

As he waited for her to explain, he linked his hands behind his back, to prevent himself from pulling her into his arms and smoothing away that look of sadness on her face. In the ensuing silence, he thought of the woman who stood between them.

Pearl. Her addictions were worse than he first thought. Since her return, he couldn't remember a moment when his wife had been fully lucid.

He wanted to share his worries with Laney, ask her how it had been with her mother, but he could see she had her own concerns. For an instant, he broke his first and only rule—never touch Laney—and bent down to take her hands in his. "I want to help you. But I can't if you don't tell me what's occurred."

"Oh, Marc, it's the children," she said. "They were banned from school today. They were so upset. I went straight down to that school to tell the teacher just what I thought of her banning innocent children from the classroom."

Noble, to be sure. But he'd seen Laney when she was all worked up. She could have easily made matters worse if she'd gone over to the school in a furious state of mind. "You think that was a good idea, charging over there like that?"

"Maybe not. But I was so furious." She threw her hands in the air and stomped through the room in big, angry strides. "How dare she, I thought. What gave her the right to judge my precious children?"

"Slow down." Marc reached out and grasped her arm. "You're making me dizzy."

She pushed away from him and went back to pacing, or rather stomping. "It wasn't even her fault and I'm still angry just thinking about this morning."

"I see that."

"Did I tell you Prescott was behind their banishment?"

That was new information, the kind that had Marc's temper rising right along with Laney's. "You saw him at the school?"

She shook her head. "No, but it turns out he's the main patron of the school. How dare he misuse his authority like that?" She spun in a circle. "The man is an awful, horrible human being."

Marc couldn't agree more. So he focused on soothing Laney's outrage. Something about her behavior made him sense this was more than a fight about a school refusing the children. This was also Laney's personal battle against all the humiliation she'd endured as the daughter of a prostitute.

For the first time Marc caught a glimpse of what Laney must have braved as a child. She'd spent her life as an outcast. And now the children of Charity House suffered a similar stigma because of the same unfortunate circumstances of their birth.

"I can help you find another school for them to attend."

"I can't ask the children to go through that humiliation again."

"Then tell me what I can do. Say the word and I'll make it happen."

"I don't have any concrete answers yet." She buried her fingers in the fabric of her skirt. "I have some ideas, but I need to do some more thinking before I commit to any of them."

Willing his hands to stay by his side, Marc stared hard at her, scrutinizing every feature on her face, trying to decipher the words she wasn't saying. "You aren't planning to do anything drastic are you?"

She shifted a vacant stare to a spot just over his shoulder. "Of course not."

A loud knock came from the other side of the door. Marc ignored it. "I want you to come to me before you make any firm decisions about the children's schooling."

"I—" The knocking came again, louder and more incessant. "Don't you think you should answer that?"

"Not until you agree to let me be a part of the solution to this problem of yours."

A slurred, high-pitched voice accompanied the next round of knocks. "Marc, are you in there?"

Pearl. Laney jumped back, shame and guilt evident in her features.

"Don't, Laney. Don't look like that. We haven't done anything wrong."

"Marc Allen Dupree. I know you're in there. I can hear you talking to someone. Who's in there with you?"

The door flew open and Pearl stumbled forward,

heading face first for the floor. Moving quickly, Marc caught her before she fell all the way.

He barely had time to catch his balance before Laney rushed passed him and out of his office. With his arms full of an incoherent, spitting-mad wife, he had no other choice than to let her go.

The rest of the evening brought a new form of torture. Sitting in a chair facing the bed in his room, Marc dragged a wet cloth across Pearl's feverish forehead, wondering why she did this to herself. This was the second time in so many days that she'd taken too much laudanum.

When he'd realized she had a problem that first night of her return, he'd tried to talk to her about it. But he'd only received oaths and curses in response, so he'd begun throwing out the bottles as fast as she could buy them. He still wasn't sure where she was getting the money to fund her habit. Not from him, not directly. She could be stealing from the restaurant, or unsuspecting customers or…any number of places. He made a note to find out where.

Pearl awakened with a cough, her eyes peeling slowly open. In a shaky voice, she made a request for water.

Marc moved out of the chair, cradled her head and eased a glass to her lips. He could no longer see the woman he'd married in this pale, rail-thin creature. She looked more apparition than person, her dull sallow skin carrying the permanent stench of her illness. Her once vibrant eyes had sunken into their sockets, small and unremarkable now.

It hurt to look at her. He'd seen enough death in his life to recognize he was staring at its ruthless cousin now.

As Pearl choked down a sip of water, Marc wondered how much longer she could do this to herself. A day, a week, maybe a year?

"I need more laudanum," she croaked. "There's some in my red dress."

He'd not thought to search there. Where else was she hiding the elixir? "Pearl, I beg you to stop this madness."

She collapsed against the pillow. Pain swam in her eyes as her unfocused gaze hastened around the room. "Not now, Marc."

Despite her hostility and the pounding headache behind his eyes, Marc refused to let the matter drop. "Look at what you're doing to yourself."

Her lip curled. "Holier-than-thou, that's what you are."

He thought about how he was failing Pearl and how much he'd hurt Laney recently. "There's nothing holy about me."

Pearl snorted. "Just give me the medicine. I'll feel better after a little taste."

"A temporary cure, at best. Let me help you, Pearl." He'd uttered those same words a lot lately, with the same fruitless results.

"You want to help me? Give me money when I ask," Pearl said, her voice thick with the coarseness of dehydration.

"That won't solve anything." Money could only buy *things*. Nothing more. Certainly not Pearl's health.

Marc couldn't pinpoint precisely when it had happened, but in the last few weeks, Marc had begun to feel trapped in his chosen lifestyle. He no longer experienced pleasure from the luxury he once found so comforting. He should sell his hotel and start over, but now wasn't the time to think about such things.

Now was the time to alleviate this pitiful woman's pain as best he could. But he wouldn't do so by feeding her the drug that was causing as much harm as it was helping.

Pearl curled her legs up against her chest and rolled onto her side. She whimpered. The sound reminded Marc of a wounded animal caught in a trap. "Give me my medicine."

"I can't. Not in good conscience."

"I don't want to hear about your conscience." She found enough strength to pick up one of the glasses off the bedside table and throw it at him. "Just give me my medicine."

"No."

She bared her teeth. "I get it. You want me dead so you can marry your latest project. I'm not stupid, *husband*. I see how you look at her. Well, I don't think I'll oblige you by dying tonight. In fact," she sucked in her breath and tossed her head against the pillow, "I plan to live for a very long time."

Marc blew out a hiss, a very real sense of loss clutching at his heart. Such a waste.

"I don't want you to die, Pearl." He meant it. As much as he loved Laney and wanted her in his life, he could never wish his wife dead in order for that to happen.

Although he harbored much anger toward Pearl, he still wanted to see her return to the vivacious woman he'd met all those years ago in Cripple Creek. "I want you to get healthy again, to find joy in life like you once had. It's not too late."

A haunted look passed in her gaze. He'd never seen

her look so vulnerable, so scared—like a lost, lonely child.

"I want that, too," she admitted in a small voice.

"Good." He rose, decision made. "I'll go fetch the doctor."

"I don't want no stinkin' doctor anywhere near this room." Terror stole into her gaze. "He'll butcher me, sure as I lay here."

"Not this doctor."

"*No.* Marc, please don't do this to me."

Not sure where her fear was coming from, Marc decided to change her mind with the most obvious strategy. "Shane's young and handsome."

She gave a snort of laughter. "You think I care about that right now?"

Marc didn't feel the need to answer that question, when they both knew the truth. "I'll be back shortly."

He opened the armoire and searched the pockets of Pearl's red dress. The new dress *his* money had purchased. Where was his anger?

Strange how his perspective had changed in a matter of weeks. Money was just a means to an end, not the goal. But not too long ago he'd come close to losing his soul in the pursuit of gathering more and more wealth. He'd nearly turned money into his god.

Forgive me, Lord.

Marc wrapped his fingers around cold glass. Frowning, he tucked the bottle into his palm.

"That's mine," Pearl screeched, apparently more aware of her surroundings than she'd let on.

Marc turned to face her. "It's mine now."

"Don't you dare take that away from me." She tried

to push to a sitting position but the effort appeared to be too much for her and she fell back on the bed.

Nearly relenting at the pathetic picture she made, Marc shored up his resolve and strode toward the foyer of his suite. "I'll return with the doctor shortly."

With the sound of her cursing in his ears, he clicked the door shut behind him, praying he hadn't left the fox in charge of the henhouse. He'd found three other bottles of laudanum earlier tonight, all in unusual hiding places. He hoped there weren't any more. For Pearl's sake.

Chapter Twenty-Three

MARC paced outside his room while the doctor examined Pearl in privacy. Every so often, he glanced at the shut door.

Sorrow twisted in his gut. He'd made many mistakes in his life, a direct result of his own selfish need to acquire massive amounts of wealth. Now he had more money than he could ever spend. Yet he couldn't buy back his wife's health.

The door to his suite swung open, slamming Marc back to the matter at hand.

Dr. Shane Bartlett stepped into the hallway, his eyes world-weary and wise beyond his years, as if he'd seen more than his share of tragedy in his life. His dark, rumpled hair had a wild look, as though he'd run his fingers through it too many times. Whatever the doctor had to say, Marc knew it wouldn't be good.

"How is she?" he asked, not sure he wanted to hear the truth.

Shane shook his head. The previously alert eyes of just an hour before now had a red rim of fatigue ringing them. "She's uncomfortable, but resting at last."

"Give it to me straight." Marc exhaled slowly. "Is she dying?"

"Maybe. Maybe not. I can't give you a definitive answer." Shane speared his fingers through his hair. "It seems the more I learn about the human body, the less I know."

"I'm not sure what you mean."

"For all the scientific breakthroughs of this century, there are still too many mysteries yet to be solved." A line of deep concentration drew Shane's brows together. "The body's potential for self-healing is surprising at times."

"Are you saying Pearl's going to be all right?"

"For now."

Marc's relief was staggering. But then he noted the caution in his friend's manner. "What are you not telling me, Shane? Out with it."

"Your wife could live to grow a full head of gray hair. *If* you can convince her to sober up, and…" he broke off, his gaze darting around. "I don't know quite how to say this, it's a delicate situation."

At this point, nothing Shane could say would shock Marc. "You may be candid with me."

"She must stay away from the liquor, the laudanum and the…men."

The good doctor was clearly embarrassed by the situation, but Marc had long since given up pretending propriety mattered, at least not when it came to Pearl and her sinful life choices. "And if she doesn't make the changes you suggest?"

"Hard to tell. She could continue this lifestyle for an indefinite amount of time."

"Indefinitely?" Marc's gut twisted into a tight knot.

"How could anyone sustain that sort of lifestyle for any length of time?"

"Look, Marc. I honestly can't predict what will happen to your wife. I wish I could, but I don't know her history and she wasn't very forthright with me when I asked. The truth of the matter is, she could last a month, a year, maybe even ten."

"Ten years?"

"It's unusual, but not unheard of."

Marc repeated the doctor's words aloud, more to anchor his spinning thoughts than for any other reason. "Ten years of drunkenness and addiction."

How would he bear to watch Pearl destroy herself for that long?

"Of course," Shane said, "all this guesswork is pointless if she ends up overdosing. You must do everything you can to get her sober and keep her away from the laudanum."

Marc shoved his hands in his pockets, trying not to feel as though the weight of the world had just landed on his shoulders. "I've tried."

"Then keep trying."

"What do you suggest I do, short of locking her in that room behind you?"

"You could speak to the apothecary, make it clear he's not to sell her any more laudanum."

"I've done that already. She finds someone else to buy the drug for her."

"Then don't give her any money."

Marc's gut coiled in helpless defeat. "She has ways of earning it herself."

"Right." Shane sighed. "Could you have someone follow her, maybe step in before she goes too far?"

"I've tried that, too." In fact, Marc had tried every-thing the doctor suggested, with varying degrees of fail-ure and not an ounce of success. "Pearl can be stealthy when she wants to be."

Alarmingly so.

"There is one more thing you can do."

At this point Marc was willing to try anything. "I'm listening."

"Pray."

In her position behind the front desk, Laney was thankful for the intricacies involved in addressing vari-ous requests from the hotel guests. Unfortunately, her concentration kept wandering upward, to the suite of rooms on the top floor. Moments after her shift had started Laney had watched Marc escorting Dr. Shane Bartlett to the elevators, their heads bent in conversa-tion.

Retrieving the young doctor could mean only one thing—Pearl was in real trouble this time.

Laney had watched Pearl slowly destroying herself over the past week. The thought of the woman's unhap-piness sparked memories of the last days of Laney's own mother's life.

Before Pearl, Laney had thought her mother had been happy in her chosen profession, or at least content. She'd assumed the whiskey and laudanum just another part of the lifestyle her mother had chosen for herself.

But as Laney witnessed Pearl's mindless self-destruction, she realized her mother had been en-during one day at a time, medicating away her shame in the most expedient manner possible.

Out of the corner of her eye, Laney caught sight of

Marc accompanying the doctor back through the lobby. Both looked beaten and Laney's heart constricted.

After speaking with the doctor on the outside sidewalk, Marc strode back inside the hotel. He stopped for a brief moment at the front desk. Although he didn't owe Laney any explanation, he gave her a brief sketch of Pearl's condition. He ended with a solemn vow. "I have to try to get her sober."

"Of course you do." Offering her support, Laney covered his hand with her own, squeezed, then let go. Tears edged to the tips of her lashes. Blinking them away, she stared into the haunted eyes of the man she loved, and her heart ached even more. "I wish there was something I could do to help."

"You can come see me before you go home tonight."

"You don't want to talk now?"

"No," he said, not quite meeting her eyes, looking as though his mind was still upstairs with his wife. "I need to be alone to think."

"I understand."

She worked the rest of the evening with half her mind linked to Marc's problems, while the other half considered the situation at Charity House. The task of educating so many children at one time was turning out to be more complicated than she'd expected.

She could ask Marc for his advice and maybe even request his assistance in coming up with a solution, but she knew she wouldn't. Marc's obligations were to his wife right now, not Laney or the children or Charity House. She would handle her problems on her own. Like always. And thereby avoid complicating Marc's life any further.

With that thought in mind, she made a decision. Tonight would be her last night in Marc's employ.

The thought depressed her. But it was the only way to ensure they both honored their individual commitments.

Sighing, she handed over the registration book to Rose then went of search of Marc. She knocked on his office door. Seconds ticked by before she heard a muffled, "Enter."

Stepping only partly into the room, she looked at Marc's bent head. "I need to speak with you."

His head rose from his paperwork, but he didn't speak right away.

Laney fiddled with the doorknob, then decided to say what was on her mind as quickly as possible. She shut the door and turned back to face him. "I've come to give my notice. Tonight will be my last night in your employ."

He looked affronted at first, blinked several times, then nodded slowly. "I suppose it's for the best."

"I wish things had turned out differently between us, but you're married and I can't—"

Before she could finish he came around his desk and caught her against his chest. "I'm going to miss you, Laney."

"I'll miss you, too." She pressed her cheek to his shoulder. "So very much."

With slow, seemingly reluctant movements, he set her away from him. Far enough for propriety sake but close enough she could still smell his clean, masculine scent.

"Will you keep me updated on the children and the orphanage?" he asked. "Let me know if you need something from me, anything at all?"

Braiding her fingers together at her waist, she carefully considered his offer, wondering what his involvement would look like and where they would draw the line. "How would that work, exactly?"

"I'll send Hank out to Charity House on a regular basis. He'll report back to me, let me know if you need anything, see to carrying out any specific action. Laney, I might not be a part of your day-to-day life anymore, but I won't walk away from you and the children completely."

"I—"

He pressed his hand over her lips. "Say yes. Say you'll let me do this for you and the children."

Touched, she worked the idea around in her head. "I suppose it wouldn't hurt to have Hank come out every so often and check up on us."

"You won't regret agreeing to this." He dropped his hand, but didn't move immediately away from her.

She stared into his eyes and a silent promise flowed between them, one that went beyond words. So caught up in the moment she didn't hear the door swing open, until it banged against the wall.

"Get away from my husband, you little tramp."

For a moment, Laney couldn't make her mind grasp what was happening.

Marc reached up as though he was going to touch her, but then he pulled his hand back. "Let me handle this."

Still unable to comprehend why the pain in her heart was suffocating her ability to speak, she nodded. But then a slurred, overloud oath hissed in her ear and a jab on her shoulder spun her around. "Leave him alone. He's mine."

Laney's head cleared. "Oh, Pearl, I know that. I was just telling him goodbye."

"You expect me to believe that?"

"It's the truth."

Before either Laney or Pearl could say anything else, Marc moved between them.

"You're drunk, Pearl." He grasped her shoulder and turned her around to face him. "You need to follow the doctor's orders and rest."

Pearl shrugged off Marc's hand. "You can't send me off like this." The venom in her tone ripped a gasp out of Laney. "I won't let you."

"I'm not sending you away. I'm sending you upstairs to rest." He caught her under her arms. "You can hardly stand on your own."

Staggering in his grasp, Pearl shifted her blurry eyes to Laney. "*You.*" She stabbed a finger in the air between them. "I've done some checking. I know all about your mother and what she was."

Laney shuddered at the memories Pearl's words conjured up in her mind. The endless fear, waiting and wondering when her mother would be through for the evening. The humiliation of keeping time, thirty minutes a customer.

"You know what they say, the apple doesn't fall far from the tree. You might act all innocent and pure, but you're the same as me."

"I'm not."

Pearl dug deeper into the open wound. "Perhaps you don't sell your body nightly, but you take money from men all the time."

Marc's distraught voice meshed into her thoughts. "Don't listen to her. She's not in her right mind."

Laney's heart broke a little more. "She's correct, though. I do take money from men. I allowed you to pay off my loan. What does that make me if not the same as my mother?"

"It makes you my friend."

Pearl snickered with distain. "Is that what they're calling it these days?"

"I didn't buy your services, Laney." His voice turned pleading. "I paid off your loan because you're my friend. And friends help each other in times of need. I would have done the same for Trey."

She wanted to believe him, *needed* to believe him, but Pearl had done her damage. She'd put an ugly spin on Marc's act of kindness, tainting it forever in Laney's mind.

She had to get away, before she broke down in front of him, in front of Pearl.

As if sensing her desperation to escape, Marc reached out to her, but Laney shoved past him. "Goodbye, Marc."

She strode purposefully through the lobby, not once looking back, not even after she'd pushed through the revolving doors and turned on the sidewalk in the direction of Charity House.

This wasn't how she'd wanted matters to end between them. Nevertheless, she was better off without Marc Dupree in her life. *Right, Lord?*

Right?

With Pearl's voice screeching in his ears, Marc set out after Laney. Hank stopped him at the threshold of his office. "Haven't you hurt her enough already? Can't you leave her with some dignity?"

The scorn in Hank's voice stopped Marc cold. The other man was correct, of course. Marc had to let Laney go. That didn't mean he had to ignore her safety. "Will you see she gets home without incident?"

"Sure, boss. I'll watch over her." Hank's gaze filled with a mixture with accusation, sympathy, and pity. "I always do."

"Holier-than-thou Marc Dupree." Pearl snorted her disgust from behind him. "Always trying to protect his woman of the moment."

Marc gathered his temper with two hard swallows then turned to face Pearl. For the first time since she'd plowed into his office he looked directly into her gaze. Her eyes swam in their sockets, her skin ashen and bloodless. Pearl had gotten ahold of another bottle of laudanum since Shane had left the hotel.

"Where'd you hide the bottle?"

"Does it matter?" She swayed but caught her balance by clawing at his arm. "Now, about your precious little Laney."

"Not another word out of you, Pearl. I mean it."

Her balance wavering, she clutched his arm harder. "Oh, I'm just getting started."

"I'm warning you, now is not the time to push me. I'll take care of you, provide food, clothing and shelter, but I won't stand here and listen to you speak ill of Laney."

A bitter, sinister snarl slipped out of Pearl. The look on her face wasn't human. "Is that threat supposed to scare me? You may be a lot of things, but like I said once before, you don't have it in you to hurt a woman."

Yet he *had* hurt a woman. He'd hurt Laney.

"Perhaps I've changed," he said, his voice low, menace riding under the surface, toying with the last shreds of his control.

"You haven't changed one bit since I first met you." She reached up to pat his cheek, her clammy fingers leaving traces of sweat on his skin. "Such a good man. You might have tried to save my wretched soul, but you never even came close. That makes me your greatest failure."

She buckled over, a violent cough racking her frail body.

Pity running deep, Marc held on to her while she struggled to gain back her control. When she raised her face to his again, the look of utter despair beneath her bravado splintered his anger and gave him hope that he could perhaps save her yet.

"Enough, Pearl. Time for you to get back in bed." He grasped her by the shoulders and with very little effort herded her to the elevators.

She wheezed through another cough. "You're coming with me?"

"I'll get you settled, yes."

They took the first step out of his office side by side. He supported her full weight by the second. On the third, her knees gave out. He scooped her into his arms. "Get Dr. Bartlett," he yelled to Rose.

"It's too late," Pearl whispered.

Marc remembered the countless ugly thoughts he'd had about this woman since she'd run off with his money, all the times he'd rejoiced over her absence from his life.

Yet now that she was back, he didn't want her to die like this. He wanted her to live, to fight for another day. And then another. "Don't give up on me now, Pearl."

Gulping for air, a spasm contorted her face. "I'm sorry, Marc."

A lump formed in his throat. "I'm sorry, too."

"You were too good for the likes of me, Marc Dupree, always too good."

"We've both made our share of mistakes."

Her eyes fell shut, right before she uttered the two words that set him free at last. "Forgive me."

Chapter Twenty-Four

Three mornings later, Laney dragged herself reluctantly awake. Gray, depressing light filtered through the curtains, declaring the start of a new day. As it had every morning since rushing out of the Hotel Dupree, dawn showed up far too soon.

A memory tugged at her tired brain, but Laney brutally shoved it back into a dark corner of her mind and slammed her eyes firmly shut. Her sanity demanded she remain inside her blissfully muddled state a little while longer.

A pounding drummed in her head—rap, rap, rap—growing louder and more forceful with each bang. Still groggy, Laney cracked open her eyes and peered around the room. She tried to focus on anything solid in the shadows, but only watery images danced in front of her.

At least, she slowly realized, the banging had finally stopped.

"Praise the Lord."

She buried her head back into the pillow's softness and tried to relax a few more moments before her day began in earnest. Unfortunately, the sound of the door creaking on its hinges intruded into the silence.

"Laney?" Katherine slipped inside the room. "Are you awake?"

"No," she mumbled into her pillow.

A low chuckle met her response. "Yes, you are."

"Go away, Katherine." Laney tugged the blanket over her head. "It's too early to talk."

"Perhaps with me, but surely you'll speak to Mr. Dupree. He's downstairs, waiting for you on the front porch."

At the mention of Marc's name, all the dreadful memories of three nights ago came crashing through her mind. The scene in his office, the accusations in Pearl's words, the reminder of who Laney's mother was, the apology in Marc's eyes. *No.* She couldn't face him again.

"Tell him to come back later."

Katherine walked to the window and threw open the curtains. A thin thread of light spilled across Laney's bed. "Laney O'Connor, this cowardice isn't like you. You should listen to what Mr. Dupree has come to say to you."

"I can't speak with him. Not now."

Not ever. She was too ashamed, too humiliated over how close she'd come to forging a real friendship with him, one that could have grown into something solid and lasting. For all she knew, she might have become dangerously reliant on him, perhaps even turning to him for help and advice on a regular basis.

What had she been thinking? Even through his proxy, Hank, Laney couldn't continue a relationship with Marc. He was married. Married, married, married. It was imperative she keep reminding herself of that important detail.

Katherine moved to her bedside and sat next to her. "He looks devastated, like he needs a friend."

Unable to bear knowing that he was hurting, Laney nearly relented. "I still can't face him." But, oh, how she wanted to go to him, to ease his pain, to offer him the compassion he must surely need. "It would be wrong."

"You've done nothing but fall in love with a man who obviously loves you very deeply in return."

Laney covered her eyes inside the crook of her arm. "He's married."

Katherine tapped on her raised elbow. "I'm not saying run away with him, I'm saying go talk to him."

Lowering her arm, Laney lashed out at her friend. "Are you defending him, me? *Us?*"

"Do you need defending?"

No. Not yet. But she loved Marc, knowing he was married to another woman. What did that say about her, about her character? "Why did I have to fall in love with him at all?"

"We don't get to choose who we love." Katherine nudged her shoulder. "Go on, Laney. Go talk to him. Maybe it's time you found out what you're made of."

"What if I'm made of the same stuff as my mother?"

Regarding her with blank, patient eyes, Katherine held her gaze. "Loving a man doesn't make you a woman of questionable virtue. Even loving the *wrong* man doesn't make you one."

"Stop being so wise, it's irritating."

"Good. That means I'm getting through to you. Now, get out of that bed." Katherine tugged her to her feet. "And be the woman of faith and honor I know you are."

Laney sighed, wondering if she really was the woman Katherine thought she was, one who could walk away from the man she loved because it was the right thing to do.

Or was she a woman willing to do anything, no matter how wrong or inappropriate, for the love of her man? The only way to find out was to face Marc again. "Tell him I'll be down shortly."

Katherine pulled her into a tight hug. "I'm proud of you."

"You might want to hold off on that opinion until after I talk to him."

"I know what I know. I'll go keep him company while you change."

After her friend left the room Laney didn't waste time waffling over what to wear. A simple dress and hairstyle would have to do. After dressing as quickly as possible, she hurried down the stairs. At the bottom, she stopped and drew in a shaky breath. This was her moment of truth.

She could hear voices coming from the front porch. Katherine was speaking softly with Marc. Laney couldn't quite make out what they were saying, but she thought she heard the word school and house and maybe…books? Was Katherine discussing what they'd come up with so far for the children's education?

Would Marc have some ideas? Would he guide them? Would he—

Enough stalling. This eavesdropping was beneath her.

Stepping onto the porch, Laney's gaze sought and found the only man she would ever love. As he stared back, unmoving, she took in his disheveled clothing, the fatigue and pain etching across his features. Katherine had been right. The man was indeed distraught.

And his eyes held the yearning that lived in her own soul.

Even after Katherine returned inside the house, Laney still hesitated, trapped in her moment of indecision. She wanted nothing more than to rush to Marc, to soothe away his sorrow, to give whatever he needed from her.

But he was a married man. And although she'd made many mistakes in her life, becoming Marc's mistress would not be one of them. "I'm sorry," she said, lowering her head. "I can't do this. I thought I could, but I can't."

Spinning around, she dashed back into the house.

"Laney. Wait." He caught her by the arm before she could climb the staircase to her room. "Stop for a moment and listen to me. I need to tell you—"

"No. I won't sneak around meeting you behind your wife's back, rationalizing my actions because I love you."

His gaze gentled and, for a moment, a portion of his pain seemed to lesson. "I love you, too."

Her stomach dipped. "You're not playing fair."

"I suppose I'm not." He moved closer, touched her arm. "Laney, Pearl is—"

"Your *wife*," she finished for him.

Before he could say another word she rushed to the back of the house. Afraid he might follow her, perhaps wear her down with one of his compelling arguments, she looked frantically around her. The washroom would have to do. She hurried inside, shut the door behind her and pressed her forehead to the hard wood.

Oh, Lord, why? Why are You putting us through this temptation, this trial?

When the expected knock came a few seconds later, she sighed. "Go away, Marc."

"Let me in, Laney."

"Go…a…way."

"I'm not leaving until you hear what I've come to say."

She flattened her palm against the door and thought she felt his warmth, as though he were pressing his hand to the other side in the same spot.

"You're going to have to trust me long enough to listen to what I've come to tell you. But I won't do it through a locked door."

"Don't you understand?" she asked. "I can't keep drawing close to you, knowing how wrong it is."

In a low, firm voice he made one simple appeal. "Trust me."

Trust him. They were back to that, coming full circle, with Laney no closer to surrendering than she had been weeks ago. If only she believed all would turn out well, that the Lord had everything worked out for their good. "I don't know how to trust you, Marc."

"No, I guess you don't."

She'd failed him. She heard the truth of it in his voice. Yet she couldn't make herself take the final leap of faith, couldn't let go of her own self-reliance long enough to give Marc a chance to have his say.

Lord, how do I give Marc what he needs without crossing a line? How do I show him support without losing my honor in the process?

After a long, excruciating moment of silence, Laney dared to whisper his name. "Marc?"

No answer.

Her heart stopped then started again, beating too fast, too erratic. "Marc? Are you still out there?"

Silence.

Hands trembling, she slowly opened the door and peered into the hallway. The *empty* hallway.

Marc had given up on her.

Three days passed without Laney hearing from Marc again. With the children fed and getting ready for bedtime, she lay on her bed, alone, staring up at the ceiling for a moment of respite before saying evening prayers with each of them. If she was honest with herself she'd admit that Marc's silence hurt.

Of course, she hadn't sought him out, either, hadn't once tried to find out how Pearl's health was holding up. She should have at least done that. First thing in the morning Laney would seek out Hank—not Marc, *Hank*—and ask him about Pearl. Perhaps there was something she could do to ease the woman's suffering, especially after living through a similar scenario with her own mother.

Flipping onto her stomach, Laney cradled her chin on her hands and sighed. She hated seeing Pearl suffer, hated watching Marc suffer with her.

Several days of hard thinking had brought her to a few conclusions about herself, none of them pleasant. Laney had not tried very hard to make Marc's life easier. She certainly hadn't been gracious when he'd offered her gifts.

Instead of acknowledging his generosity she'd pushed him away at every turn. She'd been afraid to rely on him, even in small matters. Now he was nursing a sick wife while Laney had thought only of herself, and how Marc's situation affected her. She'd always been willing to take chances for others, but never for herself.

The Laney O'Connor that had walked into the Hotel Dupree a month ago hadn't needed help from anyone. She'd been determined to fix her own problems. She hadn't even tried to rely on God, through prayer and patience.

Now she had to ask herself why?

Had she craved the heady satisfaction of facing and beating the odds on her own? Wasn't that the definition of pride?

And wasn't pride the root of most sin?

Laney knew what she had to do.

Her foray into the land of self-pity and misery was at an end. She had to return to work and do whatever she could to help the man she loved, even if all she could offer was a smooth-running front desk.

Taking action was what Laney O'Connor did best. Now was the time to gather her courage and face Marc again, proving to him—and to herself—that their friendship mattered to her, more than her prideful need to rely only on herself.

Decision made, she jumped off her bed and went in search of Katherine. Once she knew what Laney had planned, her friend was only too happy to take over and settle the children in bed for the night.

Upon entering the Hotel Dupree less than an hour later, Laney wasn't prepared for the shock that stole the air right out of her lungs. Her first impression was that she'd somehow walked into the wrong hotel. But after checking the sign over the entryway two more times, she knew she had the right place.

Taking in the changes, she circled her gaze around the lobby. She was snarling by the time she finished her inspection. Confusion and astonishment made her faint with worry. And anger.

It wasn't just the rancid smoke filling the air, or the layer of grime that had already begun to form on the once shiny fixtures. It was the *feel* of the place. The Hotel Dupree felt more like a saloon than an upscale hotel.

What was Marc thinking?

The clientele mingling in the lobby was not up to his standards. Armed with a temper, Laney headed toward the back of the lobby, stopping short as she came eye to eye with Thurston P. Prescott III.

A sense of foreboding rooted deep inside her soul. "What are *you* doing here?"

Instead of answering her question, his gaze traveled past her face, stopping several inches lower. Under different circumstances Laney would have given into the urge to slap that look off his face. But she needed answers, and from the self-satisfied look on the banker's face, she knew he was the man to ask.

"The question, Miss O'Connor, is what are you doing here?"

She didn't like the hint of triumph in his tone. "I've come to work my shift at the front desk."

"I have all the clerks I need at the moment."

Her stomach rolled. "I don't understand. Where's Mar— Mr. Dupree?"

With an amused, predatory smile, Prescott poked a lit cigar to his lips and grinned around the tattered end. "He's no longer a part of this establishment."

"What does that mean?"

Prescott's smile never wavered. "He sold the hotel to me."

Sold the hotel? The sickening churn in her stomach kicked harder, making it difficult to speak clearly. "But Marc would never sell the Hotel Dupree."

"I can assure you, I speak the truth. We finalized the transaction two days ago."

"But it can't be true. He's worked too hard to make this the most respectable hotel in the West." She spun around, soaking in the changes, understanding them now. Placing her hand against her heart, she took a calming breath. "You've ruined this hotel. What have you done with all the fine crystal and the imported furniture?" She glanced up at the ceiling. "And the exquisite chandelier?"

"Unnecessary extravagances, all of them." He took a long drag from his cigar and blew the smoke in her face. "I sold the most expensive pieces immediately— at a hefty profit, I might add."

Prescott placed a solicitous hand on her arm but she shrugged him loose. "You're nothing but an outlaw."

"Miss O'Connor, I'm in the business of making money. Now come with me."

She narrowed her eyes. "Come with you where?"

He offered his hand with such charm she almost took it, before she noticed the malice behind the gesture. "We'll discuss the terms of my agreement with Mr. Dupree in my office."

His office? Oh. *Oh*. Prescott really was the new owner of the hotel. "What could your arrangement with Marc possibly have to do with me?"

"You'll have to wait and see." He headed to the back of the hotel, not bothering to see if she followed.

Laney dashed after him, the sinking feeling in the pit of stomach churning into waves of despair.

Entering the office behind him, she watched as he went directly to his desk and rummaged through the top drawer. While she waited, Laney surveyed the changes here, too.

Where there had once been order now stood chaos. Papers were strewn everywhere. The pictures on the mantel—gone. The armoire—gone. The grand pieces of furniture carefully selected and placed in perfect harmony with one another—replaced with a serviceable desk and three hardback chairs.

Angry righteousness replaced her confusion. "How dare you do this to him?"

"It would appear, Miss O'Connor, that you don't know your lover so well, after all."

She cringed at both the accusation and the ugly summation of her relationship with Marc.

"Do you want to know why he sold me the hotel?"

"Yes."

"It was for this." Prescott shoved a paper at her.

She took the document, but didn't look down, choosing to keep her gaze planted on his. "What is this?"

"The deed to the house next door to your orphanage, listed in your name."

"What?" She couldn't have possibly heard him right.

Impatience replaced Prescott's previous self-satisfaction. "Try to keep up, Miss O'Connor. Marc Dupree sold this hotel and then purchased the house next door to your orphanage. He mentioned something about turning it into a school for those brats of yours."

Marc had bought them a house to turn into a school?

But that couldn't be true. He wouldn't sacrifice this hotel, not even for the children.

Would he?

He'd paid off her loan, yes. And he'd given her a crate of fruit. But the Hotel Dupree was his security, his future. He'd put his heart into this place.

"I can't believe this," she whispered. But she could believe it. Marc Dupree was the best man she knew, the most generous. Purchasing a house to turn into a school was exactly the sort of thing he would do.

"When did you say Marc sold the hotel to you?"

"Two days ago, he came to my office, offering to sell this hotel for a price I couldn't refuse." He smiled in wicked satisfaction, as if he'd duped Marc somehow. Laney doubted that.

"Once we settled on terms," Prescott continued, "I worked out the details for him to purchase the house next to yours."

At last, she looked down at the document in her hand, read the name on the deed to the house. Her name.

Oh, Marc, you kind man. What have you done?

"Tell me he had money left over after buying this house."

"How would I know that? Once our business was complete he asked that I give you the deed when next I saw you. He must have known you would come here looking for him."

He'd trusted that she would come to him eventually. He'd known her better than she'd known herself. Suddenly there was too much information for her brain to take in. "I...thank you."

"Don't thank me, thank him. To be honest, Miss O'Connor, I can't fathom why the man did this, especially when he'd only just laid his wife to rest. Or perhaps," he gave her a patronizing grin, "I can fathom why he did it, after all."

Her thoughts snapped to attention. "What did you say?"

"I'm not in the habit of repeating myself." He wrapped his fingers around her arm and began ushering her out of his office. "Now, it's time for you to leave."

Laney dug in her heels. "Wait. What did you say about his wife?"

"Tragic, really. She died about three or four days ago. An overdose of laudanum, I heard. But you already know that, don't you?"

"Pearl's dead?" She'd known the woman was on a path of self-destruction. But...dead?

Oh, Lord, no. Laney didn't want Marc. Not like this.

It must have happened just after Marc had come to Charity House, pleading with her to listen to him. She'd been so tangled inside her own despair she hadn't realized he'd needed her compassion.

Thinking back, she recalled his glassy eyes, the sorrow lying just below the surface of his appeals.

He'd come for comfort, and she'd banished him without honoring his request. *Oh, Marc, what you must have gone through.*

"Miss O'Connor." Prescott shoved her forward again, impatience meshing into his words. "I insist you leave my hotel."

Too deep inside her confusion, Laney allowed the man to escort her through the hotel lobby. At the revolving doors, she wrenched her arm free and walked outside on her own steam.

Her mind tried to work through all she'd just learned,

but one thought kept rising above the others. She'd refused Marc's assistance every time he'd offered it. Yet he continued to provide for her and the children, with the final sacrifice of his hotel.

Urgency had her increasing her pace. She had to find him, had to tell him she understood. And beg him to forgive her.

She stopped dead in her tracks.

What if Marc had left town? What if that was the reason he'd given the deed to Prescott?

The clip-clop of horses' hooves and the creaking of wagon wheels streamed together with the chaotic noises in her mind. She glanced around her, looking at everything and yet seeing nothing. The longer she stood rooted to the spot, the more she grieved for Marc, for Pearl, for what might have been had Laney been a kinder person.

She had to find him, had to tell him how sorry she was for his loss, and then she would thank him for his extraordinary gift. As she marched through the streets of Denver, Laney could only think of one person who would know where Marc was staying.

Marshal Trey Scott.

Turning in the direction of the jailhouse, Laney prayed she wasn't too late. She prayed, with all her heart, that Marc hadn't left town.

Chapter Twenty-Five

As it turned out, Marshal Scott had left Denver abruptly, not Marc. Trey's newly appointed deputy, Logan Mitchell, had revealed where Marc was staying, after a little wheedling on Laney's part.

Now that she knew where to find Marc, all she had to do was prepare for the most important conversation of her life. She started with prayer.

Lord, I pray You give me the words that will bring forgiveness and healing, not add more pain, I... She took a deep breath, braced herself, and finally, simply, let go. *I surrender my future into Your hands.*

Peace filled her, the kind she'd never experienced until this moment. Trusting the Lord was so much easier than she'd expected. A hard lesson learned, one she vowed to remember the rest of her life.

Thankful she'd accepted Sally's gold dress as a gift, Laney studied her reflection in the full-length mirror with a critical eye. Tonight, every detail had to be addressed purposely—nothing could be left to chance.

After making a few more adjustments from different angles she focused once more on her reflection. Perfect. She looked just as she had that first night she'd entered the Hotel Dupree. The dress hugged her figure as though it had been made for her, setting off her coloring and adding an air of contentment that hadn't been there the last time.

She took special care with the finishing touch. Twisting her hair on top of her head, she pulled a few tendrils loose and smiled at the result.

"You'll do." She picked up her reticule and secured the strings around her wrist.

She was ready.

Or so she thought. The moment she crossed the room a wave of nervousness shot through her stomach, making her knees buckle. She reached out and steadied herself on the doorjamb. The next hour could very well decide the rest of her life.

No. Anxiety had no place here. She had to surrender her need for control. And just…believe.

Head high, she pushed away from the door and marched briskly down the stairs to the front parlor.

"Well?" She spun in a slow circle. "How do I look?"

Katherine smiled. "Exactly like the first time you went to the Hotel Dupree."

Laney plucked at an invisible thread on her skirt then smoothed the material with surprisingly shaky fingers. "Do you think he'll understand why I'm wearing this dress?"

"Mr. Dupree is a smart man." Katherine leaned forward and kissed her cheek. "He'll know what you're up to."

"Is my timing off?" Laney's heart tumbled to her stomach then bounced back up to her throat. "I don't want Marc to think I'm only coming to him now that Pearl is dead."

"Then tell him that." Always the voice of reason, Katherine squeezed her arm. "Explain how sorry you are for his loss."

Laney considered her friend for a moment. "You're very wise. I'm glad I have you in my life."

"I'm glad, too."

Casting a quick glance around the parlor, Laney pulled one giant gulp of air into her lungs and then stretched out her hand. "Gloves, please."

Smiling, Katherine slapped them into her palm. "I'll be right here waiting for you. I'll want all the details."

"And so you shall have them."

For all her bravado, for all her conviction to trust the Lord, Laney still found herself hesitating on the front porch. She took a slow, calming breath. The gesture did little to dispel her nerves. She was, after all, about to tell the man she loved she wanted him in her life, even if he only wanted her friendship for now.

A wave of doubt crested. *Rely on God's will*, she reminded herself, *not your own*.

With a hard swallow, she shoved the unwanted emotion into submission. This was no time for uncertainty. Yet her feet felt as though they'd accumulated ten pounds of lead, making every step across the porch agonizingly slow.

What happened to all her spunk and fortitude? Where was the Laney O'Connor that only a month ago had defied an arrogant hotel owner, a shady banker and a stern-looking U.S. marshal?

This reluctance was just plain absurd. Pulling herself together, she stepped to the edge of the porch and studied the evening sky. Stars twinkled overhead like white diamonds secured against black fabric. And although the sun had set hours ago, modern gaslights bathed the neighborhood streets in a golden, welcoming glow, as if lighting her path.

Would she find her happy ending tonight?

She had to believe that she would.

But try as she might to think only of what she would say once she found Marc, thoughts of Pearl intruded. Tears pushed at the back of her eyelids, a reminder of the poor woman's struggles, the same Laney's mother had suffered.

No matter how it might seem to outsiders, Laney had never wanted her own happiness at the expense of Pearl's. But she had to remember that she hadn't brought on the woman's agony. Marc's wife had already been on a path of destruction long before she'd come in search of him at his hotel.

Regardless of how she died, Laney had to make sure Marc understood how sad she was for him, how much she loved him and was willing to wait for him to grieve for his wife, no matter how long that might take.

What if he doesn't want me anymore?

No. She couldn't give into doubt now.

At the bottom of the steps she felt her attention pulled to the other side of the fence. Lifting her chin, she connected her gaze with a compelling pair of steel-blue eyes.

Her breathing hitched in her throat. For one, insane moment, every rational thought receded from her mind. But then, the chaos in her head cleared. And she thought, *well, of course he'd come looking for me at the same moment I was heading to find him.*

Riveted into immobility, she continued staring at the handsome man on the other side of the fence. He stared back. Boldly, insistently. *That look*, she thought, that soft, loving gaze sent a shiver tripping along her spine.

His lips curved around a fixed smile.

Oh, my.

You love him, she told herself. *With all your heart.*

The reminder helped her recover the necessary courage to open the gate and motion Marc forward.

He stopped within feet of her and ran his gaze over her from her head to toe and back again. "I must say, you look especially lovely this evening."

"You're looking quite handsome yourself." As though by some sort of silent understanding, he too wore the exact clothing he'd donned the first night they'd met.

Rather than taking away from his severe good looks, the crisp white shirt, red silk vest and matching tie added to the classic elegance and dignity that defined him.

Her feet itched to cross the short divide between them, to throw herself into his arms, but she forced her feet to remain where they were. This was her one chance to show him how much she'd changed since last he'd been here.

He'd given her many gifts during their short acquaintance. She hoped to give him one in return. The one that mattered most. Her trust.

"I have something important to say to you," she began. "But first, I want you to know how sorry I am for your loss. You must know I never wished Pearl dead."

"Nor did I." His eyes clouded over with sadness.

She wanted to reach out to him, to comfort him, but she could see he still had more to say.

"I thought I could change Pearl, save her from the life she'd chosen." Threading fingers through his hair, his eyes darkened to a turbulent blue. "But she didn't want my help. I guess she never did. Her life was a tragedy begun long before I ever met her."

He was probably right. But Laney could see how Pearl's determination to destroy herself hurt him. Although Prescott had told Laney about Pearl's overdose, she wasn't sure she could trust the man to have told her the truth. "How did she die?"

"She took an overdose of laudanum shortly after she railed at you in my office."

Laney's heart sank. "I hate to think our confrontation in your office pushed her over the edge."

"Neither of us killed her. That much I know. Pearl made her choices. She consumed an entire bottle of laudanum after she'd already had too much whiskey in her system. Shane said she might have survived had she stuck to one or the other, but together…" His words died off, the rest of his explanation unnecessary.

Laney sighed. "I'm sorry I didn't listen to you when you came to me the other day. I never stopped to think that Pearl might have died and you needed my comfort."

"These weeks have been hard on us all."

"Forgive me," she said.

"It's I who needs forgiveness." He folded his arms across his chest, as though needing to keep his distance still. "When I first met you, I had a hard heart. I was consumed with taking back what I thought others had stolen from me. But knowing you and loving you changed me. I looked at everything I had worked so hard to accomplish and it all seemed meaningless. Like I was chasing the wind."

"Oh, Marc, I wasn't much better, intentionally misleading you to believe I was untrustworthy. Can you ever forgive me for my foolish pride? For thinking I could face the world alone, without your help?"

"It's never been about me forgiving you. It's always been about you forgiving yourself."

He was right. So, so right. "I know that now. Most of my mistakes were rooted in my pride. I pushed your help away because I wanted to cling to the very independence that in the end provided me with only loneliness and misery. I want you in my life. However you'll have me."

At last, he closed the distance between them and pulled her into his embrace. Burying his face in her hair, he breathed in deeply. "Laney, honey, it was your willingness to fight the odds on the behalf of the children that showed me the meaning of love. I want to live like that, to love like that, to make sacrifices for the people in my life."

Laney's heart constricted, knowing he'd already done so, by selling his hotel. "I know you sold your hotel and bought the house next door for us to start a school. I... That is... Thank you." She tightened her arms around him. "*Thank you* for sacrificing your future for Charity House."

He lifted his head, and gave her the smile she loved so much. "I'm still a very wealthy man. Even if I'd given the hotel away for free I would have had plenty of money to keep our orphanage afloat for a very long time."

It wasn't the revelation of his wealth that took her by surprise, but the way he referred to Charity House as *our orphanage* that told her everything would work out for them.

But just to be sure...

"Are you saying you want to be a part of all this?" Laney waved her hand in the general direction of the house behind her.

"I'm all yours. However *you'll* have me."

She nestled deeper into his arms. "Does that mean you're going to make me an honest woman someday, once you're finished grieving for Pearl?"

"Laney O'Connor, is that your subtle way of asking me to marry you?"

"Only if your answer is yes."

He crushed his mouth to hers for a long, slow, sweet kiss. "That's a yes, in case I didn't make my intentions clear."

Oh, how she loved this man. "Well, then, to avoid any further confusion..."

She sealed her lips to his, the gesture silently promising them both a lifetime of trust in one another, faith in the Lord, and love.

Lots and lots of love.

Epilogue

Six months from the day she'd first walked into the Hotel Dupree, Laney waited for the preacher to give her the cue to enter the main parlor of her home. She couldn't think of a more fitting place to marry the man she loved than right here at Charity House in front of all the children.

Marc had eased into his new role at the orphanage with the same focus and integrity he'd displayed in all other aspects of his life. For a man who had no children of his own, he'd quickly become a much-needed father figure around the house.

After the wedding, he would officially become a permanent member of their family. And Laney couldn't be more pleased.

So far, her wedding day was turning out far better than she'd hoped. The snow had held off another day, despite spitting out a warning the evening before. The sky was a brilliant blue, the sun a bright orange ball of fire, the air crisp and dry.

The children were on their best behavior. Even more surprising, the preacher had arrived on time, a minor phenomenon since he was a traveling man of God who spent most of his time ministering in mining camps, brothels and saloons. They'd been fortunate Pastor Beau had been able to make the trip to Denver this week.

Everything about Laney's wedding day was turning out perfect, except for one minor detail. Katherine. Or rather, Katherine's unusual behavior.

The young woman stood beside Laney, shifting from foot to foot, wringing her hands in a way women twice her age were known to do.

"Katherine, what's the matter?" Laney had never seen her friend so ill at ease. "Anyone looking at you would think you weren't happy about this wedding."

"Oh, Laney, I'm happy for you and Mr. Dupree. So very, very happy." She released a heartfelt sigh. "Truly, I am. Your future husband is the best thing that ever happened to you, to us, to Charity House."

Katherine sounded sincere, yet the tight seam of her mouth and the lines of worry around her eyes spoke of a tension that belied her words. "Then why the sudden nerves? Are you concerned about Marc moving into the house? Is that what's put you in this odd mood?"

"No, of course not. The children need a father and Mr. Dupree is such a good influence. It's..." she leaned backward on her heels and tossed a quick glance into the parlor "...his friend."

"Hank?" But that couldn't be right. Hank wasn't even here. He'd left for San Francisco days ago, having secured a job as a manager at a brand-new hotel.

"No. I'm talking about Marshal Scott. It's...he's... I'm..." She lowered her voice to a whisper. "I'm not comfortable around him."

"Are you afraid of Trey?" Laney couldn't blame

Katherine if she was. Marc's brother-in-law could be rather intimidating. Until he smiled. Then he looked like a big kid in a grown man's body.

Laney would have to make sure Trey smiled at Katherine more often. That gesture alone would help put her friend at ease. Above all else, Laney wanted Katherine comfortable around the lawman, as comfortable as she herself had become despite their initial rocky start. Not only was Trey Marc's family, but he was surprisingly good with the children. In fact, they liked him almost as much as they liked Marc.

Shuddering slightly, Katherine glanced in the parlor once again. "I'm not afraid of Marshal Scott, precisely. It's just, he's so big and he scowls a lot and…" Katherine shook her head "…I'm not being truthful, am I? All right, yes, I find the man a bit daunting. Maybe if he wouldn't frown so much or if he'd try to speak in full sentences around me, maybe then I would find him less…overwhelming."

Overwhelming? Katherine found Trey *overwhelming*? Now wasn't that an interesting word choice? Laney would definitely have to make sure the man smiled at her friend more often. That might actually do both of them some good.

"But today isn't about me, or my silly anxieties." Katherine yanked Laney into a hug and held on tight. "Today is about you and Mr. Dupree and your happily-ever-after. Now." She stepped back and gave Laney a genuine smile. "Are you ready to marry the man of your dreams?"

The question sent Laney's heart kicking hard against her ribs. "Yes, please."

"Well, then, stop stalling and get a move on." Katherine's eyes twinkled with affection as she spun on her heel. "All you have to do is follow me. I know the way."

Smiling after her friend—and relieved Katherine had returned to being, well, Katherine—Laney counted slowly to ten. When she was satisfied she'd waited long enough, she entered the parlor.

Gasps filled the air, as well as a few raucous hoots from the older boys. Everyone she cared about was in this room waiting to witness her wedding. Yet all Laney could concentrate on was the man smiling at her from the other end of the room. Marc. The love her life. The most handsome, kind, honorable man she'd ever known. In a matter of minutes he would become her husband.

But not if she stayed rooted to the spot, staring at him like a lovesick cow. At least he had a smitten expression on his face as well.

Laughing at herself, at him, at them both, she picked up her feet and trekked through the room. Toward her future.

When she stopped in front of Marc he broke with tradition by pulling her into his arms and planting a kiss on her lips. When he finally pulled his head away, he looked very pleased with himself.

Laney was rather pleased with him, too.

"Ready to become my wife?"

"More than ready." She leaned in for another kiss but a masculine clearing of a throat stopped her mid-pursuit.

"Perhaps we should proceed as quickly as possible."

Laney dutifully took her place because, just as Pastor Beau had suggested, she wanted to become Marc's wife *as quickly as possible*.

Instead of reprimanding them for their untraditional

behavior, Pastor Beau gave both the bride and groom an indulgent smile.

Most of the girls at Charity House were a little dazzled by the young rebel preacher. No wonder. Not only was he on fire for the Lord, but he had tawny hair, classically handsome features and mesmerizing eyes. He could have easily found success on the American stage as he had as a traveling preacher. In fact, it was rumored he came from a famous Shakespearean acting family that toured all over the world.

As if to prove Laney's point, a few female sighs filled the air, and then a few more.

Unaware of the attention he was drawing, Pastor Beau opened his Bible and began. "Dearly beloved, we are gathered here to join this man and this woman in holy matrimony…"

With happy tears welling in her eyes, Laney listened intently to every word of the ceremony. When it was her turn to promise to love, honor and cherish Marc, in sickness and in health, for as long as they both shall live, she did so in a bold, strong voice.

She stared lovingly into Marc's eyes as he did the same, silently thanking the Lord for turning their sorrow into joy and their weeping into laughter. Over the last six months, prayer and a shared faith in the Lord had healed the pain of their individual pasts.

Although the wait had seemed interminable, Laney knew they'd been right to hold off getting married until all remnants of the past were truly behind them.

The ceremony came to a close all too quickly. "…I now pronounce you husband and wife."

When Marc pulled her into his arms a second time, he sealed their union with a long, lingering kiss that had the children cheering, Katherine no doubt blushing and Trey laughing as loudly as Pastor Beau.

With her family and friends in the room, with the sound of their happiness ringing in the air, Laney couldn't think of a better way to start her life as Marc's wife. God had protected them through several trials already. And Laney knew that as long as she and Marc continued to allow the Lord to guide them they would be able to face any challenge that came their way.

They had a wild adventure ahead of them and she was ready for every twist and turn to come. Because she knew Marc would never leave her side.

And she would never leave his.

* * * * *

A mother of two young boys, **Naomi Rawlings** spends her days picking up, cleaning, playing and, of course, writing. Her husband pastors a small church in Michigan's rugged Upper Peninsula, where her family shares its ten wooded acres with black bears, wolves, coyotes, deer and bald eagles. Naomi and her family live only three miles from Lake Superior, and while the scenery is beautiful, the area averages two hundred inches of snow per winter. Naomi writes bold, dramatic stories containing passionate words and powerful journeys. If you enjoyed the novel, she would love to hear from you. You can contact her via her website and blog, at naomirawlings.com.

Books by Naomi Rawlings

Love Inspired Historical

Sanctuary for a Lady
The Wyoming Heir
The Soldier's Secret
Falling for the Enemy

Visit the Author Profile page
at Harlequin.com for more titles.

THE WYOMING HEIR

Naomi Rawlings

"What doth the Lord thy God require of thee, but to fear the Lord thy God, to walk in all his ways, and to love him, and to serve the Lord thy God with all thy heart and with all thy soul, To keep the commandments of the Lord, and his statutes, which I command thee this day for thy good?"
—*Deuteronomy* 10:12–13

To Nathanael and Jeremiah, my amazing little boys. May you "grow in grace, and in the knowledge of our Lord and Savior Jesus Christ" (*2 Peter* 3:18).

Acknowledgments

No book could ever make its way from my head to the story in front of you without help from some amazing people. First and foremost, I'd like to thank my husband, Brian. What would I do without someone to cook dinner and watch the kids and love and encourage me through each and every book I write? Second, I'd like to thank my critique partner, Melissa Jagears, for trudging through all the hills and valleys of this story with me. My writing would suffer greatly without your keen eye and brilliant mind. I also want to thank my agent, Natasha Kern, for teaching me about writing and putting up with me even when I'm not that pleasant to put up with (which happens more often than it probably should). And my editor, Elizabeth Mazer, for her helpful suggestions and enthusiasm about my stories. Beyond this, numerous others have given support in one way or another—Sally Chambers, Glenn Haggerty, Roseanna White and Laurie Alice Eakes, to name a few. Thank you all for your time and effort and helping me to write the best books I possibly can.

Prologue

Teton Valley, Wyoming
October 1893

"Hello, Ma." Luke Hayes removed his Stetson and stepped over the threshold to his mother's room. His boots echoed against the sturdy pine floorboards as he moved to where Ma sat at her vanity. A faint, sour scent wound around him, tickling his nose and turning his mouth bitter. The vase of purple coneflowers on the dresser nearly masked it, as did the rose water Ma dabbed at her throat. But the subtle smell of sickness clung to the shadows and haunted the corners, a constant reminder of the enemy that would steal her life.

"You've come to say goodbye," she whispered, her voice tired though she'd barely spoken.

Luke hooked a thumb through a belt loop. "It's time. Can't linger if I want to be back before the snow comes."

She turned to him, and the dreary, lifeless blue of her eyes hit him like a punch to the throat.

"You should be in bed."

"I thought I'd go riding…could ride down the trail with you a ways. To the end of the property at least."

Just like we used to, his throat ached to speak. How many times had they gone riding together? Felt the wind in their faces and the sun on their backs as they galloped through the shadows of the mountains?

Before. Not anymore. Never again.

But a person couldn't convince Ma of that. Luke ran his gaze over her gaunt frame. She'd dragged herself from bed and pulled on some clothes, her shirtwaist and split skirt hanging on her emaciated figure as though more skeleton than flesh. "No more riding. Pa told you as much over a month ago."

She huffed, her skinny shoulders straightening. "Doc Binnings didn't bar me from riding."

"The answer's still no." His words sliced through the room, and he winced. He'd come to say goodbye, not get into an argument, but there seemed to be little help for it with Ma convinced she could go riding.

"There's a letter for your sister on the dresser." She nodded toward the white envelope.

A smile slid up the corner of his mouth. "I'm carrying one from Pa, too, and another from Levi Sanders."

"Levi?" A flush tinged Ma's pale cheeks. "Samantha will like that."

"She'll like hearing from everyone, I'm sure. She'll be even happier to finally come home."

Ma stopped, her hands frozen midway through fastening the gold locket about her neck. "You're bringing her back?"

"Of course. What did you expect?"

"No. Deal with the estate as we discussed, but leave Samantha there."

Not get Sam? The thought stopped him cold. Even if he didn't need to leave for New York to settle his late grandfather's affairs, he still would have gone to fetch his sister home. With Ma nearing the end, Samantha belonged with her family. "It's time she came home."

"I read her letters. She loves that school, makes good grades, will graduate come spring. She needs to stay."

"Ma…" Luke scrubbed a hand over his face.

"I've got a letter for Cynthia, too, on the dresser over beside Samantha's. You'll take that one, won't you?"

Cynthia? His hand stilled over his eyes. He hadn't heard the name of his brother's widow for three years and didn't care to hear it again for the rest of his life.

But Ma was staring at him, hope radiating from her weary eyes.

"You know how I feel about Cynthia." And if Ma wasn't half delusional from her illness, she never would have brought up the confounded woman. "Just mail the letter yourself."

"You're not even going to see—?"

It started then, one of the coughing fits that spasmed through Ma's body. She grabbed the rag sitting beside the rose water and held it to her mouth, planting her other hand on the vanity for support.

"You should have been in bed." Luke strode forward, slipped one arm beneath her knees, and used the other to brace her back before he swooped her in his arms. The coughs racked her body, shaking her slight form down to her very bones. "Breathe now, Ma. Remember what the doc said? You need to breathe through this."

He laid her on the bed and sat beside her, holding the rag to her face. Blood seeped into the cloth, staining her teeth and lips and pooling in the corner of her mouth. The doc had also told him and Pa not to touch the foul cloths, or they could end up with consumption. But he wouldn't watch his mother struggle to keep a simple rag in place.

He braced her shoulders and gripped the cloth until she lay back against her pillows, eyes closed, stringy chestnut hair falling in waves around her shoulders, most of it knocked loose from her bun because of the jerking.

And she'd wanted to ride with him to the edge of the ranch.

He tossed the rag into the pail in the corner, already a quarter filled with sodden cloths, washed his hands in the basin, then moved back to her. The scents of rose water and blood and chronic sickness emanated from the bed.

She opened those dull blue eyes and blinked up at him.

"Are you…" *All right?* He clamped his teeth together. Of course she wasn't all right. Every day she crept closer to death. And every day Sam stayed East was a day forever lost between mother and daughter.

"Luke…promise me." Short breaths wheezed from her mouth.

"Promise you what?" He knelt on the floor, his eyes tracing every dip and curve and line of her features, branding them into his memory lest she not be alive when he returned.

She wrapped her hand around his, her corpselike skin thin and translucent against the thick, healthy hue of his palm. "Th-that you won't tell Samantha how sick I am."

"What do you mean? Haven't you told her yet yourself? Doesn't your letter explain?"

She looked away.

"Ma?" He stroked a strand of limp hair off her forehead. "You have to let Sam know you're sick."

"No." A tear streaked down the bony ridges of her cheek. "If I tell her, she'll come home. She needs to stay and finish school."

"She deserves to make that choice on her own. Deserves the chance to see you before you…" *Die.* He couldn't move the wretched word past the knot in his throat. Ma might not want Sam told about her condition, but Sam would never forgive herself if Ma passed without her saying goodbye. "Surely you want to see Sam again? Surely you miss her?"

Ma squirmed. "Let her finish her schooling, and we'll see each other next summer."

Except Ma wasn't going to live that long. "Sam needs to know. Now."

"I won't let her give up the life she loves to watch me die." She shook her head, her sunken eyes seeking his. "You mustn't tell her. Promise me."

He couldn't do it. He could barely stand to leave Ma as it was, wouldn't if he had any choice in the matter. How could he promise to keep her condition from Sam? Maybe Ma was right, and Sam wouldn't want to come home, but she should know what was going on.

"Luke? Promise?" Ma's voice grew panicked, even desperate.

Something twisted in his gut.

His twin's death three years earlier had been quick, nearly instant. Watching Blake die had hurt, but watching the life slowly drain from Ma? No one should be asked to endure such a thing.

But he couldn't very well leave her knowing he'd denied her last request.

He might never see her again. Even if he got Sam and brought her home, he might be too late.

"I promise." The words tasted bitter on his tongue. "Goodbye now, Ma."

He stood, swiped Sam's letter from the top of the dresser, and left, taking long strides out of her room and through the ranch house before she could thank him.

Before delight from his agreement could fill her face.

Before common sense forced him to rescind his promise.

Chapter One

~❧~

Valley Falls, New York

The simple cotton curtains on the classroom window fluttered with a whispered breeze, while autumn sunlight flooded through the opening in the thin fabric and bathed her in a burst of gaiety. But the warm rays upon Elizabeth Wells's skin didn't penetrate the coldness that stole up her spine, numbing her lungs and turning her fingers to ice.

Elizabeth tightened her grip around the envelope in her hand. She could open it. It wasn't such a hard thing, really, to slip the letter opener inside and slit the top. She just needed a moment to brace herself.

The envelope weighed heavy against her skin, as though it were made of lead rather than paper. She ran her fingers instinctively along the smooth, precise edges. A quadrilateral with two pairs of congruent sides joined by four right angles. The mathematical side of her brain recognized the shape as a perfect rectangle. But the contour of the paper didn't matter nearly so much as what was written inside.

She sighed and glanced down, her gaze resting on the name printed boldly across the envelope.

Miss Elizabeth Wells
Instructor of Mathematics
Hayes Academy for Girls

Forcing the air out of her lungs, she slit the envelope from the Albany Ladies' Society and slipped out the paper.

Dear Miss Wells...

The jumble of words and phrases from the letter seared her mind. *Regret to inform you...revoking our funding from your school...donate money to an institution that appreciates women maintaining their proper sphere in society.* And then the clincher. The Albany Ladies' Society not only wanted to stop any future funding but also requested the return of the money they had already donated for the school year.

And they called themselves ladies. Elizabeth slammed the letter onto her desk. Two other organizations had also asked that money previously donated—and spent—be returned. Then there were the six other letters explaining why future funding would cease but not asking for a return of monies.

This request galled more than most. If even women cared nothing about educating the younger generation of ladies, then who would? She'd spoken personally to the Albany Ladies' Society three times. Her mother was a member, and still, at the slightest bit of public opposition to the school, the society had pulled their funding.

She stuffed the letter back into the envelope, yanked out her bottom desk drawer, and tossed it inside with the other letters—and the articles that had started the firestorm.

She shouldn't even be receiving letters from donors and disgruntled citizens. Her brother, Jackson, was the head accountant for Hayes Academy for Girls, not her.

But then Jackson wasn't responsible for the mess the academy was in.

She was.

She'd only been trying to help. With the recession that had hit the area following the economic panic in March, the school had lost students. A lot of students. Many parents couldn't afford to send their daughters to an institution such as Hayes any longer. And without those tuition dollars, the school risked being seriously underfunded. So she'd written an editorial delineating the advantages of female education and girls' academies and had sent it to the paper.

She'd hoped to convince a couple families to enroll their daughters or perhaps encourage donations to the school. Instead, she'd convinced Mr. Reginald Higsley, one of the reporters at the Albany *Morning Times,* to answer her.

On the front page.

She pulled out the newspaper, the headline staring back at her with thick, black letters.

Excessive Amount of Charity Money Wasted on Hayes Academy for Girls

Since the economic panic in March and the ensuing depression, countless workers remain unemployed, food lines span city blocks, four railroad companies have declared bankruptcy, three

Albany banks have failed and myriad farmers have been forced to let their mortgaged lands revert back to lending institutions. But not six miles away, in the neighboring town of Valley Falls, community and charity money is being wasted on keeping open an unneeded school, Hayes Academy for Girls.

It has long been recognized that the overeducating of females creates a breed of women quick to throw off their societal obligations to marry and raise children. It is also well-known that educated women are more concerned with employment opportunities and their own selfish wishes rather than fulfilling their roles as women....

Elizabeth's stomach twisted. No matter how many times her eyes darted over the words, the opening made her nearly retch. The article went on to compare the lower marriage rate of women with college educations to those with only grammar schooling. It examined the divorce rate, also higher among women with college educations. And then the reporter turned back to the topic of Hayes Academy's funding, questioning why anyone would waste money teaching women to throw off their societal responsibilities while the poor of Albany were starving.

Elizabeth shoved back from her desk and stood. Charity money "wasted" on keeping an "unneeded" institution open? How could the reporter say such a thing, when the academy prepared young women to attend college and qualify for jobs that enabled them to support both themselves and their families? An educated woman could certainly make a fuller contribution to society than an uneducated one.

Yet since the article had appeared, the academy had lost half of its financial backers.

A burst of giggles wafted from outside, and Elizabeth rose and headed to the window. In the yard, groups of girls clustered about the pristine lawn and giant maple trees with their reddening leaves. They laughed and smiled and talked, flitting over the grass alone or in packs, their eyes bright, their spirits free, their futures optimistic.

She sank her head against the dark trim surrounding the window. "Jonah, why did you go and die on me?" The words swirled and dissipated in the empty room. As though she'd never spoken them. As though no one heard or cared what a mess Hayes Academy had become when its founder unexpectedly died three months earlier.

If Jonah Hayes were still alive, he would know how to get more donors. He would write an editorial on women's education, and people would listen, enrolling their daughters at the academy. And in the interim, while the school struggled through the recession, he would likely donate the money Hayes Academy needed to continue operating.

But Jonah Hayes was gone, and his estate had been tied up for three months, waiting for the arrival of his grandson heir from out West. In her dreams, the grandson came to Valley Falls, filled Jonah's position on the school board, convinced the other board members to keep Hayes Academy open, obliterated all opposition to the academy.

Of course, the heir had to arrive first.

And at this rate, the academy would be closed and the building sold before the man got here.

The students returned from lunch, a cascade of laughter and conversations fluttering in their wake. Elizabeth tried to smile, tried to straighten her shoulders and stand erect, tried to be grateful for the chance to teach her students—an opportunity that she might not have in another month.

Tried, but failed.

"Miss Wells?" The shining blue eyes of Samantha Hayes, Jonah's granddaughter and one of the academy's most intelligent pupils, met hers. "Meredith, MaryAnne and I are going to have a picnic along the stream that runs through Grandfather's estate tonight. Do you want to join us?"

Elizabeth did smile then, though it doubtless looked small and halfhearted. How enjoyable to spend the evening chatting with the girls beside the clear stream, watching autumn swirl. If only she didn't have to find a way out of the financial mess she'd created for Hayes Academy, which meant she had an appointment for tonight with the extra set of ledgers she kept for the school. "I'd best not. Thank you for asking."

"Are you feeling all right?" Concern flitted across the young lady's face. "You look pale."

"I'm fine, but…well, now that I think of it, I could use your help on a certain project tomorrow."

Samantha's eyes danced, light from the window streaming in to bounce off her golden tresses. The girl was breathtaking. More than breathtaking, really. Elizabeth smiled. Little surprise her brother, Jackson, had started courting Samantha Hayes last spring. Half the men of Albany would be courting her if they had any sense about them.

"Is it more calculus?"

She did smile then, full and genuine. If only all her students were as exuberant over calculus as Samantha Hayes. "I'm afraid not. I've some ciphering to do tonight, and I'd like for you to check my sums."

Samantha excelled at finding discrepancies in account books, whether they be the school's or Jonah Hayes's or Elizabeth's personal ledgers. "Sounds fun. Should we meet at the picnic spot around lunchtime tomorrow, then?"

If Samantha knew the state of Hayes Academy's accounts, she wouldn't be nearly so happy. Oh, well, the younger girl would find out tomorrow.

"Yes, that will be fine, but you'd best take your seat now." Elizabeth moved to the chalkboard and turned toward her students. Thirteen expectant faces stared back at her. Last year, she'd had twenty-three in her advanced algebra class.

"Today we're going to learn about…"

But she couldn't finish. How could she, with the school struggling to pay its bills and teachers' salaries? Did the girls understand how much funding had been pulled from the academy within the past five days? That they might not be able to finish their final year of high school if more students didn't enroll or if new funds couldn't be raised?

And part of it was her fault. Oh, what had ever possessed her to write that editorial?

"Miss Wells, are you feeling okay?"

"Can we do something for you?"

"Did you forget what you were saying?"

The voices floated from different corners of the room. Elizabeth plastered a smile on her face. "Forgive me, class, but I've decided to change the lesson. We'll review today."

Her hand flew across the chalkboard as her mind formed the numbers, letters and symbols without needing to consult a textbook for sample equations. "I'm giving you a surprise quiz. Take the next half hour to finish these quadratic equations, and we'll check them at the end of class." She wiped her chalk-covered hands on a rag and turned.

A shadow moved near the open classroom door, and the darkened frame of a man filled the doorway.

A man. At Hayes Academy for *Girls*. What was he doing here?

"Can I help you?"

He entered and dipped his head. "Excuse me, ma'am." A Western drawl lingered on the rusted voice.

"You're here!" Samantha screeched.

Elizabeth nearly cringed at the unladylike sound, but Samantha took no notice as she sprang from her desk and rushed toward the gentleman. "I can't believe you finally came. I missed you so much!" Samantha threw her arms around him for all the world to see.

Most unladylike, indeed. Did Jackson know about this other man? These were hardly fit actions for a girl who'd had an understanding with another man since last spring.

"Samantha…" Elizabeth drew up her shoulders and stepped closer. Their quiz forgotten, the other students watched the spectacle. "Sir, if the two of you would accompany me into the hallway. Students, please continue working."

The girls returned to their work—or attempted to. Half still peeked up despite their bent heads.

Elizabeth moved to the door and held it for Samantha and the stranger. Neither moved. She anchored her hands to her hips and ground her teeth together. Of all the days. Didn't the Good Lord know she hadn't the patience for such an interruption this afternoon?

The man hugged Samantha, bracing her shoulders with a hand that held…*a cowboy hat?* Elizabeth blinked. Surely she didn't have a cowboy in her classroom. Her eyes drifted down his long, lanky form. He wore a blue striped shirt, some type of leather vest, a brown belt and tan trousers complemented by a pair of what could only be called cowboy boots. And was that a red kerchief around his neck?

Plus he was covered in dust—whether from traveling or working with cows, she didn't know—but she could well imagine the dust embedding itself on the front of Samantha's—

A cowboy. From out West.

No. It couldn't be.

But it was. She knew it then, as surely as she knew how to solve the quadratic equations on the board. Samantha clung to her brother.

The Hayes heir.

The man who held the power to either continue Hayes Academy or close the school for good.

"Samantha?" Elizabeth's vocal cords grated against each other as she spoke, but she had to get her student and Mr. Hayes out of the classroom.

Finally, the girl pulled back from her brother and looked around the roomful of staring students. She flushed and moved into the hall, the dark skirt of her school uniform swishing about her ankles. The cowboy followed but only to crush his sister against him in another embrace.

Elizabeth wasn't sure whether to roll her eyes or scream.

Luke Hayes hadn't hugged his sister in three years, two months and thirteen days—not that he'd been counting—and he didn't plan to stop hugging her because some fancy teacher squawked at him like a broody hen dead set on guarding her eggs.

"I'm sorry, Sam. I didn't mean to get you in trouble," he spoke against her head, still unable to unwind his arms from her.

"It's all right," came her muffled reply.

She'd grown taller and curvier since he'd seen her last. Looked grown-up, too. Her hair was done up in a puffy bun, not long and free as it had been in the Teton Valley. And she smelled different, no longer of sunshine and wildflowers but like fancy perfume. He tightened his hold. He should have come and yanked her out of this school sooner, regardless of what Pa had to say about it. "I missed you. Can't rightly say how much."

Inside the classroom, the teacher said something in that stern voice of hers. Then the distinctive clip of a lady's boots on wood flooring grew louder, and the door closed with a *thunk*. "Samantha Hayes, what is the meaning of this?"

Sam pulled away from him, her eyes finding the floor. "I'm sorry, Miss Wells. I didn't mean to make a scene. This is my brother, Luke, from Wyoming."

The hair on the back of his neck prickled. Sam didn't need to cower like a whipped dog because she had hugged him. He crossed his arms and met the teacher's stare.

Hang it all, but she was a beautiful little thing, with deep hazel eyes and a wagonload of reddish-brown hair piled atop her head.

Her name should be Eve, for if ever God had created a perfect woman, she was it. Adam would have taken one look at that long, smooth face, milky skin and sparkling hazel eyes and been lost.

Good thing he wasn't Adam.

"Sir?"

He swallowed and took a step back, while Sam snickered beside him. Why was he staring? Pretty or not, she was a city woman—just the type he avoided. Citified women didn't fare well out West. They squealed when a bear meandered into the yard, left the door open on the chicken coop and complained about getting water from the hand pump—he knew. His twin brother had up and married one of the useless critters.

He scowled, but still couldn't pull his eyes from the gentle curve of the teacher's cheek or the soft pink of her lips. "Excuse me, ma'am, but I didn't catch your name."

"Miss Elizabeth Wells."

Did she know a strand of hair had fallen from her updo and hung beside her cheek? Or that she had a big smear of white—most likely chalk—smack on the front of her plum-colored skirt?

"I'm Samantha's mathematics instructor and private tutor." She arched an eyebrow, a rather delicate and refined eyebrow.

He snuck a hand atop Sam's shoulder. "Your letters haven't said anything about having trouble with mathematics."

Sam smiled up at him, that familiar toothy grin that had always wriggled straight into his heart. Except the grin didn't look quite so toothy anymore, and her lips had a rather refined curve to them. "Oh, no, Luke, not trouble. Miss Wells instructs me in preliminary calculus after school. That way I can head straight into the calculus class when I attend college next fall."

College next fall? He pulled his hand from her shoulder. "Sam, we've got a load of things to talk about, what with Grandpa's passing an' all. Go on and gather your belongings. You're coming to the estate with me. I've already arranged it with the office."

Her face lit up like sunlight sparkling off a cool mountain stream. "May I be excused from classes early, Miss Wells?"

The teacher's gaze went frigid, those beautiful eyes likely to turn him into a pile of ice. "If the office has granted you leave, I've no authority to say otherwise."

Luke bit back a cringe. He wouldn't say the office had said yes. Exactly. He'd just handed a letter explaining the situation to the secretary, who would probably give it to the boss lady.

"Thank you, Miss Wells." Samantha gave him a brief, tight hug before pulling away. "It'll only take a moment to pack a bag."

"No, Sam, not a bag." He slung his Stetson atop his head. "All of your belongings. You won't be returning."

The teacher let out a little squeak, her hand flying up to clutch the cameo at her neck. "Surely you don't mean to pull one of our brightest students from the academy. Why Samantha's..."

He shut out the teacher's prattling and focused on Sam. Her face had turned white as birch bark.

Confound it.

He should rip out his tongue and hang it up to dry. He hadn't meant to tell Sam she was leaving like that, but he'd spent most of his trip out East pondering things. He'd promised not to tell Sam about the consumption, but he'd never promised not to take her out of her fancy school. If he could get Sam to make a clean break from this place, convincing her to come home with him should be easy as coaxing a thirsty horse to the drinking trough. She could help him sort through Grandpa's things for the next few weeks, and then she'd be off to Wyoming before she had a chance to think about missing her school.

He stepped forward and rubbed Sam's back. "Now don't go bawling on me, Sam. It's just that—"

"How could you take me from here?" Her voice quivered.

How could he?

How could he *not*? Grandpa was gone now—there was no kith or kin anywhere in the whole of the state of New York to tie her here. Surely she didn't expect to be left here without anyone to look after her. She must hanker to see Ma and Pa and the ranch. To fall asleep to the sound of coyotes yipping and awake to the scent of thin mountain air. To see Ma before she died.

"Samantha." The teacher laid a slender hand on Sam's arm. "Why don't you head to your room and freshen up? I've a matter to discuss with your brother." Her eyes shot him that ice-coated look again. "Privately."

Sam fled toward the staircase, muffling her sobs in her hand. And something hollow opened inside his chest, filling him with a familiar ache.

"Mr. Hayes, I do not appreciate having my class interrupted or one of my students upset."

He turned back toward the teacher. Though the woman only reached his shoulder, she acted like she commanded an army. A firm line spread across those full lips, a hint of fire burned beneath her cool eyes, and her face looked as blank as a riverboat gambler's.

He'd gone and raised her hackles, all right. She probably had a hankering to sit him in the corner or send him to the office or apply some other schoolboy-type punishment.

He tipped his hat. "I'm sorry. I'd no intention of disrupting anything, miss—" or of sending Sam away in tears "—but I haven't seen my sister for a fair piece, and I wasn't keen on waiting any longer."

Not that he was about to plop down and explain the bad blood between Pa and Grandpa to the woman.

"I understand that, sir, and I appreciate your apology."

"If you'll excuse me, then." He dipped his head and shifted toward the stairs. "I best find her and get on to the estate."

"Mr. Hayes." The teacher stepped in front of him, a bold move for someone so tiny. "You can't take Samantha from here."

He crossed his arms. "My sister's not rightly your concern."

"Yes, she is. You made her my concern when you sent her here."

"Now listen. I never sent her here and neither did Pa. This school thing was all Grandpa's idea. Pa just wanted to get Sam away from the Teton Valley while we dealt with a few troubles. We figured she'd come live with

Grandpa and go to the local high school hereabouts. No one ever mentioned Sam coming to this fancy school until she was already here."

But that bit of information seemed to have no effect on the teacher. Her eyebrows didn't arch, her jaw didn't drop and her eyes didn't flash with questions. Instead, she pointed her finger and shoved it in his chest. Hard.

"Be that as it may, she has been a student here for over three years without your interference, and she has done exceptionally well. I'm sure you want the best for your sister's future, and she thrives in this environment. She'll make an excellent student at Maple Ridge College a year from now."

College. There it was again. That lousy word that threatened to keep Sam out East for good rather than home where she belonged. "Look, I appreciate what you're doing here, trying to educate women and all. And if you want to teach fancy mathematics to the girls in your classroom, you go right ahead."

"It's advanced algebra."

"Call it whatever you want. But with no more family in the area, there's nothing to keep Sam here. My sister will finish her schooling in Wyoming and won't be attending college next fall. She's coming home with me as soon as I straighten Grandpa's affairs."

The teacher raised her chin, her small nose jutting arrogantly in the air. "This conversation is becoming ridiculous."

"I agree."

"I'm sure if we schedule an appointment to discuss the situation with your sister and the headmistress, we could reach a more satisfying conclusion for all affected."

Oh, he could think of a satisfying conclusion, and it involved him and Sam hightailing it out of this confounded school, never to return. "I said my sister won't be returning, and I meant it. She's got obligations at home."

"Mr. Hayes, you are making a grave and regrettable mis— Is that a *gun?*" Her voice squeaked, all semblance of propriety fleeing while she stared at the Colt .45 holstered on his right hip.

Somewhere down the hall a door closed, and the clip of shoes on flooring resonated against the walls. He shifted his weight to his left leg and cocked his right hip, purposely exaggerating the firearm's presence. Not that he wanted to scare her, but she was a sight to behold with her perfect little feathers all in a ruffle. "We use them where I come from."

Unfortunately, she didn't stay flustered quite long enough. She clamped her hands to her hips and glared. "I'd thank you to remove it from the premises at once. We've no need for guns at Hayes Academy. Why, the entire class probably saw it."

Luke crossed his arms. "I seem to recall something in the U.S. Constitution about citizens bearing arms."

"Yes, well, certainly not in a school."

"Now look here—"

"Mr. Luke Hayes, I presume."

Luke flicked his eyes toward the tall woman coming down the hall. She moved the way a shopkeeper did when suspecting someone of pocketing a gold watch— quickly and full of purpose.

The woman stopped and extended a wrinkled hand. "What a pleasure to meet you. I'm Josephine Bowen, headmistress here at Hayes Academy."

"Luke Hayes." He gave the hand a hearty shake.

"I trust there's no problem?" The headmistress slid a stern gaze toward Miss Wells.

He'd seen similar looks on teachers' faces plenty a time in his youth. It always preceded him being dragged to the front of the schoolroom for a switching.

But Miss Wells didn't so much as flinch under the heated stare. "Mr. Hayes and I were discussing his sister's schooling. Now if you'll both excuse me, I should return to my students."

"Yes, Miss Wells." The headmistress nodded. "Do return to your class, please, and thank you for taking time to make Mr. Hayes feel welcome."

He rubbed his jaw. Hopefully the rest of Valley Falls didn't plan to "welcome" him the way the fiery little teacher had.

Miss Wells gave a tight smile as she opened the classroom door, then disappeared inside.

"Mr. Hayes, we're simply delighted to have you." The headmistress's overly bright voice echoed through the hallway, but she wasn't lecturing him on pulling Sam out of school. Then again, she probably hadn't read his letter yet, or she'd be bawling like a cow in labor.

"Hayes Academy has benefited greatly from your grandfather's generosity, and we look forward to doing the same with you," she continued.

Seeing how he'd never met his paternal grandfather, he hadn't the foggiest notion what Grandpa's *generosity* entailed. "I haven't talked to Grandpa's lawyer yet. In what ways, exactly, has my grandfather aided you?"

Miss Bowen beamed up at him. "Where, sir, do you think the name Hayes Academy comes from?"

He'd figured as much.

"Twenty years ago Jonah Hayes donated the land that this school sits on and a good portion of the funds to build it." The headmistress clasped his hand. "Three years ago we used another donation to replace the windows on the second floor and renovate the grounds. Surely you noticed the horticulture as you came in? But right now, we're simply hoping to—"

"I'm sorry, but I…" *Won't be making any donations.* The words turned to dust in his mouth. The headmistress's severe face shone with delight, and he'd already upset enough womenfolk since walking into this school. Two an hour ought to be his limit. "Settling Grandpa's estate is a mite complicated. I don't know how much I can promise."

Her shoulders sagged—if that were possible for a woman who exuded perfect posture. "Of course, I understand it will take time to fully grasp the reins of your grandfather's financial concerns. But I do hope you'll bear in mind that, while your grandfather left a wonderful legacy, in order for it to be enjoyed by future generations, we must all endeavor to keep the legacy alive. Perhaps the board members call fill you in on some of your grandfather's other contributions when you meet them."

"Board members?" This whole school business was growing a bit too involved. He took a step backward and glanced toward the stairway. The hot, stale air inside the building clung to his skin, and the hallway's white walls and dim lights were a mite too suffocating. He needed to get outside, breathe some fresh air, feel the sun on his face. What was keeping Sam?

"The school board meets once a month." Miss Bowen's grip tightened on his arm, her nails digging in a tad too forcefully. "Of course you'll fill your grandfather's seat. What a shame you missed last night's meeting, though. We truly needed someone present to keep the needs of Hayes at the forefront. Otherwise I'm afraid our precious institution gets eclipsed by the needs of the nearby college and boys' school. Unfortunately the most I can do now is provide you with a copy of the minutes."

"Uh, sure," he mumbled, then stuck a finger in his collar and pulled, but that didn't stop the tight feeling in his throat.

"But I will be able to introduce you to the board at the banquet tomorrow night. How marvelous that you've arrived in time to attend!"

"Banquet?" he croaked.

"Yes, the annual banquet for Maple Ridge College and its two preparatory schools, Hayes Academy for Girls and Connor Academy for Boys. All are located here in Valley Falls, but as most of the board members are Albany businessmen, the banquet is held in Albany. The Kenmore Hotel. Seven o'clock."

Seven o'clock. Albany. Tomorrow night. These fancy eastern women wanted money, his gun off, his sister in school, his presence at some uppity banquet and him seated on a stuffy school board. And he'd only been off the train an hour.

What demands would they come up with tomorrow? And how was he ever going to survive a month?

Chapter Two

Mug of coffee in hand, Luke stood at the French doors in his grandpa's study, looking out over the estate's immaculate back lawn. To the west, the Catskill Mountains, shadowed in blue and gray, rose over the fields and trees like sentinels guarding the land below. Pretty enough, but not anything close to the untamed wilderness he hailed from.

He rubbed a hand over his face.

What was he even doing in New York State, standing in a fancy house that he'd somehow inherited rather than Pa?

You be careful out there, Pa had told him before he left. *Your old codger of a grandfather was awful wily. Wouldn't surprise me if he found some way to chain you to that wretched estate of his, even from his grave.* The tension had risen like an old, unhealed wound still festering between Pa and Grandpa despite one of them being cold and buried. *Probably ruined Sam in the few years he had her.*

Not once in his twenty-eight years had Pa said anything good about Grandpa. Luke had about fallen over three years ago when Pa sent Sam off to the man. But the ranch had been no place for a young girl after Blake's death, and she'd needed to go somewhere.

Someone rapped at the office door, and Luke turned.

"I'm here…like you asked."

Oh, Sam was there all right. With a face chiseled in granite.

His boots sunk into some highfalutin gold and burgundy rug as he walked behind Grandpa's desk. With lions' heads carved into eight columns and sprawling paws to serve as feet, the desk belonged in a king's throne room rather than a study and wasn't something he cottoned to sitting behind. Still standing, he gestured to her. "Sit."

Head high, back rigid, she took dainty steps toward a gilt chair with blue cushions that faced the desk. She still wore that lifeless school uniform of a white shirtwaist and navy skirt, the black armband around her right sleeve indicating she was in mourning for a man he'd never met. And yet, she carried herself like a lady. Maybe that was the problem. She wasn't so much the girl he remembered anymore, but a woman.

A *citified* woman.

He cleared his throat and placed his half-empty coffee mug on the desk.

She tilted her nose into the air. "You shouldn't set that on the wood. It could ruin the finish."

He lifted his eyes, and their gazes collided. He set his jaw. She straightened her spine. He narrowed his eyes. She raised her chin. Somewhere outside, a bird chirped and a servant called. A door closed on the floor above, and footsteps plodded down the hall. But neither of them moved.

"Since I inherited this desk, along with the rest of the estate," he said slowly, his eyes still burning into hers, "I reckon it's not your concern how I treat it."

"You shouldn't use phrases like 'I reckon,' either. It's most unbecoming."

He gripped the edge of the desk and leaned over it. "I'm not interested in being 'becoming,' Samantha. I'm interested in settling this slew of money Grandpa left me and taking you home. Where you were born, where you were raised and where you belong."

"You can't make me leave."

Figured stubbornness was the one thing that fancy school hadn't stripped from her. "Don't you tell me what I can and can't do."

"I can't tell you what to do? What gives you the right to tell me?" She jumped from the chair, her hands balled into fists at her sides. "I'm staying here and graduating, then I'm going to college to study mathematics and architecture. Because I want to be an architect one day."

Her tongue lingered over the word *architect,* and her eyes burned with a fierce passion. "Not that you've bothered to ask why I want to go to college."

He didn't know whether to laugh or bang his head against the wall. At least Sam had something she wanted to do, some reason for avoiding their family—though she'd evidently had the good sense not to mention such a ridiculous notion in her letters to him.

Had probably told Ma all about it, though.

A woman architect. Who'd ever heard of such a thing?

"Well, aren't you going to say something?" she snapped.

He rubbed the back of his neck. "That's a fine dream

you've got, Sam." Or a crazy one. "But I've got to take you home before you go off chasing after college."

"You don't. Ma would want me to stay here. I just got a letter from her last week saying how much she loved hearing about how happy I am in Valley Falls."

Of course Ma would say that. But then, Ma hadn't exactly told Sam about her consumption, either. And if Ma were here, watching his conversation with Sam right now, she'd be upset with the way he was handling things.

He rolled his shoulders, trying to loosen the knots tightening his muscles. If he could manage a ranch with five thousand head of cattle, he could convince Sam to go back home while still keeping his promise. Couldn't he? "Look, I'm sorry for how I brought up your leaving at school. I didn't mean to yammer about it in front of your teacher. The words just slipped out, when you talked about packing a bag. But you can't stay in New York now that Grandpa's passed. Who would look after you? Besides I need your help around the estate for the next few weeks while we get ready to leave.

"You can start going through the things in Grandpa's room. You know better than me what should be kept or sold off. I figured Pa might cotton to a couple of keepsakes." Which was probably more a dream than anything, given that Pa hadn't talked to Grandpa in over thirty years. "The sooner we sort through this estate, the sooner we can get home."

"I cared about Grandpa," she said, nodding toward the black band around her upper arm. "And I'm happy to sort through his things, but don't you try using that as a way to get me out of school. There will be plenty of time for me to sort through things outside of school hours. Come Monday morning, I'll be back at Hayes Academy. And I'm not going to Wyoming."

Had Sam been this disagreeable three years ago? He tried to envision it but ended up with the mental picture of a sweet girl crying over her injured cat in the barn. "I happen to love you, and I happen to want my sister with me, under her family's care."

"If you loved me, you'd let me stay. I love it *here!* This place is my life."

Love it. She once said that about the Teton Valley. "What about Ma and Pa? You haven't seen them for nigh on three years." *And Ma might not be around in another year.*

She ducked her chin and toyed with the fabric of her skirt. "Do they know you're trying to take me away, trying to quash my dream?"

A fist tightened around his heart. His sister stood before him, her body tall and womanish, her eyes alive with hope and passion, her mind determined to win their argument. He'd had a dream once, too—one he shared with Blake about buying a cattle ranch. No one had told him that he couldn't. If anything, Ma and Pa had encouraged him and Blake to make their own ways in life. And they had.

And while he'd been out West, grieving Blake and seeing to the cattle ranch that now belonged solely to him, Sam had grown up, become a woman.

But woman or not, she still had a dying ma in the Teton Valley, and he had a promise to keep. Except didn't he also have a duty to reunite his sister and mother before it was too late? "I'm not trying to quash anything, Sam. Ma and Pa miss you. Is it so hard to believe they want to see you again?"

Her back went rigid as a fence post. "*They* sent me away."

"Come on now. Once you get back home and see some of your old friends, things won't seem so bad. Levi Sanders took over his pa's ranch a year back, and he's looking for a good wife who knows the ways of a ranch. Not a silly city woman who can't tell the front end of a horse from the rear. Here." He dug in his pocket and held out the creased envelope. "Levi sent you this letter."

She clutched her hands together defiantly, but her actions didn't hide the moisture shimmering in her eyes.

He blew out a breath. What was he to do with a girl who was hard as iron one minute and all weepy the next? "Take the letter, Sam, and stop being so all-fired stubborn."

"What about Cynthia and Everett? Are you forcing them to go back, as well?" she whispered furiously.

He froze, a flood of bloody images he couldn't erase scalding his mind. "I wouldn't take them back West for all the land in the Teton Valley."

"They're—"

"Enough." He slashed the air with his hand, cutting her off. "We're discussing you, not the woman responsible for Blake's death. Now take the letter." He shoved the envelope across the desk as a knock sounded on the door.

The butler poked his head inside. "Mr. Hayes? Mr. Byron, the lawyer, is here for your meeting."

"Thank you." But his gaze didn't leave Samantha.

She huffed, stood and snatched the letter. "Fine. I'll read it. And I'll reply. But I'm not going back to Wyoming. I'm graduating from Hayes Academy, and then

I'm attending college. I'm going to become an architect one day. You just see if I don't." A tear slipped down her cheek before she flew out of the room.

Luke blew out another breath and rubbed the heel of his palm over his chest, but the action didn't quell the pain in his heart. He should have never let Pa send her away, should have stood up to his sire the moment Pa had suggested Sam had to leave after Blake died. But he hadn't, and now he was good and stuck.

He couldn't drag his sister, crying and screaming, away from a place she loved. And she wasn't about to come willingly…unless he told her about Ma. But then he'd be breaking his promise, and a man couldn't just up and ignore a promise like that.

His fingers dug into the polished wood top of the desk. If he did nothing else on this confounded trip, he'd convince Sam to come home on her own.

If only he could figure out how.

Elizabeth's head ached, her neck muscles had turned into a mass of knots and her stomach roiled as though it would heave out her lunch—despite the fact she hadn't eaten any.

She could blame most of her discomfort on Luke Hayes.

She'd grown up with a politician father. She'd seen him, her younger brother, Jackson, and even her mother wheedle donations more times than she could count. Goodness, *she* had wheedled donations before. She knew the best way to go about it. Smile. Look pretty. And agree with everything the potential donor said.

Not three hours earlier, the man who could save Hayes Academy had stood in front of her. She hadn't smiled. She'd probably looked a fright with chalk on her skirt and her hair askew. And she'd disagreed with everything he had said.

Goodbye, Hayes Academy.

She sighed. Was she was being too hard on herself? Luke Hayes had interrupted her quiz and then pulled her brightest pupil out of school. Certainly he didn't expect her to smile and say, "Yes, that's fine. Ruin your sister's future. I don't care in the least."

She opened her bottom desk drawer and stuffed into her satchel the letters she needed to work on the ledgers. He had no right to rip Samantha out of class then spout off about his sister not being her concern. Of course she was concerned—she knew exactly what the girl was going through. The battle was all too familiar.

What do you mean, you're going to college?

A pretty girl like you should find a husband.

Just because one man jilted you, doesn't mean the next will.

A college degree? What's wrong with the schooling you already have? Why do you need more?

The sharp comments twined through her memory. Why should her desire to teach mathematics matter, when she could get married and have children? People had been asking her that for six years, and now Mr. Hayes had said the same about Samantha.

Maybe if she had explained the possibilities that awaited Samantha after she had a high school diploma and college degree, he'd let his sister continue her education.

Maybe.

But how many people understood her own pursuit of

mathematics? Mr. Hayes would likely squelch his sister's dreams just as so many people had tried to kill hers.

Elizabeth straightened and slipped her satchel over her shoulder. She wasn't doing herself any favors by stewing over Luke Hayes, and she needed to stop by the kitchen and inventory the recent food delivery before she even went home.

She closed and locked her classroom door, then walked down the hallway toward the large double doors at the opposite end of the building. The tinkle of girlish giggles from outside floated through the main entrance to the school, and the clear autumn sun filtered through the windows beside the doorway.

If only she didn't have the cook to meet with and ledgers to refigure, she could enjoy that picnic with her students. But some things weren't meant to be. She pushed through the doors leading into the dining hall, then weaved her way through the maze of tables and chairs toward the kitchen at the back.

Dottie McGivern, the school's cook, stood at the counter just inside the kitchen.

"There you are. Been wondering whether you were going to show up." Dottie's plump hands dove into a bowl of dough and began to knead. "We need more flour, apples and sugar."

Elizabeth sighed. Of course they did. It only made sense. She already had the ladies' society, Samantha's brother and the school's financial woes to deal with. Why not add trouble with the food order, as well?

"I'm assuming you didn't get the amounts you ordered?" *Again?*

Dottie pointed to the half-empty shelves lining the wall of the kitchen. "Now look here, Miss Wells. I've been cooking for a long time, and I know how much money it costs to feed a slew of girls. Or at least how much money it *should* cost. So when I say I need a hundred and fifty dollars each month to pay for food, I mean a hundred and fifty dollars, not the fifty dollars' worth of foodstuffs that showed up this morning. That look like a hundred and fifty dollars' worth of food to you?"

"No, it doesn't." This could not be happening again, not with the school in such dire financial straits. It seemed every time Dottie had a load of food delivered, something had gotten mixed up and only a portion of the needed food was delivered. "I don't understand. Jackson says he authorizes the food money to be released every month. You should have plenty of supplies, not be running out."

Dottie wagged a flour-covered finger at her chest. "Talk to your brother, then. Maybe you got your messages mixed up, but the delivery that arrived today wasn't no hundred and fifty dollars' worth of food."

Yes, she would talk to Jackson. Indeed, she hoped something had become mixed up. Otherwise, the academy was being cheated somehow. And not just with groceries. This was the fourth time such a thing had happened since the school year started. Jackson said enough money for materials and bills had been released, yet the gas company claimed they never received payment, the store they ordered teachers' supplies from was missing money as well, and Dottie said only a third of her food arrived.

"Miss Wells, there you are. I feared you had gone already." Miss Bowen's head poked through the swinging kitchen door, her perfect coiffure and straight suit grossly incongruous against the counters piled with potatoes, messy casserole dishes and frazzled works in the kitchen. "I'm sorry to interrupt, but I simply must speak with you. In private, that is."

Miss Bowen sent Dottie a brief smile and then disappeared back through the door.

Elizabeth squeezed Dottie's arm. "I'll be back tomorrow to figure this out."

The fiery-haired woman nodded. "Thank you."

Elizabeth headed out of the kitchen and toward the far corner of the dining hall where Mrs. Bowen stood. The lines of her gray dress looked so stiff that the woman couldn't possibly be comfortable walking. Or standing. Or sitting. Or doing anything at all. But a smile softened the creases of her face.

"I need to speak with you about the school board meeting last evening."

Of course. Why not discuss the school board meeting? It was just one more thing to add to her list of disastrous events. At this rate, she'd better not bother to go home later. She'd likely find her house burned to ashes or swallowed by an earthquake. "What about it?"

"Well, naturally the board is concerned about the bad publicity Hayes Academy received earlier this week."

Which the school board undoubtedly blamed on her, since she'd written that editorial. "Do they plan to file a complaint with the *Morning Times*? To the best of my knowledge, no one, not a school board member, nor you, nor I, nor anyone associated with Hayes Academy, was asked to defend it in an official article. I suppose it will be left to me to write something in response."

Miss Bowen blanched. "No. I'm afraid that won't be necessary. In fact, I do believe several of the board members requested you not write anything more for the paper."

"Does someone else plan to write an editorial, then?" Surely the school board didn't intend to let Mr. Higsley's article go unanswered. "Or perhaps the board could invite the reporter to the school? The man might well retract some of his comments, were he to see firsthand how beneficial—"

"The school board is considering closing Hayes Academy. Immediately." The words fell from Miss Bowen's mouth in a jumbled rush.

Elizabeth's heart stuttered, then stopped. She opened her mouth, hoping something intelligible would come out, but all she could do was stare at Miss Bowen's pale, pinched face. She should have known. She'd suspected the school board would lean in this direction, of course. But so quickly? Before she even had a chance to refigure the ledgers or write another article or find more donors?

"I see. Did...did my father..." She pressed her eyes shut, hated herself for even asking, but she had to know. "...support closing the school?"

Miss Bowen's eyes grew heavy, and Elizabeth's gaze fell to her feet. Of course Father would pull his support. He discontinued support of anything politically disadvantageous. He wouldn't care that he had championed the school during his past two reelection campaigns.

"Elizabeth? Are you all right?"

"Yes. Fine." Except her throat felt like sawdust had been poured down it, and her stomach twisted and lurched as though it would lose its contents again.

"The decision hasn't been finalized yet. There's hope in that, I suppose, though I must confess the majority of the members seemed to have already made up their minds. Still, the school board wants a detailed report from your brother on Hayes Academy's financial status by the end of next week. They're scheduling another meeting two weeks from now."

"That's when they'll decide whether to close the school?"

"Yes."

"So there's hope."

"A glimmer." But no hope shone on Miss Bowen's face.

And rightly so. One week, maybe two. That wasn't much time.

"Elizabeth." Miss Bowen touched her shoulder. "Where do we stand financially? I know several letters from our sponsors have come this week. I'm assuming your brother has received more?"

"I'm heading home to calculate numbers."

"Surely you must have some idea."

She glanced toward one of the small dining room windows. The sun still burned clear and bright outside, but the little shaft of light barely seemed to penetrate the dark, empty room. "It's not good."

"Well." Miss Bowen's lips curved into a painfully brilliant smile. "Perhaps things will improve shortly. I asked Mr. Hayes about the possibility of another donation."

Her head snapped up. "When he was here earlier?"

"Why of course. When else would I have seen him?"

Lovely timing. He'd probably pasted a grin on his face and agreed to everything asked of him, especially since she'd just finished lecturing him about bringing a gun into school and pulling his sister out. "What did he say?"

"He didn't say no, but he didn't rush to make a commitment, either. I'm sure he just needs more time."

The headmistress's voice held a fragile kind of promise. Elizabeth rubbed her temples. She didn't want to shatter it, not when it would shatter soon enough on its own. "That's something at least. He probably doesn't realize how much responsibility for this school he's inheriting. I'm assuming his lawyer will inform him sometime over the weekend."

"I'm sure Mr. Hayes will want to continue in his grandfather's stead, or he wouldn't have come East at all. But I want you to speak with him about a donation."

"Me? Speak with him? Certainly you're in a better position to solicit funds."

"Don't be foolish, Elizabeth. You have such a convincing way about you, when you're passionate about an issue. I doubt the man will be able to tell you no."

Elizabeth raised her eyebrows. Luke Hayes certainly hadn't found saying the word difficult earlier that afternoon.

And he likely wouldn't have trouble saying it again.

Chapter Three

"Sell it all," Luke said from behind his grandfather's desk. "The companies, the estate, everything but the stocks."

The lawyer, Mr. Byron, cleared his throat. "You can't."

"Why?" Luke waved his hand over the will spread across the desk. "Is there some sort of stipulation that prevents me from selling?"

"It's not done." Mr. Byron folded his stubby arms across his chest and peered through his spectacles. "Your grandfather intended for you to continue running the companies he worked so hard to establish, not to sell them off."

Luke stared at the papers he'd spent the past two hours poring over, the lines of neat handwriting growing blurry beneath his gaze. He'd inherited nearly everything his grandfather had owned. Fifteen accounting offices with an insurance company attached to each branch, and a smattering of investments both in Albany businesses and on the New York Stock Exchange. "This shouldn't even be mine. My father should inherit it."

"Your grandfather was very clear. He wanted the estate and businesses to fall to his only living grandson." The lawyer spoke without inflection, as though the words didn't threaten to shatter the life Luke had built out West.

The unreachable little spot between his shoulder blades started to itch. Had Grandpa thought Luke would feel obliged to stay, once he saw the vast holdings? According to Pa, Jonah Hayes had manipulated everything and everyone around him. When the old codger tried forcing Pa into a marriage all those years back, Pa left, and Grandpa disowned him. Was Grandpa trying to get back at Pa by pulling his pa's only living son back East?

Luke stretched his arm behind his back and tried to scratch the nagging itch. He couldn't spend his days in an office, staring at lists and numbers, instead of ranching. Falling asleep to the distant howl of wolves and breathing the sharp air of the first mountain blizzard. Working with his hands to brand the cattle, round them up and drive them east. Seeing the prairie change from summer to autumn to winter to spring, all while the bold, jagged Tetons to his west watched like slumbering giants.

No. He wouldn't leave the West. Not for all the wealth of his grandfather's estate. "If Grandpa left everything to me, then he shouldn't care what I do with it, and I want it sold."

"You don't realize the scope of what you ask." The lawyer shoved his spectacles back up on his nose, only to have them slide halfway down again. "Think of all the problems selling such large holdings will cause. With the economy as it is, you'll get maybe half the true value of your grandfather's companies."

Luke clenched his jaw. Beating his head against a brick wall would be easier than talking to the lawyer. "I don't care about the money. My ranch does well enough. But if Grandpa was bound and determined to leave me his estate, the least I can do is take the money from it back to Pa, who should have gotten all this in the first place."

"I appreciate that you want to reconcile things between your father and late grandfather, but you must consider some of the other people caught in your decision. What will happen to all the employees at Great Northern Accounting and Insurance if you sell?"

How was he to know? The new buyers would likely keep some of the employees. It wasn't as though he put thousands of people out of work just by choosing to sell Grandpa's companies. He wouldn't be shutting down the businesses, merely putting them in the hands of men actually interested in running them.

"And what about the staff here at the estate? Do you realize how many people's livelihoods you will be terminating with the single command to sell?"

Luke raked a hand through his hair. He hadn't thought of the servants, either. Whoever bought the estate would probably have his own slew of servants to replace Grandpa's. He'd need to have a meeting with the staff next week, explain the situation and let all but the minimum go.

No. That seemed too abrupt. Maybe he would keep them on for an extra month and give them time to find new employment.

But how would they look for other jobs if they were working here? Perhaps he should give them each a month's salary and then release them.

And where would they sleep and eat for the coming month? The servants all lived on the estate, and kicking them out meant they had no home, even if he sent each of them off with a heap of money. Would his former employees even be able to find other jobs? He didn't need to live out East to know that many of the country's wealthy had lost money since the panic had hit. People were cutting back and getting rid of extra staff, not hiring more.

"Have you ever fired a person before, Mr. Hayes?" Byron leaned over the opposite side of the desk, his brown eyes extra large behind his glasses.

Luke bristled. "Of course." Cowhands who were lazy or dishonest or lousy with cattle. But he'd never before fired a good, honest worker. It seemed a shame for decent people to lose their jobs because of a business decision. *His* business decision.

This whole affair was too complicated by half. Why had Grandpa left everything to him in the first place? He'd made a big enough mess of his own family. What made Grandpa think he could run an estate, and one of the largest insurance and accounting corporations in the East? He needed to get Sam, take her back home and see Ma through until she passed. Surely Grandpa would have understood that he didn't have time for servants and accounting companies and whatever else.

"You could look for a manager," the lawyer supplied. "Someone who would run the companies in your absence and report back to you in Wyoming. Then you could travel here every two or three years to see that things are being managed properly."

Luke rubbed the back of his neck. The manager idea

wasn't half bad. It made more sense than anything else at the moment.

"You would continue to make a profit off the companies, as well." The lawyer pounced on Luke's moment of deliberation like a cougar on an unsuspecting rabbit. "Think of it as an extra source of income. It's a rather sound business decision to make. Of course, you'll have to interview potential managers while you're here. But once you've found a man, you'd be free to return to Wyoming."

"I don't want to commit to anything like that just yet."

"Why don't you ponder the decision over the weekend?"

Yes, he'd better think it through. He didn't want a lot of strings tying him to the East. And yet… "Then the employees would be able to keep their jobs?"

"All but the ones on the estate."

"I'll give you an answer next week."

"Excellent." A smile curved at the edges of Mr. Byron's pudgy lips. "Let's move on to your sister-in-law's inheritance then, shall we?"

The world seemed to freeze around him, his blood turning frigid at the mere mention of her. "My grandfather left money to Cynthia?"

"Yes, a tidy sum of—"

"I don't want to know." Luke turned away and crossed his arms, but the image came back to him like hot, glowing embers buried beneath layers of ash. Cynthia with her pregnant belly cradled between her body and legs while she kneeled on the ground. Her fiery hair tangling in the mountain breeze, her eyes shining with tears, her voice pleading with him. And lying beside her, his dead, blood-soaked twin.

"Your sister also stands to inherit a nice amount," the lawyer continued.

Luke walked to the French doors and pushed them open, then sucked in a breath of cool outside air.

"Samantha will receive ten thousand dollars either when she marries or turns twenty-five."

Luke drew in another deep breath and tried to wrap his mind around the lawyer's words. Samantha. They were talking about his sister now, weren't they? Not the woman who'd let his brother die. "Has Sam been told?"

"Yes."

He stared out into the darkening valley, rife with the music of insect sounds and toads and the faint rustle of the breeze. Returning to Wyoming beautiful and single, Sam would have been the talk of the Teton Valley. But with a ten-thousand-dollar inheritance, she'd attract every bachelor west of the Mississippi.

"In addition to her inheritance, your sister also has a separate fund to pay for the rest of her schooling."

"What?" The calming air he'd just inhaled deserted his lungs.

"The remainder of Samantha's year at Hayes Academy is, of course, already paid for. But this fund contains money for further education. College—not just a bachelor's degree but a master's program, even a doctorate, if your sister so desires."

Luke turned back toward the lawyer and stalked to the desk. Grandpa's will just kept getting better and better. "That's ridiculous. She needs to go home to her family. Not chase some dream she has little hope of achieving."

Perhaps if she wanted to be a teacher or a nurse, he could understand her desire to attend college. But architecture? She'd be laughed out of her classes. And even if she managed to graduate, who would hire her?

The lawyer cleared his throat. "Educating women was one of your grandfather's passions, and something he devoted much time and money toward. He wouldn't want any less for his granddaughter."

Educating women. Why wasn't grade school enough of an education? That was all the education he had, and he managed just fine. In fact, he'd wager Grandpa didn't have more than a grade school education either, and the man had built a financial empire.

Luke poured what was probably his third cup of coffee and sank down behind the polished mahogany desk, brow furrowed as he stared at the pages of the will.

Why was God doing this to him? He hadn't asked to inherit this estate. He just wanted to put his family back together and go home where he belonged, but now Grandpa's will made it possible for Sam to stay with or without his approval. He took a sip of coffee and set the mug on the desk.

You shouldn't set that on the wood. It could ruin the finish.

He blew out a breath. His sister was right—not that he cottoned to being reminded. Still…he grabbed a page of the will and stuck it under the mug.

His head ached, he was covered in road dust, and his face needed a shave. What he wouldn't give for a good scrubbing in the stream, but first he needed to talk to Sam again. Or at least try talking to her. Hopefully their next conversation would go a little better than the first two they'd had. "Can we continue this discussion tomorrow? I've had about all I can take for tonight."

The lawyer turned from where he stood shuffling through his own copies of the papers. "We're about done, as it is. Let's cover the charities quickly, then you can have the weekend to look over the will. Perhaps you'll stop by my office in Albany on Monday with any further questions? Or if you wish, I can come here."

"Albany on Monday's fine." He'd walk there barefoot, if doing so would end this fiasco for the night.

"Here's the list of institutions your grandfather contributed to over the past five years." Mr. Byron handed him three sheets of paper. As though the twenty-five names on one sheet wouldn't have supplied his grandfather with enough philanthropic opportunities. "I'd expect the majority of these charities will send representatives to speak with you about donations in your grandfather's memory."

He'd figured that much when he'd talked to the headmistress at the academy earlier. He'd probably spend a week doing nothing more than explaining to the representatives that he would be heading West before he decided what to do with the funds.

"This is one you need to be particularly aware of, though." The lawyer slid yet another piece of paper across the desk. "You may not know it, but your grandfather was the founder of Hayes Academy for Girls and stayed rather involved in that institution. It's assumed you'll fill the role he vacated."

Luke frowned as he glanced at the papers for Hayes Academy—lists of finances and supplies, students and faculty. Easy enough to make sense of and not so very different from the accounts he kept of the ranch.

"There's a projected deficit. Am I in charge of raising money for my sister's school?"

The lawyer shoved his drooping spectacles onto his nose yet again. Following the pattern, they slid right back down. "Either that or donating it yourself."

He was never going to get back home. It took every ounce of pride in his body not to bang his head on the desk.

"Hayes Academy for Girls was your grandfather's crowning social achievement. He remained rather proud of the school and very involved in its running, right up until his heart attack."

Luke ran his eyes over the lists of expenses on the papers again. Looked like things could be managed a little better, but what was he going to do with the mess? He might be able to tell his lawyer to sell an estate, but he couldn't exactly tell the lawyer to sell a girls' school that he didn't even own, could he? "All I see is projected expenses based on current enrollment. There's no ledger?"

"The manager of the accounting office in Albany has the official ledgers, but the mathematics teacher, a Miss Elizabeth Wells, keeps her own ledgers and reports to the accountant. You might check with her about the school's current financial state, particularly in regard to the day-to-day details. She stays more informed about such things than the accountant or the school board."

Miss Wells. Lovely. He could just imagine how that conversation would go. *Howdy, Miss Wells. Now that I've pulled my sister out of your school, I want to scrutinize every last figure you've recorded in your books.* "How much, then?"

Byron's eyebrows furrowed together. "How much what?"

"How much money did Grandpa's will bequest to them?" Luke spread the papers into a bigger mess across the top of the desk. "For all the figures on these papers, I can't find the amount."

"Your grandfather made no bequests for a single charity. Everything was given to you, with the exception of the sums for Cynthia and your sister. He probably assumed once you saw the extent of his philanthropic endeavors, you would continue donating in his stead."

Luke stuck a finger in his collar and tugged. Likely another way for good old Grandpa to trap him in this uppity little eastern town. "How much did my grandfather usually donate?"

The lawyer pointed to a number on one of the sheets.

"Two thousand dollars for *one* school year?" Luke jumped to his feet, the thunderous words reverberating off the office walls. He could understand five hundred dollars, or maybe even a thousand. But two thousand dollars so girls could learn fancy mathematics? "That seems a little extreme."

The lawyer's eyes darkened, and he jerked the paper away. "On the contrary. As I already mentioned, your grandfather advocated educating women, and it's only natural he use his money toward that end. Since its inception, the school has been very successful at seeing its graduates enter colleges across the country."

Luke leafed through the pages. "But it looks like donations are down…enrollment, too. It isn't much to say the graduates go to college, when there's no one to graduate."

"That is hardly the fault of the school," Byron insisted. "The current economic state has, of course, caused some students to delay their educations. And of late, there has been a bit of local opposition to the school."

Byron handed him two newspaper articles: An Editorial on the Necessity of Educating Young Women by Miss Elizabeth Wells, and Excessive Amount of Charity Money Wasted on Hayes Academy for Girls by a certain Mr. Reginald Higsley.

Luke let the papers fall to the desk. "The derogatory article appeared at the beginning of the week. Has the school board printed an answer?"

The lawyer shook his head. "Your grandfather always handled situations such as this personally. But if you're concerned about the articles, you may find it interesting that your grandfather was a rather large investor in the *Morning Times*."

Luke sunk his head in his hands. "I see."

And he did. He hadn't even been in Valley Falls a day, and his life had been upended, flipped around and spun sideways a couple times. He was never going to survive here for a month.

Chapter Four

"These numbers don't look good." Samantha frowned and glanced up from the ledger she'd had her face buried in for the past fifteen minutes. "Do you think the school will close?"

"I don't know." Elizabeth moved the chalk in her hand deftly across her slate, finishing up some ciphering with yet another depressing result.

She and Samantha had spread a blanket beneath a large maple tree overlooking the back fields on the Hayes estate. The afternoon sky boasted a brilliant blue, and the breeze snapped with autumn's crispness; birds circled the air above, and the nearby brook babbled gaily as it flowed over rock and sticks.

In short, it was a perfect autumn afternoon. But Elizabeth could hardly enjoy it when her time with the ledgers last night had revealed a frighteningly small amount of money left in the bank account. The academy barely had enough funds to pay teacher salaries and outstanding bills, and it was only October. They hadn't even purchased the coal for the boiler system yet.

Elizabeth set her chalk down. "The school board will

make the final decision about the academy closing. But Jackson's findings will be a big part of it."

Samantha blushed and ducked her head at the mention of Jackson's name. "That doesn't sound very promising."

"No. Did you spot any mistakes in my mathematics?"

Samantha shook her head and shifted the still-open book to the ground beside her.

Elizabeth sighed. If only there had been a mistake, an extra five hundred dollars tucked into an account somewhere. But Samantha would have caught something so glaring. Goodness, Samantha would have caught a mistake ten times smaller than that. The girl was a pure genius when it came to ciphering.

"I don't suppose it matters much either way for me." Samantha gave a careless shrug of her shoulders—hardly a ladylike gesture—and slumped back against the tree trunk. "It's not as if I'll be around."

An image of Luke Hayes, standing in the school hallway with his arms crossed and that frown on his face, flashed across her mind. "Is your brother still determined to take you out of school? If there was such a problem with your attending, why didn't he or your father protest earlier, when you first started?"

"It's not my going to the school that's the problem. It's staying in Valley Falls now that Grandfather is gone. Luke's decided I have to return to Wyoming."

The breath stilled in Elizabeth's lungs. Pulling Samantha out of school was bad enough, but to take her all the way back to Wyoming? Samantha's future would be ruined. "Why would he want such a thing?"

Samantha tucked her knees up into her chest and huffed. "Because he's a tyrant, that's why."

"I'm sure there's more to it than that." There had to be. No one would be so cruel without a reason, not even the intimidating man she'd argued with yesterday.

"Not really. All he'll say is that Ma and Pa miss me, there's no one left to care for me here and I belong back on the ranch."

Elizabeth reached over and squeezed Samantha's hand. "Do you think it would help if I talked to him? Maybe if I explained all the opportunities graduating would give you, he'd let you stay."

"It won't work, not with my brother. Once he gets an idea into his head, he doesn't listen to reason."

Elizabeth let the silence settle between them, punctuated by the chirping of birds, the nattering of squirrels and the constant trickle of water over rocks. There wasn't much she could say, really. She'd speak with Luke Hayes, all right, do anything she could to keep Samantha here. But Samantha knew the man better than she did, and if Samantha didn't think anything was going to change Luke Hayes's mind, the girl was probably right.

"How long since you've been home?"

"Three years."

"That is rather long." Elizabeth bit the inside of her cheek. "Christmas doesn't afford a long enough break for you to travel home and come back, but maybe if you offered to return to Wyoming for a visit after you graduate, your brother would let you stay until then."

"Actually, I've been thinking of something else..." Samantha drew in a breath and fixed her eyes on the ground. "Do you think it's wrong to...to hope Jackson proposes? Then I could stay here, marry him and not bother with anything Luke says."

The meadow grew silent around them as she stared at Samantha's flushed cheeks. Her brother and Samantha certainly showed signs of being a good match. But Samantha had dreams of being an architect, and she was still so young...

"I—I think marriage is a very serious decision, one that affects the rest of your life. If you marry Jackson, you should do so for the right reasons. Because you love him, want to spend the rest of your life with him, and will be happier with him than you'd be without him. Marrying for any other reasons will just cause trouble."

It was a lesson she'd learned far too well when she'd been Samantha's age.

A horse nickered somewhere in the distance, and the ground reverberated with the steady *thump-thump, thump-thump, thump-thump* of the beast's gallop.

"I suppose you're right." Samantha looked up from the speck on the ground she'd been staring at. "That sounds like Triton's gait, but who would be riding out this far? The stable hands don't usually head this direction."

A moment later, a rider in a cowboy hat appeared atop a magnificent dark brown steed at the far edge of the field.

Samantha scowled. "I should have guessed. My brother has to spend at least six hours of his day on a horse, or he goes crazy."

Elizabeth tried not to watch as Luke Hayes approached, but in truth, she could hardly take her eyes from him as he raced across the field. He seemed to move as one with the strong horse, his legs hugging the beast as though it were an extension of his own body. It hardly seemed possible to imagine the man stuffed into Jonah Hayes's office, going through the endless papers.

"Good afternoon." Mr. Hayes reined the horse to a stop beside the blanket, towering over them like a king; then his eyes narrowed on his sister. "You didn't say anything about coming out here, Sam."

Samantha's eyes flashed, and she crossed her arms over her knees. "I wasn't aware I needed to ask permission to go for a walk on the estate."

He raised one of his arrogant eyebrows and scanned the blanket, ledgers and slates sprawled on the ground. He didn't need words to express the thoughts clearly written across his face: *this doesn't look like an unplanned walk.*

Samantha huffed and picked up the ledger again, interested anew in the endless columns of numbers.

"Miss Wells, I can't say I expected to find you here either, but I've a need to speak with you." He glanced briefly at the equation-filled slate on her lap, and the side of his mouth quirked into a cocky little smile. "Do you ever take time off from that fancy mathematics?"

"Do you ever take time off from being a cowboy?"

The smile on his lips straightened into a firm, white line, and he swung off his horse. "I own five thousand head of cattle in the Teton Valley. I'm a *rancher.* That's a mite different than being the hired help we call cowboys."

"Indeed." She nodded curtly and drew in a long, deep breath. With Samantha sitting beside her, she couldn't exactly persuade him to let his sister graduate, but she still needed to ask about donating money to the academy. If only she could be polite long enough to make her request.

It was going to be very, very hard.

She blew out her breath and forced herself to smile.

"Can I help you up?" Mr. Hayes extended his hand.

She stared at it for a moment, hesitating to reach for him. But really, what was the point of being rude when she still had to ask about that wretched donation? She placed her palm firmly in his.

Mistake.

His wide, callused palm engulfed her small fingers, and heat surged through the spot where their skin met. He raised her to her feet without ceremony, as though he didn't feel the impact of their touch somewhere deep inside. As soon as she was able, she tugged away her hand and shoved it behind her back, where it could stay safely away from Mr. Hayes.

The rascal didn't even seem to notice, just pinned her with his clear blue eyes. "It seems you've taken quite an interest in the business affairs of Hayes Academy here lately." Afternoon sunlight glistened down on Mr. Hayes's head and cowboy hat, turning the golden-blond tufts of hair beneath the brim nearly white.

Elizabeth forced her gaze away from his hair. Why was she staring at it, anyway? So the man had beautiful blond hair. His sister did, as well. Blond hair wasn't *that* uncommon.

Except when it shimmered like silvery-gold in the sunlight.

And she was still thinking about his hair. Ugh! "I teach at the academy. It's only natural I'd be interested in it."

"Interested enough to write editorials for the newspaper?"

Every bit of blood in her face drained to her feet, and

her limbs felt suddenly cold. Did he hate her for interfering? Feel she had no business fighting for new students? Resent the negative attention she'd drawn to the school when that dreadful reporter retaliated?

The emotionless look on his face gave nothing away. His eyes stayed that cool blue, the same shade as a winter sky, without a hint of either understanding or disdain as they waited for her answer.

"Educating women is important to me."

"I gathered that much yesterday. A bit hard to miss, actually, but I'm curious about the school ledgers at the moment." He nodded toward the books, the one lying on the blanket and the other still in Samantha's lap. "My lawyer informs me you're keeping a set. I assume these are them?"

Oh, perfect. Just what she wanted to discuss. "My brother in Albany has the official ledgers. Perhaps you should talk to him."

"I intend to, but I'd like a look at yours, as well."

"No." The word flew out of her mouth before she could stop it.

Samantha slammed her ledger closed. "Why do you want them? So you can look for some excuse to close down the school? As if pulling me out isn't bad enough."

Mr. Hayes glanced briefly at his sister. "This has nothing to do with you, Sam. I'm only doing the job Grandpa left me. Miss Wells, you must be aware that since I've been given my grandfather's seat on the school's board, I can request your books at any time."

She knew very well what he could request, and what he'd likely do if he saw the books. He'd take one look at how little money was in the account and want the school closed immediately.

"Mind if I borrow your rag?"

"Excuse me?"

Mr. Hayes held up his hand—the same he'd used to help her stand. His palm was practically white, smeared with chalk dust.

Heat flooded her neck and face. She didn't need to look down to know her own hands were covered in fine powder.

"Messy place, these fields."

She reached into her pocket, grabbed a hanky—one of the ones she was forever using to wipe her chalk-covered hands on—and held it out to him. "I apologize. I don't usually forget to clean my hands."

"Thank you." He rubbed the cloth over his palm and returned it.

She wiped her hands furiously, even though she'd be back to work the second he left.

He simply watched her, a half smile quirking the side of his mouth. "You missed a spot." He pointed to her right sleeve, where a huge smear of white stood stark against the yellow of her dress.

"Thank you," she gritted.

"So can I take those ledgers now?"

"I'd—" ...*rather eat a toad!*

Could she lie? Tell him things were going well—or at least as well as they had been before the newspaper article appeared on Monday morning—and tear out the last pages of the ledgers so the school appeared to have money?

She rubbed her fingers over her temples. No, of course she couldn't do such a thing. She'd never been one to lie for convenience, and she wasn't about to develop the habit now. He'd find out the truth soon anyway; just as he'd learned of the article she'd written to the paper. Better to be honest.

No, better to ask for another donation, and *then* be honest.

Except she didn't want to ask the arrogant man in front of her for a penny.

Taking her requests to Jonah, with his kind smiles and grandfatherly manner, had been easy. But the man who had stormed into her class yesterday and torn Samantha out of school wasn't exactly grandfatherly.

Or approachable.

Or kind.

"Miss Wells?"

She stared into Luke Hayes's rigid face, his mouth and eyes stern and unreadable, and forced herself to form the words. "Actually, I've been wanting to speak to you about the ledgers and the academy. We've recently had difficulty with several of our donors, and I was hoping you could make a donation to Hayes Academy."

There. She'd said it. Surely she deserved some type of award. A medal of honor, a golden cup, a life-size statue of herself erected in the town square.

"Yeah, that would at least be something nice you could do for the school." Samantha crossed her arms over her chest. "Seeing how you're dead set on pulling me out of it."

But Mr. Hayes didn't bother to look at his sister. "Grandpa donated slews of money to Hayes Academy. I don't understand why you can't be happy with what it's already received."

She threw up her hands. The man's brain was as dense as a piece of lead. "Happy? You think I want a donation to make me happy? Girls' futures are at stake, not my happiness. It's an issue of keeping the school open, so we can train young women, not pleasing me."

Mr. Hayes rubbed his hand over the back of his neck. "Why is girls getting high school diplomas so all-fired important? I never graduated from high school, and neither did Grandpa. Yet here I am, doing a fine job of running my ranch without any piece of paper from a high school."

She opened her mouth to respond, then snapped it shut. What did she say to that? Was it true Jonah Hayes never finished school? Probably. A lot of young people left to find work before graduating even now, let alone sixty years ago.

Mr. Hayes's face remained set, his jaw determined, but sincerity filled the little sun lines at the corners of his eyes and mouth. He wasn't furious with her as he'd been yesterday but was asking an honest question.

And here she was, parading the importance of educating women in front of him, when he'd never finished his own education. Did he feel slighted or belittled? That hadn't been her intention. "Well, you see, a high school education is important because—"

"Never mind. I read your article last night. I don't need to hear some highfalutin list of arguments in person. Just give me the ledgers, and I'll be on my way."

"Oh…um…" And there again the man had her speechless. From ledgers to donations and back again, she could hardly keep up with the conversation. "Will Monday be all right? Samantha and I have a bit more work to do on them this afternoon, and I've some issues to discuss with my brother. I truly need the books over the weekend."

Mr. Hayes blew out a long, tired breath, the kind that

held a world of weariness in the exhaled air. "Monday, then. Sorry to disturb you ladies." And with that, he swung back onto his horse and galloped off.

Elizabeth tucked a stray strand of hair behind her ear and sighed. The conversation surely could have gone worse. At least she hadn't stormed away in a rage, and he hadn't refused to give money to the school—

Though he hadn't agreed to give any, either.

So why did she have a sour taste in her mouth?

She turned and offered Samantha a weak smile. "I feel like I handled that wrong."

Samantha shrugged as she settled back down beside the tree. "It's Luke. Anytime you disagree with him, he'd say you handled something wrong."

Chapter Five

Covered in dust and smelling of sweat, Luke hurried through the back entrance to Grandpa's house. After spending the first half of the day sorting through the things in Grandpa's office, he'd decided to take a peek at the stable. After all, if he shut down the estate, he'd need to sell off whatever horseflesh Grandpa had acquired. But at a glance, some of that horseflesh had looked a little too good to be sold. So he'd hopped astride Triton, the finest beast in the stable, for a little ride.

He certainly hadn't expected to find Samantha and Miss Wells. He glanced down at his hand and couldn't help but smile. The white stain from her chalk dust had long since faded, but he'd never forget the memory of first looking at his hand and seeing white, then watching the color rise in Miss Wells's face.

With her bright hazel eyes, perfect mouth and head of thick mahogany hair, the teacher was just as beautiful today as she had been yesterday…and terribly determined to wheedle money for the school out of him.

Luke rolled his shoulders as he headed through the back hallway and out into the grand hall. Should he give the school some money? It wouldn't hurt anything. Grandpa had left him more than enough. And it might help Sam to see he wasn't some type of greedy tyrant.

But then, he didn't rightly know what he wanted to do with any of Grandpa's money yet, besides give it to Pa. And how unfair would it be to all the other charities Grandpa had supported if he discounted them and wrote out a bank draft to Hayes Academy because a pretty little teacher with shiny hazel eyes smiled at him?

Twenty-four hours in Valley Falls and his brain was already half mush. He had to get out of this place. Soon.

Luke strode through the grand hall toward the bright marble staircase. He'd stayed out riding Triton for too long after meeting up with the womenfolk. Now he needed to bathe fast, if he didn't want to arrive at that fancy banquet late. He could always scrub up quicklike in the stream behind the house, but this place crawled with enough servants that someone would probably venture along while he washed. Plus Sam could probably list a good ten rules about why a man couldn't take a simple bath in a stream these days.

A knock sounded behind him on the front door, not more than three feet away. He glanced around the large empty room with its glittering chandelier and polished white marble. "I'll answer it."

The butler emerged from a doorway on the left, but Luke pulled the door open anyway. A dark-haired young man stood there, dressed in a tuxedo and top hat, his skin smooth and pale as though he'd never seen a day in the sun.

The man pondered him for a moment, then a polished smile curved his lips, and he thrust his hand out. "Good evening. You must be Mr. Luke Hayes."

Luke shook the offered hand, the scent of his body's odor rising as he moved his arm. The other man deserved some credit for not gagging.

"I'm Jackson Wells."

Wells. As in related to the mathematics teacher? Couldn't be. Miss Wells was proper all right, but she didn't come off as slick, like the spiffed-up man in front of him. "Howdy, Mr. Wells."

"I'm manager at the Great Northern Accounting and Insurance office in Albany." He rubbed the brim of his top hat.

"Nice to meet you." So this was the accountant for Hayes Academy—who also happened to share the same surname as his little mathematics teacher? He scratched behind his ear. The lawyer hadn't said anything about the accountant and teacher being related, but he supposed it was possible.

And either way, he had a couple hundred questions to ask the man, if not for needing to be ready for that banquet thing he'd gotten roped into.

"Your grandfather hired me a few years ago. I imagine you own the accounting office now? It's a pleasure. I've been wanting to meet you."

"Thanks for coming around, Mr. Wells. But I've got a banquet to get to. Let's schedule an appointment at the office on Monday. About nine o'clock?"

"Yes, sir." Wells's gaze drifted down Luke's sweat-encrusted clothing, and the man frowned. "Were you planning to travel with us tonight? Should Samantha and I wait for you?"

"Samantha and you?"

"Of course."

"Traveling?" Luke's scalp heated. The man spoke

too easily, as though he expected to wrap Sam up in a blanket and haul her off to…to…

Well, it didn't really matter where the man wanted to cart her off to. The dandy was too old for his sister. "Sam's not taking visitors today."

Something flashed in Wells's eyes. A challenge? It was gone too soon, replaced by that overly polished face once again. "Is there some trouble with Samantha accompanying me to the banquet tonight?"

Samantha at the banquet? Luke slammed the door in Wells's face. "Sam!" He grimaced as his shout echoed up the polished stairs.

"Mr. Hayes, sir." The butler stepped forward. "Perhaps I can show Mr. Wells into the gentlemen's reception room, where you can discuss the situation."

Luke turned to the butler. What was his name again? Stebbens? Stevens? "Thank you, no."

Sam appeared at the top of the stairs, dressed in a long silvery-lavender gown. "Is Jackson here?" A thousand bursts of sunlight radiated from her face.

He should speak, send her a look, do something to show his displeasure. But he only stared as her beautiful figure descended the stairs. It couldn't be his sister. Her hair, a mixture of honey and spun gold, piled atop her head in curls, a few of which hung down to frame her soft face. Her cheeks glowed the perfect shade of pink and her lips…she'd dyed them red with something.

Sam glided to the base of the stairs, an uncertain smile curving the corners of her mouth.

A fist pounded on the door.

The butler cleared his throat.

His sister sniffed the air. "Goodness, you stink, Luke."

"Where did you get that dress?" His voice was too hoarse, and try as he might, he couldn't look away. Oh, he knew she was of marrying age. Had handed her a letter from Levi just yesterday, likely with a proposal inside. But giving her a letter from an old friend was a far cry from letting her traipse around town dressed like that with the spiffed-up stranger outside.

"Grandfather ordered it made for a ball earlier this summer. I didn't attend, of course, after his heart failed, but I was able to have the color switched from blue to lavender. It's appropriate for attending the banquet, with my still being in half mourning, don't you think?" She spoke eloquently and smoothly, with a gentle lift of the shoulder here, and slight ducking of the chin there. She was practically a grown woman, wearing that beautiful gown and honoring her late grandfather.

But none of that changed the two most important things. She was still his sister and… "Did you say you were going to the banquet, the one *I'm* attending?"

He opened his mouth to add she was too young, then stopped and attempted to blow out his frustration in one giant breath.

It worked great—until his shoulders tightened into knots.

Sam frowned. "No. I'm wearing satin to a banquet in the town park. Yes, the banquet you're attending. I gave Jackson my word. Now, if you would please step away from the door so Stevens can let Jackson inside. He came all the way from Albany just to pick me up." Her dress swished, catching the light from the chandelier as she waved toward the door.

Luke raked his hand through his hair. Mourning indeed. Why couldn't the gown be some other color? A bright childlike yellow or pink. Not shades of lavender and silver that shimmered in the lighting and caused her skin to look as creamy as warm milk. He wanted his old sister back. The one that skinned her knees trying to climb trees and didn't cry when she fell off a horse.

Again, the knock.

Luke gritted his teeth and looked between his sister, the butler and the door. He'd give his grandfather's estate away in a second, if he could be instantly back in Wyoming, Sam by his side. But since that wasn't an option, what else could he do? Keep the slick-looking man outside, and haul Sam upstairs to hog-tie her to her bed for a day or two?

She'd never speak to him again. "Stevens, please show Mr. Wells into the..." He snapped his fingers, the name of the room escaping him.

The butler raised his eyebrows. "The gentlemen's reception room, sir? Or would you prefer the drawing room since the lady is present?"

Wasn't one room the same as another?

"The drawing room will do nicely." Samantha moved toward the double doors on the right.

Luke followed her into the room and nearly had to step back out. The carpet. The molding. The drapes. The furniture. Gold gleamed at him from every direction, and the few things that weren't gold were white. Someone had painted the walls a blindingly pure shade, and the white cushions on the furniture looked so bright they'd likely never been sat on. A large marble fireplace, also white, dominated the far wall, while floor-to-ceiling windows sent shafts of sunlight into the room.

He narrowed his eyes at his sister, who stepped daintily across the room. "Hang it all, Sam. Why didn't you tell me you were going to this banquet earlier?"

Samantha sat on a small fancy sofa thing with perfect cushions, her chin quivering slightly. "I didn't feel like being yelled at."

"I'm not…" *Yelling.* Though he was close. He pressed his lips together to keep from saying more.

"Mr. Hayes." Stevens stood in the open doorway. "Miss Hayes. May I present Mr. Jackson Wells."

Wells cast Luke that too-polished smile but walked straight to Sam. "Ah, Samantha, your beauty this evening is riveting." The man settled onto the dainty couch, somehow confident the fragile furniture would hold two people.

Luke eyed the chair beside them. Those spindly gold legs would likely collapse if he sat down, and if the chair didn't break, his filthy clothes would ruin the cushions.

"Thank you, Jackson. It's lovely to see you, as well." Samantha sent the dandy a smile despite her still trembling lips and extended her hand, palm down, which Wells kissed.

Kissed.

He should burn the man's lips off.

"Luke, allow me to make introductions." Samantha sniffed, her nose tilted into the air, but something wet glinted in her eyes.

Certainly he wasn't being a big enough fool to make her cry, was he?

"This is Jackson Wells, son of our esteemed local assemblyman, Thomas Wells. He also works for you, as manager of Great Northern Accounting and Insurance's office in Albany."

"I know he works for me." And the knowledge didn't curb his urge to chase away the scoundrel with his Colt.

"Jackson." Samantha's smile seemed more genuine as she glanced at her suitor. "This is my brother, Luke Hayes."

Wells's gaze, sickeningly friendly, rested on Luke. "We've spoken."

"Mr. Wells." Luke nodded, his voice vibrating like a dog's low growl. Probably wouldn't do to fire the man just for being sweet on his sister, but it was tempting.

Wells leaned forward and whispered something in Sam's ear, and she laughed softly.

Luke flexed his fingers. "Don't eastern folk ask permission from the man of the family before they start courting a lady?"

Samantha stopped midwhisper, and Wells stood. "I spoke with the late Mr. Hayes before he passed. He was thrilled when I requested to call on Samantha. He and my father are acquainted, of course, and—"

Luke cut the boy off with a wave of his hand. "And you expect to take her to the banquet."

"Yes, sir."

"Plans have changed. Samantha is accompanying me. You can meet her there."

Sam sprang from her seat. "Luke, you can't—"

"Perhaps you're concerned about a chaperone?" Wells interjected. "My sister is awaiting us in the carriage. She's a spinster and a perfectly acceptable chaperone."

"Miss Wells, Luke." Sam held her chin at a determined angle, but she blinked against the tears in her eyes. "The mathematics teacher you met at the academy yesterday."

So Miss Wells and the dandy were related after all. And that also made her the daughter of the local assemblyman. No one had bothered to tell him that, either.

What was the daughter of a politician doing teaching mathematics like some spinster?

Not that it mattered. Nope. Certainly not. Whatever Miss Wells chose to do or not do, whoever she happened to be related to or not related to, was no concern of his.

Luke rubbed his hand over his forehead and glanced back at his sister, only to find more tears glistening in her eyes. Confound it. Why did she cry at everything he did? Made him feel like an ogre—which he most definitely was *not*.

Or so he hoped. Maybe he had some questions for Sam, and needed to have a long chat with her suitor, but now was hardly the time to go into all that. Clearly Sam and Wells had arranged to attend the banquet, and it hardly seemed fair to stop them just because he'd arrived in town and hadn't known about their plans.

But he still didn't cotton to the idea of Sam going off without him. "How about this. Sam and I will go to the banquet together. Sam, if your *friend* and the mathematics teacher want to tag along, so be it."

Sam bit her bottom lip and sent him an uncertain glance. "Does that mean you're going to change clothes?"

Chapter Six

Elizabeth scooted toward the far side of the carriage, giving the *rancher*—not cowboy—more room as he sat beside her. She hadn't considered that he and his sister would attend the banquet together, or that he would insist they take his carriage, not Jackson's. She didn't want to share a carriage with the man after offending him earlier that afternoon.

Though she still wasn't sure how she'd offended him. Surely the man couldn't be upset because she'd asked for a donation, could he?

She clasped her gloved hands together on her lap. What had Jonah been thinking, anyway, to leave the estate to his grandson? It would have been much simpler had Jonah divided up his legacy before his death and donated everything to charity. Then again, maybe he'd planned to do that in a few more years. No one had been expecting that sudden heart attack.

"Good evening, Miss Wells." Mr. Hayes's voice rumbled from beside her.

She glanced his way, then down at her lap. My, but he did look dashing in a tuxedo, all the wild strength of the

West, thinly veiled in dark evening attire. Now if only he would trade in that cowboy hat for a proper top hat.

But cowboy hat or not, he'd still be the most sought-after man at the banquet. He had too much money and too-fine looks for people to ignore him. Not that she cared in the least.

And she'd best find something productive to talk about, lest she sit here contemplating his appearance for an hour. "Jackson, about our previous discussion, have you—"

"Not now, Elizabeth." Jackson flicked his hand as though getting rid of a fly. "I'm sure Mr. Hayes has more pressing things to discuss than your preoccupation with food costs at the academy."

"I'm not—"

"Mr. Hayes." Jackson nodded at the rancher. "Please accept my sincere condolences about your grandfather."

Mr. Hayes's hands gripped the edge of the seat, and his body tensed as though he would vault from their bench and squeeze between the courting couple across the carriage. The man was quite good at issuing threats with his eyes, and this one read: *Jackson Wells, touch my sister, and you'll regret it.*

"Jonah Hayes was a great businessman," her brother continued. Whether oblivious to Mr. Hayes's disapproval or purposely ignoring it, she couldn't tell. "Not to mention one of my father's most faithful and generous supporters."

"Yes." Mr. Hayes's eyes glinted with studied coolness. "I understand my grandfather was a faithful supporter of a great many things."

Jackson laughed, the overly loud sound bouncing off the carriage walls. "Have you considered following in your grandfather's footsteps and donating funds to one of New York's longest sitting and most popular assemblymen? My father has personally passed legislation that…"

The sun cast its fading orange rays inside the carriage while the familiar discussion about politics and campaigning swirled around her. Elizabeth shifted in the seat and made herself comfortable as the carriage wheels rumbled over the road.

If they were exactly 5.2 miles from Albany and they reached Albany in 56 minutes, that meant they traveled at a rate of 5.474 miles per hour. So say the wheels on the carriage were twenty-four inches in diameter, what would be the wheels' rate of rotation? She closed her eyes, letting the numbers and equations dance before her.

But even with her eyes shut, the scents of grass and sun and musk emanated from the person beside her, and the seat dipped ever so slightly in Mr. Hayes's direction, making him rather unforgettable—even with her equations.

It was going to be a long ride.

As the carriage threaded through the crowded streets of Albany, Mr. Hayes and Jackson continued to discuss Father's politics. Jackson talking about Father's campaign and funding for an hour wasn't unusual, but Mr. Hayes not agreeing to give away a penny?

Amazing.

Across from her, Samantha stared blindly out the carriage window, bored with how Mr. Hayes had kept Jackson's attention away from her this whole time. An intelligent man lurked behind the rancher's cowboy hat and country slang—now if only he shared his grandfather's passion for educating women.

Instead it seemed he'd come into town convinced he needed to undo half of his grandfather's strides in that area. Elizabeth folded and unfolded her hands in her lap.

"Are you looking forward to the banquet?" Mr. Hayes's breath tickled her ear.

She turned to face him. Had he and Jackson finally finished their conversation? They must have, because he was leaning over, his attention riveted to her.

"Yes, of course."

The bright glow of streetlamps shone through the carriage window, bathing that bold, handsome face in a mixture of shadows and light, while subtle wisps of cologne teased her nose. She stared at the ceiling. She could breathe. Nice calm breaths not remotely affected by the fragrance of sun and grass and musk tingeing the air. "I…um…thank you for your concern."

"I'd like a word with you once we step inside," he whispered as he leaned closer.

Her heart pounded. She wanted words with him, too—about keeping Samantha in school, about contributing to Hayes Academy. But not at the banquet.

"I'd like to discuss things, as well." She glanced across the carriage as it rolled to a stop in front of the Kenmore Hotel. The lovers whispered together much the way she and Mr. Hayes did. She edged as far away as she could, pressing herself against the wall. "But not tonight."

His eyes narrowed and blood throbbed in her ears.

She averted her gaze and focused on a streetcar clunking past, but she didn't let out her breath until he shifted away. How foolish to let him bother her. First with getting her ire up that afternoon, and now by act-ing so polished and intelligent she could hardly think. A man hadn't stirred her this way since her former fiancé.

But she was older now, and stronger, no longer a child to be swayed by flattering words and handsome looks. She'd even gone to college and gotten her math-ematics degree to avoid being trapped into a marriage with someone like David again.

"Miss Wells?"

She glanced up.

Mr. Hayes stood in the doorway of the now empty carriage, his hand extended, his eyes assessing. Did he know what went on inside her? How handsome she found him? How hurt she was by his disregard for any-thing and everything concerning Hayes Academy?

Of course not. He could only see what the lights il-luminated, which was precious little, as she clung to the far corner of the conveyance and shadows filled the space between.

"Are you all right?"

Of course she was all right. She was Miss Eliza-beth Wells, daughter of the esteemed and long-stand-ing assemblyman, Thomas Wells. Educated woman and teacher of mathematics. And she wasn't about to let a few whispered words from Mr. Hayes bother her. She leaned forward and gave him her hand.

"I'm sorry for barging into your class yesterday and disrupting the test, and for that comment this afternoon about a diploma not being important. I didn't mean to upset you. Not either time." His low voice rolled over her, smooth as polished glass.

She nodded slightly as she climbed down from the

carriage. "You apologized about interrupting class yesterday."

He rubbed a hand over his chin. "Didn't exactly mean it then, but I do now."

She couldn't stop the smile that curved her lips. "Thank you, sir. We've still much to discuss, but I'm afraid this evening simply isn't the time. Now we'd best head inside."

"As you like." He took her hand and placed it firmly on his arm.

She glanced around and tried to tug free. But Mr. Hayes only settled his other hand atop hers, giving her little choice but to follow him into the Kenmore. She didn't intend to let him escort her. She had plans for the evening, and they involved speaking to the school board members about keeping Hayes Academy open, not standing around on the arm of a rich bachelor and fluttering her eyelashes every time he deigned to look her way. Arriving at the banquet together had been merely a matter of convenience, hadn't it?

Once inside, Mr. Hayes helped her with her cloak before she could take it off herself, and handed the garment and his hat to the clerk. When he extended his elbow this time, she stepped back.

"If you'll excuse me." Her heart thudded slowly, as he turned those cool blue eyes—eyes that always seemed to see too much—on her. "There is a gentleman I must speak with. Do forgive me if I slip away."

Before he could answer, or take her hand again, or stare into her eyes for too long, or do something else equally unnerving, she turned and hurried toward the banquet hall, alone.

The room held the dimly lit, quiet ambiance of formal dinners but lacked some of the usual glamour. The rich array of women's dresses should have looked beautiful beside the men's crisp tuxedos, but the gowns and suits appeared old and overworn. That only made sense, as her own dress was more than four years old. No one had money for new dresses or properly tailored tuxedos these days.

Even the hall itself reflected the hotel's attempt to save money. On the tables, crystal goblets glittered beside sparkling china plates and polished silverware. But the tablecloths weren't bright white, more gray in hue with an occasional faded stain, and the chandeliers and windows looked in need of a good scrubbing.

The depression had hit New York hard, and her family felt it more than most. The force of the panic struck home last April, when a mob had descended on her father's bank. Nearly all her parents' campaign financing and personal savings had been lost, along with the trust funds set up for her and her brother—which she hadn't been able to access until she married anyway. Indeed, few people had escaped the panic and depression unscathed. Fortunately for Luke Hayes, his grandfather had been one of them.

Elizabeth weaved quickly through the room, searching for a board member not already engaged in conversation. She finally spotted Mr. Wilhem standing beside a window and surveying the crowd. Perfect.

"Elizabeth. Don't you look becoming this evening." Mr. Wilhem swirled the wine in his glass as she approached.

"Thank you, sir. You're looking rather fine yourself."

The middle-aged man chuckled, his bushy black-

and-gray-specked eyebrows rising. "Come now, child. There's no need to flatter an old man's vanity."

Child. The word struck her in the stomach. He didn't think her that young, did he? But then, he'd known her since she was a little girl. "I wanted to let you know how much the students at the academy are enjoying their studies this year."

Mr. Wilhem patted her on the shoulder, much like a grandfather would. "Are they now? Always a pleasure to hear students are excited about learning. Though I must admit, I'm a little concerned about those newspaper articles, both the editorial you wrote and the one the reporter penned in response. Did Miss Bowen tell you—"

"Samuel, there you are."

Elizabeth turned as Mr. Taviston, the head of the school board, approached.

"Good evening, Charles." Mr. Wilhem extended his hand to Mr. Taviston. "Miss Wells and I were just discussing Hayes Academy. It seems the students are enjoying their studies."

A thick, wooly sensation wrapped itself around her tongue. She hadn't anticipated any trouble discussing the benefits of keeping the academy open with an old family friend. But the head of the board of directors?

Mr. Taviston watched her like a fox would a rabbit.

"Thank you for allowing the school to stay open," she managed. "The students are doing quite well, and I've spent time working on the books this weekend, looking for ways to allow the school to function on a reduced budget."

Mr. Wilhem smiled, but Mr. Taviston ran his gaze slowly down her body, his eyes observing every subtlety of her blue silk gown. A flame she couldn't stop started at the base of her neck and licked onto her face.

"I don't understand how students being happy will help the school to stay open, Miss Wells. But I'm very interested to see your brother's report in another week. I doubt we've enough money to keep the school running for the remainder of the year."

"Of course we'll be able to keep things running." Her voice sounded overly bright, even to her. "We'll find a way."

"Are you aware how many letters board members have received from the public since those articles appeared? I've gotten over a dozen myself from people imploring us to find better use for our funds. It seems the people of the Albany area are very much of the opinion that young women should marry and have children, not fill their heads with calculus formulas and astronomical charts, which any good mother would find rather useless, wouldn't you agree?"

If he thought education useless, why was the man on the board of directors? But she knew the answer. He thought educating *women* useless, but not men. And he was a businessman who would invest in a girls' school if he saw the potential for immediate profit. If the profit disappeared, so did any vision for the school.

"No, I wouldn't agree," she mumbled.

"Well, it certainly seems to be in the best interest of both our banking accounts and society as a whole to close Hayes Academy."

"Of course we should close it. Was there any doubt after the meeting a couple nights ago?"

Elizabeth nearly cringed at the familiar blustery voice. Father wedged himself between her and Mr. Taviston, his wide shoulders and thick middle forcing her to take a step back. "Good evening, Father."

"Daughter, you're not discussing business with these gentlemen, are you?"

If a school banquet wasn't an appropriate time for her to discuss school business, when was? "Just Hayes Academy, where I happen to teach."

"I'm sorry to say we must close it, dear. The public is simply outraged after the appearance of that reporter's article, which you encouraged by that ridiculous editorial you wrote. Have you any notion how furious your mother was when she saw what you'd penned? It isn't appropriate for a lady like yourself to express your opinions in such a public way." He spoke the words without so much as a glance her direction.

"Well said," Taviston interjected.

"You're aware you should have gotten consent from the school board before you published such a thing, aren't you?" Mr. Wilhem patted her shoulder again.

Elizabeth licked her lips and took another step back. Was there any point attempting to argue? The men had already made up their minds. "Yes, I'm sorry. I see I made a mistake. But I was only trying to help boost enrollment."

"Help?" Father adjusted the lapels on his tuxedo. "We can't afford that kind of *help.* It cast the school board and others involved in a bad light, and hurt the public's opinion of us."

You mean hurt potential voters' opinion of you. She bit the inside of her cheek to keep from spewing the words. And to think, she'd already agreed to give a speech to educators for her father in a little over a week, to help convince them to support her father in next year's election. Yet when he stood here now, he tossed any and all support for her school aside.

She should have never told him yes when he'd asked. "I think closing the school would be a great disservice to both young women and society as a whole."

Father glared. "Elizabeth, I believe Edward needs to speak with you. Why don't you go seek him out?"

Oh, sure he did. Her father's head of staff always needed to see her when she started causing trouble, which seemed to be every time she was with her father these days.

"Gentlemen. Elizabeth."

Elizabeth sighed at the sound of the crisp English voice. One would think, after thirty years in America, the accent would mellow, but Mother still sounded as though she recently stepped off the ship from London.

"Mother." She offered the group a tight smile as Mother squeezed into the foursome.

"Good evening, Mr. Wilhem, Mr. Taviston. Hasn't the weather been wonderfully mild for October? I trust you're taking the utmost advantage of it." Mother looked elegant in a new rose-colored gown, likely one Father couldn't afford.

"Why of course, Mrs. Wells," Mr. Wilhem responded. "I've enjoyed several walks with my wife during the evenings."

Mother smiled, a flawless half curve of lips and slight raise of eyebrows. "Have you gentlemen met the Hayes heir? I was informed Elizabeth arrived with him this evening, and I think I smell romance in the air."

Elizabeth's entire body grew rigid while four pairs of eyes turned to her. If only she could grit her teeth and pretend she didn't know the woman beside her. Instead she kept her forced smile in place. "Mother, my arriving with Mr. Hayes is not what you make it seem. He decided to chaperone Samantha, and as Jackson had already asked me to chaperone, we traveled here together. Mr. Hayes and I are merely..." *friends?* No, too strong of a word. "...acquaintances."

Mr. Wilhem raised those bushy eyebrows once again. "Then you're not seeing Mr. Hayes?"

"No. I'm not accepting any suitors. Now if you gentlemen will excuse us, Mother and I have some important matters to discuss." She squeezed her mother's elbow so hard the woman's perfect smile pinched.

"Yes, do excuse us, gentlemen."

Elizabeth pulled her mother away, leaving the men to whisper furiously, probably about how soon they could announce the closing of Hayes Academy. Why even ask Jackson for a report when they'd already made their decision?

"Dear, you should have had something special made for this evening." Mother's lips sank into a frown as Elizabeth led her toward a vacant corner of the room. "That dress is so old I'm afraid you'll not attract a single man."

"I'm not here to attract men." This time she couldn't stop her teeth from gritting.

Mother reached up to touch a stray wisp of hair at the side of her face. "Really, Elizabeth, a girl of your wealth and beauty should be married."

Wealth. That was laughable considering the money her family had lost in the panic. And if her beauty wasn't enough to keep a suitor faithful, then what good was it? "I'm a mathematics teacher, Mother, and a rather good one according to my students and the headmistress. I don't plan to stop what I'm doing."

She should have expected the crestfallen look, the way the light deserted her mother's eyes and turned them a dull green. But something inside her deflated anyway.

"We never should have let you walk away from marrying David when you were younger." The tone of lecture in Mother's voice, the hint of implied guilt, the soft way her eyes entreated Elizabeth to agree all coalesced into a giant wave of regret. Did Mother stand in front of the mirror and practice these speeches? "You were so young, and I thought we were helping, that maybe you should wait another year before you married. Now it's been eight years and I see how foolish a mistake we made."

"No. The mistake would have been marrying David. I'm happy remaining a spinster and teaching."

"I expect you to care about your family's happiness, not just your own. You're still a Wells, after all." Mother's face paled beneath her face powder and rouge, and she blinked an absent tear from her eye. "And it…it happens that your family needs you right now."

Her family needed her? Since when? They always seemed to manage fine on their own. Elizabeth reached her hand out and clasped her mother's. "What's wrong, Mama?"

"Oh, do forgive me, dear. I didn't intend to get so overwrought." Mother wiped another tear from beneath her eye and fanned her face, though the jerky movement did little good in the overly stuffy room. "It's nothing really. At least I think it's nothing. But well…oh, how I worry about your father. He's not been the same since the panic, losing all his savings and having to mortgage the house, so he can build his other assets back up. Some of the voters are speaking out against politicians, claiming people like your father were responsible for the panic itself. He's under so much strain."

Elizabeth patted her mother's hand. "Father may have happened upon hard times, but he'll ride it out. He always does. A year from now things won't seem nearly so terrible, but if there's anything I can do, you know I'll help."

"Do you understand how much a good marriage could aid us in a time like this? You know I married your father because of the benefit it brought my family, even though it meant I had to leave England. Every daughter should be willing to make such a sacrifice."

She dropped her mother's hand. The argument was far too familiar. "I want to help Father, but I'm not willing to spend the rest of my life chained to someone like David. It's unfair of you to expect such a thing."

"But what if your father can't make payments on the house? What if he loses it?" The whispered words hung in the air between them. "We'd lose everything then."

"No." Elizabeth spoke the word quickly, almost harshly. In her mind, she drew up an image of the century-old stone home she'd grown up in, the room in the top right corner that even now held some of her things. "That won't happen. It's ridiculous to even think it. Father's been managing his own money and investments since before I was born. Perhaps the panic set him back, but he's still a smart businessman."

The lines around Mother's eyes and mouth only deepened. "Don't you see? This is why we need you, dear. You say your father won't lose the house, but it's possible. If you were to marry someone who could help support the family, everything would be taken care of. I've invited several guests to dinner next weekend, and you should have a new gown made for the occasion. It's a time to look your best."

Elizabeth rubbed her temples. "I'd be there, you know I would. But I told you last week, the school play is that Saturday."

Mother's shoulders slumped, as though the very world would end if her daughter missed one of the weekly family dinners. "The guests are coming specifically for you."

Lovely. She so enjoyed being paraded around like a horse for auction. In fact, she could almost hear the auctioneer's announcement. *Marry Elizabeth Wells, and you'll land yourself a spinster mathematics teacher with an overbearing mother and debt-laden father.* "Why don't you reschedule for the following week?"

Mother sighed, the unladylike sound only further evidence of her distress. "Elizabeth, dear, I have your best interest in mind by wanting you at that dinner. Your family should be more important than your students."

She wanted to scream. She wanted to howl. She wanted to beat her head against the wall. And she would have, if any of it would make Mother understand. "You are, but this play is only once a year. I'll attend dinner the week after next, I promise."

"Sometimes I hardly know what to do with you," Mother huffed. "Now, just look at the Hayes heir over there. He would make a choice husband."

She glanced at Mr. Hayes, standing among a small crowd, tall and devastatingly handsome with layers of sun-bleached hair falling around his tanned face. Mr.

Brumley, the manager of the orphanage, spoke with him, while several others circled like vultures waiting to descend upon his vast inheritance.

If Mr. Hayes's handling of Jackson was any indication, he wouldn't be giving away a penny.

Directly beside him, Mrs. Crawford stood with her daughter, a young lady Samantha's age, wearing pink and flounces. Indeed, every mother in the room seemed to keep one eye trained on Mr. Hayes, waiting for that perfect chance to introduce her daughter.

"He'll return to Wyoming," Elizabeth muttered, more to herself than anything.

"He can't." Mother's face pinched. "He'll need to stay and manage his grandfather's estate, unless he wants to see Jonah Hayes's life's work run into the ground."

As though that would bother him.

"You simply must go over there and stand beside him." Mother gripped her shoulder and nudged her forward. "The man escorted you here, and now he's not paying you the least attention. It's nearly scandalous."

Probably wiser not to tell Mother *she* ignored *him,* not the other way around. "The man didn't escort me anywhere. We—"

The announcement for dinner interrupted her.

"What excellent timing. Come along now. I've already arranged for him to sit across from you."

Chapter Seven

Luke shifted sideways ever-so-slightly in an attempt to put some space between himself and the gentleman crowding his left side. Unfortunately that placed him a little too close to the girl wearing butter-yellow and ruffles standing on his right. He looked around the banquet hall. With dinner and the speaking long finished, people sauntered toward the exits.

But for all the people leaving, he stood surrounded. He stuck a finger in his collar and pulled. Four hours of chattering. Meet him, meet her, donate money to this, donate money to that. He needed a break.

And he spotted his excuse to escape, right by the back double doors. Jackson stood in a corner alone with Samantha, far too close and looking ready to eat his little sister for dessert.

Where was Miss Wells? Wasn't she supposed to be chaperoning? He glanced around the room. There she was, on the far side of the hall, engaged in a fierce conversation with an older gentleman. The woman probably wouldn't be paying attention to Jackson or Samantha anytime soon.

Luke shifted his gaze back to the rotund man earnestly yammering about beds and quilts for the hospital. "If you'll excuse me, sir. There's a matter I must see to."

The man's mouth dropped slightly. "Yes, well, can we look forward to that donation, then?"

"I'll speak with my lawyer." Luke dipped his head and scooted toward the door, their shirts brushing as he squeezed past. He didn't glance back at the girl in yellow, but another mother waiting with a different young lady gave him a furious glare.

Reaching Jackson and Sam, he grabbed Jackson's shoulder and jerked the younger man backward. The city boy landed against his chest with an *umph*. "You best step back from my sister. Or you'll not be seeing the likes of her again."

"Yes, sir," Jackson squeaked.

Samantha scowled at him. "Let him go, Luke. He wasn't doing anything wrong."

"He doesn't need to stand so close." Luke let go of the slippery accountant, and with another three steps, he burst through the doors and into the yard. Muted voices from inside floated to his ears, horses clomped past on the road and an electric railcar clunked along the street. No one else appeared on the patio, but he stood awful close to the banquet room. Anyone who stepped outside could see him, and one of those calculating mothers was sure to send her daughter out. He ducked around the far side of the hotel, where shadows shrouded the ground.

A gate or wall of some sort blocked the far end of the pathway leading to the street. Probably a wise decision on the hotel's part. One too many men had likely gotten bored with a fancy to-do and escaped thataway. Hang it all, *he* would escape if he didn't have two women to escort home.

He leaned against the brick and inhaled the thick city air, not nearly as stale as the air inside that banquet hall, but a far cry from the clean air of home. At least he had a break from all the badgering. How many young women could a man be expected to meet in one night? He didn't remember what half the ladies looked like, let alone their names.

And he wouldn't go back inside until he figured out some way to stop the constant requests for donations. Maybe he could be generous with some of his money before he returned to Wyoming—Grandfather had evidently been so—but a man needed a chance to breathe, didn't he?

A door thudded and footsteps clattered against the stone pavers.

"Don't be infantile. You know we must have the money back."

Luke grimaced. Probably time to show himself and get back to the banquet.

"You simply can't revoke the funding from the school. Half of it's already spent."

The steely voice laced with sugar stopped him. Was Miss Wells out here? Alone with a man?

"Well then, unspend it." Frustration grew in the older masculine voice.

Luke rubbed his chin. He should make himself known. But wouldn't it look strange, him appearing from the side of the building with no good reason for being there? Still, whatever was going on between Miss Wells and the other man wasn't his business.

He shifted farther down the wall. Maybe he could

hop over that gate near the street, then make his way back to the banquet through the front of the building.

Crack. A snapping sound reverberated against the brick building. He'd stepped on a twig. Now the arguing voices would come around the hotel and spot him plain as day. Then he'd have a heap of explaining to do.

Except they kept right on talking. He raked his hand through his hair and slumped against the wall. Did more twigs litter the ground? Maybe there was an old can he might kick? Anything else that would draw attention his way? Looked like he'd gotten himself good and stuck.

"It's public money, already approved and given to Hayes Academy. How are we to give the money back?"

"Cancel whatever you ordered with it," the male voice blundered. "Surely you understand why this must be done. Your father's in a precarious political situation, and those newspaper articles have made the academy widely unpopular. If the public were to find out the school received state funds, your father's reputation might not recover. We need the money returned by the end of next week. Your brother understood perfectly when I explained the situation to him yesterday."

Luke held his breath. Miss Wells's *father* was taking money away from the school? What kind of father took money away from his daughter because of some embittered newspaper article? If Sam needed a large amount of money for building a house in Wyoming or saving her husband's ranch or some other cause, he'd give her the funds in an instant. Of course, she would have to be home where she belonged before he gifted her any such thing, but still, he'd never be able to hand her money one day and take it back the next.

"My brother doesn't care about the academy," Miss

Wells's voice quivered, whether from rage or tears, he couldn't tell. "The school's no more than a nuisance to him. Besides what will you do with the money after we return it?"

"As a matter of fact—"

"No, just leave. I don't want to know what frivolous things it'll be wasted on."

"It won't be wasted."

"It's not being wasted now."

"There are differing opinions on that."

"Yes, I see there are. Good night, Edward."

Elizabeth pressed her back to the cold brick wall and stared up at the sky, vast and dark with only a handful of bright stars shining down. The chilly night air wrapped around her, causing gooseflesh to rise on her arms, but she couldn't seek the warmth inside. Not when curious eyes and wagging tongues filled the banquet room.

Dreams were a bit like stars, weren't they? Most swallowed up by the city lights, and only a few so bright they shined through all the busyness trying to snuff them out. She'd once thought her dreams were brilliant enough to sparkle on their own—graduate from college, get a teaching job, train young women. But even after achieving so much, her dreams risked falling pale and dry to the ground. Father remained too busy to know she had dreams, Mother wanted her married despite her dreams and Jackson smiled and promised to help with her dreams, then ended up doing nothing at all.

She'd thought she'd been following God, pleasing Him in some way by refusing to marry a man like her ex-fiancé and then training to be a teacher. She'd thought she'd be helping young women not too different from herself when she'd gotten her teaching position at Hayes. She'd thought she'd been helping the academy when she'd written that editorial about female education. But somewhere along the way, she'd ceased helping anyone and started causing trouble. When had she strayed from the path God intended for her?

Father, what have I done? She sunk her head into her hands, a foolish move, since the jostle to her precariously positioned coiffure sent the side of her hair cascading down. Lovely. Just lovely. Now when she appeared back inside, the people present would think she'd been in the yard with a man.

She felt about for the loosened pins still stuck in her tresses. She could probably shove her hair back atop her head and arrange it in a manner that wouldn't attract too much attention.

If only fixing her other problems was as easy as jamming pins into her hair. Maybe she should stop fighting for the academy and tell the board she would abide by their decision if they closed the school. Tell Mother she'd attend that dinner next Saturday and meet whatever gentlemen had been invited. Tell her students they couldn't return after the semester break because no one cared enough to defend the school they attended.

"Miss Wells?"

The unfamiliar masculine voice sent a chill down her spine. She looked toward the patio doors. A tall figure in a painfully crisp suit approached, his dark hair gleaming in the lamplight though his face remained shadowed. She took a sudden step back.

"May I help you?" The night seemed to swallow her words, leaving only emptiness around them.

"You most certainly may. I'm Reginald Higsley from the Albany *Morning Times*."

He didn't need to say where he worked. His name had imprinted itself on her mind, when it first appeared beneath the headline of that wretched newspaper article.

"Why are you here, sir?" *Outside? Alone with me?* Though her stomach twisted, she raised her chin. "At an event to which you weren't invited?"

"I was indeed invited. Your father asked me to attend."

Betrayal blazed through her gut. Of course Father would invite the reporter and try to schmooze good publicity from him.

"I've hoped for a word with you all evening." He moved close, so close the sleeve of his coat brushed her gloved arms and the soft puff of his breath on the chilled air floated into her face.

She took another step back, bumping the wall. "Would you like a statement, then, for the paper?" She cringed at the quiver in her voice. "Perhaps next week you're going to run an article on the importance of educating young women rather than the dangers of it?"

His mouth curved up into a shadowed smile. "Yes, I suppose you could say that."

"Very well, then. I believe the importance of educating women cannot be ignored despite the current economy. Young women are not to blame for the panic or the recession. Why should they be the first to suffer?"

"So you feel women should be educated at all costs, even at the expense of feeding hungry children?"

She ground her teeth together. This was why she hated reporters. "I think both causes are important, and one shouldn't be sacrificed for the other."

"So you would starve children if it allows you to keep teaching trigonometry?"

Advanced algebra. First her mother tried fixing her up with Luke Hayes, then her father revoked the funding from Hayes Academy, and if that wasn't enough, now this polished reporter was twisting her words. It was enough to drive even the most sane of people mad. "I didn't say that. But how like a reporter. You ask questions fifteen different ways until you get an answer you half like. Then you go on your merry way and make up false quotations for all the world to read the next day."

And she'd just ruined any hope of Mr. Higsley's next article repairing the damage from the last one. Oh, why couldn't she keep better control of her tongue? It was like she had a little monster inside her mouth, popping out and saying whatever it willed at the worst times.

"I don't appreciate being called a liar." The man loomed over her, barely contained fury radiating from beneath the lines of his stiff suit.

She shrank back against the wall. Yes, she should cut out her tongue for all the trouble it got her into. Tongues were such a useless part of one's anatomy, anyway. One didn't need them for practical things like quadratic equations or theorems or integration.

Except one could use a tongue to scream when in danger. A sure benefit in her current situation. But if she cried out now and someone came, everyone would see she'd been outside with a man. And with her hair in such a state of disarray, it would appear that…that…

Well, the incident would get her fired.

"Tell me, Miss Wells." Mr. Higsley placed one arm on either side of her, trapping her against the cold bricks. "Does it feel good knowing that students at your extravagant academy continue their education in luxury while most young women their age work ten-hour days to bring bread home for their families?"

"Leave the lady alone."

The reporter jerked back as though stung.

Elizabeth felt more than saw Mr. Hayes approach from the far side of the building. Trembling, she blew out the air in her lungs and took a hesitant step away from Mr. Higsley, only to have her next breath clog in her throat. Had Mr. Hayes been there this whole time? Listening around the side of the building?

But then, perhaps his eavesdropping wasn't so terrible. At least he wouldn't assume she'd set up a secret rendezvous with the reporter.

Mr. Hayes stopped beside her, his gaze narrowed on the reporter. "Why don't you take yourself back to whatever hole you climbed out of. The lady's spent enough time with you."

Mr. Higsley extended his hand. "I'm Reginald Higsley, sir. And I'm afraid this situation is not as it appears. You see, I'm a reporter for the Albany *Morning Times,* and I just stepped outside to get a—"

"You could be President Cleveland for all I care. If the lady asks you to leave, you leave."

"I'm sorry, sir, but I didn't catch your name." The reporter's voice turned icy.

"Because I didn't give it. Now go." The growl in Mr. Hayes's voice must have convinced the other man to obey, because he departed.

"Are you all right? Did the scoundrel hurt…?"

Luke's words fell away as he turned to face Miss Wells. He'd thought her beautiful before. She *had* been

beautiful before, in that midnight-blue gown that reminded him of the sky just after sunset and with her
hair swept up into that mass of fat curls. But now half
of those thick mahogany locks fell about her shoulders
and shimmered under the lighting.

She wasn't simply beautiful, she was magnificent.
Beyond magnificent. Luke edged closer, compelled
partly by a desire to ensure she was safe and partly by
some invisible pull he didn't understand.

He should be drawn and quartered for leaving her
unprotected with that man for so long. But she didn't
seem harmed. Her body didn't tremble nor did tears
streak her cheeks. If anything she seemed more courageous than before.

"No. I'm not hurt, and I can explain," she answered,
but she refused to meet his eyes.

"Go on, then." His fingers itched to slide up into
those burnished mahogany tresses. Surely they couldn't
feel as soft as they looked. He crossed his arms solidly
in front of his chest—a good way to make his hands
stay put.

She began to babble then, a torrent of words about
not doing anything untoward with the reporter, and
being upset earlier and grabbing her hair, at which time
half of it fell down. Then she claimed if he just went
back inside, she'd take a few minutes to set herself to
rights, and they could leave for home.

Her brain had plumb run off and deserted her body,
if she thought he'd leave her alone again. After he'd
overheard her conversation about the money for the
academy, he peeked around the side of the building to
find Miss Wells still outside, clearly distressed. Then
he'd wandered over to the gate near the street to try get-

ting out somehow. A crying woman hardly needed to know that a man she despised had witnessed her being humiliated.

But the exit had been shut up tight, with no way to break the lock, short of putting a bullet in the thing. And since he didn't rightly want to climb the fence and mess up his fancy getup, he waited awhile, figuring to give Miss Wells some time to herself. He hadn't thought some brute might approach her.

"So if you please, Mr. Hayes?"

If he please what? Had she asked him something?

"I only need a moment of privacy."

Oh, so they were back to him leaving again. "Not likely."

She took a step away from the wall, maybe to chase him off, maybe to head somewhere herself, but the bricks at the back of her head must have pulled something loose in her up-do. The moment she moved forward, the rest of her hair tumbled down, a waterfall of velvet glinting traces of red and brown where the lights touched it.

She gasped, the quiet sound clambering through his head as though she'd screamed, and she started sifting through the heavy locks. "Oh, I've done it now. I'll never be able to get this back up. I'm terrible at putting it into anything but a twist, you see. This is why most women who attend such events have maids. To pin up their hair properly, so it doesn't fall at the slightest bump. But I simply must become a better hairdresser, living on my own as I do." She sank to the ground, her hands still moving frantically about.

"What are you doing?"

She glanced up. "Searching for pins, of course."

Searching for pins. She'd just been told her father was taking back money from her beloved school, then a reporter nearly accosted her, and she became upset over her hair?

Most times women made little sense, but at moments such as this, they made no sense at all. He hunkered down to help anyway.

"The things are impossible to find in the dark." Her hand brushed his, slender and warm even through her glove, then went about searching the ground. "And I can't go back into the hall with my hair like this. Everyone will assume your hands have been in it, or worse, and—"

She stopped and stared at him, then pressed a hand over her mouth, her eyes rounding. "Oh, no. I didn't mean it like that. Forgive my tongue. It gets carried away far too often."

"Calm down." He laid a hand over hers. "If you can't go back through the banquet hall, we'll go 'round the side of the building and have the carriage brought out." He'd find some way to break the lock on that gate if it meant saving the woman from rumors. Then again, maybe there wasn't a gate on the other side of the building.

"Oh." She breathed the word like a sigh. "I hadn't thought of that."

He would have released her hand and drawn back, but she held him with her eyes, those wide, vulnerable orbs shimmering with a tearless pain that pulled words from him before he even realized he'd opened his mouth to speak. "I'm sorry about your evening—the money, the reporter, the whole lot of it."

Her face hovered so close to his that her breath

warmed his neck. His gaze drifted to her lips, full and dark in the night. They'd taste as sweet as that fruit-and-sugar voice of hers. He'd give up his Colt .45 and saddle if he was wrong.

The breeze stirred, and a strand of hair fanned across her cheek. He swept it away and anchored it behind her ear, then let his fingers linger at the tender spot behind her earlobe. Did she know how beautiful she looked in that dress? Bathed in moonlight? With her hair falling to her waist?

Her jaw trembled slightly. Would she tremble more if he pressed his lips to hers?

"Mr. Hayes."

Her whisper, soft as it was, slapped him. He pulled back and dropped his hands. Here he thought about kissing the woman senseless, and she called him Mr. Hayes.

"It's Luke," he said, his voice rough as gravel. "And we best be going." Because if he stayed here any longer with her, he was going to kiss her—the woman who didn't want to let Sam come home and lectured him for wearing his gun.

Yep, that would have been a disaster, all right. He stood and extended his hand. "Let's get you to the carriage, then I'll go hunt up Sam and Jackson."

She hesitated for the briefest second, something unreadable flashing across her eyes, before she placed her gloved hand in his.

Confound it, did that have to be small and delicate, too? Couldn't the Good Lord have made some part of the woman undesirable? Blessed her with a big nose or unseemly freckles? Carrot-orange hair or a laugh that sounded like a pig snort?

He swallowed and helped her up, brushing his thumb

over the top of her knuckles. Shafts of silvery moonlight filtered through the sporadic clouds above, illuminating the gentle curve of her pink cheek, the fragile column of her creamy neck, the spilling waves of her mahogany hair.

Disaster. Kissing her would be a disaster. He'd just keep repeating it until he and the woman were safely surrounded by a slew of other folk, and he forgot all about his urge to kiss her.

Because he would forget—he hoped.

"Come on," he said a bit too roughly and pulled her forward. She followed silently, her dress swishing softly over pavers, then grass, as they rounded the far side of the building.

He led her down the narrow dirt path between the Kenmore and a similarly massive structure. Darkness shrouded the walkway, and moonlight barely slanted through the small space above. But streetlights illuminated the far end of the path, a good sign there wasn't a locked gate before them.

A gasp. A rustle up ahead. He quickened his pace, tugging Miss Wells behind him. Through the shadows, a silhouette of two lovers locked in a passionate kiss emerged. Getting around them in this confined space would be interesting, if not embarrassing.

A breathy sigh filled the air, and the man pressed the woman's back against the building while her hands clutched at his hair. Heat stole across the back of Luke's neck.

He shifted farther in front of Miss Wells, hopefully blocking her view of the careless couple. Then falling gold curls caught the dim light, and fury rushed his blood, a swelling tide he'd no desire to stop. He dropped

Miss Wells's hand, strode forward and heaved Jackson back by the collar.

Jackson gagged, the sound similar to the noise a man made as a noose tightened about his neck. Luke jerked the fabric harder, and Jackson gagged again, his hands flying up to loosen his shirt. Well, the man deserved to choke for a bit after touching his sister.

"Jackson?" Miss Wells gasped.

"Luke!" Samantha cried.

He didn't glance at either woman but leaned his head close to Jackson's ear. "Don't you *ever* touch her again. Don't you *ever* come calling again. And don't you *ever* try contacting her again."

He released Jackson's shirt enough so the man could suck air. "Say 'Yes, sir.'"

"Luke, stop. You're hurting him." Samantha rushed forward and gripped his arm, trying to yank it away from Jackson.

"Luke, please release my brother and let's discuss this." Miss Wells, ever calm, appeared behind Samantha.

"He was touching Sam." Maybe the boy didn't deserve to die, but so help him, Jackson Wells wouldn't touch his baby sister again.

He finally let go of Jackson. The other man stumbled forward, and Samantha rushed to his side.

"I love her." Determination carried on Jackson's voice.

Luke stared into Jackson's eyes, his stomach sinking. Not his baby sister. She wasn't old enough to be loved by a city slicker like Jackson Wells. She was just a girl at heart, a beautiful girl caught in a woman's body. Not big enough to be kissed that way, touched that way. "If you loved her, then you wouldn't take advantage of her."

"I wasn't taking advantage. It was merely a kiss."

"It was more than a kiss."

"Luke, I'm sorry. We didn't mean to. We just…got caught up." Samantha tucked herself beneath Jackson's arm.

Did she fancy herself in love with Jackson, too? Luke closed his eyes as tiredness flooded him. *Please, Father, no. How will I ever get her to come home if she's moonstruck?* "Say goodbye and get to the carriage." His voice, soft but firm, carried through the air. "You'll not be seeing him again."

"No, wait. You can't do that. I said I was sorry." Samantha wound her arms about Jackson's waist, and Jackson settled his hands around Samantha's back in return.

Luke raked a hand through his hair. How had he gotten into this mess?

"Jackson, obey Mr. Hayes. You were wrong in kissing Samantha like that. Even if you do love her," Elizabeth stated from beside him.

But Jackson didn't obey, and why should he? The way he and Sam had wrapped themselves around each other, nothing short of an army could pry them apart.

Luke could still hear Samantha's gasp echo between the buildings, still see the way her hands dove into Jackson's hair. She had no business kissing a man like that until after she was married. "Jackson, we'll discuss this further on Monday. How convenient we already have an appointment scheduled. And, Samantha, if seeing him meant so much to you, you'd not have kissed him."

"Oh, like you've never kissed a woman before," Sam

shot back. "Or maybe you've forgotten about the time I found you and Mary Baker behind the barn."

"Jackson was devouring you." Luke thrust his hand toward the spot where he'd found them against the wall. "That was a heap more than some stolen kiss behind a barn."

"You've still got no right to keep us apart."

"Watch me." Luke rubbed the back of his neck. Where was his sister's guilt? Or Jackson's? Oh, Sam had apologized, but more because she'd been caught than because she felt she'd done wrong, and now she stood defending herself. Had Samantha and Jackson done this before? Exactly how familiar were they with each other?

"Samantha, go to the carriage." Miss Wells's firm voice stole over them.

"Tell my brother, Miss Wells, tell him he's being unreasonable."

Miss Wells edged forward and laid a gentle hand on Samantha's upper arm. "It's best you and your brother discuss this tomorrow, when you've both calmed down."

"But what about Jackson?" Sam's words tumbled out, caught somewhere between a sob and a whine.

"Jackson's a grown man, accountable for his own actions. You, on the other hand, are still under your brother's protection."

Sam glared at Miss Wells, but the look mellowed into calculation as she swept her eyes over the teacher's hair. "And what, dear brother, were you doing between these buildings with Miss Wells?"

"I'm wondering the same thing." Jackson scowled at Miss Wells.

"That's not your business." Luke crossed his arms.

No need for Samantha and Jackson to know what type of evening Miss Wells had.

"No?" Jackson asked in a deceptively quiet tone. "It appears Samantha and I are getting into trouble for the very thing you were doing with my sister."

"I didn't..." *Touch her.* Except he had. Not in the way Samantha and Jackson implied, but he'd held her hand, stroked behind her ear, almost kissed her. *Almost.* "...do anything inappropriate." The words sounded pathetic even to him.

"Elizabeth?" Jackson watched his sister like a wolf watching a deer before it pounces.

"She looks as though you mauled her." Samantha slapped her hands on her hips and tapped her shoe impatiently on the ground.

Luke rolled his eyes. Where had his sweet, innocent sister gone? The woman who stood before him couldn't possibly be the same girl he'd taken to the train station three years ago. "Get to the carriage, Sam. Jackson, hire a hansom cab to take you home. I'll see your sister back to Valley Falls."

"I'm not going anywhere," Samantha declared. "And I won't let you stand there and berate me for kissing the man I love while you were trysting with a woman you haven't known for more than a day."

The man she loved. The words packed a wallop to his gut.

"Samantha!" Shock seared Miss Wells's voice. Whether because of Sam's accusations or her attitude, he couldn't tell. "You mustn't blame your brother. It's my fault. I got myself into some trouble, and then I accidentally knocked my hair askew when I put my head in my hands."

Luke took a step toward Miss Wells. "You don't owe—"

"Your brother came to my aid," she continued. "Yes, my hair is down, but if not for your brother stepping in, I may well look worse."

"Are you all right, Elizabeth?" The words were appropriate, but doubt tinged Jackson's voice. Instead of going to his sister's side, Jackson wrapped his arm tighter about Samantha's shoulders. He didn't ask why her head had been in her hands or if anyone had tried to hurt her, didn't even sound like he believed her.

Miss Wells raised her chin a notch, masking whatever she felt beneath that polished veneer of calm. "Thank you, I'm fine."

So she claimed. But she swallowed as she stood there. So still, so alone, his arm ached to reach out and pull her against him.

A bad idea to begin with, and definitely not something to attempt with Jackson and Samantha around. Still…couldn't Sam hug the woman or something? Then she wouldn't seem so abandoned.

"Right." Sam's gaze darted between Miss Wells and him, and the hairs on the back of his neck prickled.

Samantha and Jackson were in the wrong, not Miss Wells and him. And he wasn't about to stand around while someone else threw accusations at the poor teacher. "We're leaving, Samantha. Now." He pointed toward the front of the building, then turned to Jackson. "You'd best say goodbye. You won't be seeing my sister for a while."

The finality in his voice must have resonated with Jackson, because the younger man reached up, touched the side of Sam's face, and whispered against her ear.

Luke scowled. Something still told him this was the first time Sam had been caught, not the first time Jackson had kissed her that way. But as he took Samantha's shoulders and steered her toward the street, he couldn't block the sound of her quiet sobs.

Chapter Eight

"How could you?"

Samantha's whimpers floated from the opposite side of the carriage. Elizabeth shifted uncomfortably and glanced out the window while the conveyance rocked and swayed toward Valley Falls.

"I love you, Sam." Tenderness filled Mr. Hayes's—she couldn't bring herself to call a man she'd known for so little time by his first name, even if he'd asked her to—voice. "I'm trying to protect you."

Indeed he was. After sneaking off with Samantha and kissing her that way, Jackson deserved a belt to his backside.

"I don't want your protection." Tears, rather than venom, choked Samantha's voice.

Through the darkness shrouding the opposite side of the carriage, Elizabeth made out the combined silhouette of the two siblings: Mr. Hayes holding Samantha on his lap and the girl crying into his chest.

The moment seemed oddly tender, and something she'd no business witnessing.

"I'm your brother. I can't just stop protecting you or caring about you."

"But I love him."

"I'm sure you love him, Samantha. But you're only seventeen," Elizabeth said, then licked her lips. The same age she'd been when she had fancied herself in love with David. "You've much to learn yet."

"You don't understand." Samantha sniffled. "Neither of you do. You've never been in love."

Elizabeth's heart twisted. If only she didn't understand. If only she'd never been in love. "Perhaps so. But your brother is simply trying to help."

"If he wanted to help, then he'd let me see Jackson rather than tear the two of us apart."

"Samantha, it's not like that," Mr. Hayes rasped, his voice a mixture of tiredness and frustration.

Fabric shifted across the carriage, likely Samantha moving away from her brother, and Elizabeth sighed. The girl didn't realize how blessed she was to have a brother willing to protect her from ill-intentioned suitors. If her own family had been half as concerned about her as Mr. Hayes was about Samantha, then breaking off her engagement with David all those years ago might have worked out better. Namely, her family wouldn't still think her a villain for her decision.

Instead, she'd had to fight her family to get away from David, rather than fight to be near him.

"Do you mind?" Mr. Hayes appeared from the shadows and settled onto the seat beside her. "I'm not exactly welcome on the other side of the carriage at the moment."

His presence seemed to fill the entire bench, which was ridiculous, as he only took up 33 percent of the black leather seat. Though it seemed like more with the way the mixture of grass and sunshine and subtle cologne filled the air.

Elizabeth shivered. Because of the draft creeping in from under the carriage door. Not because Mr. Hayes shifted subtly closer. Not because he watched her with those piercing eyes. Not because he smelled so good she wanted to lean toward him.

"Why don't you tell me what's putting those worried lines around your mouth and eyes?" He spoke gently, that deep, rusted voice full of concern.

The carriage rocked and bumped—common, lulling movements—and somewhere outside coyotes yipped. Across the conveyance, deep, rhythmic breathing had replaced Samantha's soft sobs.

Elizabeth picked at a speck on her dress, unwilling to meet his eyes. "It was a long night."

"Because you learned your father's revoking public funding from the academy?"

"You overheard."

"Not intentionally."

Embarrassment flooded her anyway. "Yes, in part because of Father, but even more so because of that reporter." She folded and unfolded her hands in her lap. "You see, with the panic last spring and now the recession, enrollment at the academy is down, and—"

"My lawyer explained the situation. Why do you think I asked for your ledgers?"

"I'm afraid you still don't understand. The reason I didn't want to give you my ledgers…that is, well…a lot of donors have pulled their funding from the school… like, like my father." She could barely force the last words over her tongue. Maybe if she said it over and over in her head, it wouldn't be so hard to speak it aloud. *My father revoked our funding. My father revoked our funding. My father revoked our—*

"Your father shouldn't have pulled your funding."

She stared at him. "I beg your pardon?"

"I said your father shouldn't have pulled money out from under you."

"Why would you be bothered by such a thing, when you're taking your sister out of school without so much as a thought about her desires?"

"Because no father should deal with his daughter like that."

Her lungs suddenly stopped drawing air. Was he defending her? This man who'd come into town with a will of iron and a desire to make everyone bend to his wishes?

"It's cruel enough to give you something and then ask for it back. But the old man didn't even tell you himself. He sent his little minion to do it." Resentment dripped from Mr. Hayes's voice. "Then that reporter appeared, and where was your father? Or your brother? Not keeping an eye on you. Not making sure you were safe. Your brother wasn't even concerned you may have been hurt. Instead, the scoundrel thought I'd taken your hair down and refused to listen when you tried to tell him otherwise. No person should suffer that kind of treatment from family."

Something thick rose in her throat, and she looked down toward her feet. Surely her family didn't treat her as poorly as he made it sound. They were just caught up in their own lives and wanted her to support their endeavors rather than her own.

So how should she answer Mr. Hayes? Say she was

used to it, that they'd treated her this way since she had called off her engagement? "Thank you for your concern. But I'm a spinster. It's ridiculous to expect my father or brother to watch me as though I were a debutante."

"I wouldn't have figured you for a spinster." He shifted forward and moved a strand of hair from her face. Then he trailed his fingers beneath her jaw and tilted up her chin.

Her skin burned beneath his touch, tiny agonizing fires that paralyzed her, despite her mind screaming to slap him or push him away.

"Well, I am." And being one was better than being a wife to the wrong man.

"You don't want a husband? Children? A family?"

She used to. And maybe somewhere deep inside, she still did. She'd had numerous opportunities to marry, good men whose faces lit up like the sun when she'd walked into the room. But no matter how kind or interested a gentleman might seem, her experience with David had taught her that she wouldn't be able to keep him happy. The man would probably be content with her for a year or so, then lose interest. After all, David hadn't been engaged to her half a year, and he'd found himself a mistress. "No. I'm quite comfortable remaining a spinster. Thank you."

Mr. Hayes released her jaw, though the pressure of his fingers against her skin still lingered. "Why? You're still young enough to have a gaggle of little ones."

She looked away. Of all the things to discuss, why her spinsterhood? "My marital status isn't your concern."

"Is it teaching, then? Does that mean so much you'd give up a family?"

The inside of her mouth turned painfully dry. The man didn't understand. Teaching was all she had, her only escape from life with an unfaithful husband. And if the academy closed, she would lose the little security she'd found. "We've discussed enough about me. Now what about you? Tell me what you'll do with your vast inheritance. Obviously you're not planning to give to charities or to further educational opportunities, like your grandfather did."

"Sell what I can and go back home."

He said it so simply, as though he was discussing the dinner menu or the weather rather than his grandfather's life work. "All of it? Even the companies and estate? You could keep something in your name for an investment, at minimum."

"Every bit and as quick as I can."

"Oh, that's noble. What happens when you get home? Do you sit around on your pile of money and congratulate yourself on a job well done? You sold a man's life work in record time. What a hero you are."

"I wouldn't expect you to understand."

"No. Rest assured I don't. You're planning to yank your sister away from her dream and run back home when you have opportunity to do so much good here. Did you know Samantha wants to study architecture?"

"Yes, and it's ridiculous."

Rage burned under her skin, flushing from the tips of her toes up to her hairline. How dare he say such a thing and of his sister, no less. "Why, because she's a woman? A woman can study architecture as well as any man."

"I'm sure a woman can. And let's say for just a moment that you're right. Let's say that Sam doesn't go home, where she belongs, and goes off to college instead. What happens after college? Does she graduate and get a job? As an architect? No architectural firm is going to hire a woman. And even if she does get hired, how would she deal with the builders? You think a crew of men is going to listen to her when she tells them they have the wrong dimensions for a parlor, or that they need to frame a doorway at a different angle?"

Elizabeth swallowed. He had a point, of course. Most of society would agree that architecture was hardly an acceptable field of work for women. Women could do things like nurse and teach, but becoming something like an architect or lawyer was a bit different. Still, Samantha shouldn't have to give up her dream so easily. The goal she'd set for herself would be difficult to achieve but not impossible. "Louise Blanchard Bethune is a professional architect. She even lives in the state."

"A woman as a professional architect?" Mr. Hayes snorted. "She probably runs an architectural firm with her father or brother."

"Husband. But that doesn't mean she couldn't run one on her own."

Mr. Hayes gripped her wrist, his fingers closing around her skin until she brought her eyes up to meet his. "It does, Miss Wells. No businessman in need of architectural work is going to hire a woman for such a thing."

"So, because of that, what some man might tell your sister in the future, you'll deny Samantha the chance to be an architect? She could end up like Louise Bethune. Even if Bethune works with her husband, she's still doing the thing she loves. It's wrong for you to steal such a dream away from your sister and force her back home."

He released her wrist. "I don't have a choice."

"But you do."

The muscle in his jaw clenched and unclenched. "No. I don't."

The man was three sides of stubborn and an oaf on top of it. "How can you say that?"

"It's not just about me or Sam. It's about my ma…" His eyes dipped down to his boots, nearly shrouded in the darkness. "She has consumption."

Consumption. The word echoed through the dark carriage, the heaviness behind it seeming to drain the very life from Mr. Hayes.

"If Sam's going to see Ma before she dies, Sam's got to get home soon."

Elizabeth drew in a long, slow breath. She'd assumed the man beside her was being selfish in demanding his sister return to Wyoming. She hadn't thought, hadn't expected, hadn't dreamed something so serious drove him.

"I—I'm sorry." The words sounded inane. A paltry offering that couldn't begin to make up for the grief Mr. Hayes must be feeling—or the pain Samantha would feel once she found out.

"Yeah, me, too."

Elizabeth glanced at the other side of the carriage, where Samantha's breathing had grown deep and even with sleep. "She must have no idea. You clearly haven't told her yet, or she'd be packing her bags and heading West on the next train."

Mr. Hayes's hand clenched around her arm again, squeezing so tightly her hand grew pale and cold. "I can't tell her and neither can you. My ma and I aren't fools, Miss Wells. We read Sam's letters and know she likes her schooling. Neither of us wants to take her away from something she loves. That's why Ma made me promise."

Promise? What kind of promise could he be talking about? Likely not a good one if it prevented Samantha from finding out about her mother. "What did you promise?"

"Not to tell Sam about the illness. The doc says Ma's got a year to live. She's ailing faster than that. Everyone can see it. Pa, me, any of our friends, but she's gone and convinced herself she has plenty of time, so Sam doesn't need to come home until she graduates. Then she thinks Sam will spend the summer with her before she passes.... But she won't last until summer."

Elizabeth clasped her hands together on her lap and glanced down. His mother was dying, and he and his sister were stuck two thousand miles away. What must that feel like? For all the antics she put up with from her own mother, she'd be devastated were her mother to become seriously ill. "So instead of telling her about your mother, you're not giving her any choice in leaving."

"Yes."

The clomp of the horse's feet and rumble of the carriage wheels grew louder as the carriage moved from the dirt road onto the cobbled streets of Valley Falls. A few more moments, and she would be home, the conversation finished whether she'd spoken her piece or not.

The soft moonlight filtering through the window cast Mr. Hayes's hair and eyelashes in a silvery glow, outlining half of that strong, handsome face while leaving the other in shadows.

She understood him now, at least partly. It made

sense that this man would storm into Hayes Academy and announce his sister had to leave, made sense that he'd want to sell everything and get back to his mother's bedside as quickly as possible. She'd do the same in that situation. And yet, Samantha was trapped between his desires and his mother's wishes, and all the answers she needed were being withheld. "You need to tell your sister anyway. She deserves a chance to decide for herself what she's going to do."

"No man with any bit of character can just up and break a promise like the one I made to Ma."

"Then maybe you shouldn't have made the promise in the first place."

"You try telling the woman who raised you no, while she's lying on her bed coughing up blood."

The carriage rolled to a stop in front of her house, and Elizabeth took her reticule and stood as the coachman opened the door. "If you don't tell Samantha, you'll end up breaking her heart in a worse way than Jackson ever could."

His eyes widened even as his jaw took on that familiar, determined set. She turned and stepped down from the carriage before he could think of something else to say, because in the end, her words would turn out true. He knew it. She knew it. And even his mother, sick and dying back in Wyoming, had to know it.

Luke's boots sank into the plush carpet as he carried Samantha across the floor and laid her on her bed. Lavender and lace decorated the room, from her bed to her curtains to the wallpaper. Girlish colors in a childish room. He swiped a hand over his eyes, trying to dispel the image of Sam kissing Jackson, but it clung to his mind like a wood tick on a buffalo.

Sam's dress rustled as she curled on her side without waking. Lamplight spilled off the silvery-blue material, making it glisten in the half-lit room. He should probably rouse a servant to help her change. But she looked so restful he could hardly wake her.

Her face lay peacefully against a white, flowery pillow. Tears had streaked the black around her eyes and the pink smudged onto her cheeks. He rolled his shoulders and took a clean handkerchief from his pocket to dab her face.

The girl was too young for makeup, and too young to be kissing Jackson. She'd looked like a gullible child beside the accountant. But society deemed her old enough to attend the banquet, old enough to find a husband, old enough to graduate from school. And she seemed so grown-up in that confounded dress, such a mixture of girl and woman he hardly knew what to do with her.

She wasn't supposed to start crying when he protected her from a man. Wasn't supposed to claim she loved the scoundrel. And she wasn't supposed to come out East and make plans for her life that didn't include her family. She should chafe for home at that ridiculous academy, not want to graduate. Not think about going to college or becoming an architect. Luke raked a hand through her hair. He didn't want to crush her dreams or the life she'd built in Valley Falls, but to protect her. If her dreams were doomed to fail, then wouldn't she be better off back home, with her family looking out for her? Wouldn't she be happier in Wyoming, the place where she belonged and where she'd have time to spend with Ma before it was too late?

Maybe Miss Wells was right, and he should tell Samantha about Ma's consumption, regardless of the promise he made. But that felt wrong somehow. He'd only been in Valley Falls for a day and a half, and he needed to try to honor his promise for more than two days.

But would anything short of the truth draw his sister away from here?

I love you, Jackson. The scene beside the Kenmore flashed across his mind once again. The tremble in Sam's voice. The tears in her eyes. Getting her away from Jackson Wells was going to be harder than starting a campfire during a rainstorm, especially with her accusing him of being so unreasonable. It was *not* unreasonable to protect his sister from a wily city slicker. Why couldn't she see that?

Then again, him pulling her out of school with little explanation probably had something to do with her anger.

What if he went ahead and made that donation to the academy? That might temper Sam some, at least convince her that he didn't hate her school and wanted the best for her.

An image of Miss Wells rose in his mind. Her eyes soft and vulnerable as she explained that her father had pulled state funding away from her school. No, it couldn't hurt to make the donation.

And what was he thinking? He was *not* going to pledge away two thousand dollars of his grandfather's money just because a pretty teacher had gotten misty eyed with him. Something was happening to his brain. He'd been clearheaded and competent enough to run a ranch for the past decade, but put him around Miss Wells, and his mind suddenly turned to mush.

He rose and left the room, taking the stairs down to the grand hall two at a time. "Stevens!" He'd consider giving money to the academy, but he'd do so based on sound logic—and the possibility of it helping his relationship with Sam—not because of a pretty mathematics teacher.

And before he gave a dime, he was going to learn everything he could about the woman asking for the money. He walked into the drawing room and blinked against the bright lights glinting off the gold and white furnishings.

"You called, sir?" Stevens appeared in the doorway.

"What do you know of Miss Wells?"

"Miss Wells? The mathematics teacher and daughter of Assemblyman Wells?"

"That's the one." Luke leaned back against the wall and crossed his arms.

Stevens pursed his lips together and paused, as if trying to reach into the back drawer of his mind for information. "She thinks rather highly of female education, and went off to college instead of marrying her intended several years ago."

"She had an intended?" His pulse accelerated. He'd been daft not to see it sooner. With her family and looks, the woman had probably been offered more proposals than there were men in the Teton Valley.

"Yes, sir, one of the most acclaimed men of Albany. He's in Washington, D.C., now. A congressman."

"How convenient for her father." He could imagine it all too clearly, Miss Wells in a shimmering silk gown like tonight, her hand tucked gently into the arm of her

politician husband as he smiled and schmoozed and ca-
joled. And after growing up in a politician's home, Miss
Wells was surely practiced at playing the perfect role
of supportive female. Yes, on the surface, she would
make a fine politician's wife. "Why didn't they marry?"

Stevens kept his face set in austere lines. "It's not my
business to speak of it. Perhaps you should make your
inquiry to Miss Wells herself."

A servant that didn't like gossip. Just his luck. "You
know something. Tell me."

"Really, sir. I'd prefer not to—"

"Stevens!"

Stevens cleared his throat. "Ah, yes, sir. I don't know
much of the situation, but before Miss Wells was to
marry Mr. DeVander, it is my understanding that she
learned the gentleman kept a mistress, so she refused
him."

He stilled even as his blood began to simmer. What
type of cheating crook would do such a thing? "I assume the family ran off the scoundrel with a shotgun."

"No, sir."

He glowered at the butler, who again didn't seem inclined to give more information. "What do you mean,
no?"

"The family didn't seem to mind Mr. DeVander's
indiscretion. He had a rather large bank account and a
bright political future."

"So she stood up to her family." That made sense. He
could almost picture her telling her father she wouldn't
marry a cheat as she stood with her chin high, her shoulders back and her gaze cool.

"She would have still ended up married had your
grandfather not stepped in."

"What?" Now that he couldn't envision. Especially since the old codger had tried forcing Pa into a similar marriage. Oh, as far as he knew, the bride picked out for Pa hadn't been a cheat, but Pa hadn't loved her. Marrying her would have been nothing but a business transaction, arranged for Jonah Hayes's benefit. Grandpa would have been more likely to help the Wells family marry Elizabeth off, not protect her. "Doesn't seem like it would even be his business."

"Your grandfather and Thomas Wells were rather close, and he was always something of a godfather to the Wells children. They seemed to replace the grandchildren he never saw, until Samantha arrived, that is."

Luke glowered. As though he needed to be reminded that he'd never met his grandfather. "Go on."

"I never inquired into your grandfather's motivations regarding Miss Wells, sir. It wouldn't be proper. He did smooth things over with her parents regarding the broken engagement, however. And he was most supportive of her studies. It pleased him greatly to see her teach at the school he'd founded. And then, in his will, he gave her the house she'd been making payments on."

"Grandpa did all that for her?" Luke scratched his head. This didn't seem like the man Pa'd told cruel stories about, but hadn't the lawyer said something about giving someone a house when they were going over the will? He just hadn't been paying much attention.

"Perhaps you should speak with Mr. Byron about it, if you have any further questions. All I know of the situation regarding Miss Wells is what I've overheard."

"Thank you, Stevens. You may go."

"You're welcome, sir."

The butler turned and left, and Luke rubbed the heel

of his hand over his bleary eyes, his blood still boiling at the thought of what her former fiancé had done.

And why should his blood boil? Why should he care at all? She was just a teacher who wanted a donation from him. No different from any of the other people who had asked him for money tonight.

So why couldn't he get those fiery hazel eyes out of his mind?

Chapter Nine

Elizabeth's breath clogged in her lungs, and the air around her turned thick and heavy. One would think she stood held at gunpoint, with the way her heart raced and her body went from hot to cold and back in an instant. Instead she stood in church, exactly one pew behind Mr. Hayes.

People filled the small sanctuary, their voices singing and bellowing and crooning on this bright Sunday morning. Smiles radiated from faces as though heaven itself had descended and implanted a spark of divine joy in the hearts of the worshippers. But she could hardly focus on singing with Mr. Hayes blocking her view of the song leader—and everyone else.

She held the hymnal open and scanned the page. She'd known the words to "Rock of Ages" since childhood, and the song rolled over her tongue with little effort. Maybe that was the problem. The hymn proved too familiar to offer a distraction.

Not that being distracted from those muscular shoulders would be easy. She glanced around the small church. A handful of farmers carried themselves the way Mr. Hayes did, with wide shoulders and thick necks and strong bearings.

But the farmers looked rough in their coveralls and flannel shirts, while Mr. Hayes's tailored suit lay smooth against his body. And if she leaned close enough to Mr. Hayes, she could probably even smell the sun and grass and cologne that had entranced her last night.

She looked around the congregation as the pianist continued playing. Every woman present, whether married or single, watched Mr. Hayes—not that she was paying attention. If the man decided to sit right at the front of the church, of course women would stare. He was likely the richest man within a hundred miles.

But he hadn't held another woman's hand last night. And he hadn't rescued someone else from the reporter. And he hadn't smoothed hair from another woman's face or stared into another woman's eyes. She swallowed. He had looked at *her* as though she mattered. He'd caressed her jaw and pinned a strand of hair behind her ear, his face close enough that his breath warmed her cheek.

And she would have kissed him. Oh, why hadn't he leaned forward just a bit? Let their lips brush? Then she'd know how his mouth felt on hers and wouldn't be left wondering.

And *what* was she thinking? Why kiss at all when he would leave in a few weeks?

The minister motioned for the congregation to sit while the pianist played the introduction to "Amazing Grace." Elizabeth sang the opening line, letting her soprano voice ring out above the others.

Samantha turned and looked at her, giggles sounded from the pew behind, and Mrs. Weldingham, seated to her left, glared. Elizabeth looked around. Was something…?

She clamped her mouth shut as more snickers erupted. A rich alto voice filled the air. *One* rich alto voice. She shifted to see past Mr. Hayes. Indeed, one woman stood at the front of the church, singing the solo Elizabeth had tried making into a duet.

Elizabeth pressed her eyes closed until the last strains of music faded away, and she could open them to find everyone staring at the pastor rather than her.

"Take your Bibles, and turn with me to 1 Samuel 15." The aging minister's voice filled the crowded church. She flipped through the delicate pages of the pew Bible, then followed along as the minister began to read.

An invisible band tightened around her chest. Minister Trevnor wasn't preaching on Saul disobeying God. He couldn't be. But the pastor's voice boomed through every wretched word of the passage, causing one verse to reverberate through her mind, the verse Mother had quoted when she'd refused to marry David DeVander eight years earlier. *Rebellion is as the sin of witchcraft, and stubbornness is as iniquity and idolatry.*

"We're going to examine what the Bible teaches about obedience and disobedience this morning," the minister continued. "The Bible promises happiness to those who obey God and His commandments, but sorrow and punishment to those who disobey. When God looks at you, does He see obedience or disobedience? Children, do you obey your parents? Laborers, do you obey your bosses…?"

Elizabeth crinkled the pages of the Bible between her fingers. She didn't need to hear a sermon on obedience, not now.

Have you any notion how furious your mother was when she saw what you'd penned? It isn't appropriate for a lady like yourself to express your opinions in such a public way. Father's words from last night about the newspaper articles flashed through her mind.

Had she disobeyed some unwritten law, some sacred commandment, by writing that editorial? Mother and Father seemed to think so.

Her parents had also said she was disobedient and rebellious for refusing to marry David. No matter what she did, what grades she'd gotten in college or how far she went out of her way to please them these days, she was somehow always "disobedient." She likely would be until she married a suitable man. And by "suitable" her parents meant some rich public figure who would help her family's political connections. Her husband could behave in countless despicable ways beyond the public's eye, so long as he looked good in the papers. And she was disobedient for refusing to comply.

She fidgeted and looked about as casually as she could manage. She ought never to have made a habit of sitting in the third pew from the front. How easily she could slip out if she sat nearer the back.

Mrs. Weldingham eyed her again, and Elizabeth straightened, staring ahead and trying to shut out the sermon.

Certain words slipped through anyway. *Disobeyed. God. Punished. Destroyed.*

Was God punishing her for not obeying her parents? Was that why Hayes Academy would likely close? Because she'd written an editorial rather than sitting back and accepting whatever happened to the school? Was that why her parents never seemed happy with her?

Because she'd disobeyed them by teaching rather than marrying?

Her head began to throb, and she glanced toward the front of the church. But instead of seeing the minister, rambling about the horrors Saul's family faced because of his disobedience, Mr. Hayes filled her view.

He already knew she disagreed with her father about the school's funding, and he hadn't condemned her. Nor had he said anything about how she shouldn't teach last night. He'd simply said her family should treat her better and then had asked if she wanted to start her own family. Would his opinion of her change if he knew how she'd defied her parents by not marrying? Or if he knew her intended had found her so unsatisfying he'd run into the arms of a mistress before they'd even married?

And why did Mr. Hayes's opinion matter so much anyway?

Luke entered the drawing room and stopped. He hadn't expected there to be so many people. Sure, he'd seen a servant moving about the premises here or there, inside the house or on the grounds. But to have everyone in the same place—why there were nearly twenty of them.

And they looked terribly uncomfortable. Not a one sat on the dainty furniture—not that he could blame them—but half of them tiptoed about as though they'd never even seen the drawing room before.

Had he told Stevens to assemble them in the wrong place? Where did one meet with his servants? The kitchen, perhaps? Or the servants' dining room?

Stevens stepped up to him. "Everyone's in attendance, as you requested."

Luke cleared his throat and moved to the front of the room. "Thank you all for taking time from your usual duties to be here."

The milling and soft chatter stopped, and every eye turned his way. Fear and dejection filled most faces. Some eyes burned hot with anger, while others shone dull with resignation. But all knew why they stood there.

"Is he the new master?" A girl of no more than twelve or thirteen whispered to the maid beside her.

The woman made a shushing sound and cut her gaze toward him, her cheeks pale.

Luke looked away and surveyed the other workers in his grandpa's employ. No, not Grandpa's employ, *his* employ. "I know you all worked hard for my grandfather, Jonah Hayes, and I appreciate that. As most of you are aware, some changes need to be made. The estate is being put up for sale, and I will not be staying long in Valley Falls. I'm sure whoever buys this home will want to hire his own staff, so I…"

The words crusted in his mouth. Confound it. He couldn't do this. He'd planned to only keep on six of them and give the rest two months' salary plus a month of room and meals while they looked for other jobs. Now it hardly seemed enough.

What do you plan to do with your vast estate? Miss Wells's words from last night ran through his mind. *What happens when you get home? Do you sit around on the pile of money that got handed to you and congratulate yourself on a job well done?*

Luke rubbed the back of his neck. He might not want this estate, Grandpa's money, responsibility for the servants, or the rest of the mess that had been handed him, but hang it all, it was *his* mess, *his* duty. And he wasn't going to put nearly two dozen good workers out of a job because he found cutting back convenient. Let the next owner fire them, but he wouldn't have that on his conscience.

"Sir?" Stevens sidled up beside him. "Are you unwell? Do you need something? A glass of water, perhaps?"

"No." He didn't need anything another person could offer. He was the one who needed to do something, to provide for those Grandpa had left in his care. "As I was saying, whoever buys this house will most likely hire new staff, but your job here is secure for as long as I remain owner. I also have a monetary gift of two months' salary for each of you, as a thank-you for the years you spent serving my grandfather. Stevens and Miss Hampstead will distribute the envelopes accordingly."

The servants hushed completely, creating an awkward silence as gazes riveted on him. He turned on his heel and left before he could think too hard on what he'd just done.

The sun was just rising in the eastern sky as Elizabeth stopped before the four brick walls of Hayes Academy. She stared up at the towering three-story school and flicked her gaze over the windows. Her classroom and Miss Torneau's, Miss Bowen's office and the dining hall.

She didn't need to step inside to know how the classrooms looked, painted the standard white with blackboards at the front, the desks filled with bright-faced students. She could almost smell the chalk and wood polish, hear the giggles of young ladies and the clip of boots against flooring.

An empty dream.

The school would close at Christmas. The board may not have made their official announcement yet, but they'd already decided. Without the report on finances from Jackson. Without thought for where she or Miss Bowen or any of the other teachers would work next. And without concern for students themselves.

Mr. Taviston would likely have the blackboards, desks, beds and other supplies sold within weeks of closing the school, and then he'd sell the building itself.

Who would buy it? Another school? Not likely, with the way private institutions were struggling in the midst of the recession.

The Hayes Academy would probably go to some company who needed a warehouse. The inner rooms would be torn down, the walls stripped of any remembrance of the school, and the structure would become a simple building, not a place that held girls' futures and cultivated their dreams.

A breath of cold air teased her face, and she shivered in her coat. The morning was cool, with frost crusting the grass and birds slow to start their songs. She wasn't dressed to be outside long, hadn't planned to come here at all. But when she'd opened the door to retrieve the morning paper, she simply kept walking, the academy calling to her from the end of the street. She'd needed to say goodbye, here in the quiet light of dawn, without anyone to interrupt her.

But now she'd best get home before someone saw her and asked questions. Saying goodbye to a building? She could only imagine the look she'd get if she attempted to explain.

She turned, headed down the sidewalk, wrapping her coat tighter about her and not looking back at the brick structure that would soon stand empty. Instead, she looked ahead toward her house, the yellow paint and protruding turret barely visible between the stately trees lining the road. What would she do with it after the school closed? Sell?

No. She could never do such a thing. She was blessed to own her own home. Indeed, most teachers spent their lives renting rooms in houses that belonged to someone else. And those teachers who did manage to buy their own property, well, they weren't nearly as young as she was.

After she'd started teaching at Hayes Academy, Jonah Hayes had approached her about buying a house, specifically the one which she and two other teachers had been renting from him. He'd said she needed the property in her name for investment purposes, and she could make monthly payments to him. She'd nearly swooned when the lawyer came to her house after Jonah's death and told her that he'd left her the house in his will.

She lingered a moment on the walkway and gazed up at the two stories. Hers, from the peak of the gabled roof to the flower beds at the base of the walls. And she took care of it, tending the lawn and gardens, calling a repairman at the first sign of trouble, filling the interior with furniture and decorations.

She climbed the steps to the porch, the paper she'd passed earlier still resting on the wooden planks beside the door. Sighing, she picked it up and unrolled it.

At least nothing about Hayes Academy was printed on the first page. She opened to the second page, and the letters stood bold and stark at the top.

> Hayes Academy for Girls Employs Bribery and Accusations While Continuing to Waste Money
> Charitable organizations and taxpayers have already wasted an exorbitant amount of money on Hayes Academy for Girls. Yet in the face of our current economic depression, that institution seems determined to waste more. Saturday evening…

And Higsley went on to describe the banquet. "Overly elaborate," he called it. "Wasteful…a disgrace to the area's needy," with his own invitation to the event derided as "an attempt to bribe him into silence." Then he claimed to endure the rudest behavior and most harrowing of accusations from a certain Miss Wells.

> Surely this teacher's qualifications must be examined, as no one with such a venomous mind ought be allowed anywhere near society's young ladies.

She gulped air and fanned her face with the paper, even as tears stung the back of her eyes.

Venomous mind? Qualifications examined? What nonsense. Yet if people believed the raving reporter's words this time, as they had his previous article, the wretched man might well see her fired before the school even closed.

The front door opened and Miss Loretta Atkins, the literature and drama teacher, poked her head out. "Oh, there you are, dear. Miss Torneau made some oatmeal for breakfast, but we couldn't find you."

"I just…" she fisted her hand in the paper "…went for a morning walk, is all."

Miss Atkins's eyes landed on the *Morning Times*. "Oh, no. That reporter didn't print another, did he?"

Elizabeth handed over the paper. No point in hiding what the rest of the world would be reading in another hour or two.

"My, my." Miss Atkins clucked her tongue. "You don't think the school will close because of this reporter, do you?"

She watched the older woman, her forehead wrinkled as she glanced at the article. It would be nice, just for a moment, to be like Miss Atkins—a pleasant old spinster who had never fallen in love or had any suitors, to hear her tell it. She'd started teaching decades ago, always living in a house or apartment somebody else owned. She smiled gently when she heard news, whether good or bad, and never took it upon herself to take a stand or push for change. In another week or two, when she learned the school would close, she would frown and cluck her tongue. Perhaps she would say something like "such a shame, that is" and then go about her daily routine.

Elizabeth swallowed. Would it be better to live out her days like Miss Atkins? Not overly involved in anything? Not caring when she failed because she never tried to achieve anything in the first place? Maybe she should attempt it, the calm complacency, the blind acceptance of whatever was handed her.

"Do you mind if I take this back to the kitchen? Miss Torneau will want to see it."

"Fine," Elizabeth croaked.

Miss Atkins stepped back inside and held the door open. "You come in, too, dear. Those fingers look to have a touch of frostbite."

She glanced down at her red chapped hands, nearly numb from the cold. "I'll be in shortly."

The door closed, and she leaned against the post, sucking the chilled air deep into her lungs. She needed one moment, maybe two, of peace before the whirlwind of her day began. Miss Bowen would have seen the article, as well as the students, the other teachers, the school board members. Goodness, but the article might well bring a couple board members to the academy today. If only she could hide in bed and claim she was ill. It wouldn't be a lie, not really. Because somewhere deep inside, where her heart beat heavily and her stomach twisted into knots, she was very, very sick.

Chapter Ten

"Sir, I'm afraid your sister is missing."

Luke turned from where he stood in his bedroom, threading a tie around his neck. "What do you mean, 'missing'?"

The butler handed him an envelope. "Well, sir, she wasn't in her room this morning, but this letter was resting on her bed."

Luke knotted his tie and tore open the letter. Sam had gone straight back to the school he'd told her to stay away from. Stubborn girl. He looked out the north-facing window toward town. Morning sunlight danced off the frosted grass and painted the maple trees an even brighter red, while silhouettes of whitewashed houses darkened the horizon. "What time does Hayes Academy start?"

"In about half an hour."

Confound it. He had a half hour to catch the train to Albany as well, and he needed to make that appointment with Jackson.

"Did she go to the academy, sir? Would you like someone to bring her home?"

Luke set his jaw and stared out the window again, in the direction Sam would have walked. He'd embarrassed her on Friday by pulling her out of class, and he didn't cotton to doing it a second time. Maybe he'd talk to her when he got home later and set some boundaries. Calm, reasonable boundaries. Like she couldn't leave her room again until they headed West, or see any friends, or study any mathematics books.

Hang it all, he may as well beat the girl for smiling— not that she'd done much smiling since he showed up.

Luke sighed. Maybe Miss Wells was right, and he just needed to tell Sam about Ma. Perhaps Sam would hate him for doing so, perhaps Ma would hate him even more for not keeping his promise, but things were getting ridiculous. Sam was already close to detesting him, and leaving Valley Falls was going to break her heart. Ma thought she'd been doing Sam a favor by hiding the truth, but didn't Sam deserve to know what was going on?

And somehow he'd gotten himself stuck smack-dab in the middle of the mess. "Sam wants another chance to see her friends. She can attend the academy for the day."

"Yes, sir." Stevens dipped his head and left.

Luke slid into his suit coat and glanced in the mirror. Had Grandpa liked always getting duded up? Because Luke looked like a corpse in the rigid black and white garments. But he couldn't help pausing, lingering an extra moment at the too-familiar face in the mirror.

If only he and Blake hadn't looked so similar, hadn't shared the same bright blue eyes and sun-streaked hair. If only he could change his face and replace it with another. Black hair. Gray eyes. Less prominent cheekbones. A softer chin. Anything so he didn't have to stare at his brother's face whenever he looked in the mirror.

"I'm sorry, Blake," he whispered into the empty room. And indeed he was. Sorry for Blake's death, for the sudden way Pa had sent Sam out East afterward, sorry for not trying harder to keep his family together. Something had shattered the day of Blake's death, and the pieces of that tragedy still lay like splintered shards on the hot Wyoming ground.

He straightened his tie and suit coat as best he could without looking back at the mirror. He didn't have time to think about Blake or the way his family had been torn apart after his twin's death. He had a train to catch, more meetings scheduled than he wanted to think about and a scoundrel to scare away from his sister.

Luke's boots hit the wooden platform as the train that had returned him to Valley Falls hissed and steamed behind him.

"Mr. Hayes, sir, your carriage is ready." A young coachman instantly appeared by his side.

"Thank you." He spoke absently, then followed the boy to the conveyance.

A certain part of him, the part that loved the Teton Valley, wanted to say he'd hated his day and found the meetings dull and stifling. But while sitting round a table with a bunch of other suits wasn't near as fun as riding the range, it wasn't terrible. He'd never been slow at ciphering, and the columns of numbers he'd glanced over made sense. The businessmen he'd conferenced with hadn't been half bad, either. They were, after all, still men underneath their fancy getup. And the meetings weren't much different than managing a crew of cowhands around a campfire.

In fact, sitting in those meeting rooms, making decisions that would affect other people's lives, was almost kind of nice. Like how to offer a home insurance plan that was affordable and yet would provide adequate coverage in case of a fire or flood. Or sending a corporation-wide memorandum out to all Great Northern Accounting and Insurance employees explaining that there would be no change in operations or job layoffs at present. A lot of his workers would return to their homes happy after getting news like that.

All in all, hadn't been bad in the least—which made that familiar spot between his shoulder blades start to itch.

The lawyer, too, had been thrilled when Luke told him to go ahead and start interviewing men for an overseer's position. If he was going to keep the house staff on for as long as possible, he could at least find an overseer to manage the accounting and insurance offices. If the setup didn't work after a year or two, he could always come back to Valley Falls and sell the companies.

But campfires and managers and meetings aside, he now had another stack of paperwork to get through, and he still needed to have that conversation with Sam. "Did my sister enjoy her day at school?"

The boy turned back to him, a frown plastered across his face. "Wouldn't know, sir. I don't usually ask her such things. And besides, she hasn't returned yet."

Luke stopped, despite the people milling in the crowd around him. "She hasn't returned? As in she's still at school?"

"No, sir. She's at Miss Wells's house for her calculus lesson. Goes there every Monday and Wednesday, she does."

"And no one thought to fetch her home?"

The boy shifted nervously from one foot to the other and glanced at his boots. "I wasn't aware I needed to."

Luke scrubbed a hand over his face. So help him, he should shove Sam on the first train West. Here he was trying to be nice by letting her go to school one last time, then she up and headed to a lesson without so much as asking. There was no keeping the girl happy. "And where does Miss Wells live?"

"She owns a place just down from the academy. Rents rooms to two of the other teachers."

"You'd best take me."

The coachman nodded and scampered toward the carriage.

The conveyance took him to a quiet tree-lined street where neighbors sat on porches and children played in the yards. Just the sight of the two-story house, painted a buttery-yellow with soft green shutters and gables, calmed him. He could well imagine Miss Wells up in the little turret on the north side of the house, knitting or painting or doing some other ladylike craft while she looked down on the street below. Not that he needed to think about Miss Wells all cozy in her home.

He headed up the walk and knocked on the door, then waited.

Nothing.

He knocked again, a little louder this time.

Still nothing.

Turning the door knob, he slipped inside. Muted female voices floated from the doorway on his left. He followed the sound, trying to force his boots to step quietly through the otherwise silent house.

Samantha sat at a writing desk against the far wall of the parlor, while Miss Wells stood beside his sister, her shoulders and head bent, her soft voice filling the room with odd sounding words: *derivative, function, linear approximation, tangent line.* Sam's head bobbed back and forth as she scrawled something across a slate.

A teacher. The woman standing beside the far wall surely was one. She'd said as much to him the other night in the carriage when she'd insisted she was content to remain a spinster and had refused to answer his questions about why she didn't want a family. When he had first seen her at the school, she'd been so beautiful he couldn't envision her doing anything but marrying a distinguished gentleman.

But would she marry if it meant she'd spend her days at home rather than lecturing or whispering encouraging words to her students? Rather than covering her hands with chalk dust?

He walked closer. They'd have to hear the rustle of his suit or the floor creak beneath his feet. But with their backs to him, neither woman noticed until he stood close enough to touch.

"Mr. Hayes?" Surprise lit Miss Wells's eyes.

"Luke." Sam turned, guilt rather than astonishment etching her face. "What are you doing here?"

He crossed his arms. "Seems I should be asking you that."

Sam stiffened. "I'm studying calculus with Miss Wells, like I do every Monday. Grandfather never had a problem with it."

Miss Wells's gaze flitted between them, her lovely

hazel eyes filled with questions. "Samantha, did your brother give you permission to be here?"

Sam hunched back over the desk. "I understand the first one. It's this second derivative I can't quite grasp."

"No." Luke shifted and tapped a finger against the slate, filled with as many letters and symbols as digits. How did they even call this stuff mathematics if it hardly used numbers? "She didn't have permission to be here or at school today. She was supposed to sort through Grandpa's room. I need her help at the estate, if we're going to make it home anytime soon."

"Oh. I'm sorry." And the round, sad look in Miss Wells's eyes showed she truly was. "When I saw Samantha this morning, I assumed that you…well…had become more sensible about your decision and had given her permission to attend classes until she left Valley Falls."

"My decision's perfectly sensible." He not only needed Sam's help at the estate, he needed to break her away from the things she'd grown to care about here and get her excited about going home. None of that would happen if she spent her days at school, fixated on heading to college. "Sam, get to the carriage."

"Mr. Hayes, if nothing else, please let her continue these private lessons with me. It's the least you can do, if you're going to be taking her away soon." Miss Wells looked away, blinking and biting her lip.

He swallowed a groan. The last thing he needed was for the woman to start crying.

"I understand that you miss your sister," she went on, her shoulders straightening. "And I realize you have reasons for wanting her home. But can't you wait a few more weeks? Maybe she could return home with you at Christmas, after the end of the semester."

"Go home at Christmas? Now *you* expect me to leave, too, Miss Wells? I'm not going to Wyoming at Christmas or anytime after that." Samantha gripped the back of the chair, her knuckles whitening. "You'll have to drag me to that train, and I'll scream the entire way. Then I'll—"

"I don't care how much screaming you do." What was the point in being reasonable with the girl anymore? Nothing he did made a dent in Sam's stubbornness, and he could be just as mule-headed as she. "And I'm done trying to be nice about it. You're on a train West as soon as I find a chaperone to take you."

"No!" Horror filled his sister's face. "I'll turn around and come back, I swear it. I'm finishing school. I want to graduate and go to college. I want to be with Jackson. He says I can still attend college after we marry."

Luke balled his hands into fists. "You're not marrying that scoundrel."

Miss Wells gasped, and heat burned the back of his neck. Probably shouldn't have called the lady's brother a scoundrel while she was present. But what else was he supposed to do while Sam was hollering at him?

"This is about Blake, isn't it?" Sam sprang from her chair.

"Blake? You've gone daft." He'd been about four years old when he figured out most women were batty, but nothing illustrated it better than Sam's cockeyed statement.

"I'm just going to slip into the kitchen and make some tea," Miss Wells squeaked and scurried through the doorway.

Sam held his gaze. "I'm not daft. You're not happy I left after he died. You never wanted me to leave, and now that you see me here and happy, you can't stand that you were wrong about me leaving the Teton Valley."

She'd gone haywire. Sam needed to go home because of Ma, not because of something that had happened in the past. But her words brought back the memories anyway, an image of his twin's body lying on the blood-soaked dirt.

Blake had discovered some things missing around the ranch, and when he'd pegged the thief as one of their seasoned cowhands, Blake had fired him. The man had ridden up to Blake's place the next morning, called for him while he was sitting at breakfast with Cynthia, and shot him the moment he stepped outside.

Luke's stomach twisted at the image in his mind, and an insatiable well of regret opened inside him. He hadn't known what was happening to Blake. His brother's cabin was on the other side of the ranch property, out of view from the big house, but when Blake hadn't shown up in the stables at his usual time, Luke had ridden out, only to find Cynthia crying over his bloodied twin.

He'd jumped from his horse and kneeled beside the body, ripping off his shirt to stanch the bleeding. *"Who's riding for the doctor? Why don't you have rags here to stop the blood?"*

Cynthia shook her head while tears coursed down her face—a face she'd powdered that morning, as though she still lived in Boston rather than the Teton Valley.

"I tried. The horse..." She hiccupped. *"I couldn't... h-he wasn't hitched to the wagon."*

"Answer me, Cynthia! Who did you send for help?"

"No one was around. I tried to saddle the horse, but..." She broke off in a fresh torrent of sobs while the sticky warmth of Blake's blood soaked his shirt and coated his hands.

"I'm not going home," Sam spoke quietly from somewhere above him.

Luke looked up at his sister. Somehow, he was sprawled in the green wingback chair by the front window of Miss Wells's parlor, though he didn't remember moving there or sitting. "You don't have a choice, Sam."

"You should give me one instead of ripping me away from the place I love."

Luke didn't even glance at her, just watched the street through the lacy window covering. It was time. He couldn't keep putting off the truth about Ma if it was going to destroy their relationship. "Ma needs you. You have to go home."

But Sam didn't ask what he meant about Ma needing her. Instead, she thrust a finger into his chest. "No. It's not Ma. It's you. You don't like that mathematics makes me happy. Or that I want to marry Jackson. You don't want me to go to college and become an architect.

"You storm back into my life and try taking everything away." Sam tossed her head to the side and blinked furiously against the moisture glistening in her eyes. "Well, I won't let you. I have dreams, too, Luke. And they've got nothing to do with a cattle ranch in some forgotten valley. If my going home had to do with wanting family to be together, you'd be taking Cynthia and Everett home, too. Goodness, you have a nephew, Blake's very own son, and you've never even seen him."

Luke clenched his jaw. Why did Sam keep dredging

up Cynthia when Ma was dying? "Confound it! You're not listening. Coming home—"

"No. You're right. I'm not listening to you anymore." Sam stormed past him and out the parlor door.

Luke followed her into the hall as the sound of the front door opening and then slamming echoed through the house. He buried his forehead in his hands and groaned.

How had he messed that up so badly? He was only trying to help, only attempting to tell her about Ma.

"Mr. Hayes?" Miss Wells emerged from the door at the far end of the hallway, a tray with tea service balanced in her hands. "Is everything all right?"

He rubbed the back of his neck. "Yeah, yeah. Look, Miss Wells, I'm sorry about all this…." He gestured toward the parlor. "We should have saved our shouting match for the ride home."

"I don't mind so much. Truly." She swayed gracefully inside the room, set down the tray, then returned to the doorway leading from the hall to the parlor. "Every family has words at one time or another. I'm sorry about your brother, though. I can tell he meant a lot to you, and I can't imagine how hard it must be to lose your mother, as well."

"You're a blessed woman, Eliz— I mean, Miss Wells. To still have your family alive and well."

She sighed, her chest rising and falling with the motion. "I suppose you're right. My family might not be overly supportive of my teaching, but they're all living."

"You should cherish that."

A sad smile tilted the corner of her mouth. "I should. More than I do at times."

"Right." He looked away but couldn't help seeing her

as she'd been the other night. Those full lips so near his own, the soft curve of her cheek in the moonlight, the mesmerizing swirl of gold and green and brown in her eyes as she had stared up at him.

"The knot in your tie is lopsided," she stated, those beautiful eyes filled with somber thoughts.

The knot in his tie? He nearly choked. "I hadn't noticed."

And he hadn't.

Then again, most men looked in the mirror when knotting them, because most men didn't see their dead brother's face staring back from the glass. He lifted a hand and fumbled to straighten the offending piece of cloth.

"Mr. Hayes—Luke. Can you try doing something for me?"

There was a hint of deliberation in her voice, a vague trace of calculation. His hand stilled on his tie as he narrowed his gaze. Miss Wells's large, perfect eyes; her full, pink lips; the sincerity in her face. This felt like a trap, if he'd ever seen one. "Depends on what you're wanting."

"Can you try working out something with the school? For Samantha, that is. Perhaps your sister could arrange for a long break at Christmas and travel home to see your mother then. Or maybe she could still attend classes for the length of time you remain in Valley Falls and try to graduate early. Whatever you decide, you have to do something, if you want to make peace with her. I'm sure exceptions can be made, if you'll talk to Miss Bowen."

Luke rubbed his hand over his forehead. The woman was a teacher through and through, always thinking about her students over anything else. "This isn't a simple situation."

"No, but it would help if you found some way for your sister to graduate."

"Tell you what. I'll let Sam go to classes at Hayes for as long as we stay." One of the servants could probably sort through Grandpa's bedroom, or even him—if he ever dug himself out from underneath all the paperwork in Grandpa's office.

Miss Wells gasped, a small, happy sound, and her hands flew up to cover her mouth. "You mean it, then? You'll really let her come back to school? And you'll speak to the office about arrangements after that so she can graduate?"

He scowled. "You care an awful lot about my sister graduating."

"I care an awful lot about every student graduating. Have you thought anymore about making a donation to Hayes?"

"Yes," he grumbled. Far more than should have.

"Yes? As in you agree? Or as in you've thought of it?" Miss Wells's hands gripped his forearm, her tiny nails digging through the fabric of his sleeve. Her eyes sparkled with hope, and her lips curved in a full-out grin.

And how could he say no when she looked at him like that? He was making a new business policy, here and now. No more decision making when womenfolk were around. They could get a man to sign over his entire life's holding by looking at him thataway.

"Yes, as in I've thought on it, but I'll have to do some more thinking before I've got an answer."

"I understand." She released his arm and stepped away, her brilliant smile fading.

And now he'd just let her down. Teach him to open his mouth and answer without thinking while she was around.

Miss Wells shifted from one foot to the other, as though suddenly nervous, and gestured to the parlor and tea service. "I would offer you tea and discuss the possibility of a donation further, but, um, my housemates are still at the academy, and with Samantha gone, your being here is hardly proper."

He looked around the quiet hallway and parlor. Yep, they were alone all right, and he'd probably broken a couple dozen rules of society by coming here at all. "I'll get on home."

But as he turned, he knocked an already-open newspaper off the small table in the hall. "Sorry about that." He bent and reached for it, then his eyes landed on the headline, and he sprang back up. "He did this? That scoundrel of a reporter published another article?"

Miss Wells's eyes seemed to dull even more. "What did you expect Mr. Higsley to do after Saturday evening?"

"Turn tail and run. What else?"

"That's not the way reporters work. Indeed, one can't have a worse enemy than a reporter."

"Perhaps if I hadn't scared him off…"

"My tongue angered him before you arrived." She wrapped her arms around herself. "I anticipated an article such as this."

He ran his thumb over a crease in the paper, his eyes scanning the basics of the article. "He attacked you personally."

She shrugged, the gesture small and hopeless for a woman comprised of steel and fire and determination. "It's nothing new."

"Does this mean the board will close the school?"

"I told you as much on Saturday."

But he hadn't quite believed her then. Holding this paper, with an article he could have prevented had he cared to, made the situation more real. More his fault. He glanced at the writing desk against the far wall, where Miss Wells had been not twenty minutes ago, instructing Samantha in a subject too complicated for him to comprehend. "You're so concerned about Samantha not graduating. What will happen to the other girls in Samantha's class if the school closes? Will they be able to finish out the year?"

"There are sixteen other students in Samantha's class. And I don't know what will happen to them. The school board will decide that, not me."

"But you think they'll just close the school and wish the girls well, as they find various other places to finish out their last semester of high school?"

"Yes, very much so."

"That doesn't seem fair."

She shrugged. It was the first time he'd seen such an unladylike gesture from her. "I hardly think treating the students fairly is the board's foremost concern."

And suddenly it became clear. Like it had yesterday, when he'd stood in the drawing room filled with his servants, and today when he'd told Mr. Byron to start finding potential managers for the insurance and accounting corporation. He could stop Hayes Academy from closing, at least for this school year. The school was as much his responsibility as the corporation and

his servants—at least until he returned West and handed
the reins to somebody else. And he wasn't going to be
responsible for sending nearly a hundred students off
in the middle of a school year.

"I think I'll be making that donation after all, Miss
Wells. And having some visits with a few of the school
board members."

Chapter Eleven

"I know you say there should be money here, Miss Wells, but I certainly can't find it." Samantha raised her head from where she sat in a chair in Jonah Hayes's office—or rather, his *former* office. The office now belonged to the man with sun-streaked blond hair standing on the other side of the room with his lawyer.

Elizabeth pulled her eyes away from Mr. Hayes and frowned at Samantha. There should be several hundred more dollars. Somewhere. If only she could find the mistake buried in the endless columns of numbers. Here she was, a mathematics teacher defending the need for higher-level academics to people like her parents and Mr. Hayes, and she couldn't even add. "You're certain?"

"Maybe it's in one of the other accounts? The food money could have gotten mixed up with the funds for teacher supplies or something."

Elizabeth flipped back several pages in the ledger on her own lap and ran her eyes down the columns once again. "I've already checked twice. There's nothing extra."

But the missing food money had to be tucked somewhere. Either that or the school's food supplier was cheating them out of produce.

"Are you saying the school's missing money?" Mr. Hayes glanced up from the paper he'd been studying with Mr. Byron.

"No." Or if so, she certainly couldn't prove it. She scratched the side of her head, causing a lock of hair to tumble down from its pins. "The books balance perfectly."

Which would be fine, if she was getting a hundred and fifty dollars' worth of food delivered to the school each month, and if she didn't have letters from the gas company and general store saying they'd never received payment for overdue bills. The books showed every expense paid in full.

She simply must have made a mistake somewhere. She'd probably recorded a donation in the wrong place and thus had incorrect fund levels in several of her accounts. If only she could find the discrepancy.

Sam flashed a bright smile at her brother. "See, nothing to worry about."

Elizabeth forced herself to nod, but Mr. Hayes's sky-blue eyes riveted to hers, as though he knew something wasn't quite right.

"Operating on a budget as tight as the one at Hayes Academy, I'd expect you to have some difficulty spreading your funds around to pay outstanding bills, am I correct?" Mr. Byron shoved his sagging glasses back up on his nose.

"Something like that," Elizabeth mumbled.

Mr. Hayes scowled at her. "You realize that if I'm going to convince the board to keep the school open, I have to prove it to be financially stable?"

"Yes, of course. I—"

"If you've any concerns, you should talk to Jackson Wells about this." The lawyer shifted closer to Mr. Hayes. "His books are likely in better order."

Samantha jabbed a finger at Mr. Byron. "That was uncalled for. Miss Wells can answer your questions better than Jackson, and I should know, since I'm close to both of them. Hayes Academy is just another client to Jackson. He doesn't pay its ledgers anywhere near the amount of attention Miss Wells does."

"Yes, Mr. Byron—and I regularly check my books against my brother's." Elizabeth stood, her face burning. She didn't need to sit here and be accused of mismanaging the ledgers after already giving Mr. Hayes and Mr. Byron three hours of her afternoon. "You'll find both sets of ledgers match perfectly. Now if you gentlemen will excuse me, it's growing late, and I've tomorrow's lessons to prepare."

She set the ledger on the ornate desk dominating the far side of the office and headed for the door. Mr. Hayes and the lawyer could spend their time attempting to make sense of the pages if they wished, but she was done for the night.

And possibly forever, if Mr. Hayes didn't manage to charm the school board.

"I'll see you out." Mr. Hayes appeared by her side, extending his elbow her direction.

She nearly groaned as she slipped her hand onto his arm. She must look a fright, with her hair starting to fall from its pins, and her skirt rumpled after a long day of teaching and studying books, and…she looked down. Yes, the front of her plum-colored skirt sported a large patch of white chalk dust.

A fright indeed.

"I appreciated your help tonight." Mr. Hayes led her down the large hallway filled with floor-to-ceiling windows, sparkling chandeliers and elaborate gold trim. The sky outside had darkened to a deep blue, turning the view from the front of the estate into a perfect scene for an artist's canvas.

"I'm happy to assist."

He sent her a lopsided grin, the kind that transformed his entire face from handsomely serious to irresistible. "You're lying."

She couldn't help but smile back. "Not really. I mean, yes, the afternoon was long, and perhaps a bit frustrating, as I feel like I've done nothing to prove the school's financial stability. But I'm willing to do whatever you need, if you think you can convince the school board to change its mind."

He placed his other hand atop hers, strong and warm over her small fingers. "I'll convince them. Don't worry."

"But how?"

He stopped at the top of the marble staircase leading down to the grand hall and turned her to face him. "You're not one to trust people, are you? I tell you that I'll take care of things, and you need to see a detailed battle plan before you'll believe me."

She paused, the words striking somewhere deep in her chest. Not one to trust people? Perhaps she trusted her students or even her fellow teachers. But not men, no. "I didn't mean to offend you. Do forgive me."

His gaze latched on to hers, watching, probing, as though looking into her very soul to find…what?

"You don't even deny it, do you? Just apologize and

hope you didn't cause any hurt feelings. But you've no intention of trusting me the next time around, either."

She had no answer she could give to that, not without lying, so she smiled weakly and looked away.

"Somebody's hurt you before."

She attempted to tug her hand away from his, but he only settled those wide, callused fingers more firmly atop hers. "Really, Mr. Hayes—"

"You can call me Luke."

She glared at him.

"You just spent an entire afternoon in my study, working with me and my sister. It's entirely appropriate that you call me by my first name. Just like it's appropriate for me to start calling you Elizabeth."

Her face turned slightly warm at the sound of her name on his tongue. "Fine, then. Luke…but I hardly see how my past, or what we call each other, pertain to keeping the academy open."

"If I get the board to keep the school open, will that convince you to trust me a little more?"

"Probably not." She'd trusted a man once before, and it wasn't something she planned to do again.

Elizabeth slipped out the front door on Friday morning, picked up the paper, and nearly dropped it back onto the porch boards. There it was, written in black lettering across the bottom corner article.

Hayes Academy Creating Jobs and Opportunities for Women

Mr. Hayes—or rather, Luke—had done it. Not only had the school board members been curiously silent throughout the week, but now the paper itself seemed to be retracting its first two articles.

Her hands trembled as she glanced over the specifics. Another reporter had written this one, and Luke had been quoted as pledging five thousand dollars to the academy.

Five thousand.

And then inviting others to do likewise.

She pressed the paper to her chest and grinned up at the sky. "Thank you, Luke."

Chapter Twelve

❧

"Miss Wells, your mother's taken ill."

Elizabeth stared at her parents' coachman and gripped the molding along the doorway until wood dug beneath her fingernails.

"She's asking for you directly," he added.

Giggles and squeals rang out from the parlor of her house behind her, where would-be actresses dressed in costumes and applied makeup for their production of *The Taming of the Shrew*. Miss Atkins's calm voice tempered the insanity of laughs and chatter—when it could be heard above the noise.

"Ill? How ill? What's wrong?"

"I was merely sent to fetch you, miss."

"Yes, of course." Something hard fisted in her chest. Mother's illness would have to be consuming for her to cancel the dinner party tonight. She'd hosted such events before in spite of fevers, headaches and nerves. Unless…

Mother wouldn't be using some illness as a ploy to get her away from the play, would she? Mother had a way of getting what she wanted, but surely a weekly dinner party wasn't important enough to pull antics such as this.

"Miss Wells?" the coachman asked.

"Is she truly ill? Not feigning something?"

The coachman shifted back and forth on his feet. "As far as I know, miss."

Elizabeth licked her lips. "Did you see her? Was she lying down?"

"I only see your mother when she needs use of the carriage."

"Yes, of course." Elizabeth glanced down at the tips of her shoes, part of her ready to bolt outside and head to Albany, and another part aching to ignore the summons and return to her students. The tinkle of feminine voices and laughter rose from behind her. But what had Luke said earlier, about her having family? Something about her being *blessed* to have family alive and well and close at hand?

Yes, that was it. She had family, and she needed to cherish it, because one day she might find herself in a situation like Luke and Samantha, with her brother in the grave and a parent heading there. "Just give me a moment. I'll be right out."

The coachman nodded and moved down the steps. She closed the door, reached for her coat, then headed into the parlor.

MaryAnne, dressed in trousers and a waistcoat for her upcoming role as Petruchio, stopped her at the entrance. "Miss Wells, are you all right?"

"Pardon? Oh, yes…I'm f-fine, dear. But I'm afraid I'll have to miss your performance this evening."

The students nearest them fell silent, and MaryAnne

inched closer. "Then you're not all right. Something has to be wrong, or you wouldn't miss the play."

"You're leaving?" Miss Atkins asked from across the room.

Elizabeth swallowed. The chaos existing only moments before turned to heavy silence as every student's gaze riveted to her. If only she could find some way to be both here and in Albany. Some way to see the hours of work and effort acted out on the stage while also supporting her mother.

"You promised to stay backstage and help with the scene changes," Miss Atkins insisted.

"I'm sorry. I just..." Elizabeth blew out a long breath. Mother wouldn't want rumors spread if whatever ailed her could be easily treated. But how else to explain leaving? "A family emergency has come up. I'm terribly sorry, but I must go to Albany immediately. Please forgive me. I know you've been working hard, and I so wanted to help with your play." She turned and hurried outside before more accusing words could be flung her direction.

"Miss Wells. Wait!" Samantha rushed into the yard, a dish of powder and a cosmetic brush still in hand and more makeup spread across her dress. "It's not Jackson, is it? I was supposed to see him at the dinner party tonight, but decided to help with the play instead."

"No, no. Mother's fallen ill and sent for me. I can only assume the dinner party is canceled. But please don't speak of it. I don't yet know what ails her, and I might arrive to find it something so slight as a headache."

Concern clouded Samantha's flawless face. "I hope everything turns out all right."

Elizabeth swallowed. "I hope so, too."

And with that, she turned and climbed into the carriage.

"How is Mother?" Elizabeth demanded as she burst through the front door of her parents' Albany home.

Connors, the butler who had been serving their family since before she was born, raised his eyebrows at her. "Quite well. She is in the drawing room."

"The drawing room? She's not in bed, then? Has she taken a turn for the better?" Without waiting to be announced, she rushed into the drawing room—and then stopped cold.

Mother sat on the settee, her face round and healthy, and a beautiful gown of green silk draping her figure. Jackson, dressed in a suit, lounged in a chair opposite Mother. And Father stood by the fireplace, deep in conversation with...

No. Anyone but him... Her body trembled as her eyes latched on to the "dinner companion" leaning against the mantel.

"Good evening, Elizabeth." Mother smiled brightly.

She should excuse herself, rush from the house and never step foot in it again. And she would, if her tongue didn't weigh like lead in her mouth and her stomach didn't lurch until it threatened to heave its contents. Instead she stood planted to the floor, staring at the one man she forever wanted to blot from her memory.

He turned slowly. "Ah, Elizabeth, darling. How kind of you to join us. A bit late though, aren't you? And..."

The eyes of her former fiancé skimmed down her. She didn't need to follow his gaze to know what he saw: a plain white shirtwaist and serviceable blue skirt. Both probably dusted with a mixture of chalk from a calculus lesson and stage powder. And her hair…she shoved some of the loose strands hanging about her face behind her ears.

All while Mother sat there, wearing soft silk and a hopeful smile.

"…a bit underdressed, perhaps," David finished.

"Mr. DeVander." Scanning the room again, she raised her chin. "We seem to be missing your wife this evening. Is she not joining us?"

Surprise lit his deceptively handsome face. "She passed away. A carriage accident over the summer. I assumed you'd heard." His voice sounded like coffee, rich and deep and entirely too smooth.

"I'm sure you were devastated," she snapped.

"Elizabeth, that was uncalled for." Mother fanned her face. "Do forgive my daughter, David. Sometimes her tongue gets the better of her."

"I was, actually. Quite devastated." David glanced at his feet, as though truly pained.

Elizabeth sighed. Perhaps she was being unfair. He may well have loved his wife. Simply because he hadn't loved Elizabeth when they'd been engaged didn't make him incapable of loving anyone else. "I'm sorry for your loss then. Truly."

"Thank you." He flicked his gaze over her once again, lines of disapproval wrinkling his forehead and mouth. "You'll want to clean up for dinner, I'm sure. We'll wait for you before we adjourn to the dining room."

The controlling snake. He was a guest here, yet he had no scruples at hinting she wasn't good enough to dine as she was. He may have lost his wife, may have even been upset by the death, but the man hadn't changed. "Mother, I'd like a word with you. Now."

Mother straightened. "Surely any conversation we have can wait until after we eat, dear."

"No." She clenched her teeth. "Either we talk now, or I leave."

"You're not leaving, when we've waited the better part of an hour for you to get here," Jackson piped up. "I'm famished."

"Yes, daughter, is this truly necessary?" Father added.

She gripped her skirt in her hands and turned. "Then watch me leave."

"Very well, very well." Mother stood slowly, as though trying to temper Elizabeth's quick movements with her own languid ones. "This won't take but a moment, gentlemen."

Elizabeth marched straight across the hall and into her father's office.

"Really, child. You're going to ruin your chance with David all over again." Mother closed the door behind her. "'I'm sure you were devastated'? You don't say such things to a man grieving for his late wife."

"If he still grieved, he wouldn't be here, expecting to have dinner with me." Fury built inside her, an angry storm of rage and betrayal and past regrets. "You lied. I had plans for this evening, a play to help with, and you deliberately misled me to get me away from it."

"Oh, don't be so dramatic." Mother sank fluidly into a chair. "I had a headache when I sent for you, and it cleared up before you arrived."

"You didn't send for me because of a headache. You

sent for me because you wanted me to have dinner with David while he was in town."

"Why you're here hardly matters now that you are. So stop blabbering, fix your hair and come in to dinner. Wait. Don't you have one of your dresses here, up in your old room? That ivory velvet?"

"Hardly matters? Have you gone daft?" She paced in front of Mother's chair. How could the woman sit and wear that guileless smile after what she'd done? "No, don't answer that. You must have. Or you wouldn't have called me away from my commitments. My students have been working since the beginning of the school year on the production, and I promised I'd be there for them.

"Maybe the play and how I got here hardly matter to you. But they matter a great deal to me." She stopped her pacing and headed straight for the door. "Good evening, Mother. I'll see myself out. Thank you."

"No, you won't." Mother sprang up, a terrifyingly quick movement for someone so elegant, and rushed to the door. "You'll go into the dining hall and eat with the rest of us. You have a responsibility to aid your family, not spurn it, and this is your opportunity to do so."

"Opportunity? For what? I know you didn't want me to walk away from my engagement to David all those years ago, but that's over and done. And you *did* let me. Why do I suddenly have to marry now, when you've survived the previous twenty-six years of my life with an unwed daughter? And don't tell me it's because I wrote an editorial in the paper. I'm not a fool."

"We're going to lose our house if you don't marry him."

She barely refrained from rolling her eyes. "Yes.

You told me so at the banquet. But I highly doubt it's going to happen tonight, so that still doesn't answer my question."

"No. You don't understand. The bank sent a man to… to our house yesterday. He was here when I returned from the Ladies' Society meeting. He apparently spoke with your father and assessed the value of the property. There were papers from the bank and…and…I don't know." She waved her hand, as though the simple gesture would shoo the problem away. "I had hopes of you and David reuniting while he was in town. What mother wouldn't dream of such a thing? But after your father told me about the bank man…"

Mother's lips tightened into a straight white line. "I had to get you to dinner. I didn't want to lie, but there seemed no other way."

Elizabeth gripped the bookshelf behind her for balance and pressed her fingers to her temple. Could her parents truly lose the house she'd grown up in? At the banquet, it had seemed like an idle threat, another of Mother's endless dramatics to try to keep her in line. But Mother's face had gone pale beneath her cosmetic powder, and her eyes pleaded for understanding.

"Things can't be that bad," Elizabeth argued. "Look at you, you're dressed in a fine gown and still maintaining a full staff here. If there was so little money, wouldn't Father be cutting back?"

"Oh, stop with this ridiculousness about expenses and cutbacks. I've never paid attention to how your Father manages his accounts. I simply trust him to do so, as any good wife would. And I know what he told me this morning, that the bank will take our house before

Christmas if we don't come up with money. Which is why we need you."

The worry in Mother's eyes faded into a dreamy sheen. "David DeVander has money and position. The panic barely touched him. And he needs a wife. Someone elegant and refined, someone who can charm the crowds in Washington and here at home. He's willing to marry you and willing to help your father get back on his feet."

Elizabeth wrapped her arms around herself and stared at the plush blue carpet beneath her feet. Mother couldn't understand how deeply David had hurt her. If she did, Mother would have never asked such a thing. "I can't, Mama. He cheated on me."

"Don't you see, dear? David would take you back."

"He would take *me* back?" She paced across the floor again, four steps to the fireplace and four steps back. She had to do something to burn off the fury raging inside her. "How very gracious of him, but I refuse to take *him* back. I can't ignore what he did."

"Well, you should. Any woman of breeding ignores—"

"Ignores what? That her husband sleeps with other women?"

"They're called mistresses, Elizabeth."

Mother spoke calmly, so coolly, that Elizabeth stilled, all her fury draining from her at the mention of that one terrible word.

"Father has one, doesn't he?" The whispered accusation slipped from her mouth. Her lungs felt as though they would shatter if she breathed wrong, and a steel band, heavy and unbreakable, tightened about her heart. But still, it couldn't be true. Father wouldn't

take a mistress. He couldn't. Perhaps he had his faults—
she'd be the last person to proclaim him perfect—but
he wouldn't betray her mother, her family, in such a
manner.

A faint blush rose on Mother's cheeks. "Your father is very discreet, both personally and profession-
ally. How should I know whether he has a mistress?"

"Don't lie to me. You know." Oh, goodness, she
wanted to be sick. But she couldn't, not here in front of
Mother, not with David and Father and Jackson across
the hall. "A woman always knows that kind of thing."

She had with David. She'd just been too young and
trusting to pay attention to the warnings inside her head.

"Don't you understand why you need to marry?"
Mother stepped close, her eyes framed with unfulfilled
dreams and glittering like bright, hard diamonds. "Mistresses don't matter, not in the grand picture of things.
But a good marriage can take care of both you and
your family."

Obey your parents. Honor them. The minister's
words from Sunday's sermon curled like smoke around
the recesses of her mind. But surely honoring her parents didn't mean she had to spend the rest of her life
married to a man like David. Surely God wouldn't ask
that of her, would He? "I'd never be able to keep him
happy."

"Happy? What has happiness to do with duty?"

"You speak as though I neglect you, but I help the
family whenever an opportunity arises. I make appear-
ances with Father, attend your social events and give
speeches on his behalf. I'm even giving a speech next
week. Why can't that be enough?"

"We're going to lose our house, and you have the

ability to stop it from happening, yet you refuse. Oh, dear, you're going to make me cry." Mother blinked her eyes frantically, but two large tears streaked down her cheeks. "Have you a hankie?"

Elizabeth reached into her pocket and handed Mother a chalk-dusted handkerchief.

"Thank you." Mother sniffled and dabbed at her face, unwittingly smearing the tears, cosmetic powder and chalk dust together into a pathetic mess on her skin. "I simply don't understand why you can't marry David and leave that wretched teaching job."

Elizabeth sighed. No. Mother didn't understand, not how important teaching was to her, or how miserable she'd be if she married David.

Perhaps Mother didn't understand because she didn't care to, or perhaps she was simply incapable of recognizing that some women had dreams which extended beyond marriage to a prominent husband. So round and round they went. Mother would never look at her life and see success, would never say, "Well done, Elizabeth. You're making a difference." She would only, always, see the world through her unchanging, marriage-hungry eyes.

"Good evening, then. I'm quite done here." Elizabeth hurried out of the study and to the front door, not stopping to ask for her coat or reticule. The cold air cloaked her as she rushed outside and down the steps. Then she halted, staring at the empty street.

The carriage. How could she have forgotten she'd ridden here in her parents' carriage? Mother certainly wouldn't offer to have the coachman return her to Valley Falls, and without her reticule, she could hardly pay to take the train home.

"No way home?" a cool voice asked from the steps.

Her body tensed. If only she could find some way not to turn around, some way not to face the man she'd once promised to wed. But that would involve walking down the street and into the night without either her coat or reticule. Her knees trembled and her hand locked onto the iron railing beside the steps as she turned.

"If you'll please step aside, I need to retrieve my things." She tried to move around David, but he shifted to the middle of the steps and extended his hands until they touched both railings, completely barring her way.

"You've changed."

"Yes. A great deal." She shivered. Didn't he realize that she needed her coat?

The lantern on the porch slanted down, illuminating David while his eyes narrowed and traveled down her once again—as though he hadn't learned enough from his earlier perusal in the drawing room. "I'm trying to determine if the change was for the better."

She stared into the smooth face, the hair black as midnight, and the brown eyes full of secrets. Most would call him handsome, but then, most people saw his outward charm rather than the blackness within. "And what about you? Have you changed? Or do you still keep a mistress in the house around the corner?"

He laughed, a bold, raucous sound. "Still upset about that, darling? No, if you must know. I tired of her long ago."

"And moved on to another, no doubt. Probably one who stays in Washington. Tell me, did you bring her with you on your trip here?"

"Come now, Elizabeth. No gentleman discusses his mistress with a lady. You know that."

No. You only discuss your mistresses with other gentlemen. The old wounds, long buried under the busyness of her current life, opened fresh as she stood before him, David DeVander, the man who had caused her untold hours of tears and heartache.

The man who had taught her never to trust another man again.

Of all the nights to have this conversation, all the times to face him, did it have to be now? Tonight? After Mother's lie and news of the house and missing her students' play?

She glanced down at her skirt, still splotched with chalk and cosmetic dust, and her shirtwaist tucked crookedly into her belt.

"I'm not much of a lady anymore," she whispered. Was it a bad thing?

"You would make any man a fine wife and if you marry me, I'll see that your family is taken care of. I'm sure you know your father's about to lose his house."

She tried to breathe, clean deep breaths that would calm her, allow her to think rationally. But the air choked off in her throat, and her entire body turned cold, then hot, then cold again. Mother had given her the same ultimatum inside, so why did the words seem more terrifying coming from David himself?

Perhaps because David's offer laid the choice bare in a way Mother's hadn't. Mother was always imploring her to marry one man or another, but never before had her family's house been at stake. Never before had someone made her so clear an offer: Marry and save your family or refuse and…and what?

She looked up at the house, the strong brick walls that had sheltered her family for nearly thirty years, the bedroom in the upper left corner where she'd spent the first seventeen years of her life, the room that her parents shared on the opposite corner of the second floor. She could save it, allow Mother to keep her silks and Father to keep his dignity. Just one single, tiny word. *Yes*.

She licked her lips. The word wasn't hard to say, not even two syllables. So why did her tongue refuse to form it?

Because she didn't want a marriage based on a business contract. Perhaps some young ladies married for the reasons David delineated. But her? She'd shrivel up and die. Was the sacrifice worth it, her family for her soul?

"What are you thinking?" David's dark voice pierced her thoughts. "Tell me."

She took a step away from him. "You wouldn't want me. I've changed too much."

"You know how to behave, even if you've been off on this…" he twirled his hand in the air as though too bored to find the right word "…teaching escapade for several years. Your recent antics with newspaper articles have been a little much of late, but they merely prove a woman like yourself ought not be living on her own, without parents or a husband to answer to. It's nothing a solid hand couldn't correct once you're wed."

Solid hand. Correct. Did he think her some errant child?

"Furthermore, my late wife left me with two young sons. They need a mother. I need someone to host dinner parties and appear at political gatherings. You're a rather good orator and would do well speaking to ladies' groups and so forth."

A mother. A hostess. An orator. All the things he

required in a wife. Still the man said nothing about *her* as a person. What she dreamed of, what she liked or disliked.

Because he didn't know. She'd been raised with him, their families were longtime friends. Then they fell into courtship and got betrothed at the proper ages. But he only knew her in the way one knew an objet d'art. A person could study the lines and forms of a sculpture, the position and facial expressions. But a statue was only clay or stone or marble, incapable of feeling or emotion, of behaving in any way other than what the sculptor designed.

That's what David wanted: a marble wife.

His golden-tipped words would have been enough once. But she'd changed; David was right in that assessment. And she'd rather spend her life teaching mathematics and offering her students a glimmer of hope instead of hanging on the arm of David DeVander or anyone of his ilk.

"I thank you for your compliments, Mr. DeVander. But truly, I must be going. Now if you'll let me pass so I can fetch my belongings." She tried to brush by him, but he grasped her shoulder and turned her face to his.

"You're beautiful, Elizabeth." He tucked a strand of hair behind her ear.

She lurched away, the feel of his fingers so near her face burning despite the cold seeping through her clothing. "Don't touch me."

He tightened his grip and dragged her closer. "I leave for Washington in two weeks. I need a wife before I return, and your family needs money. You think I don't know how badly off your father is? He can barely keep his house and staff and you can change all that—if you marry me."

"Elizabeth?" a rusty voice called from the direction of the street.

Elizabeth gulped a breath and closed her eyes. She'd imagined the voice, she must have. Luke couldn't be here, not now. She merely needed to open her eyes and see that no one stood on the walkway, particularly not a tall, lean man wearing a cowboy hat.

"What's going on here?" the voice growled.

She opened her eyes and took in the shadowed figure in the unmistakable cowboy hat. There was no denying Luke was here, all right, staring straight at her.

Luke wasn't sure whether to run up and yank Elizabeth from the scoundrel who held her on the steps or turn and head home. When he'd left Valley Falls an hour ago, he'd figured on finding any number of things at the Wells's house, but Elizabeth standing outside, practically in the arms of another man, wasn't one of them.

She tried to step down, probably to greet him, but rather than release her shoulder, the other man pulled her back against his chest. Luke curled his fingers into hard fists.

"Can I help you?" the dandy asked in a voice as smooth and liquid as water itself.

Luke flicked his gaze to Elizabeth. "Since you're not keeping vigil near your mother, I assume she's feeling a mite better."

"Yes, I—"

"The students were worried, especially Samantha. I volunteered to come check on you. Though I see they got their dander up over nothing."

"Is that what your mother did to get you here?" The other man laughed, a chilling sound. "Sent word she was ill?"

The laugher must have loosened his hold, because Elizabeth jerked away and headed down the steps. "It's not funny. My students were counting on me."

"I'm sure they were, darling. I'm sure they were."

She stopped before Luke, and he stilled as the words sank in. Her mother had tricked her by sending word she was ill? Why would she do such a thing? Surely Mrs. Wells didn't begrudge her daughter helping with a play.

Luke shifted closer, running his eyes down Elizabeth's slender form. Her face didn't carry the flushed look of anticipation one might expect from a woman meeting with a lover, but glowed pale and taut with tension in the dim lamplight. Lines etched the corners of her mouth, while smudges haunted the hollows beneath her eyes, and her dirty, serviceable clothing hung limp and twisted on her frame. Not the way a woman would look if she had a rendezvous with a man.

She shivered under his gaze—no, not under his gaze. She was freezing. Hang it all, he'd been too all-fired frustrated to notice how cold she was.

"Where's your coat? Did you leave home without it?" He shrugged out of his and wrapped it about her shoulders. "And why are you outside without something to keep you warm?"

"My coat's inside with my reticule." She hunched her shoulders against the cool air and stretched the coat tight around herself. "I was heading inside to retrieve them when I was…intercepted."

He glanced toward his carriage, then back to her disheveled form. "You need a ride home?"

"She most certainly does not," the other man interrupted. "She's coming inside to dinner. Aren't you, darling?"

"Stop calling me 'darling.'" Her body stayed slumped as she spoke, as though she hadn't the energy to straighten and raise her chin in that familiar, haughty angle. As though the man on the steps had already defeated her.

"Aren't you going to introduce me to your friend, *darling?*" Something sharp glinted in the man's eyes.

Luke shifted in front of Elizabeth as the scoundrel came forward.

"Mr. DeVander, this is Luke Hayes, grandson of the late Jonah Hayes, whom I'm sure you remember." Gone was the usual steel behind Elizabeth's voice, replaced by a small quiver. "Mr. Hayes, this is David DeVander, United States Representative of our congressional district."

DeVander. The name set off warning sounds. Luke looked the scoundrel up and down, from the top of his sleek black hair to the tips of his shiny shoes. Where had he heard…?

DeVander. Luke hardened his jaw while Stevens's words echoed inside him. This was the man who had offered to marry Elizabeth and then taken a mistress.

"The Hayes heir." DeVander straightened and extended his hand, his eyes assessing, probably trying to figure whether he could hit up the new heir for a donation. "It's a pleasure to meet you."

Luke stared at the offered hand and pushed some spittle around in his mouth. If only the lady wasn't present…

He settled a hand on Elizabeth's shoulder instead.

"Do you want to leave? I can take you in my carriage and send a footman later for your things."

"I already said she was attending dinner," DeVander barked. "And she can hardly ride back to Valley Falls with you unchaperoned."

Unchaperoned in a carriage. Did that break one of the social rules? Probably. Simply breathing was enough to break half those highfalutin guidelines. But at the very least, he could take the train and give Elizabeth his carriage.

"As though you would complain if I rode unchaperoned in a carriage with you," Elizabeth snapped at DeVander, then turned. "I appreciate your offer, Luke. I can use a ride home."

Luke extended his arm, and she took it.

"Very well, Elizabeth." DeVander glowered at them through the darkness. "I'll be waiting to hear your decision."

A shudder rippled down her slender frame as she headed to the carriage.

Chapter Thirteen

"What happened back there?"

Elizabeth's bottom had barely touched the carriage seat before Luke asked his question.

What *had* happened? She pressed her shaking fingers to her temples. She wasn't sure. Mother had deceived her and arranged an engagement to David. Father had a mistress—which evidently wasn't a shock to anyone but her. And David had proposed.

No it wasn't just a proposal. David had offered to help her family out of their current disastrous situation *if* she married him. The hard timbre of his voice as he made his offer resonated through her memory.

"Elizabeth?" Luke's fingers, firm but warm, took her chin and lifted it up until their eyes met.

She pulled back and sank deeper into the carriage seat. If only she could be home. In her own bed, that sat in her own room, that was part of her own house, surrounded by her own soothing things, in the comfortable world she'd created for herself.

She would be there in a little over an hour. She just had to endure the ride home with Luke first.

The carriage lamp burned above them, casting the inside of the conveyance in a soft orange glow. She shrank farther away from Luke. Why did it have to be lit? Darkness had cloaked their ride back to Valley Falls after the banquet, but now he could see everything about her, from her dirty clothes to her falling hair to the tears brimming in her eyes.

She shouldn't be in the carriage with him at all. David had been right in that respect. She'd get in trouble if someone at the academy found out she'd ridden alone with Luke Hayes, and David would likely announce her lack of propriety to the world if doing so served his purposes. But still, letting Luke, with all his assessing looks and uncomfortable questions, escort her home seemed a small difficulty compared to walking back inside her parents' house.

The carriage wheels clattered against Albany's cobbled roads. Snorts, groans, creaks and shouts from all manner of conveyance, beast and persons echoed through the space she and Luke shared, but the noise from outside didn't thwart the quiet that lingered between them.

She looked down at her hands, curled atop the soft brown leather of his duster, and settled deeper inside the warmth it offered. The scents of sunshine and grass and Luke Hayes clung to the material, as though she need only close her eyes and she could be with him in some Wyoming meadow, the sun beating down upon her back and wildflowers surrounding her. So very far away from the chaos her life had become.

"Elizabeth?"

She glanced up. Luke leaned forward, his eyes intent upon her face, probably still waiting to hear what had happened that evening. She could evade, of course. Change the subject or flat-out refuse to speak of the evening. Except she couldn't ride the entire way to Valley Falls with his gaze boring into her and silence strangling the air.

"My family…" she started, but tears welled up to choke her throat.

"Your family is the biggest bunch of conniving rats I've ever met."

She gasped and blinked against the burning in her eyes.

"Your ma tricked you out of helping with the play so you would come here and have dinner with that snake DeVander. Am I right?"

She looked away.

"But you didn't stay."

She sank her head in her hands. "Oh, goodness, what have I done? I was so disrespectful. Mother will never want to speak to me again. And Father, how will I ever stand up and give that speech for him?"

She was still supposed to speak to her fellow educators in two days' times. And now that David was in town, he was sure to be there as well, giving a speech on the benefits of education. His attendance had likely been planned—and concealed from her—from the beginning.

She couldn't do it. It simply wasn't possible for her to stand up and smile and speak to educators on David's behalf.

Luke's fingers gently wrapped around her wrists, tugging her hands away from her face. "You did the right thing. You shouldn't have stayed, not when your ma used deceit to get you there."

"You heard the sermon on Sunday. 'Children obey your parents. Rebellion is as the sin of witchcraft, and stubbornness is as iniquity and idolatry.'" The scripture tasted bitter on her tongue, and try as she might, she couldn't stop a tear or two from slipping down her face. "Mother's right. I'm a terrible daughter."

"No." He wiped one of her tears away with his thumb. "You're a strong, courageous woman. A tad bit independent but beautiful for it. You like teaching and helping your students. You challenge those girls to be better, more educated people than they were before you met them. You've got nothing to be ashamed of."

His words swirled around her. Supportive and hopeful and kinder than anything she'd heard all night, probably even all month. Was her independence truly beautiful? Did she mean that much to her students? And if so, how could she mean so much to them and so little to her family? "You don't understand."

"No?"

"Maybe my students appreciate me, but according to Mother, I'm sinning by refusing to marry someone who will support Father until…until he can…"

The torrent of sobs building inside her chest broke in one violent gush. She pressed her hand to her mouth, trying to stem the swelling flood.

Luke watched her for a moment, then pulled her against himself and held tight. Tears dampened the front of his shirt, and her petticoats crinkled awkwardly against his legs; but he didn't unleash a harsh rebuke about puffy eyes, unlady-like behavior or tears ruining his clothing. He only tightened his hold, his muscled arms offering strength and protection, his solid chest lending stability and support. She buried her face into his shoulder and cried until she had no tears left.

Then she cried harder, after the tears refused to come but her soul still ached.

He simply held on.

"Hush now, there's nothing wrong with you. I doubt you're disobeying God."

The words soaked through slowly, seeping in layer by layer, and filling the icy cavern inside her chest.

"What does God want for your life?" He stroked his hand down her back then up again, gentle, soothing movements. "We're to obey God over men. Have you read the story of Jonathan in the Bible? He didn't always obey his parents. He was best friends with his father's worst enemy, but he still honored God by saving David from his father's hands."

"Jonathan." She sniffled. "Mother always quotes that verse about Saul and rebellion. And here God's answer lies in Saul's son."

"There're consequences for disobeying your parents. The Bible tells us to obey both God and the family He's given us. If God and family are at odds with one another, the person caught in the middle will have heartache, to be sure. But we ought to always obey God first."

She wiped her face with his coat sleeve. "I hadn't considered Jonathan, my parents and God being at odds, any of it."

"And now you have." His hand continued to rub up and down her back, comforting even though her tears had stopped. "Feel better?"

"Yes, thank you," she croaked, her voice hoarse and froglike.

He shifted to offer his handkerchief, and with the simple movement, his side pressed hard into hers.

Entirely too hard.

Where was she sitting? *How* was she sitting? She glanced down and found herself nearly on his lap, with her head touching the crook of his shoulder and his arm tight around her back.

She scrambled away. "I'm sorry. I shouldn't have… that is, it was very improper for… I mean…"

He laughed, actually laughed. Not a raucous sound at her expense like David's cackles but an encouraging guffaw from deep inside. "No need to get your feathers in a ruffle. I can keep a secret."

"Thank you." She glanced down, then back up. "It seems that's all I'm doing this evening, thanking you and then apologizing."

His lips slid into that lazy half smile and he handed over a handkerchief. "Everyone's allowed a bad night once in a while."

She glanced away, her cheeks suddenly hot.

"You feeling a bit better after that cry?"

She nodded without looking up.

"Good. So now we've got that business over your parents settled, tell me about this DeVander fellow."

She dabbed her face with the hankie. "Nothing much to tell, really. Just my mother's latest suitor for me."

"Who you were once engaged to."

Her eyes snapped to his. "How'd you know?"

"My butler told me."

"Why would your butler—?"

"I asked."

"You just happened to ask if I had any former fiancés?" Ugh. She could just imagine that conversation.

The side of his mouth twitched up into that smile again. "No. I asked why you weren't married."

"Oh…"

The carriage rumbled over the road that had turned from cobblestones to dirt. A faint draft stirred around the boxed-in conveyance, and a coyote yipped in the distance. She stared down at her lap, folding and unfolding her hands, unable to bring her eyes to meet his. "And why would you ask about a thing like that?"

"Seemed relevant."

"I can assure you, it's not."

"Then why were you standing outside with your former fiancé?"

"Because Mother…Mother…" Should she continue? And why was she even tempted to blurt her life's troubles to Luke Hayes?

She slid her eyes toward him, his firm jaw and solid shoulders. The man seemed strong enough to carry any burden she unveiled—and determined enough not to let her out of the carriage until she answered.

"David's wife died recently. So he needs another, you see, for appearance's sake. Mother wants it to be me. Did you know Father lost a lot of money in the panic?" She swallowed. "Actually he lost everything. His bank collapsed, and his campaign finances, his personal savings, his investments in the railroad… Everything is gone.

"So after the panic, he mortgaged his house, thinking that he only needed a little time to build his investments back up. But now Mother and Father are through that money and on the brink of losing their home and… um… David is still well off. So if I marry him, he would take care of my fam—"

"No." The single word sliced through the carriage.

She stared down at her hands, still curled in Luke's coat. "He can save my parents."

Luke shifted close, so close his broad shoulders blocked the carriage lamp. He trailed a finger from her cheekbone to her jaw, then laid it over her lips. Probably to silence her, though she could hardly speak with his hand warm against her face.

"You'd be wasting your life." The breath from his whispered words brushed her face. "And you'd hate marriage to him."

She knew as much, but how did he? What enabled him to discern such a thing after spending only five minutes' time with David?

His other hand came up to caress her cheek, and he inched forward until his face obliterated everything else from her vision. Her gaze dipped to his mouth. The slightest movement from either of them, and their lips would touch.

What would it feel like, being kissed by a cowboy? David's kisses had been smooth and seductive, but something told her kissing Luke Hayes would be in no way similar.

She should pull away. Shift back. Slap him. Move to the bench on the opposite side of the carriage. Anything to distract her from those lips.

But she didn't.

Instead, she leaned forward, propelled by some inward desire she didn't understand, part curiosity, part defiance, part longing.

Their lips brushed, and a wave of warmth started where their mouths met and traveled to her toes. She closed her eyes against the tender contact, the way time suspended as her lips rubbed briefly against his. Then she sighed and pulled back.

"Not yet," he whispered, taking her shoulders and covering her mouth with his own.

The man was controlled strength, no pretense or secrets. His lips were firm but not hard, demanding but not reckless. His muscled arms wrapped around her, drawing her closer. His unyielding lips kissed her slowly at first, his mouth whispering a silent message as it lingered against hers. *Trust me.*

Kissing Miss Wells was like unwrapping a present. Slowly drawing off the ribbon, then the wrapping. Taking the lid off the box, and digging through the tissue. She had so many layers—the proper lady, the dignified teacher, the steely politician's daughter, the soft woman. He peeled them back until her heart shimmered like diamonds in his hands.

He knew the moment he had gained her trust. Her muscles relaxed, her breathing grew deeper and her hands became restless as they slipped from his neck to his shoulders.

And what was he doing? Kissing Miss Wells in a carriage, while she hadn't even a chaperone? She was a city woman who lived thousands of miles from his ranch. A politician's daughter who faced bigger decisions than kissing him. A teacher who did unfathomable good for her students and didn't need him getting in the way of her dreams or hurting her reputation.

He leaned back, abruptly breaking the kiss. But she clung to his shirt, her eyes closed, her face upturned, her breathing erratic. Then her eyelids flickered open, and he stared into pure, dreamy hazel.

He should have never ended that kiss.

He should have never started it.

A splotch of red stained her cheeks and spread until it covered her face and neck. She put a hand to her cheek. "Luke, I—"

"You don't kiss me like that and then try apologizing," he growled, more frustrated with himself over what he'd started than whatever she called him.

He hadn't thought it possible for her face to grow redder, but it did. She fixed her eyes on some teeny speck on the floor and wrapped her arms around herself in a halfhearted hug. "This... I... We can't do this. It will lead to trouble." Her eyes shone large and luminous in the lamplight; her lips full and swollen from his kiss.

He should take her in his arms and repeat the kiss. Only this time, he wouldn't stop to worry about where she lived or who her parents were or what she did for a living. This time he'd kiss her and hold her like a man who planned to be in Valley Falls for the next fifty years. Because right about now, he wanted to be that man for her.

But he couldn't.

He didn't have time to get involved with Elizabeth, and even if he did muddle into a relationship, what happened when he returned to Wyoming? He couldn't take her with him. Where would she teach? The Teton Valley already had a teacher for its tiny schoolhouse.

And why was he thinking about taking her West? A man didn't up and pick a bride after one kiss.

Did he?

He swallowed. No. Definitely not.

"I, um..." Some of the flush had left Elizabeth's face, and her skin took on that irresistibly creamy hue again as she pushed words through her stammering mouth. "That is… I want you to know, that…I—I…don't really kiss…" Her finger traced an imaginary pattern on her lap. "Well, you remember what I told you? About how much I enjoy teaching? And the board of directors feels very strongly about its teachers behaving with the utmost propriety. So, you see, um…I can't really…"

"You won't kiss me again, but you'll consider marrying a scoundrel like David DeVander." The realization twisted something deep inside him. Maybe he was a tad crazy to get so moonstruck over one kiss. But the thought of her going to DeVander, kissing the snake the way she'd just kissed him, ignited fire in his blood.

"If you could please just keep from telling anyone about this, this…indiscretion. I didn't mean to kiss you, and it won't happen again."

"That's two indiscretions in the past hour I'm supposed to keep secret."

"Indeed. I'll be more careful in my future encounters with you."

"Tell you what. I'll keep your secrets, if you refuse to marry DeVander."

Her eyes flew up to his. "You can't make such a demand. My relationship with David is hardly your business."

"I'm making it my business."

Her spine straightened, inch by inch, revealing the steel hidden beneath her veneer of softness. "And why is that? Are you prepared to give my family the money they need to keep their house? Or maybe you'll make me an offer like David's. Marriage in exchange for helping my family?"

"Would you consider it?"

He'd gone daft. Crazier than a senile old man. What made him say that? Sure, Elizabeth was being smart with him, but he didn't want a citified wife in the first place, and certainly didn't plan to get one by making a business deal.

"I used to think I knew what I wanted, could reach my dreams." She stared blindly at the far wall. "But I don't think I can do anything anymore—except for marry the man Mother's picked out."

And now she was thinking her life worthless. She'd had a hard enough night already, and here he was being harsh on her all over again. He reached over and took her hand. "You've reached your dreams, and you're a good teacher. Do you realize that? Every one of your students is better for having sat in your classes, for having known you as a person."

"Most of my girls would rather run screaming from the room than study advanced algebra."

He grinned. "I doubt that, Lizzie. Really."

"Don't call me Lizzie."

"Beth, then."

If a look could shoot poisoned arrows, he'd be dead several times over.

"Say you won't marry DeVander, and I'll call you Elizabeth."

"You can't talk me out of marriage by threatening to call or not call me some name."

He scratched his forehead beneath his hat brim. "It makes me furious to see you all but forced into marriage."

"Why?"

Because marriage should be more than a business arrangement. Because Elizabeth loved teaching and should pursue that rather than chain herself to a snake like DeVander. Because Pa and Grandpa had spent forty years of their lives not speaking to each other over this very issue.

"Because I don't cotton to browbeating people into marriage." And for some reason he didn't understand, he'd forfeit his entire inheritance to prevent the smart little teacher beside him from falling into that trap.

Elizabeth pressed her palm against the cold bedroom window and stared out over the street. Luke's carriage had disappeared around the corner moments earlier, but still, she couldn't pull her gaze from the path it had followed.

She rubbed her eyes, trying to dispel the image of him inside the conveyance from her mind. Or the image of him squaring off with David. Or the one of him sending the reporter scampering away after the banquet. She could alternate between the images at will, but try as she might, she couldn't fully shake those clear blue eyes from her memory.

Or his words. *What does God want for your life?*

To teach, of course. The answer was so obvious to him that she hadn't the slightest notion why he'd bothered to ask. But then, why was the answer obvious to him, and not Mother or Father or Jackson? Why did a rancher from Wyoming understand her better than the people who'd known her since birth?

He'd sat in the carriage and held her, calm despite the storm raging inside her, open and straightforward despite her family's deceit.

And she loved him for it.

Oh, goodness. She *loved* him.

No. She couldn't. Perhaps she'd grown fond of him, and perhaps she counted him a friend. But she didn't love him, certainly not. David had hurt her too badly to love again.

She let the curtains fall, shutting out the world beyond her own little room. She didn't want to love a man, especially not a man who'd come to take his sister away and sell off Jonah's life work.

She moved from the window and sank down onto her bed. She wouldn't let herself love Luke Hayes. Perhaps he played the attentive gentleman—or rancher—when she was about. But hadn't David? Maybe he kissed her as though she meant something. But hadn't David? Perhaps he would even say he loved her. But she couldn't be sure he'd love her forever, couldn't say with certainty he'd still love her five years from now.

And so she wouldn't love him. It was a simple decision, really, to close off one's heart. She'd done it once before. She could do it again.

Chapter Fourteen

"**P**roposed? What do you mean Jackson proposed?" Luke shot to his feet as his words reverberated throughout his grandfather's office.

Samantha cringed but stood her ground in front of the gargantuan desk, the sapphire on her finger sparkling far too brightly.

"I said the two of you could go horseback riding… with a *chaperone*." He blew out a breath, long and hard. Control, he needed to find a bit of it, before he launched himself over the desk and went on a warpath to find a certain accountant and wrap his hands around the miscreant's throat. "I never said anything about agreeing to an engagement. The scoundrel didn't even ask me if he could marry you."

"He's waiting outside the door to do so now, if you'd stop shouting."

"I'm…not…shouting." It was more like hollering, really. "What's the point of him asking *after* he's put a ring on your finger?"

"There's no point of him asking you at all. You're not my father, and Jackson wrote to Pa nearly a week ago."

Sam's face had turned a ghostly shade of white, and her words came quietly, without hint of defiance or menace.

Luke scratched the back of his neck and paced behind the desk. He should have strangled the boy nearly a week ago. Right around the time he found the scamp kissing his sister's face off.

"Besides, Grandpa was good friends with the Wellses and would have given his approval in a heartbeat. Asking Pa is just formality. He has no reason to refuse."

"Grandpa and Pa didn't speak. If anything, Pa's likely to say no to Jackson simply because Grandpa liked him." Luke planted his hands on the desk and leaned forward. "And do you really think Pa's not going to ask my thoughts, just give you blind permission to marry some man he's never met?"

She gasped and took a step back from the desk, moisture shimmering in her eyes. "You wouldn't deny me the man I love out of spite."

He sighed. "Not out of spite, Sam. Out of concern. I don't trust him." And not only that, but getting Sam back home was going to be a heap harder now that she had a ring on her finger.

"How can you say such a thing? Jackson's wonderful." She blinked back the moisture in her eyes, but it did little good as a tear crested anyway. "You'd see that for yourself, if only you'd give him a chance."

"Don't cry." Here he was calling Jackson a scoundrel, but wasn't he the bigger scoundrel of the two of them? Seemed he made his sister cry every time they talked. He walked around the desk and offered his kerchief, then wrapped his arm around her shoulders. "You need to go home for a bit, Sam. Not stay here and marry. We can try to work something out with Jackson, and

I'll meet with him. But that still doesn't change your needing to go home."

And it still didn't change his thoughts about not trusting the younger man.

Why didn't he trust Jackson? Because of the ten thousand dollars Sam would inherit upon marrying? If she didn't have an inheritance, would he feel differently about Jackson? Maybe he was being unfair. They'd begun courting before Grandpa had fallen ill—before Sam had become an heiress. And even if the man's parents were in financial trouble, that didn't mean Jackson was. The boy made a good salary at the accounting office, after all.

"I've told you before." Sam buried her face against his shirt as the tears fell. "I don't want to go home, not now, when I've so many things to do out here."

A hard knock sounded at the door.

"Hold on—"

"Come in," Sam sniffled.

The door swung open, and Jackson slid in. His eyes slanted immediately toward Sam, and he moved to her with the speed and agility of a wolf chasing its prey. "Samantha, love, what's wrong?"

Luke scowled but pulled his arm from his sister, who immediately threw herself against Jackson.

"Come now, our engagement is cause for celebration, not tears." Jackson spoke against her temple.

Luke took a step back from the entwined couple. Was he a monster? Some terrible ogre for not simply agreeing to the wedding his sister clearly wanted? Yet he could hardly agree when Sam needed to return home to Ma—and he wondered if the marriage would hurt Sam eventually.

"Two days," Luke croaked. "Give me two days to think about the proposal. And, Jackson, I need to speak with you when you're done attending Sam."

What was he going to do? Luke settled his shoulder against the glittering gold doorjamb of his grandfather's bedroom, a room he hadn't yet entered since arriving in Valley Falls, and rubbed the back of his neck.

Coming to Valley Falls was supposed to be simple. He'd had two goals in mind: sell off Grandpa's estate and take Sam back home. What had happened to his plans? It seemed the longer he stayed here, the more confused he became. He was supposed to hate this town, this house, the staff, the insurance and accounting company. But he didn't.

Oh, sure, he'd been slow warming up to it all; but after a week of staring at numbers and looking over his grandfather's businesses, the companies didn't seem so intimidating. He wasn't a fan of the gilt trim and pristine decorations tacked up all over the house, but the structure itself was rather pleasant, with its sprawling design and wide window-filled rooms and kind staff.

But even more than the house, his work here mattered. Ranchers were a dime a dozen west of the Mississippi and though he'd employed a handful of people, his ranch only affected the dozen men that worked for him.

As head of Great Northern Accounting and Insurance, he had hundreds of employees depending on him, and that wasn't even considering the staff he employed here at the house, or all the good Grandpa's charitable endeavors had wrought.

Time was when he'd not been able to imagine himself living anywhere but on his ranch. But now, after a mere week in Valley Falls, he saw himself here, too. Waking up every morning to those shadowed Catskill Mountains and managing the legacy his grandfather had left.

He stared into his grandpa's room, fully lit in all its gaudy, golden splendor. Did the man regret the choices he'd made? The one that had forced his son away? He appeared to have changed at some point in his life. To hear Pa speak, Grandpa was a controlling, greedy self-made man. But a greedy man wouldn't give half his profits to charity or one of his houses to a schoolteacher.

Luke ran his eyes over the walnut-and-white-silk headboard, the gargantuan bed covered in snowy white, the elaborate nightstand and dresser. Who was this man, his grandfather?

He took a step into the room, then another and another, until he reached the dresser. The sun cast its fading rays through the windows as he opened the top drawer and began to sort.

Three hours later, chaotic piles littered the room. Clothes to be donated over here, things to be discarded over there, items to be saved beside it. Sam had already gone through the closet, leaving the heaps of clothing and other items on the far side of the room, and he was making an even bigger mess.

Luke opened the top drawer of the nightstand and pulled out a Bible. Flipping through, he trailed his thumbs over the worn, note-marked pages. He stopped at a passage in Psalms where it seemed every verse had been notated, then turned a few more pages. The Bible seemed to fall open to the first chapter of Proverbs on its own. And there, at the beginning of the book on wisdom, lay an envelope with the name Luke Hayes scrawled across it.

He ran his finger over the sprawling letters. Was it truly for him? Sure it carried his name, but a letter of any importance wouldn't be tucked into an obscure corner of Grandpa's room, would it? Still, he slipped a finger beneath the seal and opened it. Inside lay a single piece of stationary and a smaller envelope with Pa's name.

My Grandson,

If you hold this letter, that means you have arrived in Valley Falls, likely as my heir, and are busy seeing to the business matters which I left you. It brings me joy knowing the son of my son is in my house caring for my legacy, and it brings me pain knowing I died without ever laying eyes on you.

Be wise, Luke. I leave you a life's work, some of it built upon ambition and greed, some of it built upon love and hard work. Do not make the mistakes I did during my early and middle years. Do not sacrifice family for ambition or love for greed. I pray when you one day reach my age and sit penning letters to your children and grandchildren, you'll look back on your own life with no regrets.

Keep the Bible, keep the house, keep anything of mine you wish. Use it wisely, and please give the enclosed letter to your father.

Sincerely
Jonah P. Hayes

Luke stared at the large, uneven handwriting until the words blurred. *Don't sacrifice family for ambition or love for greed.* The man would know. He'd made mistakes for most of his life and evidently only set about correcting them at the end.

But Luke was already on a better track than Grandpa. He sought to sell the things Grandpa left, so he could return home and reunite his family before Ma's death. Yep, he would place his family before ambition by selling the house and everything else.

And what about Cynthia and Everett? Are you forcing them to go back, as well? Sam's words rippled through his mind. But surely he wasn't supposed to take them back to Wyoming. He wasn't even obligated to see them. Cynthia had married into the family and held no blood relation.

But Everett…Everett was his twin's blood. Blake's legacy and heir.

A sickening sensation fisted in his gut. He was shutting out family—not so much for his own ambition, and not just because of his anger and grief, but to forget his own failures. And he would regret it one day. Confound it, he regretted it even now, the hard words he'd spoken to Cynthia over Blake's body, the way he'd sent her packing before she saw her husband buried.

And he was being just as controlling with Sam, in pressing her to make amends, to go back and see Ma, to be a part of the family once again. She was seventeen and standing on the edge of womanhood, yet he pushed her to settle things in his way and his time, not leaving any part of the decision up to her.

Luke sunk his head in his hands. Truly he was as bad as Grandpa. He was making all the same mistakes, just in different ways. Forcing those he loved to do some-thing, regardless of his motives, was controlling and ruthless. And he wouldn't do it anymore.

He'd find out where Cynthia lived—somewhere near Philadelphia, if he recalled—and ask her to forgive him, see how she wanted to settle things. Maybe the woman wished to move back West. Maybe she wanted her son, *Blake's son,* raised somewhere else. Maybe she longed to be a part of the Hayes family again. He would leave the decision up to her but she'd have his support no mat-ter what she chose.

As for Sam, he had to tell her about Ma. He'd prom-ised Ma that he'd keep quiet, but he never would have made that promise had he known how much Sam loved her life here. Sam was grown enough to wear some man's ring on her finger, and if she was grown enough for that, she was grown enough to make her own deci-sions about Ma. He wouldn't be like Grandpa one day, looking back from the end of his life and wishing he'd been more honest with Sam, regretting that he hadn't let her make her own choices.

He only hoped it wasn't too late for Samantha and Ma. As for Cynthia…he'd find out where he stood when he got to Philadelphia.

"Luke?" A soft voice echoed from the doorway. Sam stood there, dressed for bed in a white lacy nightgown.

She glanced around the cluttered room. "You're going through Grandpa's things? Now? I can help some more. I don't mind. I just didn't want to sort through this stuff instead of attending school."

"I'm sorry, Sam."

She blinked. "For what?"

Everything, it seemed. "For trying to force you back West."

Her eyes turned wide as a boy's who'd just been given his first rifle.

"Come sit." He patted the floor beside him.

She came, trusting and innocent, and tucked herself up against his side.

He slowly rubbed circles on her back. "I never should have tried forcing you to go home."

"*This* is my home."

He held up a hand, stopping the argument before it started afresh. "Forcing you *West*. It's your choice to make, not mine. And…" He fingered Grandpa's letter, its edges crisp beneath his touch. "I was afraid if I left things up to you, you'd choose the wrong thing."

Her eyes shot tiny sparks. "So you still think it's wrong for me to stay here?"

"Yes. No. I…" He growled and scratched behind his ear. "I have my reasons for wanting you to go back. The main one being Ma…"

His words jammed together in his throat, so many of them aching for release. But how to get them out without ruining things again?

"I know she misses me. You've told me before. And I miss her, too, but I'm not going to leave for Wyoming in the middle of the school year. Maybe later, sometime over the summer, I can come see her. I want her to meet Jackson, after all, and—"

"Summer will be too late, if you want to see her alive." The words fell from his tongue, hard and shattering and unavoidable. "She's dying, Sam. She's got consumption."

Sam grew still, her chest barely rising enough to

give her breath. Her face drained of color, starting at the top of her forehead and slowly blanching until her skin shone white as snow. She reached a hand out and gripped his forearm, and her fingers trembled as they dug into his shirtsleeve. "No, she can't be dying. I don't believe it."

He placed his hand over her cold fingers. "I should have told you sooner. Ma wanted me to keep it secret, wanted you to stay out here and continue your life without worrying about her. But I look at you, and though I expected to find the girl I dropped off at the train station three years ago, you've changed in the time you've been here. You're grown up now, thinking about marriage, planning your future. You've got a right to know about Ma, a right to make your own decision about whether you see her before she dies.

"I was wrong for keeping it secret." He swiped a stray strand of hair away from her face. "I won't try forcing you to do things my way anymore. The decision's yours, but I'm telling you, your ma's dying, and if you want to see her, you've got to go soon."

"How long?" Moisture pooled in her eyes, and she didn't look at him but stared vacantly at a spot on the wall above his shoulder. "With something like consumption, a doctor can tell how long, can't he?"

"Maybe, sometimes. But Ma seems set on hiding how sick she is from the doc. Seems set on hiding it from everyone, really. The doc said she'll last through next summer, but she gets a little sicker every day, and she won't…" The aching sadness fisted in his chest again. One would think he'd grow used to saying the words aloud, but they caught in his throat every time.

"I want to go." Tears coursed down Sam's cheeks.

"Now. As soon as I can. I can come back to school later, can't I? Come and finish up?"

"Whatever you want." He wrapped an arm around her shoulders and pushed her face into his chest, her body trembling against his. "Forgive me for not telling you sooner?"

With her face still buried in his shirt, she nodded.

He stroked his hands through her falling gold tresses in soothing, comforting motions. Or so he hoped. Because truly, one could do so very little to soothe when the pain inside ran as deep as life itself. "You'll need to decide about Jackson, as well. I won't stand in the way of you and him—"

"He can wait." She pulled back and met his gaze, determination etching her voice despite its slight wobble. "I need to see Ma. She's more important right now, wouldn't you say? And there's no need to rush on setting a wedding date, not with Ma so ill."

Sam twisted the sapphire ring, then slid it off her hand. "Maybe you should keep this for me until we sort things out. Do you think Jackson will wait for me to get back?"

Luke closed the ring in his grip and pulled Sam in for another hug. "The man would be daft not to."

"Thank you for meeting with me, Elizabeth."

Elizabeth smiled at Miss Bowen and took a chair across from where the headmistress sat behind the wide desk in her office. But rather than offer her usual prim smile or begin the conversation, the older woman looked down at her hands and fidgeted with a stack of papers.

Elizabeth swallowed. This couldn't be good.

"It's the academy, isn't it?" she blurted out. "The

school board decided to close us down despite the money Mr. Hayes has donated and that favorable article in the paper."

Miss Bowen's gray eyes shot up to hers, and the lines of her painfully straight suit almost seemed to slump with resignation. "No, Elizabeth, it's not the academy we need to discuss but Mr. Hayes himself."

"Mr. Hayes?" The sandwich she'd eaten several hours ago for lunch threatened to come up.

"It's been brought to my attention that you and Mr. Hayes traveled back from Albany Saturday night in his carriage. Alone."

She tried not to cringe. "I...um..."

"Do you deny it?"

She stared at her feet, at the swirling golden vines and leaves on the rug. "No, it's true. I hadn't planned to be unchaperoned with him. It simply..." A vision of David standing on the steps making his marriage offer seeped into her mind. "It seemed the best choice at the time. My family and I were facing some...difficulties, and Mr. Hayes offered me a ride home."

"I'm glad to know it was an exception." Though nothing about the severe lines on Miss Bowen's face looked glad. "After all, you've been here over two years, and I've never received any complaints about your conduct until this morning."

Elizabeth fisted her hands in her skirt. A complaint, and David was the only one to see her leave with Luke.

"But you are aware of Hayes's policy regarding teachers courting?" Miss Bowen's tight-laced voice echoed loudly against office's sparse walls. "A chaperone is to be present at all times."

"Yes. A chaperone." Elizabeth licked her lips, as

though she could still feel the firm pressure of Luke's mouth against hers, the way the stubble on his jaw brushed her chin.

Which was why a chaperone was needed—to prevent situations like that. Her cheeks burned, and she glanced away from the headmistress. "M-Mr. Hayes was only being gentlemanly. Being from Wyoming, he's not exactly aware of society's rules about chaperones and propriety and such. But I assure you, he didn't have any ill intentions." Except for the kiss. That exquisite, wonderful kiss. One which would likely remain unparalleled for the rest of her life.

At least she'd have something to give her sweet memories when she was eighty.

"You do remember the Code of Conduct you signed when first agreed to teach at Hayes?"

"Yes, ma'am." The document had been fifteen pages of painstakingly small rules. True, she couldn't recall every minute detail, but the chaperone one had probably been in there. "What's to be done, then? Do you need to inform the board?"

"I should. Our procedures ask that the board be notified in these types of situations." Miss Bowen sighed and repositioned her glasses on her nose. "Though your mother's illness did bring about some extenuating and unforeseen circumstances. I trust she has recovered?"

The moisture leeched from her throat. "Yes, quite."

"Well, then, since nothing inappropriate happened between you and Mr. Hayes…"

Her heart pounded. Nothing inappropriate? She'd hardly call that kiss "nothing inappropriate," but then Miss Bowen wasn't asking for confirmation so much as assuming the best.

"…And in light of all Mr. Hayes has done to keep the school open, I will refrain from informing the board this once. We can hardly have such a story leaking out and casting Mr. Hayes and the school in a bad light."

Elizabeth forced a smile. Luke wouldn't be the one seen in a bad light nearly so much as her, but if Luke's help with the school would get her out of this situation, then she'd hardly complain.

"So, Elizabeth, please make certain that you're not alone with Mr. Hayes again."

"Thank you for understanding. I'll be more careful from now on." And she refused to think about why that depressed her.

"I won't make another exception like—"

A knock sounded on the office door, and the secretary entered.

"Yes, Sarah?" Miss Bowen asked.

But Sarah didn't look at the headmistress. "Elizabeth…er, Miss Wells. There's a reporter here to see you."

"A reporter? From the *Morning Times?*" But she already knew the answer. Who else could the reporter be other than Mr. Reginald Higsley? And the man was likely seething since Luke had gotten that retraction printed in the paper. The reporter had probably come to find more lies to print.

What if he'd dug up an embarrassing piece of information from her past?

Or worse, what if he'd learned about David's recent "proposal"?

The air around her turned thick, and her hands began to tremble.

"Miss Wells?" Sarah held the door open. "He's waiting in the outer office."

Her feet weighed heavily as she followed Sarah through the door, but Mr. Higsley wasn't in the office. The man leaning over the desk and scrawling on a pad of paper was undoubtedly a reporter, but with his short stature and thick middle, he certainly wasn't the man she'd met at the banquet. He busied himself with the other secretary, Elaine, battering her with all manner of questions about the admissions process to Hayes. Poor Elaine could hardly answer one inquiry before he fired another.

"Those reporters are spectacles to behold, aren't they?"

Elizabeth gasped and turned toward the rusty voice. Luke lounged against the wall near Miss Bowen's door. As always, he wore those dusty cowboy boots, a leather vest and a kerchief around his neck, and his hands held a wide-brimmed hat. She smiled, her heart tightening as she took a step toward him.

And stopped. What was she doing? She couldn't go to him. Not after that lecture in Miss Bowen's office. Not after her decision to avoid him.

Though making that decision in her dark bedroom was a lot easier than holding to it here, when Luke Hayes stood three feet from her.

That familiar half smile curved his lips, and he dipped his head toward her, his eyes lingering on her skirt. "You look lovely this afternoon, Miss Wells."

She glanced down, and sure enough, chalk smeared the fabric just below her waist.

Once, just once, she wanted to see Luke teach advanced algebra without getting chalk on himself. "Did you need something?"

"Certainly."

His gaze landed on her lips for a moment, so brief anyone watching wouldn't have noticed, but she flushed nonetheless.

He cleared his throat and pushed off the wall. "I wanted to bring the reporter—Mr. Thompson—by. Figured after school would be a good time for the two of you to meet formal-like."

"*You* brought him? Why?"

"He needs to settle some things with you."

She'd seen reporters settle things enough to know she wanted nothing to do with it. "If you'll excuse me, I have an appointment with one of my students." She turned and started for the door.

Luke reached forward and caught her elbow, the simple touch searing through her sleeve to her skin. "Oh, no you don't. You're not turning yellow-belly over some little meeting with a reporter."

Perhaps meeting with a reporter seemed insignificant to Luke, but she hardly shared his opinion. "It's been a long day, and I have a commitment tonight. I need to go."

He glanced up at the reporter, still inundating the secretaries with questions. "He needs to talk to you."

"I tried talking to a reporter last week. It didn't turn out well, if you remember."

"Did you know my grandfather owned a rather significant amount of stock in the Albany *Morning Times?*"

She stared at him, her brain sluggish to follow the direction his words were taking. "I don't see what Jonah's stock… Oh." She bit the inside of her cheek. "You own it now."

"I do. And the man before you isn't simply 'a reporter.' Mr. Thompson is the editor and chief of the paper, and he especially wished to speak with you."

"Then why's he interviewing Sarah and Elaine?"

Luke took her hand, settled it in the crook of his arm, and patted. "Because he's writing an article on how Hayes accepts scholarship students from poorer families."

"Oh." And what could she say to that? The fervent interest the editor showed in Sarah and Elaine didn't speak of a man who hated female education, regardless of what the editor had allowed to be printed in the paper before.

"Thompson." Luke interrupted the other man midquestion.

The older man turned. "Ah, Mr. Hayes and…" He stilled when he spotted her, then came forward. "You must be Miss Wells. Please accept my apologies." The editor took her hand, his eyes shining with sincerity. "I'm terribly sorry for the trouble those articles caused you and the school. We printed what Higsley wrote without doing adequate research on the topic, and we never should have allowed such things in our paper. Do forgive us."

"Thank you." She took her hand from Mr. Thompson's and stepped back. "Your apology means much to both me and the academy."

"Indeed. We plan to remedy the situation," he went on. "We've a series of articles planned on the benefits of female education. They will appear weekly on the front page over the next month. And we'd like permission to reprint a portion of that original editorial you wrote to be used in next Wednesday's edition."

A series of articles on the *benefits* of educating women? That's what she'd been intending when she first wrote that editorial. Plus, he wanted to take the original piece she'd written and use it in a positive manner. She let out a breath she hadn't realized she'd been holding. "That would be lovely."

"Yes. We expect the series to be rather popular, and I must say, we're excited to print it."

Just then Miss Bowen's door opened, and Mr. Thompson's gaze moved to the headmistress.

"Ah, Miss Bowen." He glanced back to her and Luke. "If you will excuse me?"

He stepped around them and nearly ran for Miss Bowen. "Might I have five minutes of your time? I'm very curious about the process Hayes Academy uses when determining…"

The editor's voice faded as Luke took her elbow and guided her into the hallway.

"Thank you for bringing the editor by, Luke. You didn't have to speak up for the school in such a public manner, and you surely don't have to keep me this informed."

But in some ways, she wasn't surprised. He'd made his decision to stand by the school, and now he was unashamedly sticking to it. He wouldn't worry about what people said or thought, either. He was so strong, so unruffled by society's opinions. It was why she loved him.

And why she had to keep away from him. "Please excuse me, though. I shouldn't be here right now."

He frowned as a group of students brushed past,

their girlish chatter filling the hallway. "What's wrong with the hallway?"

"The hallway isn't the problem."

His eyes narrowed.

She sighed. Best to just tell him and be done with it. "You are."

"Exactly how am I a problem?"

She could hardly look at his face without memories of the kiss flooding back—memories of a kiss she couldn't let happen again. And she was being ridiculous! She needed to start behaving like a proper spinster, not some smitten schoolgirl. "Miss Bowen knows about the carriage ride Saturday."

"What exactly does she know?" His voice smoldered.

"Th-that you and I rode back to Valley Falls unchaperoned. She's agreed not to tell the board this once, but if they find out anyway and determine I acted improperly, I could lose my job."

"Not while I'm here." Luke's jaw hardened into a determined line.

A trio of students emerged from a classroom down the hall, and she took a step back, putting more space between her and Luke. "Please, we have to be careful. You can't be alone with me again or touch me." *Or kiss me.*

He crossed his arms over that impossibly broad chest, and his eyes glinted with untamed anger. "DeVander did this."

"How it happened hardly matters. But you'll need to call me Miss Wells in public, and you can't…can't…"

"Can't what? Talk to you? Show you any attention?" He leaned so close his breath tickled the top of her head. "Kiss you?"

She shook her head furiously. He definitely couldn't do that again, not ever. "We have to be careful, that's all."

"Fine." And with that sharp word, he turned and disappeared back into the office, leaving the hallway beside her empty.

Elizabeth bit her bottom lip and stared at the suddenly vacant space. She drew in a deep breath and let it out in one giant rush. He'd brought the editor and chief of the paper to meet her and had finagled a way to get favorable articles printed about the school. How was she supposed to resist a man who did that?

She'd known she needed to be careful around him, but would carefulness be enough? What if, despite her efforts to keep her distance, despite Miss Bowen knowing about the carriage ride and Luke's leaving in another month, she couldn't keep from loving him?

Chapter Fifteen

❧

Elizabeth sucked in a breath and leaned her head on the town hall's back door. She should have been indoors ten minutes ago, but couldn't quite manage to step inside the building. She knew what awaited her. People. Probably about three hundred of them—teachers and school board members come to hear her father and David speak on education. The speeches, of course, were an unofficial start to the campaign both David and Father would run through the coming year until the elections next fall. And who better to begin the event than her, a schoolteacher?

She rubbed her arms. Oh, why had she agreed to give this speech? She didn't know if she could look at Father or David after last Saturday, let alone stand on a platform and publicly beseech fellow educators to vote for them.

She glanced down at the paper crinkled in her hand, the wording for her speech scrawled in elaborate cursive across the page. She'd read it a hundred times and still had no idea what the paper said. The words just seemed to slip through her head without sticking.

And here she was, being a terrible daughter again. Truly she was the most hopeless daughter ever to grace the earth. Giving a speech was the least she could do to help her family, especially since she refused to marry David. She should be happy to aid them, not hiding outside the building and praying for the earth to open up and swallow her. But still, getting up on that stage and convincing people to support Father and David in the next election felt wrong somehow, fraudulent.

She closed her eyes as the cold autumn air stung her face. What had Luke said about Jonathan honoring God above his father in the Bible? Was there a way she could honor her family *and* God by giving this speech, even if she didn't respect her Father or David? It didn't seem possible.

With a sigh, she pulled open the back door and stepped inside.

"Elizabeth, there you are," her father bellowed. "Come, they've already started. Where did you disappear to?"

"I was…"

But he didn't wait for an answer, just grabbed her wrist and tugged her down the hall and toward the steps to the platform.

"…feeling a little sick," she mumbled.

"We haven't time for that. See?" He gestured up the steps, hidden by a thick curtain, to where a man in a tuxedo stood introducing the speakers. "Here, give me your cape." He yanked it off her shoulders until she stood in the faded green velvet she'd worn for the occasion. "And what are you doing with that paper?" He tore the page from her hand, scowling when she didn't let go and it ripped in two. "You've been giving memorized speeches since you were ten. You're not taking a paper up there with you."

Applause drowned out his words as he snatched the rest of the speech from her still-clenched fist and shoved her up the steps. The host stood at center stage, his smile wide and welcoming. Then, before she could even take a breath, the speaker left, and she stood alone on the platform with several hundred people seated before her.

She swallowed and stepped forward. Her hands were slicked with sweat, and her heart pounded in her ears. "I, um…" What had her paper said? "I came to speak to you about education this evening."

Of course she had. The entire event was about education. She'd hardly been asked to speak on derivatives or integration.

Her stomach tightened and lurched. She couldn't do this. Couldn't stand up here and recite platitudes to make her father and David look good.

"Education is…" She licked her lips and stared out into the audience. Mother and Jackson sat in the front row, both scowling, as she imagined Father and David were doing on the side of the stage. She forced her gaze past them to the other people filling the hall. Some she knew, like the teachers and board members from Hayes and its affiliate institutions. Some she recognized as teachers she'd met at similar events in the past, but many unfamiliar faces stared back at her, as well. All waited, thinking she had something important to say, something of value.

But what *could* she say? That her own education had saved her after she'd escaped from what would have been a terrible marriage? That if teachers truly wanted to educate students, they would endeavor to open up possibilities rather than stifle the country's future generations in societal expectations? No, she could hardly say such things, even if truth dripped from her statements.

And then she spotted them, clustered into the back right corner. Not a group of teachers from Hayes wearing polite smiles and dignified clothing, but a group of students. Samantha and MaryAnne and Meredith and Helen, surrounded by several others she couldn't make out, all beaming as though the sun rose and set on her.

Behind them stood Luke, leaning against the back wall, legs crossed and shoulders relaxed, in much the same way he probably leaned against a fence post on his ranch. He'd brought her students. She'd not mentioned more than two words about her speech to him, but evidently he'd known of it—and cared enough to come.

A bud of warmth unfurled somewhere deep inside, spreading heat to her icy fingers and a smile to her face. And with that smile came her answer. She didn't need to stand there and cite platitudes so people would support Father and David, she needed to convince people that education was significant, because students were people, with longings and desires and dreams, and their futures were important.

"Education is important." Her full voice rang with confidence over the fidgeting crowd. "Not so much because it teaches Shakespeare, quadratic equations and the War of 1812, but because it teaches students to dream."

"Your speech was wonderful."

Elizabeth stiffened at the masculine voice behind

her. She stood on the side of the platform, peering out from the edge of the curtain and into the chaos beyond.

"Your speech was delightful, as well." She spoke without turning to face David, and glanced at her father, standing only a few feet from the stage, nearly swallowed by a horde of well-wishers and supporters. "The crowd really took to it. I'm surprised you're not out there greeting people, though."

Something large and brown flashed in the far corner of the room. Luke and his cowboy hat? She'd likely imagined it. Even if he hadn't rushed himself and the girls outside by now, she had no way of getting to him without being engulfed and waylaid by all the people.

"Looking for someone?"

"Pardon? Oh, um…no. Not really." She waved her hand toward the crowd. "I'm simply watching. You really should be out there, though. Wasn't your speaking engagement intended to give you opportunity to meet constituents and procure votes?"

"As always, you have an excellent understanding of politics and publicity. But the audience tonight would have slept through my speech had they not been so captivated by yours. I think when I came onto the platform, everyone was holding their breaths and hoping you would reappear for an encore."

"Don't be ridiculous."

He moved behind her, so close the heat of his chest radiated into her back. She shivered and huddled nearer the curtain.

"Now who is it you're watching for?" David peered over her shoulder, not giving her room to shift without touching him. "The Hayes heir?"

She bristled. Luke Hayes was the last thing she

wanted to discuss with David. "You've gone from ridiculous to insane. Now please let me by. You're standing far closer than is proper."

He took a half step to the side, just enough so she could brush past. But rather than stay at the curtain, he followed her down the hallway. "And where are you going now?"

"It's none of your business."

"On the contrary. It's very much my business, if you're going to be my wife."

"David, I'm not…" She rubbed her temples, already beginning to throb, and lowered her voice. "I'm not going to marry you. Didn't I make that clear the other evening?"

His face remained firm and unyielding, as though chiseled in marble. "Step in here so we can talk." He opened a door to a meeting room and held it for her.

She halted on the threshold and looked about. It was hardly appropriate for her to be alone in a room with him…but then she hardly wanted someone overhearing their conversation, either. And David simply had to get this fool notion of marrying her out of his head. So she stepped inside, letting him close the door behind her.

"There's nothing to talk about. I don't love you, and if I don't love you, I can't possibly spend the rest of my life with you. I'd be miserable, and I'd make you miserable, as well. I appreciate your offer and…" Shame crept into her face, and she swallowed. How did she even discuss the situation without feeling like an expensive brothel girl? "…your willingness to help my parents financially, but I simply can't agree. Now if you'll please open the door. It's highly inappropriate to be in here together."

"Not any more inappropriate than you riding home with Hayes the other night."

"You shouldn't have told the headmistress."

"Who says I told and not your mother?"

She stilled at that. Could Mother have done such a thing? Surely not. Mother might not approve of her daughter teaching, but she wouldn't try to get her fired, not when the scandal would have negative implications for the rest of the family.

David came toward her, slowly, as though he had no reason to hurry, since he already had her cornered. "Your unwillingness to give my offer due consideration surprises me. What could cause you to spurn me so quickly, I wonder? Feelings for someone else? That cowboy, perhaps?"

Not a cowboy. A *rancher*.

"The only thing between me and Mr. Hayes is friendship." Or so she hoped, because if Luke loved her, too… but no. She wasn't going to love him back.

"Elizabeth."

David tapped her chin up. She met his eyes for a mere instant, and then his lips covered hers, hot and invasive and humiliating.

No. She attempted to say the word, to push him away. But his arms wrapped around her, pressing her tight against him. She clamped her lips together and tensed every muscle in her body. She might not be strong enough to fight him off, but he wouldn't get any satisfaction from holding her. Then his hands snaked up into her hair. She planted her hands against his chest and shoved, but it was too late. Her hair tumbled down in one giant mass, her hat landing on the floor at her feet.

"David!"

And the door opened.

Chapter Sixteen

"Hope I'm not interrupting," the intruder drawled lazily.

David released his hold on her, and Elizabeth sunk her head in her hands. She didn't need to see who stood in the doorway, the rusted twang of his voice gave him away.

"Fix your hair, Miss Wells."

Miss Wells. Such formal words, and this from the man whose eyes had emanated love and concern in the school hallway that afternoon, who had held her in his arms and let her tears dampen his suit two nights ago. What must he think of her? Kissing him the other night, speaking privately with him today, and found in another man's embrace this evening?

"Miss Wells." Luke spoke her name so firmly her head shot up. "The girls are waiting behind the building. They wanted to thank you for your speech. So unless you fancy parading around with your hair tangled and hanging every which way, I'd suggest you put it back up."

She flew into action, kneeling on the floor to retrieve

her hat and pins, shoving her snarled tresses up beneath the too-small creation, and squishing it into place. She jabbed pins randomly through her locks. Now if only the arrangement would hold for the ride back to Valley Falls.

"And you," Luke said. She didn't need to look up to know he pointed a finger at David. "I trust she's given you an answer about your marriage proposal."

"Yes, as a matter of fact." David's smooth politician's voice filled the room. "We've decided—"

"Good. Don't come near her again."

Don't come near *her?* Luke was protecting her? After finding her in David's arms? She stood slowly and glanced at him, but he'd trained eyes so fiercely on David he didn't notice. Somehow he knew she'd been forced, knew she hadn't wanted David's kiss. Maybe her struggle had been obvious when he opened the door, even more obvious than her fallen mass of hair.

"This is the room we were in, isn't it?" A woman's words floated in from the hallway.

"Yes, I must have left it just in here." Mother, *her mother,* answered.

All moisture leeched from her mouth, and her hands grew icy even as they started to sweat. What was Mother doing back here?

"It'll only take a moment to retrieve it." Mother appeared in the doorway with Mr. Taviston and his wife.

Elizabeth's body turned cold, but she could only stare at the trio. Mr. Taviston's eyes locked instantly on her, then ran slowly down her body in that uncomfortably familiar manner.

"Oh, dear, sorry to bother you," Mrs. Taviston exclaimed, oblivious to the look in her husband's eyes and the tension radiating between Luke and David. "We'll only be a moment."

"I do hope we're not interrupting." Mother came farther into the room, her shrewd eyes surveying everything. "Elizabeth, I didn't expect to see you back here. I just needed to get my hat. I left it before the rally, silly me. But what are you doing in this room, and with two gentlemen, no less?"

"No," she whispered, more to herself than anything. Beside her, David shifted subtly closer, and she began to shake. Mother and David couldn't have set her up. They wouldn't do such a thing. Mother was family, after all. And if David wanted to marry her, he had to care somewhat for her reputation.

But if Mr. and Mrs. Taviston had opened the door to find her in David's arms with her hair undone, she'd have lost her job and found herself in the middle of a scandal. A scandal that would have only stopped if she married David.

"Elizabeth." Mother inched closer, plucked a stray hairpin—from where, Elizabeth didn't know—and held it up, her eyebrows raised.

Heat rushed to her face, so forcefully she'd surely turned the color of a turnip. And all with the head of the school board still watching her.

"I hope you know how this looks, you being alone with two gentlemen." Mother sniffed.

"Miss Wells was just leaving." Luke's words, hard and controlled, permeated the room. "Some of her students came tonight and are waiting to speak with her outside. I believe Miss Wells was concluding a brief conversation with Mr. DeVander. Likely something to do with a business offer she's turned down." Luke nodded at her and extended his arm. "Now, Miss Wells, might I escort you to your students?"

She stared at his offered elbow. Two steps and she'd be at his side. But still standing next to David, with her knees trembling and her stomach tying itself in knots, she may as well have been on the opposite side of the Hudson River.

And then he was there, beside her and placing her hand on his arm, the hard muscles beneath his sleeve radiating strength and confidence. "Just hold your head up and leave," he whispered against her ear. "We'll settle the rest later."

So she sucked in a breath, straightened her back and went with him.

He loved her.

Luke sat in the train, one seat behind the students surrounding Elizabeth, and stared at the back of her auburn tresses and fancy hat. She laughed when her students said something funny, nodded as they asked questions and thanked each of them for going to hear her speak. He didn't need to see her face to imagine the way her eyes lit when she smiled or sparkled with understanding as she answered questions.

Yep, he loved the woman, all right. And if he had any doubts before, tonight had shot them down. She'd had every excuse not to show up at the town hall and give that speech for her father and DeVander. But what did she do? She didn't run. Didn't make excuses. Didn't gracefully bow out. Nope, she fulfilled the promise she'd made and stood composed before three hundred people. And she hadn't lied. She hadn't convinced them to vote for her father or DeVander; she'd convinced them to vote for the children. It would be interesting to know how many of the people present tonight would vote for the opposing candidates a year from now.

Wells and DeVander had followed Elizabeth's speech by throwing out platitudes, empty thanks and trite sayings about education in New York State. Elizabeth had captivated the crowd's heart and probably still held it.

And her family had thanked her by setting her up. He clenched his jaw. If he hadn't brought a group of students tonight and headed off to find her, she'd have been caught alone in that room while DeVander forced her to kiss him.

He'd nearly plowed his fist into DeVander's stomach when he'd opened the door to find Elizabeth struggling in the rat's arms, would have broken DeVander's nose had he not heard the voices in the hall. Even then, he hadn't realized who the voices belonged to, or what Elizabeth's mother and DeVander had done.

He'd figured it out a second before Elizabeth. Then she'd given him that stricken look, and he'd wanted to wrap his hands around DeVander's throat. How dare he treat Elizabeth that way? How dare *anyone* treat her that way?

Luke blew out a breath. *I love you. I'll protect you.* The words had nearly poured out of his mouth when Elizabeth had looked at him with all that hurt shimmering in her eyes. But with four others crammed into the little room, it was hardly the time to start spouting his devotion.

He shifted and smiled as a tendril of hair slipped from the back of Elizabeth's hat and down her neck. Several locks had already fallen from their hastily crammed positions. She'd probably have to put her hair back up before she got off the train in a few minutes.

And he'd enjoy watching.

Yep, he loved the woman. He'd have to tell her. Maybe even tonight after the girls left. When a man decided he loved a woman, that wasn't something to put off.

But say he told her how he felt, what happened then? He would return to the Teton Valley in another month or so, and where would that leave her? He swiped a hand over his mouth. Hang it all. He'd known getting too involved would cause a mess from the first moment he'd laid eyes on her.

But knowing hadn't stopped it from happening.

When the train finally ground to a halt in Valley Falls, he herded the girls into the waiting carriages. The students, content to ride in two carriages on the way to the train station, all swarmed into Elizabeth's convey-ance now, leaving Luke alone on the ride to the acad-emy. But as soon as the girls headed inside, he ushered them up the stairs to their rooms.

And he was alone with Elizabeth.

At last.

"Let me walk you home." He extended his arm.

She looked away. "Not tonight, Luke. Perhaps you could just lend me use of your second carriage."

"I could, if we didn't need to talk."

She shook her head and took a step back from him. "We can't. Walking outside after dark is just as inap-propriate as being in a carriage alone with you. Or in a room. Or even standing in this hallway. Please…" Her voice quivered. "Just let me go home."

"Look at me, Elizabeth." He stepped closer, peering into her pain-clouded eyes, and touched a hand to her cold cheek. "I can't let you go home like this. What will you do? Climb into bed and lie awake stewing until dawn? You can't hide from what your mother and DeVander tried to do. You need to talk about it." He knew. He'd have been a lot better off if someone he loved had forced him to face his problems after Blake died.

"I'm not hiding. Needing time to think and sort through my feelings isn't hiding."

"Then sort through them with me."

She seemed undefeatable standing there, her back stiff and chin high even with half her hair falling about her shoulders. But sadness haunted her eyes. Sure, she was strong, could handle almost anything she faced—at least on the outside. Inside, the woman seemed ready to shatter.

"Is there something you're not telling me?" He brought his hand down to cradle her neck. "Did DeVander hurt you when he had you alone?"

Her eyes turned flat. "I'm fine."

But she didn't seem fine, and she was shutting him out, much like Samantha had when he'd first arrived in Valley Falls. "Just tell me what to do, and I'll do it." He reached out and tucked a strand of hair behind her ear.

She jerked back as though he'd slapped her. "No. Don't touch me. Don't ask me to talk, and don't look at me that way. Just leave me alone."

"I only want to help. What your mother's trying to do... Elizabeth, you can't handle it on your own. Think. What if I wouldn't have come looking for you earlier tonight? You could have found yourself engaged to DeVander come morning."

She took another step back, shaking her head as tears pooled in her eyes. "I can't do this. I don't want this."

"You can't do what? Talk to me? Let me support you?"

"Be alone with you like this."

Confound it! Were all women this impossible? Her mouth said she didn't want his help, but her eyes begged for it. He'd have had her home by now, half the incident with DeVander and her mother talked out, if she would stop backing away from him and simply walk toward him. "Why can't you be alone with me? Because of what Miss Bowen said to you?"

"Because I—I…" Her gaze drifted to his lips, then back to his eyes.

"You want to kiss me." He closed the space between them.

"No."

He leaned down until mere inches separated his mouth from hers. "You do. Why else would your eyes get sleepy and your breath catch when I'm this close?"

She pushed at his chest, her hands as firm and unyielding as iron bars. "You're wrong. I don't want anything to do with you."

"Hang it all, Elizabeth. Stop pushing me away and talk to me for a minute. I want to walk you home tonight. I want to see you tomorrow and the next day and the next. I want to court you. I'm in love with you."

Elizabeth wrapped her arms around herself, a sob catching in her throat. Luke still stood too near, his body radiating heat and strength and confidence, issuing that subtle message that he'd carried with him since the first moment she'd seen him: *Trust me. I'm safe. I'll protect you.*

But she couldn't latch on to him. Not now.

I'm in love with you. She'd heard those words from a man before. How many times had David told her that he loved her? Held her in his arms? Stolen a kiss from her? And then strode from her parents' house straight to the mistress he kept?

She stepped farther back from Luke, even though doing so trapped her against the wall. "No, it doesn't matter if you're in love with me."

Perhaps she loved him. But that would remain a secret. There would be no declaration of her feelings, no public courtship, nothing but the silent ache of her heart when he walked into a room.

He didn't approach her again but stood back, his arms crossed and hip cocked, watching her far too closely. "You're terrified of me."

Not of him. Of love. He claimed to love her now, and probably did, at least a little. But how long until Luke lost interest the way David had?

"What have I done to scare you? Is it because I'm going back to Wyoming? Because I wasn't raised to be a fancy eastern gentleman? We can work through those things, Elizabeth. I don't have all the answers tonight, but give me half a chance to dig some up."

"It's not where you live or how you were raised. It's got nothing to do with you." Indeed. She'd never met a more wonderful, trustworthy man.

But was he trustworthy enough to love her ten years from now and not just today?

Was any man?

Marriage lasted until death, and Luke hadn't even

known her two weeks. "I told you before, I don't want to get married."

"Every woman wants to get married."

She shook her head. "Not me."

"What's this about? Teaching? Are you so afraid I'll make you give up teaching that you won't let me walk you home or take you to dinner? Good grief, Elizabeth, I haven't proposed. I'm just asking for a chance."

If only the reason was that simple. If only she could easily claim she didn't want to give up her students for a family. But as much as she loved the girls who walked into her mathematics classes every day, they only made up half the problem. "Luke, please. Just let me go home."

He rubbed the back of his neck. "Fine. I'll send for the carriage, but at least let me take you to dinner to-morrow night."

She nearly groaned. "No. It isn't wise."

"Samantha can come. We'll invite along a gaggle of her friends, and I'll pay for the lot of them. Call it a school outing, if you want."

Oh, how unfair. Her students had been so sweet to-night, nearly making her forget the disaster with David, and now Luke offered an opportunity for her and the girls to have some special time together. She simply had to trust him.

She looked into his eyes, that deep, honest blue that seemed to promise the world, and had to ask. "Do you… do you have a mistress?"

He went deadly still, his face turning pale, as though his veins had been slit and every drop of blood drained from it. She expected blustering rage and a haphazard denial like David had displayed when she'd accused him all those years ago.

But Luke barely seemed able to breathe. "A mistress? You think I have a mistress?"

She stared at the floor. "I…I have to know."

He came close, moving slowly, the way one would if trying to catch a butterfly. And indeed, she probably would have flown from the building had he moved any faster. But he soon stood in front of her, pinning her against the wall while she stared at the buttons on his coat.

"No." Softness permeated his rusty voice. "And I never plan to, either, if that's what this is about."

She drew her gaze slowly up his buttons, to his strong neck and firm jaw and chiseled cheeks, before finally staring into those trustworthy blue eyes. "I…I believe you."

The words twisted something inside her. Perhaps they freed her, or maybe they further chained her. Either way, they hurt, and she just wanted to go home, make a cup of tea, curl up on her bed.

And cry until the sun came up.

"My butler told me why you called off your engagement to DeVander." His breath brushed her face, warm and sweet and with the barest scent of mint mixed in. "I've known since the night I first asked about why you weren't married."

She ducked her head. At least she hadn't needed to voice her shame, to admit aloud she hadn't been woman enough to keep her last fiancé. "So you understand why I can't let you court me. I can't take a suitor, Luke. Any possibility of me marrying ceased the night I ended my engagement to David. If I opened up myself that way again and got hurt, I'd shrivel up and die inside."

He didn't back away but stayed close, so close she only need raise a hand to touch him, so close the subtle heat emanating from his body warmed her skin. What she wouldn't give to rest her head in the crook of his shoulder as she had that night in the carriage. To draw from the strength and steadfastness of Luke Hayes.

"Lizzie." He pressed his palm, warm and callused, against her cheek. "Do you have feelings for me? Tell me you don't. Just say it, and I'll back away."

She pressed her eyes shut. She should say she felt nothing. Then he'd let her go, and life would be easier for both of them.

But she couldn't lie, not to a man as honest as him.

"You're leaving." They were the only words that came out. "Whatever you feel for me, whatever I feel for you, it doesn't mean anything. It can't, unless you stay here and manage your inheritance. I won't leave my students."

"I'd never ask it." He smoothed a strand of hair off her forehead. "But I'm not requesting your hand tonight. I'm asking you to dinner. I'm asking you to be my friend. I'm asking for a chance to earn your trust. Please, Lizzie. Have dinner with me tomorrow evening, and let's see how things go."

She swallowed. Trust and marriage loomed ominously before her but giving him a chance? She gave her students a chance every day when they walked into her classroom.

How could she do any less for the man she loved?

Chapter Seventeen

The Philadelphia Society for Children buildings sat drooping and dirty on a half-forgotten street in Philadelphia. An occasional person or carriage passed by the aging brownstone, but no one bothered to even glance its way. Perhaps because it stood farther back from the road than most establishments, perhaps because it held nothing interesting or unique enough to draw one's attention.

Luke didn't care so much whether the orphanage sat in the middle of Philadelphia's business district or on a forgotten twenty acres in the country. He only cared about one thing: seeing Cynthia Hayes.

His hands slicked with sweat and his pulse quickened as he waited for her in a cramped, stuffy parlor. Would she be willing to see him? She might have the worker who had shown him in come back and send him away without even laying eyes on her.

And he'd deserve it.

He'd treated her no better after Blake's death.

Luke plopped down in a faded chair and attempted

to still his antsy legs. At least he was trying to make things right. A person couldn't blame him for that.

Something swished gently near the door, and he looked up.

She stood there, framed in the peeling blue-trimmed doorway, with no clomp of footsteps or creaking floorboards to introduce her. Then his eyes landed on the boy beside her, gripping his mother's hand with a white-knuckled fist, and the breath left his lungs.

Clear blue eyes peeked out from beneath a mop of floppy blond hair. He looked like Blake. Exactly, completely, entirely. From the way he awkwardly held his shoulders—too big for the rest of his little body—to the curiousness in his eyes, to the half smile curving one side of his mouth.

Luke swallowed. If the boy looked like Blake, then the boy looked like him, too. An ache started somewhere deep inside his chest, and he wasn't quite sure what to do with it.

Cynthia hadn't changed, save for a few extra lines around her eyes and mouth. Her flaming hair was tucked up into a haphazard bun, and a serviceable black dress with a white apron draped her figure. But otherwise, she looked much the same.

The image of her kneeling over Blake's lifeless body flashed like fire through his mind, and the pain, old and bruised, came flooding back. *Get out!* his mind screamed. And his mouth nearly formed the words.

But he wouldn't do that again. He couldn't blame Cynthia for what had happened to his brother any more than he could blame himself. Rafe McCabe had fired the gun that had killed Blake, and the man had swung from a tree for his crime. The matter should have been settled the day Rafe was hanged, but instead of letting go, Luke had clung to his pain with the same bitterness and vengeance Pa harbored toward Grandpa.

"I'm sorry," he blurted out as he stood. "For what I said over Blake's body, for the way I sent you packing seven months pregnant."

She stood still, as though etched in granite with her rigid posture, tight muscles and white skin. Her throat worked back and forth, the only sign she hadn't turned to stone, then her eyes filled with moisture.

"I don't blame you." Her voice sounded like cracked glass, thin and frail and ready to shatter if he breathed wrong. "You were right. I may have been able to save Blake that day, but I'd…I'd…chosen to be ignorant about the ranch. I'd been there a year. I should have known how to ride a horse or hitch a wagon. I should have found rags to stop the bleeding, rather than stare at Blake and cry." She reached out to steady herself on the back of a chair. "Excuse me—I need to sit down for a moment."

He offered his hand to help her into the chair.

The gesture was basic, simple. Anyone would have done it. But rather than take his palm, she stared at it, the battle flashing in her eyes. Touch him or refuse? Accept his help or decline?

Then she looked into his face, the corners of her mouth tipping up into a soft smile before she placed her hand firmly in his.

And he knew. A weight, three years old and as strong as steel fetters, fell from his chest and cracked into a thousand unrecognizable pieces. Cynthia had forgiven him. God had forgiven him. And he was finally making amends for how he had handled Blake's death.

* * *

Elizabeth let herself into her brother's office, the building empty on this early Saturday evening. Jackson probably didn't even remember the key he'd given her over a year ago "in case of an emergency." And in truth, finding out about another wrong shipment of food wasn't an emergency per se. But how many wrong shipments and unpaid bills needed to pile up before they became an emergency? This was the fifth time since the beginning of the school year that something hadn't aligned with the payments recorded in the school's accounts. Yet she'd entered everything in her ledger and had spent the better half of the afternoon poring over it to find the discrepancy.

As usual, she found nothing.

So she would compare her books to Jackson's. She'd asked him about the finances again Monday at the political rally, and he'd been too busy to answer. Not that she could blame him, enamored as he was with Samantha. But the world still spun on its axis, regardless of whether Jackson had proposed, and tonight she was getting to the bottom of this. She'd find his ledger and take it to dinner at her parents. While Jackson and Samantha spent the evening huddled together in a corner of the drawing room whispering their goodbyes before Samantha left for Wyoming on Monday morning, she'd plop down at one of the tables and review the two books until she found the errors.

She sighed. In truth, she should have looked into the wrong food shipment earlier that week. It had arrived on Wednesday, but she'd gone out to dinner with Luke on Wednesday—and Tuesday and Thursday—and hadn't stopped by the kitchen until yesterday afternoon, after Luke had left for Philadelphia.

That man. She pressed a hand to her flaming cheek. He was too handsome and understanding by far, and the added layer of Western charm only sealed her demise. He drove all sensible thoughts from her head, had been doing so since first they met. She could hardly recall the Pythagorean theorem when he was around, let alone her name or any semblance of why she shouldn't be spending time with him.

She rubbed the heel of her palm over her heart. Falling in love with him felt wonderful—at least right now. He would still leave her one day, and her heart would likely break. But that didn't mean she couldn't love him today. Couldn't let herself dream of a future with a husband who loved her and children she could cherish while teaching an advanced mathematics class or two.

And goodness. Look at her. Here she was, standing in Jackson's office daydreaming instead of finding that ledger. She'd told Samantha, waiting in the carriage, that she wouldn't be more than a couple minutes, and she'd spent those minutes thinking of Luke.

She walked deeper inside the darkening office and rounded the desk to where her brother's ledgers rested on the shelf, everything organized alphabetically. Her eyes scanned the *G*s and *H*s, before landing on a leather binding clearly marked Hayes Academy. She pulled it down. Columns detailed the academy's regular expenditures, but the accounts were from last year, not this year. Jackson must have started a new ledger at the beginning of the school year.

She slipped the binder back into its slot. But the books on either side read Gomer's Millinery and Head-

ings Mercantile, with no vacant space indicating another ledger for Hayes Academy. Standing on her toes,
she brushed her fingers over the bindings on the high-
est shelf. Perhaps Jackson had simply labeled the ledger as Academy.

But no book labeled such sat in the *A*s. She frowned
up at the too-high books. The spot where the Academy book would have stood held an unlabeled ledger.
Maybe that was it.

She pulled it down, but the book wasn't for Hayes.
The pages held random labels, with columns of dates
and items and money listed, then smaller monetary
figures running along the far right. Greater Albany
Hospital, Maynard's Bakery, Albany Ladies' Society,
Headings Mercantile, St. Thomas Orphanage, and various other names had been scrawled across the tops of
the pages. The businesses seemed to have no rhyme or
reason for the order in which they appeared, or for the
single page of accounts dedicated to each one.

Then she spied it. Hayes Academy for Girls printed
neatly across one of the middle pages, and an open column of numbers beneath. Entries for foodstuffs and
teaching supplies with larger amounts of money had
been recorded in one column, and a second column of
smaller amounts ran along the...

Coldness swept her body. She dropped the book,
and it crashed to the floor in a flutter of pages. But she
didn't need to glimpse the page again to make sense of
the numbers. She knew those figures, had them circled
in her own ledger. They weren't sums paid to suppliers.
They were the *missing* sums. The money for the food,
only two-thirds of which had arrived two weeks ago
and again on Wednesday. The new slates ordered for

the beginning of the school year that had come with a third of the slates missing. The note from the insurance company saying it hadn't received its full payment last month. The amount of bills for the school Jackson had claimed to pay pitted against the actual supplies and creditors' notes that had arrived at the school.

And Jackson had the difference recorded in his book. A book that didn't just include Hayes Academy, but hospitals and orphanages, small businesses and... She hunkered down on the floor beside the ledger and flipped through pages. The numbers blurred, but the names of the organizations branded her mind.

Jackson couldn't have. He wouldn't. He was her brother, after all. Surely he wasn't embezzling money from so many different places. Certainly he didn't have a bank account somewhere in the city where he had all these funds collected.

She found three pages for Maple Ridge College and Connor Academy for Boys. The columns on the left listed salaries, books and office supplies, among other things. On the right were the sums that must have been rerouted to a separate account. As if the girls' academy wasn't enough for him to steal from.

What was she going to do? She had to tell someone. Luke? No. He wouldn't be back until later this evening, and she couldn't wait that long. The police? But she couldn't just walk into a strange police station and accuse her brother of...of...

Oh, goodness, she couldn't even think of the full ramifications if he had indeed embezzled funds from all these establishments. So where did that leave her? She swallowed back the bile climbing into her throat.

Dinner. She was still going to dinner, wasn't she? Her family expected her, and she needed to talk to Jackson.

Maybe the book she held was some mistake. Her brother probably had a sensible explanation for the entries that meant the situation wasn't as it appeared. Yes, of course Jackson had a logical reason for everything. Why not these accounts? She needed to see him before she did anything else.

"Elizabeth?"

She straightened and slammed the book shut.

Samantha stood in the doorway, concern engraved on her too-innocent face. "Are you all right? What's wrong?"

Samantha started toward her, but she held up her hand. "No. Don't come any closer."

"What's happened? You've been in here for half an hour. Any longer and we'll be late to your parents'."

She used the desk to pull herself up onto wobbly legs, then grabbed the ledger and clutched it to her chest. Jackson was this girl's fiancé, even if the wedding was temporarily delayed. If the ledger was accurate and her suspicions correct, what would happen to Samantha? She'd be betrayed by her fiancé at a young age, similar to what David had done eight years ago. Only Jackson's mistress was money rather than a woman. Either way, Samantha shouldn't have to witness the conversation she needed to have with Jackson.

"No. You're not going to my parents'."

Samantha's mouth fell open. "But Jackson... You said..."

"Things changed. You're going home." She cringed at the harshness ringing through her voice, even as she came around the desk. "You get back in that carriage and head straight to your brother's estate. Don't stop anywhere or for anything. Simply go home."

Samantha searched her face. "Is this because of what Luke said yesterday? How he didn't think we should go to dinner at your parents? That your ma might do something she shouldn't?"

If only the situation was that simple. If only she'd accepted Luke's advice and stayed home rather than claiming she couldn't ignore her family. "No. It's got nothing to do with my mother or Luke. It's something else entirely. Trust me. Please."

Samantha reached forward and offered her hand. "But what about you?"

"I'll be fine."

She only prayed her words were true.

Chapter Eighteen

Elizabeth's heart pounded as the footman opened the door to her parents' drawing room and she stepped inside. She'd spent countless hours in this room growing up, quietly doing needlework or taking refreshments while Mother and her friends gossiped about the latest goings-on. Yet she hardly recognized it now. The room seemed different somehow—darker, emptier, even though the furniture and window dressings and people inside were much the same.

Mother sat on the settee, and David and Father stood by the fire discussing politics in muted tones.

The familiar feeling of betrayal wrapped itself around her gut. Of course David would be here. She should have expected it. It was evidently too much to ask her parents to shun the man who had nearly forced her into marriage the other night, especially when that man had money and political connections. Well, they were about to find out how deep David's love for her and the rest of the family ran. Because if the ledger she held in her hand proved true, he'd run from the house and publically denounce any relationship with them before noon tomorrow.

Elizabeth stared at Jackson, sprawled comfortably in his favorite armchair. Surely there must be some mistake. How could he sit there in his expensive suit and act as though everything was normal if he'd been stealing money from schools, hospitals and orphanages?

"Good evening, Elizabeth, how lovely to see you."

Elizabeth ignored David and headed straight for her brother. "Explain this. Tell me it's not what I think." She threw the book in his lap.

Jackson glanced down, a flicker of recognition racing across his face, then he shoved the ledger off his legs onto the floor.

A flurry of footsteps and voices rushed around her.

"Elizabeth, what are you doing?"

"Is this any way to behave before dinner?"

"I see you're as excited to see me as I am to see you, darling."

"Jackson, what's that book?"

"David, perhaps you better excuse our family for a few moments."

But despite the chaos, Elizabeth didn't pull her eyes away from her brother.

"I don't know what you're talking about." Jackson shrugged indolently, as though there was nothing wrong with the world. As though that book didn't shake the very core holding their family together. "I've never seen these accounts before in my life. Now where's my fiancée? She was supposed to come with you, wasn't she?"

Elizabeth picked up the ledger and drew in a breath—it burned like fire down her throat and into her lungs. "Never seen it? I got it from your office! The entries are written in your handwriting! Unless I'm misunderstanding this ledger—which I don't think I am—you've been embezzling money."

"Embezzling?" Mother squeaked. "Jackson's been embezzling?"

"That's quite enough, Elizabeth." Father's voice boomed from the doorway.

She turned and scanned the room to find David gone, Mother looking ready to faint on the settee, and Father glowering.

"He's been stealing money, Father. Look for yourself." She came toward him, holding the book out.

"Stop being such a ninny. I know what's in there. But bringing the matter up before dinner is hardly appropriate."

She stopped, standing halfway between her father and Jackson. "You...you know what's in it?" It made no sense. How could her father know unless...

"No," she whispered.

Father laughed, a polished chuckle he no doubt used when advocating one bill or another in the assembly. "Where do you think all that money is? In some account for your brother?"

She pressed her eyes shut and tried to block off her ears, tried to prevent her father's meaning from sinking through to her brain. Her father couldn't be embezzling, too. He was a politician, for goodness' sake. The slightest whiff of scandal would ruin his career.

But why else would Father admit to recognizing the ledger?

"How dare you." She clenched one hand around the book's binding and another in her skirt. If only she could fly at him, rage and beat and kick until she was spent. Or maybe she could simply close her eyes and disappear, be somewhere else entirely. With Luke having dinner. In her classroom teaching quadratic equations. In her parlor helping MaryAnne get ready for the play. Anywhere but standing in her parents' drawing room.

"What were you doing, keeping that ledger where someone could find it?" Father crossed his arms and glared at Jackson. "You're lucky only your sister noticed."

"Maybe you should ask Elizabeth why she was in my office," Jackson shot back.

"Will one of you please tell me what's going on?" Mother said from where she still slumped on the settee.

Elizabeth turned to her mother. "Jackson has been embezzling funds from the accounts he handles at his office." Admitting it aloud made everything somehow worse. She was no longer asking questions, but stating facts—rather irrefutable ones that would have disastrous consequences for her family. "I needed to look up something for Hayes Academy in his books, and I uncovered the embezzlement instead. Jackson didn't just take from Samantha's school, he stole from hospitals, orphanages, ladies' clubs and—"

"Enough." Father slashed his hand through the air. "We see you've familiarized yourself with the accounts. Now give the ledger to your brother."

She clutched the book to her chest. "Give it back? Have you gone daft? Do you realize how much money's been stolen?"

"Elizabeth. Do be respectful." Mother fanned herself. "Whatever you've discovered, it's no reason to call your father names."

"Respectful?" At a time like this? Her mother couldn't be serious. "Why should I be respectful, when Father's known what Jackson's been doing and hasn't stopped him?"

"It was my idea, not Jackson's." Father leaned his wide frame against the door and watched her with an amused smile, as though enjoying the show at a circus. "Your brother merely had access to the funds."

The air in the room turned so cold she could hardly breathe it without her lungs freezing in her chest. "What would possess you?"

But she didn't need to ask, not really. The dates told her when the embezzlement had started. Seven months ago, just after the panic.

"We need money to live on," Father said mildly. "And you're aware of exactly how much we lost last March."

"But you mortgaged the house. That gave you money. I know you've gone through most of the funds by now, but—"

"Don't be ridiculous." Father waved his hand dismissively. "I merely invented that story when you and your mother started asking questions about how we could maintain our household staff and so forth."

"You lied." Fury surged through her as the full implication of his actions sank in, and she turned back to her brother. "And you lied, too. What reason do you have for this? You make a fine salary and keep apartments, with no great household to maintain."

Jackson shrugged. "My trust fund went the same place yours did when our bank folded."

"You're criminals." She squeezed the ledger against herself until it was sure to leave a rectangular imprint on her clothing. "I...I have to turn you in."

Moisture, hot and traitorous, stung her eyes, but she blinked it away and stared at her father. "And you truly will lose your house when you have to repay everything you stole."

"You can't turn anyone in, Elizabeth." Mother propped herself up from where she'd been lying on the settee. "I know you're upset right now, dear, but you'd ruin the family name."

"What purpose is there in a family name when the men who carry that name have no integrity? I'm not the one ruining anything."

She whirled toward the door. She had to get away and decide what to do with the ledger. But Father stood in front of the door. He hadn't moved so much as an inch since he'd shown David out.

She stilled, as the realization hit her. He hadn't moved from the exit since David had left…because he was keeping her in. While Jackson paced in front of the fireplace, looking ready to pounce on her and rip the ledger from her hand at any moment.

"We can't let you go. Don't you understand?" Mother dragged herself to a standing position. Devastation haunted her eyes, and the wrinkles around her mouth and across her forehead seemed more pronounced than they had just minutes ago. "This is why you have to marry David. He can provide us with the funds we need to maintain everything, and your father and Jackson can stop what they've been doing. I'm sure they're already sorry, aren't you?"

Father harrumphed and Jackson kept his dark eyes pinned to her as he paced.

"See there?" Mother spoke as if they'd both agreed. "The embezzlement will stop, and David will take care of us until your father gets his investments and campaign funds rebuilt. But you can't turn them in. You'd destroy our family." Concern rang through Mother's voice, and her eyes pleaded for understanding. The woman loved her family; no one would argue that. And she'd stay loyal, even if her loyalty meant she harbored thieves or murderers. Family always came first with Mother, which was why she'd attempted to arrange the scandal on Monday night. What was a little scandal, a little dishonesty, a little wrongdoing, when the family stood to benefit?

Should she do as Mother said and honor her family? Elizabeth's stomach revolted at the thought. When God said to honor your father and mother, to obey your parents, did He intend a son or daughter to do so at the expense of others? At the expense of the law?

Jonathan had honored his father. He'd followed King Saul into battle and ended up dead. But he'd honored God before all others and had protected David's life in spite of his father's wishes. Which choice was right for her? Did she follow her family at the expense of right? Or did she do right at the expense of her family?

She closed her eyes and saw her students' bright, smiling faces as she gave her speech on education. Saw Miss Bowen rushing up to ask how much money was left in the academy's bank account, and Miss Atkins's hurt face after hearing she couldn't help with the play. Saw Luke, arms crossed and hip cocked, as he leaned against her classroom door frame and watched her conclude a lesson, Luke offering assurance after Mother demanded she marry David, Luke brushing the hair from her face and asking her to give him a chance.

Luke had said something to her in the carriage last

week. Something about family and God and obedience. What had it been?

We ought to obey God rather than men.

She'd looked up the verse the next day. The Apostle Peter had said it. He and several others had been thrown into prison for preaching, and that night God opened the doors of their cells and released them. Rather than run from the city, they'd gone straight back to the temple and started preaching again. Then soldiers came and brought them before the high priest who had thrown them in prison the day before.

And what did Peter say? Not that he would obey the priest. Not that he would cease preaching and leave the city. But that he would obey God rather than men.

Peter suffered a beating, more prison time and eventual death to obey God. Jonathan never saw his best friend and eventually lost his life in trying to honor both God and his father. And she...she'd lose her family, whom she loved and had once respected, and whose approval she still sought.

She opened her eyes. Her family stared at her, every one of them waiting for an answer. Yes, she would lose them. But she'd be following God. And she'd be protecting her students and the children at St. Thomas Orphanage, the patients at the hospital and the small business owners listed in the ledger.

She met her mother's gaze. "You've made your own choices. Now you need to let me make mine. I have to obey God and act as the law demands. I'm sorry you'll be hurt by my actions, but you've been throwing Bible verses at me since I was a little girl. You should be the first to understand why I need to obey them."

Mother's mouth fell open, then closed halfway before

it dropped a second time. "But…but…" Confusion flitted across her face. Perhaps she was considering what she'd just heard, or perhaps she was formulating yet another way to plead for her family. Elizabeth hardly knew one way or the other.

"You're being ridiculous, Ellen," Father snapped, still standing guard at the door. "Why are you even considering the tripe Elizabeth's spouting?"

She moved toward him, tucking the ledger close against her body. "Please move so I can pass."

"Certainly, right after you give me the ledger." Father extended his hand, still keeping his back against the wood of the door.

"I can't. You know I can't."

"You don't have a choice."

She swallowed and glanced about the room. One door out. Two windows facing the street, and numerous pieces of furniture. Without access to the door, she had no way to get free short of smashing through the front windows. But maybe if she stayed and talked a bit longer, she could draw Father away from the door. He had to be getting tired of standing by now. But she'd need some sort of distraction, perhaps something to do with Mother.

Jackson appeared at her side, big and tall, with fury radiating off his body in tightly coiled waves. "Father said to hand over the ledger."

She shrank back from him only to bump into Father. "Perhaps we should talk about this some more. We seem to be at quite an impasse."

"The time for talking is done." Jackson gripped the ledger and wrenched it away from her trembling fingers.

"No!" She grabbed for the pages, rushing after him

as he moved to the center of the room. But she wasn't fast enough. The proof of Jackson's deceit stayed in his hands only a matter of seconds before he flung it into the fire.

"How could you?" She raced forward as the pages ignited and reached for the poker beside the blaze. If she could pull out the book and save a few pages, one or two examples might be enough to prove what her family had been doing.

But Jackson's arms wrapped around her, hard and unyielding as he dragged her backward. "No, you don't."

"Let me go. You've no right to manhandle me." She tried to pry his hold from around her waist and kicked at his shins with her heels.

"You can go, all right," he whispered in her ear. "Just as soon as you've watched every last page of that wretched ledger burn."

She turned her face away from the fire's orange glow, but the heat of the blaze, ravenous as it devoured the papers, seared her skin. A tear slid down her face, then another. "You won't get away with this. There's other proof of what you've been doing. There has to be. See if I don't find it. See if I let you walk off with all that money."

He fisted a hand in her hair and yanked it to the right, her head turning until she'd no choice but to stare into the flames once again. "We kept our bank accounts under false names, and my office has the only records for most of those businesses. Even if you go through my office, how do you know which accounts I altered and which I left alone? You can try to prove what I stole, Elizabeth. But your only proof is in that fire."

Chapter Nineteen

❧

Luke's back ached as he turned his rented horse down the Hayes estate's long drive. He'd spent all day with Cynthia and Everett, staying so long at the orphanage he'd rushed to catch the last train out of Philadelphia and then rented a horse in Albany since the train to Valley Falls wouldn't run again until morning.

The lights from Grandpa's house gleamed in the distance, though he'd no idea why more than one or two lights would be lit at this time of night. What he wouldn't give to be in bed right now, curled up under a heavy quilt on a comfortable feather mattress.

Time was when he wouldn't have minded bedding down under the stars with a rock for a pillow, but this place was making him soft. And strange as it was, he didn't mind coming back here, welcomed the sight almost as much as he did the view of his own ranch. Returning to the place Grandpa had built felt almost right.

So if the place felt right, if he wanted to be here, why was he trying to sell it or find a manager for Great Northern Accounting and Insurance?

Luke rubbed his bleary eyes. These thoughts were

Elizabeth's fault, every last one of them. Her words had niggled in his mind ever since he'd told her that he loved her. *You're leaving. Whatever you feel for me, whatever I feel for you, it doesn't mean anything. It can't, unless you stay here and manage your inheritance.*

Besides the lawyer on his first night in Valley Falls, no one else had mentioned him staying until Elizabeth. Luke stared at the acres of trim grass, passing slowly by under the dim moonlight. Acres that *he* owned. Maybe he'd have been better off staying in Wyoming and never coming East, telling the lawyer to sell everything and send the profits West. His life would have been easier, for sure and for certain.

But then he never would have seen the Philadelphia orphanage or ensured Hayes Academy stayed open. He never would have looked into the faces of the students and orphans Grandpa had helped. Never would have realized his sister was growing up or faced Cynthia. Never would have met Elizabeth…

He shifted in his saddle. Returning to Wyoming with Sam used to mean reuniting his family, but with matters settled between him and Cynthia, and with Sam scheduled to leave on Monday for Wyoming, going back West for good took on a whole other significance. It meant ending his ties with all Grandpa had worked for and pretending the orphans in Philadelphia and the young women at Hayes Academy required nothing from him. Ignoring the needs of the staff at the estate and the hundreds of insurance agents, accountants and actuaries along the East Coast that he employed.

Was it right to rush away from the things Grandpa had left him, or was it some form of neglect? And was

Grandpa even the one who had given him this vast inheritance? Or had God done that?

The thought echoed inside him like a shout reverberating through a mountain pass. His heart thudded slowly, surely, and he knew. Here he'd been blaming Grandpa for his new heap of responsibilities, but God controlled the world, not Jonah Hayes.

God could have let Grandpa's savings and assets be lost in the panic, as had happened to the Wellses and countless others. God could have led Grandpa to disperse his assets and estate himself, donating everything to charities rather than a grandson he'd never met.

Luke swallowed as a new thought took shape. And God could have seen him shot rather than Blake on that sunny morning three years ago. Then Blake would have inherited everything.

Instead, God had given it all to him, Luke Hayes.

He couldn't leave it behind and head back to the Teton Valley. Not anymore.

He could run the businesses Grandpa had left him well enough. In fact, it almost seemed God had used his ranch to prepare him for taking over Grandpa's holdings. Sure he had a few things to learn, but numbers made sense to him, always had. And managing a business didn't differ too much from running a ranch—except the workers smelled better.

He'd still miss the wide-open prairie, with those giant Tetons looming to the east. But the ranch would be well taken care of under Pa, and like Sam, he could go back and visit. Besides, New York had its own appeal. Though not as grand as the Tetons, the Catskill Mountains loomed to the west, their blue-shadowed slopes visible from his bedroom and office. He could take day trips into the wilderness or spend a weekend camping here and there.

And besides, if he stayed in Valley Falls...

He slowed his horse in front of the house. A vision of a woman, dressed in green velvet and standing in the hallway of Hayes Academy, curled around the edges of his mind. She looked hesitant, unsure as she said she'd have dinner with him the following evening.

A smile crept across his lips as he stared up at the white three-story mansion. Such a grand house needed a beautiful woman to run it. A beautiful woman with a heart for teaching and a wagonload of reddish-brown hair. Now he only had to figure out how to ask her— and hope she said yes.

He gulped. A woman as fine as Elizabeth would have plenty of reasons not to want a country bumpkin like him.

Luke swung off his horse and took the steps two at a time. The butler opened the door before he'd even reached the top.

"Stevens, what are you doing awake? Do you realize how late it is?"

"Yes, sir, quarter of two."

Luke stepped inside and waved his hand at the fully lit chandelier. "Then why's the house lit up like there's some fancy dinner going on?"

A sob echoed from the direction of the drawing room, and he turned. He knew that sound, had heard it far too many times when he'd first arrived. "Samantha's still up?"

"Yes, sir. You have a visitor, and I'm afraid she delivered some rather distressing news."

Distressing news? Was something wrong with Ma?

Had Sam received a telegram after he'd left yesterday afternoon? He strode toward the drawing room and opened the door, only to find Elizabeth sitting on that fancy white and gold couch. What was she doing here? And in the middle of the night to boot?

He whispered her name, running his eyes over her unkempt hair and pale face. Samantha sat hunched in her arms, sobs emanating with every breath.

Elizabeth raised her head and looked toward the door.

"What's wrong?" He came closer, and she hugged Sam tighter to herself. Redness lined her eyes while devastation haunted the hollows and planes of her porcelain face. His heart thumped against his ribs. "Is it Ma? Or Jackson? Was there an accident? Is someone…"

Dead?

Sam pulled back from Elizabeth, her hands clenched into angry fists. "Oh, I wish there were some accident. I wish it was all some mistake, or maybe that I'd never met the conniver at all."

Luke strode toward his sister, his own fingers clenching in response. "What'd he do? Tell me, and I'll make him pay."

Sam leaped into his arms and started crying all over again. "I should have listened to you. You were right from the very beginning. All he wanted was money."

"Hush now." Luke stroked her hair, but the soothing movements had little effect on her. "It's all right. We'll work everything out, just calm down."

She only cried harder.

He lifted his eyes to Elizabeth's. She'd backed away from him and Sam, and stood near the fire, her arms wrapped around herself in a lonely hug.

Confound it. He should be holding Elizabeth in his arms at this moment, kissing her and whispering promises about staying in Valley Falls. But with Sam sobbing in his arms and that silent sorrow etched across Elizabeth's face, this was hardly the time. "What happened?"

"I'm so sorry, Luke." Her whispered words barely reached him above Sam's shudders. "I didn't know. I promise I didn't."

"Didn't know what?"

She shook her head, as though trying to deny whatever she needed to say.

"Go on, now. You can tell me."

"I tried to go to the police, but they wouldn't believe me."

"The police?" His hands tightened on Sam's back. "Why would you need to go to the police? What did Jackson do?"

"He…" Elizabeth pressed her eyes shut and rubbed her temples. "I'm sorry. This is harder than I'd thought."

"Here, Sam, sit for a minute." He set his sister on the couch and gave her a pillow to clutch before moving to Elizabeth. Tears glistened in her eyes, tears she seemed determined not to shed.

"Tell me." He reached for her, but she took a step back.

"No. Don't touch me. Not right now. Not after what my family did."

Her family. Dread, icy and hard, sank its claws into his chest. Had they coerced her into becoming DeVander's wife? Had she already signed a marriage license?

But then Sam wouldn't be so upset at Jackson. The

fear constricting his heart loosened just a bit. "Will one of you please tell me what's going on?"

"You need to do an audit on your Albany office." Elizabeth stared into the fire.

"What?"

Her chin trembled, and she raised it, calling on that inner strength that had mesmerized him from the first time he'd met her. "Jackson and my father...th-they've been..." She swallowed, the tight muscles in her throat working far too hard. "Embezzling. From you. Since the panic, they've been using your accounting and insurance offices to steal from you and the companies you service."

Every idea about what had happened, every thought about what he'd do to Jackson Wells, every word he'd planned to comfort Elizabeth with, deserted him.

"What do you mean, embezzling?" He heard his voice speaking, knew his mouth had somehow formed the words, but the implications of what Elizabeth had said seemed as vague and hazy as a mountain fog.

"I mean that I went to Jackson's office before dinner tonight to find his ledger for Hayes Academy. Sometimes the supplies and materials arriving at the school haven't matched the amounts that were supposedly ordered, so I wanted to compare my books with Jackson's." Her breath quivered as she blew it out. "I—I didn't find the ledger for the academy, but I found another ledger instead. It was an accident. I wasn't supposed to discover it. I never knew anything about what they were doing before tonight."

"Oh, Lizzie." He reached for her hand, but she pulled it away.

"You believe me, then?" Shock flared in her eyes.

"Why wouldn't I?"

Two tears slid down her cheeks, silent compared to Sam's noisy gulps on the couch, but almost more wrenching. "I went to the police station before I came here. The police officer—he wouldn't believe me without the ledger. Said I had no business going through the accounting office at all, and maybe I could be prosecuted for looking at Jackson's books without permission."

"Elizabeth, that's ridiculous. They're my offices, and I promise no one's going to prosecute you."

She wiped furiously at the tears on her cheeks.

"Where's the ledger now?" He didn't think it possible for her face to lose more color, but her skin blanched yet again, and she stared at the blaze in the fireplace.

"Jackson threw it... Father wouldn't let me leave, and—"

"Jackson? Your father?" He gripped her shoulders and jerked her around until she faced him fully. "You went to see them?"

She stood rigid in his arms, the warmth she'd shown him over the past week buried under layers of rigid hurt. "I had to make sure. What if I'd misread things? Imagined something that wasn't really in the ledger? You weren't here, and I couldn't walk into a police station and accuse my family of stealing thousands of dollars without knowing for sure."

He pulled her against him, pressing her head to his chest and wrapping his arms around her waist.

She only stiffened more.

"There were other companies listed in the ledger besides Hayes Academy. Connor School for Boys and Maple Ridge College with their normal operating expenses and the hospital in Albany. St. Thomas Orphanage and…" She sank her head. "I don't remember what else. I'm sorry. I should have paid better attention."

"Stop apologizing. You've done nothing wrong."

"Don't say I shouldn't apologize." Her eyes turned fierce, and she shoved at his chest.

He didn't have to let go. He was stronger and could force her to stand in his embrace. But forcing people into his will had caused him enough trouble of late. So he released her, though every muscle in his body screamed to keep her close.

"My family was stealing from my students. And what's worse, they expected me to keep silent." Elizabeth fisted her hands in her already wrinkled skirt. "They actually thought I'd marry David and let him take care of matters, while Father and Jackson walked off with the money and promised not to steal again. If I don't apologize for what they did, who will?"

He raked his hand through his hair. She stood only two feet away, but she may as well be standing on the other side of a mountain. His arms ached for the feel of her, but she wouldn't come, not now. And he could hardly blame her. She'd been hurt, and even though he hadn't been the cause of it, he was tangled in the mess right good, as he owned the company her family had used to steal. "Then let me apologize, too. I'm sorry for what your father and brother did and for the pain it's putting you through."

She shook her head and took her cape from where she'd draped it over a chair, then moved to hug Sam before turning back to him, her face as desolate as the prairie after a blizzard. "Thank you, for being my friend, Luke, and for believing me when no one else would."

You're more than a friend. I love you. I want to marry you. Didn't she see that? Didn't she understand he would stand by her through whatever trouble her discovery unleashed?

But she disappeared through the door before he could open his mouth to tell her.

Chapter Twenty

The knock sounded at two thirty-six the following afternoon. Not that Elizabeth was watching the clock. Oh, no. She had plenty to do as she sat in the parlor, rocking in an old chair and staring out the window at the side yard. She could be packing her books and belongings, going to Jonah's lawyer and asking that her house be put up for sale, writing a farewell to her students, or any other of the numerous tasks that awaited her.

But every one of those took energy, and as she'd cried through the night until the first streaks of dawn tinged the sky, she didn't have any left.

News of the rumored embezzlement hadn't appeared in the paper yet, but no doubt speculation circled through town. Indeed, with Luke likely at his office doing an audit and his entire staff knowing where he was, things could hardly be kept secret. Miss Atkins and Miss Tourneau, friendly this morning, hadn't even looked at her after they'd returned from church.

Elizabeth wrapped her arms around herself and shivered. She'd expected as much. She'd grown up in Albany and knew how gossip worked. Regardless of whether her father and brother ended up on trial and were found guilty, society had already formed their opinions. So if she planned to keep teaching, she would have to leave the area. And she had no choice other than to continue teaching. She needed to earn a living, needed food to eat and clothes to wear and a roof over her head.

Maybe she should go West. Not somewhere as remote as the Teton Valley, but newspapers always ran advertisements for teachers wanted on the other side of the Mississippi.

The knock sounded again, and the floor above her creaked. She stared up at the parlor ceiling, but no footsteps pounded down the upstairs hallway. Evidently neither Miss Atkins nor Miss Tourneau seemed inclined to answer the door. It was just as well, the callers would be there for her anyway.

She rose slowly, each step a concentrated effort as she headed out of the room and pulled open the front door.

"Miss Wells." Mr. Taviston removed his hat and offered a slight dip of his head, his lips pulled down into a frown and his eye devoid of their usual lecherous glint. "Just the person I needed to speak with."

"Indeed." She forced her lips to curve into a smile. "Won't you come in?"

She stepped back from the door, took his coat and ushered him into the parlor. If she wanted to be polite, she would offer tea and sandwiches, but why go through the flat, empty gesture? Tea or not, he would fire her.

She sat on the settee. "Mr. Taviston, let me make this conversation as quick and painless as possible. You don't need to fire me. I resign."

Tears, hot and coarse, crept up the back of her throat. Whether she loved her job or not, she'd no business facing her students again after how her family had stolen from them.

"We appreciate that overture on your part, Miss Wells." Mr. Taviston kept his frown in place, as though his actions somehow pained him. "You've always been a sensible woman, and I'm sure you understand why we can't allow you to continue teaching at Hayes Academy."

"Yes." She felt hollow inside. Like an eggshell drained of its contents and a breath away from cracking. "With the trouble my family is in, keeping me on would look bad for the school."

"Your father, of course, is also being relieved of his position on the school board. Nearly all the board members were in agreement regarding the actions to be taken toward both you and him."

"Nearly? Striking the Wellses from any association with Hayes Academy wasn't a unanimous decision?"

She was daft to ask, but something inside her had to know if Mr. Taviston's words meant Luke had dissented.

The man's eyebrows furrowed together. "Well, several of the board members couldn't be reached, but it hardly matters as more than a majority were in compliance with the recommendations."

"I see." Had Luke been one of the members left uninformed? Or perhaps he had defended her, and Mr. Taviston refused to admit it for one reason or another.

And wasn't she a heartsick fool, hoping for anything other than the obvious. Her family had hurt Luke, and there would be consequences. Losing her job was one.

Losing Luke was another. She sucked in a breath and prayed Mr. Taviston didn't notice the underlying tremble.

"You should also know," Mr. Taviston continued, "that we'll be looking closely into your actions at Hayes Academy. We would, of course, hate to discover that you'd been aware of your family's illegal activities earlier and had hidden it to protect them."

She jumped from her seat. "I would never, *never* jeopardize my students like that. I turned in my family as soon as I discovered what was happening. Do you know how that feels, Mr. Taviston? To have to choose between your family and your students? Your family and honoring God?"

The man stood. "No, Miss Wells. I can't say I do, or that my family would ever put me in a situation where I'd find out. But if you're innocent, I'm sure an adequate investigation will show—"

"Go." She pointed toward the door, her finger stiff. "I refuse to sit in the house I own and listen to you accuse me of some crime I never committed. Get out. Now."

Mr. Taviston's jaw fell, and he stared at her as though she'd lost her mind. And maybe she had, telling off a distinguished gentleman like him.

"Well then, I'll take my leave. But first, someone requested I give you this." He dug inside his pocket and then held out an envelope.

David. She recognized his script before she even took it. The letter likely retracted his offer to marry her and claimed he'd found another woman more suitable to be his wife just that morning. She smiled bitterly. Had she really considered his offer, however briefly, to help her family? She wasn't just some heartsick fool, she was the world's largest one.

She straightened her shoulders and met Mr. Taviston's gaze. So she didn't have much dignity left or any reputation to speak of, but she wouldn't let a man like David DeVander humiliate her without even being present. Tearing the envelope in thirds, she dropped it on the floor. "As I said, Mr. Taviston, good day."

"I've got another one, sir."

Luke looked down at the accountant, holding out an open ledger and pile of receipts. Hushed voices and the shuffle of papers filled Jackson Wells's office as men went from one ledger to another comparing original receipts to the amounts Jackson had written in his ledgers.

"Looks to be about a thousand dollars since March." The man pointed to a number he'd circled at the top of the page. "Though we'll have to go over it again to be certain of the amount."

Luke rubbed his hand over his mouth. A thousand dollars from an orphanage. How could people steal from such a place? He waved a hand toward the table where a wire-thin police detective sat. "You know where to take it."

Chest puffed and shoulders high, the employee weaved his way through the throng of policemen and accountants that spilled from the office into the hallway as they searched for more evidence of falsified accounts.

The frenzy had started last night, when he'd ridden back to Albany, awoken Jackson's assistant from bed and sent the man to the office. Then he'd gone to the police station to drag an officer over to Great Northern Accounting and Insurance. The accountant had found money missing from two places before they'd arrived.

Luke moved to the side of Jackson's desk and stared

at the ledger he'd left open. How much longer would the officers be here? Did they intend to break for the evening and then return come morning? Because as a man who hadn't slept last night, he was perilously close to sitting down in Jackson's armchair and dozing off.

And yet, despite the fatigue plaguing his eyes and the haze encompassing his mind, sleeping didn't seem right. Not with all these men rushing about his company in a work-induced frenzy, and not without knowing how Samantha and Elizabeth were coping with all that had happened.

Samantha was still slated to leave on the train in the morning, but maybe she'd want to postpone her trip. Sure, he'd never liked Jackson, but he could hardly blame her if she wanted the comfort of her friends and familiar places for another day or two after the stunt Jackson and his father had pulled. But even then Samantha's heartache looked miniscule compared to Elizabeth's.

Luke raked his hand through his hair. How was she? Still as upset as she had been last night? He should go to her, see how she was and if he could do anything to help. She probably hadn't slept last night, either. But hopefully one of her roommates had found a way to distract her from all the rumors floating around today— and made sure she ate some breakfast and lunch.

Hang it all, he should be with her now, taking her for a walk, seeing that she got a decent meal and promising that he still loved her despite what her family had done. Instead he was stuck here going over ledgers and listening to workers mutter about cheating politicians and arrogant office managers.

"Mr. Hayes?"

Luke turned toward the half-familiar voice and frowned at the older man in a suit and hat. What was his name? Witman? Wiltern? He'd met him the night of the banquet and then again when he'd gone to the school board to convince them the academy needed to stay open.

"Ah, Mr. Wisner, what brings you by this afternoon?" Luke extended his hand.

"It's Wilhem, son, not Wisner."

"Sorry. I remember all the faces from the school board but can only seem to recall half the names."

He chuckled, a calming, grandfatherly sound. "Doubt I'd be able to remember everyone's name either if I were in your position." He glanced around the overfilled office. "Quite the day you're having, eh?"

Luke shrugged even as a policeman bumped into an accountant, knocking him into the table where the detective sat and sending a tall stack of papers fluttering to the floor. "I didn't exactly envision myself in this mess yesterday. But you're not here to tally numbers. What can I do for you?"

"For me? Oh, nothing at all. I wanted to find out if there's anything the school board can do to help you straighten out this…er…"

"Tangle."

The man's black-and-gray speckled eyebrows rose. "Yes. That's probably an adequate description."

Luke inched a ledger closer to the older man. "Don't suppose you've a mind for ciphering?"

Wilhem shook his head. "Own a shipping company but leave the book work to others. Still if there's any way we can be of aid…" Despite the chaos of the room, a shattered silence lingered between them. "You'll be pleased to know that Thomas Wells has been relieved of his position on the school board."

Luke crossed his arms. "Probably goes part and parcel with embezzling over twenty-five thousand dollars and getting yourself locked up."

"Too true." Wilhem looked down at the tips of his shiny black shoes. "Elizabeth Wells has also been relieved of her teaching position."

The words sliced through him, cold and slick. He didn't think, didn't swallow, didn't even breathe. Just reached for the man and gripped his lapels. "What?"

Every head in the cramped room turned at his shout. Wilhem was probably just the messenger, sent to relay a decision others had made. But Luke's hands tightened on Wilhem's coat regardless, and he pulled the man closer. "Why don't you explain precisely what 'relieved of her teaching position' means?"

"Well, ah…" Wilhem gulped. "Surely you understand. I like Elizabeth, I do, and I've known her since she was a little girl. But we can't keep her in our employ when everyone will soon know her family has been engaged in illegal activities."

Luke sucked in a deep breath and let it out. He could control himself. He didn't need to explode. And he wouldn't break Wilhem's nose because he didn't like something the man said.

He hoped.

"I still see no reason to take action against Miss Wells."

"Ponder the situation a moment, Hayes. What parents would want their daughters taught by a woman of questionable character?"

"Questionable?" He dragged Wilhem closer.

"Mr. Hayes, is there a problem? Perhaps I might be of help."

Luke flicked a glance at the skinny police detective, now standing beside him. "There's a problem, all right, but I doubt you can fix it." He released Wilhem. "Why don't you explain why Miss Wells's character is suddenly questionable?"

Their eyes met, Wilhem's gaze holding an uncomfortable sympathy. "You won't like it."

Luke just crossed his arms and glared.

Wilhem's shoulders slumped. "We're looking into whether she knew of the embezzlement earlier and covered the matter to protect her family."

How could they accuse Elizabeth of such a thing? She was wholesome and honest and determined. Didn't the school board understand that the mere mention of this suspicion would destroy her? "That's nonsense. She's been nothing but honorable in this whole mess and I won't let you take teaching away from her. She's sacrificed too much for the academy and those girls to be treated that way."

Pink tinged Wilhem's cheeks. "I attempted to say as much to Taviston, but he refused to listen."

"Then we'll change Taviston's mind together." Luke whirled and stalked from the room with Wilhem's hasty footsteps following behind. Maybe he couldn't prevent Elizabeth's family from abusing her and stealing. Maybe he couldn't prevent the papers from informing the whole of New York about what her family had done. But there was one thing he could do. And he'd use everything in his power to accomplish it.

Chapter Twenty-One

Two trunks and three crates. Elizabeth had to fit everything she needed inside them, and she had so many things sitting about her house, all little pieces of the home she'd worked to create. Packing her room had been a simple matter of folding her clothes into squares, stacking them in the trunks and cleaning out the few other items she wanted to take. But downstairs she faced the settee and chairs, the curtains, the dishes, the pictures on the walls. And the two open crates on the parlor floor had filled far too quickly.

The five-shelf bookcase loomed in front of her now, full of textbooks and works by mathematical geniuses. Which should she take? Newton's *Principia* or Descartes's discourse on geometry? Leibniz on calculus or Gauss on geometry? She had room for maybe five texts total.

She moved to the shelf and pulled down *An Introductory Calculus,* the textbook from her first calculus course. Opening the cover, she ran her fingers over the letters on the first page.

Elizabeth, May you use this book and the knowledge you have learned in these classes to do great things. Professor Strohm.

This one would have to go with her, even if she had little hope of teaching calculus wherever she settled.

She reached up and took Newton down, then opened that cover.

My Dear Elizabeth, When you returned from your first year of school and I saw how much you'd come to appreciate calculus, I decided you needed the work of the man who fathered the subject. Happy Birthday.
Jonah Hayes.

She pressed the books to her chest and closed her eyes. How did one choose? How did one pack a life into two trunks and three crates? Perhaps the past two days hadn't been kind to her, but she'd lived twenty-six years in upstate New York. She couldn't wipe all the memories of pleasant times from her mind and heart because her family had been deceitful.

A knock sounded on the door. She jolted, then glanced at the clock on the mantel. Miss Atkins and Miss Tourneau wouldn't be back from the academy for another four hours. Who could possibly be here?

The pounding sounded again.

She walked to the window and peered through the lacy curtains, then stopped. Luke Hayes stood on her porch, wearing that familiar cowboy hat yet again. She stepped to the side of the glass and pressed her back against the wall lest he decide to peer through the window and see her.

Perhaps she had the strength to leave, selling her house and starting her life anew. But she hadn't the strength to face him or her students again. The ties that bound her to Luke and the girls at Hayes Academy had snapped the night she'd found Jackson's ledger, and the words *I'm sorry* could hardly repair the damage done.

Elizabeth blinked back the moisture pooling in her eyes. Crying seemed to be the only thing she wanted to do of late. But her tears couldn't fix what happened or change what needed to be done any more than the words *I'm sorry* could.

Something creaked near the back of the house, and she stilled. Had Luke broken in through the kitchen door? She clutched the base of her throat. Certainly not. The house simply groaned sometimes, all houses—

Footsteps echoed in the hallway, then his familiar silhouette filled the parlor entrance. "Miss Wells." He tipped his head and removed his hat.

"W-what are you doing here?"

"Front door was locked, found the back open, though." He watched her, those clear blue eyes seeming to bore into her soul, and held out a lunch tin. "Just got back from delivering Sam to the train station. She still wanted to go home, was more eager than I could have ever imagined to get away from Jackson. So I figured I'd stop by on my way home and make sure you got something to eat. Doesn't look like you've had a good meal in about two days."

He wanted to share a meal? Where was his anger? His rage over what her family had done? He'd been quiet and supportive when last they'd spoken, but that had been before he'd done the audit and seen the extent of her family's fraud.

"I'm not hungry. Thank you."

He snorted. "Figured you'd say something like that. It's about lunchtime, though. You won't mind if I eat?" He came into the parlor and plopped down on the floor by her crates, then emptied the contents of the sack. Cold ham, cubed cheese, crackers and *grapes*. Her favorite.

He shoved a piece of meat into his mouth and chewed. "You ever tried my cook's brown sugar ham? It's the best meat this side of the Mississippi."

She shook her head and pressed herself harder against the wall. A foolish place to stand, but she could hardly resume her packing while he watched, and if she got any closer, he'd finagle some way to have her sitting beside him. And surely she had some good reason why she couldn't eat with him—she just couldn't remember it.

"The best meat west of the Mississippi would, of course, be fresh beef from the Double H ranch in Wyoming, but Valley Falls is a little far for that." He popped a cracker in his mouth and rested a hand over his knee. He looked handsome and at ease sprawled on her parlor floor, as though he belonged there. His shoulders so broad and commanding she could hardly look anywhere else, his jaw stubbly and unshaven and begging for her to run her hand across it.

She'd been so certain she couldn't trust him, couldn't trust any man after David had betrayed her. But in the end, her family had proven untrustworthy, not the man sitting before her.

Why hadn't she been able to look past her own fears

a week ago and see the heart of the man that loved her? What she wouldn't give to have him look at her with the tenderness his eyes had held when they'd talked after the speech, to feel his arms around her as they'd been in the carriage after she'd first confronted David. She sagged against the wall and wrapped her own arms around her middle—a rather poor substitute for Luke's.

"Care for a grape?" He popped one in his mouth.

Yes. She nearly said it. But he couldn't know grapes were her favorite, could he? Or that she longed to launch herself into his arms and bury her face in his shoulder and cry until her heart stopped aching.

She needed to get out of this room before she made a fool of herself.

He swallowed another bite, and the perfect excuse hit her. "Tea. You need tea or water or milk. Something to drink. Let me get it."

She hurried toward the doorway, but his hand shot out and fisted in the front of her skirt as she passed.

"Sit." He tugged the fabric.

"Mr. Hayes. I appreciate that you're hungry and will happily get you something to drink, but then you really must be on your way. It's highly inappropriate for you to be here, in my house, without a chaperone."

"Probably is." He stuffed more food in his mouth, but didn't release her skirt. "It's also highly inappropriate for your brother to use his position at my company to embezzle over twenty-five thousand dollars' worth of funds from various accounts."

Twenty-five thousand dollars? She hadn't any idea the amount was so large. The paper that morning didn't list any figures, just said her brother and father were in jail, charged with embezzlement and without the funds needed to post bail.

As for Mother… Elizabeth blew out a breath. Mother knew where she lived and hadn't come. "I already told you I was sorry. What more do you want?"

"As I said Saturday night, I don't know why you're sorry. You didn't do anything wrong. In fact, you turned your family in when looking the other way would have made everything a heap easier for you." He dropped his hand from her skirt. "But if your heart's set on getting me a drink, get on with it. I could stand to whet my whistle—I've got a while to talk yet."

"I don't understand why you're here at all. What's left for us to say to each other? My family stole, and the school board had me fired. Not that I feel like I could ever look my students in the eye again, but you and the others didn't have to get rid of me in such a manner. I'd already decided to leave anyway. I couldn't stay here while everyone gawked and whispered behind my back."

He sprang to his feet. "I didn't vote to fire you. I didn't even know what those idiots had done until a couple hours after Taviston paid you a visit." He reached into his pocket and pulled out an envelope. "Here, see if this changes things."

She stared at it dully, the crisp, straight lines too similar to yesterday's letter from David.

"Do you need me to open it?" He pulled a knife from his belt and slid it along the top fold, then held out the missive.

She scanned the contents. "This…this can't be right. It says the school board is reinstating me."

"It's right."

"You got me my job back? Why?"

"Because you did right even though it meant turning your family in, and the people you've spent the past two years working for should support you."

She shook her head. "I don't—"

"Hush. I've more to tell you, now that you've started talking to me again. On the way back from Philadelphia, I decided something—or rather, God showed it to me. I'm not going back West. I'm staying in Valley Falls to run the businesses Grandpa left me."

"Y-you're not leaving?" She could hardly breathe, let alone think, as she waited for his reply.

"No. And what's more…" He took her hand and held it between them, her fingers dangling over his. "I still love you."

"Oh, Luke." He couldn't feel that way, not after everything that had happened. But his eyes didn't lie, and the deep blue of them shone with patience and support and love. All things she'd never had from her family. All things she'd never realized she wanted until Luke walked into her life. "I love you, too. I didn't want to fall in love with you, but it happened anyway, without me even realizing it."

A smile tilted the corners of his mouth. "Don't make it sound like a crime, Lizzie. People have been falling in love since Adam and Eve." He pulled a box from his pocket and opened it. An emerald ring gleamed dark and rich against the blue fabric. "Marry me. Spend your life with me."

Her throat shriveled into a gritty mass of sand. How easily she could accept the life he offered. How wonderful to be his wife and wake up beside him every morning, to go back to teaching and surround herself with students. She'd have a life she'd only dreamed of.

Yes. The word rested on her tongue, ready to tip over, fall out and cement her future to his.

But she couldn't.

She must have taken too long to respond, because he gripped her shoulders and pulled her so close her petticoats squashed against her legs. "You're going to tell me no. I can see it in your eyes."

She looked away.

"It's because of what happened with that cheat, DeVander, isn't it? You still don't think you can trust a husband." He trailed a finger down the line of her jaw and back up again. "I can't promise never to hurt you or disappoint you, Elizabeth. But I can promise to always be faithful. Before God and you, I promise. And if it takes another week or month or year for you to believe that, then that's how long I'll wait for you."

"Luke, stop."

But he didn't. He stroked a strand of hair behind her ear and leaned closer. "I love you for who you are, and I'm never going to take that love away and give it to another woman."

"You've been so patient with me. Too patient, really. I don't deserve you."

"Then why are you about to cry?"

She straightened her shoulders. "I'm not."

"Liar."

She shifted away and clasped her hands together. "Have you forgotten about my family? Surely you saw the paper this morning. The embezzlement scandal is huge, and it just appeared today. We haven't yet seen how voters are going to respond when they find out the politician they've elected for the past twenty years stole twenty-five thousand dollars. Or how the companies Jackson took from are going to react when everyone learns of his deceit. Why, you might lose half your accounting clients. More than half.

"And now you want to stay here and take your grandfather's place. Which is fine. It's what you should have done all along. But nobody will accept a thief's daughter as your wife. You can't…" *Marry me.*

The words stuck in her throat, but she pressed on, speaking the truth, the only logical answer despite her heart's screaming otherwise. "You're going to be a respected member of society, even with that wretched cowboy hat you like to wear, and me…I have to leave."

"Look at me." He grabbed her upper arms and waited for her eyes to meet his. His jaw had gone hard, his eyes glinting with determination. "I love *you*. I want to marry *you*. And as for what everybody else thinks about your family and the embezzlement—" he bent and kissed her forehead "—I don't care."

If only she could see the world through Luke's eyes. Black-and-white, right and wrong, and forget anybody who didn't agree. But society wouldn't hold with Luke's ideas about marriage. "You don't understand. A marriage can't work between us, not now. Maybe…" She drew in a breath. "Maybe in a few years, after the scandal settles and things calm, if you still feel the same about me, you can write to me and…"

He ran his hand back to cup the base of her neck and tilt her face toward his. "Maybe I want to marry you now," he whispered, his breath hot against her skin. Then he lowered his lips to meet hers. His mouth tasted of warmth and comfort, understanding and forgiveness.

Her knees weakened and her body went limp for the briefest of moments. Then she stiffened. Nothing good could come of kissing him. Not when she had to turn down his proposal. Not when she had to leave. But Luke Hayes had never been easily put off. He wrapped his arms around her back and pulled her closer, his lips gently lingering on hers, then broke to trail kisses down her jaw.

"I love you, Elizabeth," he whispered as his mouth trailed up to her ear.

"I love you, too. But we can't marry. You have to understand."

"Nothing to understand. We can marry without the heap o' troubles you're yammering about, and I'll prove it to you." His lips, still soft and warm, left her suddenly. Then he clasped her hand in his and pulled her toward the hall.

"Prove it? You can't prove something like that. And where are we going? I need to finish packing."

He dragged her out of the parlor and toward the front door. "There's another matter you have to settle first."

"Another matter? The house will be up for sale by the end of the week. My things are nearly packed. I answered several advertisements for teachers this morning. What's left to—?"

"Your students."

She dug her heels into the tiled floor. "I can't face them again, not after how I missed the signs of the embezzlement."

"Look at me, Elizabeth." He took her by the shoulders, rubbing her knotted muscles. "You have to see your students. Sure, you feel like you let them down. But you can't hide away in your house forever. Nor can you leave without fixing things. I know that better than anyone.

"There was a man once, a criminal who stole from the ranch." He sucked in a breath, as though telling the story robbed him of air. "After my twin caught and fired him, he returned and shot my brother, who died from the wound.

"I went a little crazy after his death. Holed myself up, let Pa send Sam out East where she'd be safe, and blamed myself over and over again for what happened. I got bitter at my sister-in-law, who I faulted for not stopping my brother's bleeding, even though the wound likely would have killed him anyway. And I shut out everyone else. In short, I wasted three years of my life blaming myself and those closest to me for something none of us could control.

"I love you too much to let you do the same." Pain etched his face and glittered in his eyes, but he gave her shoulders another squeeze. "Your family was wrong, yes. But you protected your students once you realized everything. You did right by them, and you need to go back and face them."

He was right, as always. Before God, she had nothing to be ashamed of. She'd honored her Creator above men. Of course, society didn't judge people by God's standards. No. The socialites at church would rip her apart, and the teachers at Hayes probably gossiped even now.

Still, she owed her students one last visit, didn't she? Then she could start anew somewhere else, rather than hide.

"Let's go." Luke held out his hand.

She looked down at his hand, the same hand she'd covered in chalk dust the second time they'd met. The same hand that had wiped her tears after David had proposed, had anchored her hair behind her ears too many times to count and had cupped her cheek when he'd kissed her. And she put her palm in his.

Elizabeth had never before considered how ominous Hayes Academy for Girls could appear, with its redbrick jutting three stories and its plain windows staring down at those coming up the walk.

Like a prison without the fence.

Luke held open the door and waited. "No one's going to attack you for coming inside."

If only she could be so sure. "The first time I looked at this building, all I saw were dreams, both mine in possibly teaching here one day and the students' for the expanded opportunities they would have after graduating from such a place." She stood just outside the threshold and peered in at the austere white walls. "I never thought…that is…" She rubbed her damp palms together. "I never really noticed before how intimidating it looks."

He grabbed her hand and pulled her through the doorway. "Stop stalling."

The door closed behind them, sealing her inside. She nearly pulled her hand from his and dashed back into the sunlight.

"I thought the same thing the first time I saw the building. Dull and void of life." He led her forward, so quickly she hadn't time to think of another way to slow him down. "A little teacher with rich mahogany hair changed my mind, though."

"Don't be ridiculous."

"I'm not."

She paused in front of the office and drew in a deep breath. She'd have to face Miss Bowen before seeing her students. What would the headmistress say? Then again, maybe Miss Bowen would kick her out, and she wouldn't have to worry about looking into her students' eyes.

"Stop slowing down." Luke yanked her past the office.

"But Miss Bowen. Shouldn't we—?"

"Nope. This way."

"The only thing down here is the dining hall…." Her voice trailed off as he pushed open the double doors.

Students crammed into the room, milling about and sitting at tables, eating and talking as an organized sort of chaos filled the room.

She tugged at her hand, but he still didn't release it. "Luke, I don't want to be here, not like this."

He hunkered down, placing his mouth beside her ear. "It'll be fine."

"No." She jerked harder on her hand, but the stubborn man had a grip like iron.

Then MaryAnne, who had been busily eating, looked toward the door and shot from her chair. "Miss Wells! You're back!"

The rest of the room fell silent, every eye turning to her. Her face heated, and her throat went achingly dry. She turned to go. Luke could continue to hold her hand or release her, but either way, she was plowing through those doors and heading straight back to her private little home.

"Miss Wells, wait!" MaryAnne approached her, as did Meredith and Elaine.

"Mr. Hayes said you would stop by today." Elaine

ducked her head shyly to the side, stray wisps of brown hair tickling her cheek. "So we made these for you."

She thrust out her hand, a crisp, white envelope caught between her thumb and fingers. Another letter. Elizabeth's hands trembled too much to even reach out and take it.

Mr. Hayes stroked a palm down her back, then up again, the gesture warm and comforting, but still, she couldn't stop the shaking that plagued her limbs.

"Why don't you read it for her, Elaine?" Mr. Hayes's deep voice settled over the entire room.

Elaine dipped her soft eyelashes down, pink staining both her cheeks as she struggled to get the envelope open and unfold the letter. "Dear Miss Wells..." Her voice carried its usual softness, but the dining hall had fallen so quiet that the words likely reached the farthest corners.

"Growing up, every girl has teachers—not just one, but multiple teachers of different ages and backgrounds who endeavor to impart everything we need to know about womanhood. From this group of myriad women, every so often a teacher comes along who makes a difference in her students' lives.

"She cares about her students and what she teaches. You can see it in the way her eyes light as she lectures, and the way she agrees to meet students after school for tutoring. You can tell by the smile on her face when she answers questions and gives encouragement, not just about her subject, but life in general. Like the way you said you'd help me apply to Wellesley College for next year, and the way you've tutored Samantha Hayes with all that calculus.

"Please know that you've been that teacher for me

and for my friends. My only complaint is that you teach mathematics instead of composition. Don't you know composition is a much more interesting subject?

"Thank you so much for all the effort you put into teaching us."

Elizabeth pressed her eyes shut, unable to meet Elaine's gaze. The students were thanking her? After what her family had done? She should be thanking them for letting her teach for the past two years, not the other way around.

Another voice rang out; MaryAnne's strong, clear cadence easily recognizable despite Elizabeth's closed eyes. Reading her own letter, the girl mentioned advanced algebra and having fun and not wanting her teacher to leave.

Then another voice started and another and another. Mr. Hayes kept one hand on her shoulder and his other on her back, stroking gently as the girls read, gripping tightly whenever tears threatened her. And read the girls did, letter after letter. Twelve of them, until every student in her advanced algebra class, save Samantha, had gotten her say.

Then someone near the doors started to clap. Her eyes flew toward the entrance, and there stood Miss Bowen. She must have entered the dining hall as the letters were being read, but instead of a dour frown crossing her lips, the headmistresses smiled, her eyes shining and even moist.

Someone else started clapping, Dottie McGivern, at the back of the room, a huge smile pasted on her face. Then a student in the middle of the dining hall stood and clapped, and another and another, until the entire room was standing and clapping and making so much noise, she nearly had to cover her ears.

She'd spent the past eight years studying and then teaching, trying to earn her family's approval in spite of her decision to attend college and teach. Trying to make her parents proud by doing something other than marrying a cheating scoundrel.

She'd never gained that approval.

But maybe, just maybe, she'd been searching for her family in the wrong place. Her family had betrayed her and destroyed itself, but God had given her these students and her fellow teachers. A different family that loved her despite her shortcomings and supported her when no one else did.

Her eyes moved to Luke standing beside her, so close the warmth from his strong body radiated into her, and her fingers rubbed the spot where her engagement ring would fit. God had given her that honest rancher, as well.

"You're thinking about me," the half-rusted voice whispered in her ear.

She raised her eyebrows. "You believe you've acquired the ability to read my thoughts now?"

"Not hardly, but when a woman looks at a man a certain way, all soft and moonstrucklike, he can tell what's going on inside that pretty head of hers."

"Do tell, then. I'm most anxious to hear what I'm thinking."

He glanced down at the finger she toyed with. "That you're ready to put my ring there."

All teasing fled as she looked at the finger and nodded.

He slipped his hand into his pocket and pulled out

the gold circle set with an emerald. "You know, it's terribly unfair of you to accept my proposal here." He slid the cool metal onto her finger and bent low so his lips brushed her ear. "I can hardly kiss you with a hundred students looking on. Wouldn't be proper, I'm told."

"Luke Hayes, whispering such a thing in my ear is hardly proper, either." Their eyes met and held, still and peaceful despite the chaos of the dining hall.

"You're getting married!" a student squealed, likely MaryAnne, as the noise overtook the sound of the fading clapping.

MaryAnne flung herself forward, and Elizabeth nearly stumbled as the girl's slender body plowed into hers. Before she could right herself, Luke stepped back, and Elaine hugged her from behind, Meredith slammed into her side, and Katherine encircled the three of them. Then the whole room descended into a torrent of squeals and giggles and hugs.

Elizabeth pushed to her toes and tried to find Luke through the melee. He stood watching the scuffle, his arms crossed, his hip and shoulder propped against the wall. His eyelid slid down into a wink, and her face heated anew. Then when someone bumped her from behind, she smiled. Not a forced curve of the lips, but the kind of smile that started deep inside and spread until warmth and joy coursed through every inch of her body.

With her students surrounding her and her eyes locked on the man she loved, she could hardly do otherwise.

Epilogue

~❧~

Teton Valley, Wyoming
August 1894

"This is it?"

"This is it." Luke kept his eyes riveted on Elizabeth, his wife of seven months, as she looked around the deserted cabin where Blake and Cynthia had once lived, a building he hadn't stepped foot in since Blake's death.

"I'm glad we're staying in the ranch house."

He crossed his arms and leaned a shoulder against the wall. "Why's that? You don't like the layer of dust coating everything?"

"It feels eerie, unsettling." She eyed the sagging mattress against the far wall. "And look at that bed. It's only big enough for one person. Cynthia and Blake couldn't have slept in it."

He grinned slowly and ran his eyes over the small mound on his wife's ever-growing stomach. "That wasn't the bed they shared. Some of the ranch hands have used this place a time or two, so we moved a couple old mattresses out here. But we could both fit on it."

She shook her head. "We definitely could *not*. And I can prove it. That bed looks to be about 6 feet by 3 feet, giving it a surface area of 18 square feet. You're about 6.2 feet tall and perhaps 2.5 feet wide through your shoulders. So let's say you take up 15.5 square feet. I'm approximately 5.3 feet tall with a width of—"

She squeaked as he swooped her up in his arms and deposited her on the bed, then fell beside her, squashing her against the wall. "See, we fit."

"Not comfortably," she growled. "Which is what I was about to point out before you interrupted me."

"Oh, it's very comfortable for me." He looped a hand around her back and drew her nearer. "But then, I like being close to my wife. Tell me." He ran his hand over the swell of her stomach. "How do you figure this extra lump here into your equation? That's not exactly a straight line."

"I was using averages, but calculus would give you the exact area." She elbowed him in the chest. Heaven only knew whether it was intentional with the way they lay squished beside each other. "Calculus is the study of curves, after all. But to determine the area of my belly, we could probably just take the equation for an ellipse and divide it by…"

He pressed his mouth to hers before she started spouting off a jumble of letters and numbers and symbols that would make about as much sense as starting a brush fire during a rainstorm. He meant to keep the kiss quick, a little silencing of her mouth. But her lips were too warm and her body too soft. He inched closer, using the hand not trapped between them to cup her cheek and slide down her neck…

"Luke? Elizabeth?"

He jolted upright at the sound of his sister's call, scrambled off the bed and headed to the open door. Sam and Pa each sat on a horse and watched the cabin.

"I wondered if you'd bring Elizabeth here…for your picnic." Pa's eyes twinkled.

Confound it. The man knew exactly what he'd been about in the cabin. At least Sam seemed ignorant.

"Pa and I were out riding and thought we'd stop by." Sam edged her horse closer. "Do you need us to carry anything back?"

Luke glanced at the spread blanket and empty plates beside the cabin. "Sure. It'd save me the hassle of taking things myself." He stepped down and headed toward the blanket. "You look like you're enjoying that ride on Dumplin' a little too much, Sam."

She patted her horse's neck. "I hadn't realized how much I missed it."

"Told you."

Indeed, she loved this place as much as he did—she'd just forgotten it for a while. She still planned to make it to college in another year or so, and he'd no doubt she would. But for now, she contented herself helping Pa around the ranch and filling the spot Ma had vacated when she'd passed last January.

Pa wasn't exactly happy about Luke's living out East, but the older man was coping. Of course, signing the deed to the ranch over to Pa hadn't hurt his convincing.

Reaching the blanket, Luke tossed the leftover food into the picnic basket and hefted it up to Pa, then threw the blanket across Sam's lap and gave Dumplin' a pat on the rump. "Now the two of you get on out of here and let me go back to courtin' my wife."

Sam turned Dumplin' around. "Courtin'? You're supposed to get all of that in before you marry."

Pa chuckled, low and soft. "The things you've yet to learn about life, girl."

"You sound like Elizabeth." Sam scowled and kicked her horse into a trot.

"Well now, Elizabeth's a pretty smart woman," Pa called, sending Luke a wink as he trotted away. "I'd listen to her."

The twosome were mere specks in a sea of prairie grass before Luke headed back toward the cabin. Though they'd likely as not decide to turn around, come back and ask him another question.

Annoying family. What was so good about having them all together anyway? He'd hardly gotten a second alone with his wife in the two weeks they'd been staying at the ranch. Almost made a man want to move into his brother's deserted cabin.

Luke stepped back inside the ramshackle building and paused. Elizabeth lay where he'd left her, curled on her side. Dusty sunlight filtered in from the window above, hitting her hands, belly and knees while casting the rest of her sleeping form into shadows. He moved closer and stroked a strand of hair back from her face. She slept so peacefully, as though she belonged on the lumpy straw rather than their soft feather bed.

And in a way, maybe she did. Not because the dusty cabin suited her or because she deserved the discomfort and aches she'd surely wake with, but because she filled the spot inside him that had lain empty for so long. He had his old family back, a sister-in-law and nephew who wrote him every week, and a new family starting. He had employees who depended on him and commitments to charities. He had God's forgiveness and a fresh hope brimming inside him. Indeed, for the first time since his brother's death, he was full enough to burst.

And being full felt good.

* * * * *

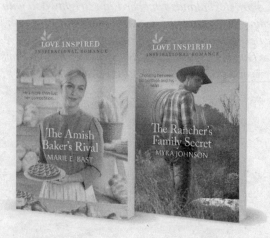

In high school, Finn had dated a girl for about six months. Once, when they'd been watching a movie, she'd fallen asleep tucked against his arm. His arm had also fallen asleep. It had been a painfully good place to be, and he hadn't moved even though he'd suffered through the end of that movie.

This time it was three little monkeys who'd taken over his personal space, and once again he was incredibly uncomfortable and strangely content at the same time.

Reese, the most cautious of the three, had snuggled against his side. She'd fallen asleep first, and her little features were so peaceful that his grinch's heart had grown three sizes.

Lola had been trying to make it to the end of the movie, fighting back heavy eyelids and extended yawns, but eventually she'd conked out.

Sage was the only one still standing, though her fidgeting from the back of the couch had lessened considerably.

Ivy returned from the bunkhouse. She'd taken a couple of trips over with laundry as the movie finished and now returned the basket to his laundry room. She walked into the living room as the movie credits rolled and turned off the TV.

LIEXP0121

"Guess I let them stay up too late." She moved to sit on the coffee table, facing him. "I'll carry Lola and Reese back. Sage, you can walk, can't you, love?"

Sage's weighted lids said the battle to stay awake had been hard fought. "I hold you, too, Mommy."

Cute. Finn wouldn't mind following that rabbit trail. Wouldn't mind making the same request of Ivy. Despite his determination not to let her burrow under his skin, tonight she'd done exactly that. He'd found himself attending the school of Ivy when she was otherwise distracted. Did she know that she made the tiniest sound popping her lips when she was lost in thought? Or that she tilted her head to the right and only the right when she was listening— and studied the speaker with so much interest that it made them feel like the most important human on the planet?

Stay on track, Brightwood. This isn't your circus. Finn had already bought a ticket to a circus back in North Dakota, and things hadn't ended well. No need to attend that show again. Especially when the price of admission had cost him so much.

"I'll help carry. I can take two if you take one."

"Thank you. That would be really great. I'd prefer to move them into their beds and keep them asleep if at all possible. If Reese gets woken up, she'll start crying, and I'm not sure I have the bandwidth for that tonight."

Ivy gathered the girls' movie and sweatshirts, then slipped Sage from the back of the couch.

Finn scooped up Reese and caught Lola with his other arm. He stood and held still, waiting for complaints. Lola fidgeted and then settled back to peaceful. Reese was so far gone that she didn't even flinch.

These girls. His dry, brittle heart cracked and healed all at the same time. They were good for the soul.

Don't miss
Choosing His Family *by Jill Lynn,*
available February 2021 wherever
Love Inspired books and ebooks are sold.

LoveInspired.com

LOVE INSPIRED

INSPIRATIONAL ROMANCE

UPLIFTING STORIES OF FAITH, FORGIVENESS AND HOPE.

Join our social communities to connect with other readers who share your love!

Sign up for the Love Inspired newsletter at **LoveInspired.com** to be the first to find out about upcoming titles, special promotions and exclusive content.

CONNECT WITH US AT:

Facebook.com/LoveInspiredBooks

Twitter.com/LoveInspiredBks

Facebook.com/groups/HarlequinConnection